FINAL
ARRANGEMENTS

COVINGTON COUNTY LIBRARY SYSTEM
403 SOUTH FIR AVENUE
COLLINS, MS 39428

WITHDRAWN

$500.00 FINE, SIX MONTHS IN
JAIL FOR MISUSE OR FAILURE
TO RETURN LIBRARY MATERIALS.
(MS CODE 1972, 39-3-309, 1989 SUP.)

F
AND
COL

6/23/15 $13.95

FINAL ARRANGEMENTS

MILES KEATON ANDREW

COVINGTON COUNTY LIBRARY SYSTEM
403 SOUTH FIR AVENUE
COLLINS, MS 39428

WITHDRAWN

THOMAS DUNNE BOOKS
ST. MARTIN'S GRIFFIN ⪰ NEW YORK

THOMAS DUNNE BOOKS.
An imprint of St. Martin's Press.

FINAL ARRANGEMENTS. Copyright © 2002 by Miles Keaton Andrew. All rights
reserved. Printed in the United States of America. No part of this book may be used
or reproduced in any manner whatsoever without written permission except in the
case of brief quotations embodied in critical articles or reviews. For information,
address St. Martin's Press, 175 Fifth Avenue, New York, N.Y. 10010.

www.stmartins.com

Title page photo by James Sinclair

Library of Congress Cataloging-in-Publication Data

Andrew, Miles Keaton
    Final arrangements : a novel / Miles Keaton Andrew.—1st ed.
        p. cm.
    ISBN 0-312-27462-9 (hc)
    ISBN 0-312-31362-4 (pbk)
    1. Undertakers and undertaking—Fiction. 2. Funeral rites and ceremonies—
Fiction. 3. Eccentric and eccentricities—Fiction. 4. Family-owned business enter-
prises—Fiction. I. Title.

PS3601.N55 F56 2002
813'.6—dc21   2001051302

First St. Martin's Griffin Edition: August 2003

10 9 8 7 6 5 4 3 2 1

For Marisa

AUTHOR'S NOTE

This is a work of fiction. In no way should this book be taken as an accurate representation of the good citizens of the Florida suncoast region, nor of the character of its people, nor of the funeral practices of that region, or any other region. The story takes place in a fictional town, which accounts for the geographical distortions contained herein.

ACKNOWLEDGMENTS

Marisa: My wife, my love, my inspiration, and front-line editor; Loren G. Soeiro, of the Peter Lampack Agency, the best damn literary agent in the world; Peter Lampack, for outstanding ethical practice; Melissa Jacobs, for taking a risk with my material; Emily Hopkins, my editor at Thomas Dunne Books, for needful encouragement during my final draft, and for being southern; Eric Nichols, for technical assistance. Special thanks to all of those who labored through my original, 839-page manuscript.

TO THE BEREAVED

Final Arrangements is a graphic, irreverent story about the funeral trade. If this book has fallen into your hands during a time of loss or sorrow, please accept my most sincere apologies, and deepest regrets.

—Miles Keaton Andrew

FINAL
ARRANGEMENTS

1

"There are only three types of men working in the funeral trade: those born into it, those married into it, and those *drawn* into it. It's the latter type that gives me pause. You were drawn here. Can you tell me why?"

A simple question, posed to me by Jerrold Anthony Stiles, manager and senior director of Morton-Albright Funeral Home and Memorial Chapel. I sat there in my black suit, praying for a simple answer to his question. I opened my mouth to speak, but nothing came out, and I could not leave Jerry's office without a job. It was my twenty-first birthday, and I had spent the last twelve years of my life waiting for this moment. Now it had arrived, and I had nothing to say.

Then I remembered the key in my pocket. The key would speak for me. I reached into my pocket and withdrew the handkerchief, embroidered with Jerry's own initials. I stood up and placed the handkerchief in the middle of Jerry's desk. I opened the handkerchief slowly, one fold at a time, to give myself a moment to think of words. None came to me, but I saw the change on Jerry's face as I backed

away. He was looking at it now, lying in the center of his own handkerchief: the key, shining like new brass—an old skeleton key, seventy-five years old. The sun, streaming in through the window, made
it gleam.

"My God." Jerry spoke in a quiet voice. With a look of slow delib-
eration, he moved his hand toward the object. Fingers set to grasp it,
he paused, and looked at me. "May I?" He asked.

I nodded, thankful that I had not yet been required to speak,
thankful that Jerry remembered the key. He picked up the key by its
proper end. He leaned back in his chair and examined it, then trans-
ferred it to his palm, as though weighing it along with my intention
to enter the funeral trade. He spoke, giving me reprieve from my
struggle for an answer. "How did this old key get so shiny?" he asked.
"It didn't look like this when I gave it to you."

I told Jerry that whenever I was scared or worried, whenever
something bad happened to me, I would wrap my fingers around the
key and squeeze it as tightly as I could. Every night, I went to sleep
with the key in my fist. Every morning, it was still in my hand. I
showed Jerry my palm. I had held on to the key so long and so tightly,
it had left a permanent indentation in my hand. Because of the depth
of the key's indentation, Jerry supposed it hadn't been easy for me,
growing up an orphan. He said, "I remembered your family name as
soon as you called for the interview. Your parents were Richard and
Nancy Kight. Fortunately, we don't hold many double funerals here
at Morton-Albright. They're hard on folks. All of Angel Shores
showed up for your folks. That plane crash was on all three channels.
Tragedy always draws a crowd, son. Nineteen-sixty, I believe."

"Sixty-two," I said. "I remember the crowd. I thought my parents
were famous."

"They were, son. The crash made them famous." Jerry began to
recall the funeral. I relaxed in my chair and let him speak. He had
watched me leave my parents' service. When I didn't come right back,
he searched the funeral home, looking for me. "I found you in the

Rose Room," he said. "There you were, standing on a kneeler, examining the body of an old man, lying in an open casket."

"You scared me," I said. "I fell off the kneeler—knocked the breath out of me. You came to me and rolled me over. I remember your face. I remember what I said to you: '*I want to be an Undertaker.*' "

I had also remembered Jerry's eyes—such a pale blue, I could see *into* them. His hair, now gray, had been as black as my suit. After finding me in the repose room, Jerry had brought me here, into the office. He told me if I wanted to be an Undertaker, I needed a key. He opened a cabinet and selected the skeleton key that now lay upon his desk. "This key used to open every door at Morton-Albright," he'd said. "Now it's yours. It's your Undertaker's key. Come back and see me when you're twenty-one. Bring your key. If you still want to be an Undertaker, I'll give you a job."

Now I reminded Jerry of his promise. "Today is my twenty-first birthday," I said. "Here is my key. I still want to be an Undertaker."

"But you still haven't told me why," Jerry said. I still had no answer—not one that I wanted to tell. It didn't matter. Jerry kept talking. He said that I had been in shock that day—nine years old. He confessed he had given me the key to get my mind off things—a distraction. He had never expected to see me again—not dressed in a black suit, looking for a job. "Most young men wouldn't dream of spending a birthday in a funeral home."

Jerry's words hit me hard. My talisman key had been a distraction. I had dedicated my life to a toy. I was headed for depression, but I was struck by my own oddity, spending my birthday in a funeral home—odd enough for a laugh, and the smile on Jerry's face was growing larger. Now we were both laughing. Jerry was warming up to me. I could feel it.

"Casey James Kight," he said my name, shaking his head. He also said I didn't need to answer his question. I had already answered it—by *not* answering. "You're here out of deep curiosity—what some call morbid." Most fellows came in spouting off about helping the bereaved, when all they wanted was a peek at the back room—nothing wrong with curiosity, but curiosity didn't make a good man. "I don't know of any man in the trade who could rightly say why he's in it. If it runs in your family, you've got an excuse, or a tradition—however you want to put it."

I promised Jerry I'd work hard. "There's something about this *place*," I said. "It calls to me."

"Don't ruin your interview with spooky talk, Casey. You were doing fine. You're a well-mannered, clean-cut kid, and I detect sincerity. You can start tomorrow morning at seven A.M. Don't get too excited—last time we hired outside the trade, I swore I'd never do it again. Think of your first day as a test—it only takes a few hours to know for sure."

"Know what?"

"Whether or not you're cut out for the work." He told me not to buy any new clothes just yet. I could wear my black suit tomorrow. I asked him what was wrong with my suit—it seemed appropriate for funeral work. He explained that it was an offense to the bereaved. "We don't mourn with our families, and they know it. We serve them from a professional distance." He told me not to worry, they wouldn't turn me loose on the public until I wore proper attire. He also promised to call the principal of Clearwater High School, for a reference.

"I didn't go to Clearwater. I went to Dunedin."

"I thought you lived here in Angel Shores."

"I did, but my aunt Margee moved us out into the county after the accident. I went to Dunedin."

"That explains it," Jerry said. "If you had gone to Clearwater, I would have met you long before now." Jerry asked if he could hold on to my key overnight. He wanted to show it to the other men. The thought of spending the night without my key brought sweat to my palms. I didn't want to risk an episode without my key, but the Presence of Morton-Albright had calmed me, and the indentation in my palm would remind me that the key was safe with Jerry.

. . .

I didn't bother with the door of the green MG. The top was down, and the Florida heat had soaked me to my underwear by the time I made it across the blacktop of the Morton-Albright parking lot and hopped into my car. I yanked at my tie, and drove out onto Druid Road, the breeze in my face. I sniffed at the air, smelled the salt spray, and headed for Angel Shores Beach. I hadn't been there since I was a kid. Aunt Margee hated the sand, and the sun was cruel to her fair skin. That was the reason I went to the beach that day, because Margee hated it so. I loved Margee. She had raised me ever since the accident, all by herself, but the time had come for both of us to begin living our own separate lives. Margee had been only twenty-three when she became my adoptive mother. She was now thirty-five, and had never taken up with a man during our time together. She had devoted her life to caring for me. She had stood by my side at Tampa airport when the plane went down.

Mom and Dad had won the Betty Beeson Home Permanent Hawaiian Getaway Sweepstakes—six days and seven nights in Waikiki, and all because Mom had been born with straight hair. It was 1962—twelve years earlier. Jackie was in the White House, and my mother was one of millions of American women who now had a reason to experiment with glamour. The days of Eleanor Roosevelt, Bess Truman, and Mamie Eisenhower were over—all respectable women, but none of them looked like Jackie. It nearly killed my dad to see the woman he married in pedal-pushers and short, wavy hair, but he got over it when the letter of notification arrived from the Betty Beeson Company: Mom had won the grand prize.

At the beach now, with my hand to my forehead, I visored my eyes against the sun and surveyed the vastness of the Gulf of Mexico. I listened to the cry of gulls mingled with the sound of the waves. Another familiar sound rose up into the air from behind me—the high-pitched noise of cicadas in the scrub across Beach Road. For a moment, the sounds all fell together, creating a single auditory event: the sound of my own name, like a whisper. *"Casey."* I whipped around, startled—it seemed to have come from behind me. I looked across the road at a vacant lot of dirty sand, scrub, a few short pines. Through the pines I saw a clearing, and a giant coquina rock—an elevated view of the Gulf.

I sat down on the big rock, careful of the only suit I owned. I removed my shoes and emptied them of the sand from climbing up the ridge. I could barely hear the waves now—the cicadas had taken over, and my view of the water was obscured by scrub. My interest diverted to the clearing itself, I noticed it was perfectly circular. A road, strewn with fallen pine needles, wound into deeper wood. I heard the sound of my name again—still in a whisper, but muffled, as though it came from under the ground. The noise of the cicadas intensified, as if in response to the voice. I began to feel dizzy, probably from the heat. The noise became so loud, I covered my ears.

It wasn't insects I was hearing anymore—it was the whine of jet engines, ready for takeoff. I was nine years old again, standing in the observation area of Tampa airport, holding Margee's hand, watching the Hawaiian Trans-Pacific jetliner surge down the runway—the jet climbing into the air, then falling out of the turquoise sky. The explosion at the end of the runway. The column of fire shooting upward, blossoming into a flower of black fire. Sick-faced adults, scrambling for the fire trucks and rescue equipment.

For a moment, the crash seemed impossible—I expected to see my parents running from the wreckage, frightened they'd worried me; but the heat from the explosion roared into my face, and burned away the calm, thrusting me into the chaos that surrounded me. I knew that Mom and Dad were in the plane, burning at the end of the runway. My breath quickened; my heart ready to explode, like the airplane. Margee and I turned to each other, wide-eyed, mirroring horror. With hardly a motion, I scaled the fence of the observation area and ran down the runway toward the fire. Margee screamed my name. My lungs burned as I ran. I saw a flash of yellow; my feet left the ground. A fireman had snatched me up. I tore at his yellow slicker, trying to free myself. I kicked at him and begged, "Let me go! They're *in* there! We've got to get them out! They'll burn up if we don't get them out!" The fireman set me down on the ground, his blackened face streaked with tears. He lowered himself, eye-level with me. "Who's in there, son?" he asked. "Your mama? Your daddy?"

"No!" I heard myself scream aloud.

I looked up into the sky from my perch on the coquina rock. I saw the big tail of a passenger jet, on its approach to the airport, screaming overhead. I wiped my face, wet with tears and sweat.

I drove back into town, gritting my teeth, awaiting the calm that always followed an episode. The calm was nothing more than a self-imposed state of shock. Over the years, I had taught myself to prolong the calm. I prolonged it by pushing everything from my mind except my path to Morton-Albright. I knew the purpose of the episodes—my own mind was trying to jolt me out of my shock and make me *remember*. I didn't want to remember—not yet, for I suspected terror in the memories: since my episodes always began with the crash itself, I believed that the memories lying beneath could only be worse. I wanted to remember them, but not until I was safe at Morton-Albright, the only place of comfort I had ever known. For now, I was postponing the memories, but it was becoming more difficult. Occasionally, some event would trigger an episode. It could be something as simple as brushing my teeth, or something more obviously tied to the crash, like the sound of a jet airliner, passing overhead. After each episode, I remembered pieces of my childhood. Today at the beach, I remembered the real reason why Margee stopped taking me there—not because of her fair skin but because the beach was on the air-traffic approach to Tampa airport.

I knew only two distinct states of mind: the episode, and the tranquil path to remembrance. Because of this, I had few memories of my childhood. I could barely remember my life before the crash. I had only faded pictures of my mom and dad in my head—Margee had thrown away the real photographs of my parents, or had hidden them from me. I suspected the latter, because Margee was not the kind of person who'd throw away photographs of her own brother.

As I drove through town, the deceitful calm of shock settled in. I marveled at the old beauty of Angel Shores. The courthouse square, shaded by ancient trees, was surrounded by family-owned businesses, including a real soda fountain, where they still served blue-plate specials and mixed Coca-Cola syrup with carbonated water. The old money in Angel Shores had ensured the town's preservation. Nobody cared about progress except in the unincorporated county, where Margee and I lived, with all the discount stores and car dealerships. In Angel Shores proper, no new construction was allowed to stand more than three stories high, and its look had to fit in with the small-town motif. The rules of preservation had impacted Angel Shores in an unexpected way: the town itself had become a tourist attraction. People came from all over to see life as it had once been in a small town of the old South, and there was nothing more old South about Angel Shores than Skeeter's Real Open-pit Barbecue.

Skeeter's family had brought the art of barbecue with them from rural Georgia. You could smell it all over town. Margee and I loved eating there, so I pulled the MG into a gas station and called her from a pay phone. I asked her to meet me at Skeeter's for dinner. She hammered me with questions about my job interview. I'd tell her all about it over a pork sandwich and Brunswick stew.

From a picnic table inside Skeeter's Barbecue, I watched Margee enter the restaurant. I didn't signal her right away. Instead, I sat there for a moment, watching Margee look nervous, scanning the place through her sunglasses. She always forgot to take them off, and would remember only when she realized she couldn't see a damn thing. I watched her fumble them into her purse. She spied me, rolled her eyes, and headed for my table. It would be our last meal together.

"Look at your white shirt," she said. "How did you manage to get dirty at your job interview? Have they got you digging graves already?"

"No, but I saw some really scary stuff. Wanna hear about it?"

"You stop that, Casey. It's a funeral home, for godssake. It's creepy"

Morton-Albright was not creepy, I insisted. It was the most beautiful mansion in Angel Shores, its lobby full of hand-crafted antiques, velvet sofas and chairs, tables of polished oak, all illuminated by a thousand prisms of a giant chandelier. "Jerry was good to me," I said. "He gave me the job."

"Mr. Stiles is a nice gentleman. I'm sure he doesn't go around scaring his aunt Margee."

"That's because he doesn't *have* an aunt Margee. I start tomorrow morning."

We ate our dinner in silence—in the silence of the argument that had grown between us over the years: I wanted to be an Undertaker at Morton-Albright. Margee wanted me to be *anything* but an Undertaker. She didn't understand—it was my calling: "The heart of the wise is in the house of mourning." A verse from Ecclesiastes. Morton-Albright was the house of mourning. I knew if I dwelt there, my heart would become wise. I would remember everything, in the only place of comfort I had ever known. It didn't matter that Jerry had given me the key as a distraction. It only mattered that he had given me a *key*. It was the key to everything. Margee knew it, too— she wasn't really worried I'd see something bad. She worried I would remember.

"All you'll find is more death," Margee said. "It will only make you more sad."

"I can't be any more sad. I've been sad all my life. I want to be happy, like everybody else." I had felt happiness today, I told her. The moment I stepped into the lobby, the warm chills began—the Presence of Morton-Albright fell upon me. I was home. I had been able to speak with Jerry about the crash, without worrying about an episode. I knew what Margee was thinking. She worried about more than my remembering. I just sat there, waiting for her to say it.

"How are you ever going to meet a girl in a funeral home?" She said it. "You're twenty-one. You've never brought a girl home. You've never even been on a date."

"Neither have you," I said. "Besides, all the girls at school thought I was a freak."

"What did you expect? How many other boys came to school in a black suit? I had good reason for staying away from men."

I knew what was coming next: Margee's lecture about how she had given up her romantic life to raise me, how she hadn't wanted some guy hanging around, pretending to be my father. I listened to her sermon all the way through dessert.

At the foot of my bed, I spied my mother's cedar chest. I hadn't opened it in a long time. It filled the room with an old, relaxing aroma. Inside were my treasures: Mom's handmade quilt, Dad's army flashlight, and a cardboard box full of fourteen Green Hornet comics, each one in its own protective sleeve. I also owned a toy replica of Black Beauty, the Green Hornet's car.

I figured on a sleepless night, so I prepared myself. Despite the warmth of April, I flung my mother's quilt onto my bed. I turned off the lights, pushed the switch on the flashlight, and laid myself down in comic-reading position. The Green Hornet looked at me from the cover of issue number three. My dad had made me wash my hands just to *look* at the comics while he turned the pages, never mind touching them. Dad liked the Green Hornet because of his clothing— a normal men's suit, a black mask, and a fedora hat. "Not like those sissy heroes with their leotards and superpowers." The Green Hornet fought like a man. Actually, most of the real fighting was done by Kato, the Hornet's sidekick and chauffeur. And although the Green Hornet himself had no superpowers of his own, his car, Black Beauty, had plenty of secret armaments, which made for great car-chase scenes, especially in the TV series. I'll never forget that first Friday night when Black Beauty roared onto our television set. "Faster, Kato!" The Green Hornet called from the backseat of the souped-up 1966 Chrysler Imperial. My toy replica looked just like it.

I had washed my hands thoroughly before bed, and was opening the comic book when Margee's knock came at the door. She walked in and sat down on my bed. She didn't say anything for a long time, as though working on exact phrasing. Her first sentences were in fragments. I aimed the flashlight toward our faces so we could see each other in the dark. She told me how she had mourned my parents, and how she had tried to save me from it. "Grieving hurts so bad," she said. "I didn't want you to feel it. Now you're going to a place where people feel it every day. I know I can't stop you, so maybe I was wrong to try. If you have to go, then go. Find what you're looking for. You can always come home." I let Margee hug me that night. I told her not to worry—maybe I'd meet a nice girl at a funeral.

2

I left the house at 6:00 A.M., an hour before work—too early for Margee's good-bye hugs and kisses. It was a fifteen-minute drive to Morton-Albright. I drove past the welcome sign and into the outer circle of Cracker homes that surrounded Angel Shores—my old neighborhood. The working class of Angel Shores lived in its most striking homes: hundreds of wooden houses painted lime or lemon or sky blue or peach, they rested atop pillars of brick or stone, every one of them crowned with a tin roof, shaded by old cypresses strung with Spanish moss. Their tropical colors were dim this morning. Fog had rolled in from the Gulf. It gathered in patches that swirled through lower ground.

I followed Druid Road into town. Straight ahead, on the right-hand side of the street, I saw it—the black, horse-drawn funeral carriage that marked the corner of the Morton-Albright property. I watched it emerge through the swirls of mist—the vision enhanced the excitement of my first day at work. I braced myself for all that

Margee had warned me about—the horrible sights that awaited me in the private areas of the funeral mansion.

At 6:15 A.M., I walked under the green canopy that led to the veranda of the main entrance. I rang the night bell. To my right, a jalousie door opened. Jerry stepped onto the veranda. He looked handsome in a charcoal suit—the man I had idolized for years. "Had a feeling you'd show up early," he said. "We're ready for you. This is the employee entrance. We take our coffee in the kitchen."

I stepped across the threshold. We stood in a dark corridor. Jerry entered a door on the right. I followed him into a large kitchen. At the dining table, two men in white shirts and ties slouched over cups of black coffee.

"Casey, meet Ray and Carl," Jerry said.

The heavier of the two men dragged on a cigarette, then extinguished it in the ashtray in front of him. He arose to shake my hand. His glasses were thick, his eyes all but invisible behind the strong lenses. "Ray Winstead." He said.

"Ray's the embalming room supervisor," Jerry explained. "Been here thirteen years. You report to him."

Ray sat down. Jerry pointed to the other man—midtwenties, mustache. His hair seemed too long for funeral work. Jerry introduced him: "This other fellow is Carl Midkiff, my Yankee nephew. He gets his funeral director's license next month. Carl needs a haircut."

Carl offered me a chair and a cup of coffee in a deep voice that didn't sound Yankee at all, more like local.

"Spend the morning with Ray and Carl," Jerry said. "Afterward, we'll talk." He left me there with Ray and Carl. I sipped my coffee. Ray and Carl studied me. Ray lit a cigarette, exhaled, and played with his lighter. He spoke to me in a slight drawl: "Dead people." Ray said. "We work with dead people here at Morton-Albright. Can you work with dead people? That's what we need to know and there's a dead person on the embalming table right now. Let's go."

I followed Ray and Carl down the corridor, deeper into the funeral home. Ray said, "Most fellas quit after the first hour. A few make it through the first day."

Halfway down the corridor, a cavernous space opened to the right. Ray flipped a light switch. The lights gleamed off a white station wagon parked on a concrete floor. The wagon pointed into sloping darkness. "Removal car," Ray said. "We use it to pick up dead people." Ray led me around to the nose of the car. He pointed into the darkness. "We call this place the bat cave—garage ramp winds down, then out the south side of the building. Car stays here, right in the middle of the funeral home."

The car sat between two walls. There was a door on each wall, one marked Supply, the other Private. Ray pointed to the Private door. "Preparation area," he said. "That's where we're going. It's divided into two rooms: Dressing room, and embalming room. Dead person's in the embalming room."

I stood in the middle of the dressing room—a room with four doors, one on each wall. To my left, a sign over a wide door read Quiet! Ray explained, the door opened into the lobby. "The Quiet sign means shut your mouth before you walk into the lobby. Might be a family out there." Three high tables were parked along the left wall—dressing tables, Ray said. He opened the door straight ahead of me, revealing the scissors gate of an old elevator. "Goes up to the casket display room," Ray said. "These doors are all wide because we move caskets through them. We put dead people in the caskets. You understand the dead part?"

I nodded, then scanned right, to the last door, narrow and stained dark. Inscribed upon the door, a single word, stenciled in gold leaf: Embalming. "The dead person is on the other side of that door," Ray said. "When you see the remains, you can do whatever you like: Scream, puke, run, faint—it doesn't matter. Most men just gulp and stare, then excuse themselves forever. One more option—you can change your mind about walking through that door and go home— nothing to be ashamed of."

I said I was ready to go inside.

I followed Ray and Carl into the embalming room. Two white enameled ceramic embalming tables lay end to end. The table closest to the door stood empty. Upon the other table lay the body of an old woman, covered to her neck with a sheet. Ray flapped the sheet off her. I had spent years preparing myself for horror and gore. Instead, I beheld an old, naked woman with pink curlers in her hair. At least eighty years old, the dead woman sported the dark tan typical of Florida retirees. Her flattened breasts stretched beyond her rib cage. Nipples pointed at her feet. Gray as the hair on her head, the old woman's pubic hair had grown sparse. I embarrassed myself with these observations and averted my eyes to her legs, a tangle of purple veins. Her feet were gross too—flaky skin and big, crusty yellow nails. A tag dangled from a big toe. "Her name is Pfister," Ray said, then spelled it: "P-f-i-s-t-e-r. *Alice* Pfister—but she's too old and too dead for you to call her Alice, so it's Mrs. Pfister to you. Rule Number One: Always refer to the decedent by name: This is Mr. Shellfish; this is Mrs. Bejesus. We already know that Mrs. Pfister's husband's name was Mr. Pfister. We've already used that joke, so don't bother." Ray emphasized that I should avoid crass terms, like *cadaver*, or *stiff*. *Corpse* was the worst. "Don't *ever* let me hear you say 'corpse.' 'Remains' is the proper term." Ray lit a cigarette. "You took a real good look at Mrs. Pfister," he said. "What struck you most about her?"

She's old and naked, I thought, but didn't say it. I posed my answer as a question: "She's dead?"

"You hear that, Carl? Casey says she's dead." Carl leaned against the counter. He nodded his head. Ray looked back at me. "Smart kid," he said. "Your answer is correct. Mrs. Pfister is dead. She did not *'pass away.'*" Ray imitated quotation marks with his fingers, then continued, "Mr. Bogart died. Miss Monroe died. Rule Number Two: Never say 'passed away' to a family member. Don't say 'expired,' either—we're talking about a person, not a library card. Don't say, "Granny's 'gone'" Granny didn't go anywhere. Granny's right here on the embalming table, dead as a doornail. You with me so far on this dead thing?"

I nodded.

"Okay, Rule Number Three: Never express sympathy to a family for their loss. It's a crude thing to do, seeing as how we all get paychecks as a result of Granny's death. We're sensitive, but in a business sense, we're not all that sorry. So be polite, look after the family, but don't say, 'Sorry about your granny.' "

Ray looked thirty-five, overweight by twenty pounds. A lot of Ray's hair had run down the shower drain. "Hang your jacket on that hook," he instructed. "Get an apron out of that drawer."

I slipped the apron over my head and tied it around my waist. I asked Ray if they had already drained Mrs. Pfister's blood, trying to impress him with what I already thought I knew about embalming.

"You're referring to *arterial* embalming," Ray said. "We did that yesterday. Today we embalm her cavities, and I don't mean the ones in her teeth. That's where Carl comes in. Carl's going to show you cavity embalming. Ain't that right, Carl?"

Carl explained the process. "Cavity embalming requires aspiration. Aspiration means 'to suck out.' To stop decomposition, we need to suck out the fluids of Mrs. Pfister's internal organs. That means we need a suction device. That device is called an aspirator." Carl positioned me at the space between the two embalming tables. The ends of the tables extended over a sink that stood between them. The sink resembled a toilet half-full of water. A faucet hung over the side of the toilet-sink. The top of the faucet had been fitted with a cylinder. Carl pointed to the cylinder. "Aspirator," he said. "Creates suction with water pressure."

The aspirator's control lever was marked with three positions: Suction, Reverse Flow, and Off—the lever now in the Off position. Carl turned on the faucet. From its nozzle, water poured into the toilet-sink. Carl then flipped the control lever to Suction—the pouring water became a high-pressure spray. Attached to the aspirator was a clear plastic hose. Carl uncoiled it and handed it to me. I heard the whooshing sound of moving air. I moved it closer to my ear for a better listen. The hose sucked itself onto my cheek, like a vacuum cleaner. It squeaked when I pulled it off. "Suction," Carl said.

"I understand the suction part," I said, rubbing my cheek. "I *don't* understand how the organ fluids get sucked into the hose."

"Trocar," Carl said. He went to a tiled wall and took the trocar from its mount, then placed it in my hands—a hollow tube of stainless steel, three feet long, the diameter of my finger. The trocar looked like a sword—a handle-grip at one end, a sharpened spearpoint at the other. I held it aloft like Excalibur. Carl took Excalibur away from me and worked the suction hose onto a fitting on the handle. The air now sucked in through small holes near the end of the trocar, as well as through slots in the spearpoint itself. Trocar in hand, Carl approached Mrs. Pfister. I fixed my eyes on the spearpoint, which now dented a cleft in the skin of the dead woman's abdomen, near her navel. Carl glanced up at me, said *"Ready?"* then thrust the trocar through the skin and into Mrs. Pfister. "Puncture the heart first thing," he said. "Any blood left inside her will be there." The hose gurgled dark with Mrs. Pfister's blood. The blood sprayed into the toilet-sink. Carl changed the angle of the trocar's attack. Every time he did so, a different color charged through the hose. "Next, go for the lungs," he said. "Sometimes there's goop in them—mucous. Poke some extra holes in the lungs so the embalming fluid permeates better. Don't poke too hard—Ray keeps the points sharp—shove the trocar right through her if you're not careful. Now the liver—see that green stuff in the hose? Bile, from the gall bladder."

The smell of human viscera filled the room— a vomit smell, sour and nauseating.

"Step on that pedal on the floor, next to the sink," Carl said. The pedal flushed the sink, like a toilet. Most of the smell went away.

Ray asked, "Any questions so far?"

"Yes. Can I try it now?"

"Jesus," Ray said. "Don't act so eager. We don't need some kid like you at the front door, handing out memorial records like they were tickets to a Jerry Lewis movie. For godssake, you can at least *pretend* not to be so eager, can't you?"

"Morbid," Carl said, still sucking fluids out of Mrs. Pfister. "Jerry was right—black suit and all—not to mention the key."

"The *key*," Ray said, rolling his eyes.

"Jerry gave me the key when I was nine years old—at my parents' funeral. They were killed—"

"In a plane crash." Ray completed my sentence. "I worked that service. We had to borrow an extra hearse from Jesup Funeral Home. Jerry told me the decedents had left a little boy behind. Now here you are. People like you mostly want to stay as far away from funeral homes as possible. I'm sure you've got your reasons, so excuse me for asking, but what the fuck are you doing here, kid?"

Carl stopped sucking fluids to listen.

Jerry had excused me from answering the question by offering an answer of his own. From the look of these guys, I knew they would wait for an answer from me, even if it took all day. It might have taken me all day to think of an answer that would satisfy them, without adding to their doubts about my right-mindedness, so I answered their question with a question of my own, hoping for a clue. "What are *you* doing here?" I asked.

Carl answered first, "I'm family. Jerry is my uncle."

"I married in," Ray said. "When you see my wife, you'll know why. She's from the Albright side of Morton-Albright, so I'm family too."

I told them what I had told Jerry, twelve years ago, "I want to be an Undertaker."

"Undertakers don't exist anymore," Ray said. "Hell, we're all funeral directors now. Rule Number Three: *Never* tell anybody you're an Undertaker. It creeps the shit out of people. You're an embalmer's apprentice, but don't tell anybody *that* either. Just tell folks you work for Morton-Albright. They'll get the picture."

"Are you telling me I passed the test? Do I get to work here?"

Ray scratched his head. "Well, you're sure as hell not afraid of dead people." He glanced at Carl, who shrugged. Ray let out a long breath. "Okay, kid," he said. "We'll give you a shot."

"Does that mean I get to work the trocar now?" I asked.

"Jesus, kid. Will you cut that shit out? You'll get your chance. We've got a never-ending supply of bodies to embalm, especially with Sunset Towers going up—largest retirement complex in the country, now under construction. It'll form a half-circle around Angel Shores. Tens of thousands of senior citizens, some of them dying every damn day. Trade in the removal car for a conveyor belt."

Carl pulled the trocar out of Mrs. Pfister and went around to the other side of the table. He rested his left hand at the beginning of her pubic crest and forced the trocar back in through the same hole, downward this time, into the bladder. Dark urine sprayed into the sink. "If we don't take it out this way, it ends up in the nice, brand-new casket," Carl said. "With men, you just ligate the penis."

"Carl means you tie a string around it," Ray said. "Tight."

Carl changed the angle of the trocar—the intestines. He explained: "Notice after each forward motion I pull the trocar out of her almost to the spearpoint. I'm checking for globules of fat or maybe even shit stuck in the little holes of the trocar. These *are* the intestines—you *will* find shit in here."

"Carl means feces," Ray said.

"Hear that sucking noise when I pull out the trocar?" Carl asked. "If you don't hear that noise, the trocar's clogged. The trocar and ten feet of hose will be full of whatever nasty shit you're trying to suck out. When the trocar gets clogged, all you have to do is flip the aspirator switch to Reverse Flow—send a big blast of water right through the trocar. All that shit stuck in there flies right out of the tip. You must, and I mean *must*, submerge the tip of the trocar under the water in the sink *before* you flip the lever to Reverse Flow. I'll demonstrate." Carl withdrew the trocar from Mrs. Pfister's abdomen and submerged the tip in the flushable sink. He flipped the switch to Reverse Flow. The water in the sink boiled brown and green. "See there. Reverse Flow sprays nasty shit out of the trocar at a hundred pounds of pressure. If the tip of the trocar is not submerged, the nasty shit sprays all over the room."

"We'll call the Reverse Flow thing Rule Number Three," Ray said.

"Important rule," Carl said. "I know from experience. Three months ago, Ray storms into the embalming room with Jerry Stiles and Colton Albright himself—all three of them looking for some lady's jewelry. I was holding the trocar up in the air and they distracted me from my work."

"Distracted, my ass," Ray interrupted. "Carl was high on that smokey-dope. Ain't that right, Carl?"

Carl rolled his eyes and continued his story. "I accidentally flipped the Reverse Flow switch with the trocar sticking straight up in the air. After the blast, nobody said a word. We all got sprayed somewhat, but Colton Albright had shit and guts all over his face. He stood there like a statue—like if he moved, it would make it worse. Albright's face reddened up, but the doctor has warned the old man about getting pissed off—high blood pressure."

"*Real* high." Ray added.

"Ray snickered and pretended like he was coughing. Ray gets away with that shit because he's Colton's son-in-law. So is Jerry. Jerry gave Albright a towel. When the old guy was done patting his face, he still had a goober hanging off his ear. We pointed to our own ears and Albright flipped the thing off—hit the wall over there and stuck to it. Then he washed his face with antibacterial soap, took a piss in the flushable sink, farted, and walked out like nothing happened. Had to call Cruel Jewell—or Mrs. Albright, I should say—to bring him another suit."

"Carl, you're scaring the kid here," Ray said. "He's afraid you're gonna talk all goddamn day. Besides, I'm the supervisor. I'm supposed to talk all goddamn day. Now tell the new kid what comes after aspiration."

"Injection of embalming chemical into the cavities," Carl said. "Then we pack the orifices and put her in the casket."

Ray said we'd put some clothes on Mrs. Pfister too. "We don't put nekkid people out for visitation—but hell, we serve all faiths here at Morton-Albright. Maybe someday, we'll hold a service for someone of the Nudist faith. Guess we'll all get nekkid for that one. Maybe just wear our ties. Ain't that right, Carl? Nudie funeral directors."

Carl looked at me, then pointed his eyes at Ray. "You can see why we're looking for a new man," Carl said. "Ray needs a day off—in Chattahoochee." Carl now held a bottle of embalming chemical high above his head. A rubber hose was attached to the bottle. The other end of the hose was attached to the trocar, which was back inside Mrs. Pfister. This time, Carl moved the trocar all around the dead woman's insides in rapid thrusts, to distribute the chemical evenly, until the last of the formaldehyde ran from the bottle.

"What about the hole in her stomach?" I asked. Carl picked a stubby white plastic screw from a box. He held it in his palm for me to see. "Trocar button," he said. With a screwdriver, Carl screwed the trocar button into the hole in Mrs. Pfister's abdomen.

"Okay boys, that's it," Ray said. "Let's go get a doughnut and we'll dress her after coffee break." Ray put a hand on my shoulder and said, "Kid, I hope you're not a custard fan, because the custard doughnut is *mine*. Rule Number Three: Never touch the custard doughnut. Carl's a jelly man. Jerry likes anything with powdered sugar. That pretty much leaves you with the glazed."

3

Jerry was already wiping powdered sugar from his mouth when the three of us entered the kitchen. I poured myself a cup of black coffee and took the glazed doughnut, as Ray had commanded, then I sat down across the table from Jerry.

"You watched the cavity embalming?" Jerry asked.

I nodded, my mouth full of glazed doughnut.

"Are you still with us?" Jerry asked.

"Yes, sir."

"The kid can't wait to get his hands on the trocar," Ray said.

"Is that true?" Jerry asked. A smile began in the corner of his eye.

"Yes, sir," I said again.

Jerry turned to Ray and Carl. "What's the verdict, boys? Is Casey the man we're looking for?"

They nodded and uttered yeps and uh-huhs through their mouthfuls of doughnut. Ray tried to say "Definitely," at least that's what it sounded like, but it came out a mumble with doughnut crumbs spraying and custard dripping from the corner of his mouth.

Jerry stood up and buttoned his suit jacket. He extended his hand. "Welcome to Morton-Albright. You'll make a good man—part of the Morton-Albright family now, isn't he, boys?"

More yeps from Carl and a "Damn right" from Ray, who had finally swallowed his second doughnut. Jerry gave me back my key. "You keep this, son," he said. "It still opens the supply room." Jerry excused himself to go call Colton Albright to tell him of my employment. Ray sat down in Jerry's vacant chair and lit up a Marlboro. "You are the luckiest kid in the world, kid." Ray said, blowing smoke. "You stumbled into the best job in the world. Morton-Albright is the finest store in the whole damn South—everybody knows it. We've had pictures of the place in *Southern Funeral Director Magazine—twice.* The antiques in this place are worth even more than the two acres of prime that we sit on. Funeral cars are brand-new. Nobody ever squawks about the pay. Morton-Albright buys all your clothes—pays to have them laundered, too. Lots of experienced men out there would give up a testicle to work here, at Morton-Albright—but Jerry didn't hire any of those experienced men. He hired *you*, kid, and I'd bet my ass you don't even know why he hired you. Ain't that right, Carl?"

"That's a mighty big wager," Carl said, eyeing Ray's behind.

"Look, kid," Ray said. "When Jerry Stiles said that you were now part of the Morton-Albright family, he meant he's got family-type plans for you. *Matrimonial* plans. Understand?"

I shook my head.

Ray leaned across the table toward me, his eyes blurry behind his glasses. He whispered out loud: "*Jerry's got a daughter.*" Ray leaned back in his chair to let the words sink in, then said, "Now, go out to your car and get your stuff. Carl and I will help you move in."

"Move in?"

Carl and Ray looked at each other.

"Hell, kid, you live here now," Ray said.

"Here? In the funeral home?"

"You're the new apprentice, kid. Hell, even my granny knows that the apprentice lives in the funeral home."

I went dizzy. "I can't believe it," I said.

"Don't worry, you'll have company. The mortuary students live here too—More or Less—that's what I call them. Their real names are Morey and Lester. Ain't that some shit? They're twins—named after both of their grandfathers. Mom and Dad didn't think that one through all the way. You can't tell them apart, so don't even pretend. Twin funeral directors. Sebring will become one confused town when those two fellas get back home. They're in the licensure program at the Taylor School of Mortuary Science owned and operated by Taylor Chemical Company, makers of the finest embalming fluids on the market. All of us Morton-Albright men went to Taylor, all the way back to John Morton. You'll go there too, kid. We all wear Taylor rings here."

"Why do the students live here instead of on campus?" I asked, wanting the place all to myself.

Ray explained—no dorms at mortuary school. They want you to live and work in a real funeral home while you're in the program. Funeral homes all over the Tampa area provided living quarters to students in exchange for a few hours' work. Morey and Lester would be happy to meet me—we could exchange weekends off. I could no longer hide my exuberance. It burst forth: "This is fantastic!" I said. "I really get to live here?"

"Will you stop acting so damn eager?" Ray said. "You're scaring Carl and me. Rule Number Three: Cut that shit out. Of course you get to live here. Who do you think answers the phone at night? You, that's who. Lots of folks prefer to die after normal business hours. Just wait till those phone bells go off at three A.M. Put you right up in Chattahoochee with the crazies, you hear those bells enough times. They're loud, because you've got to catch the phone on the very first ring—every time."

"First ring," I said, nodding vigorously.

"These folks aren't calling the Angel Cinema for show times. While they're talking to you on the phone, they're looking down at dead old Granny with her mouth hanging open and her eyeballs staring straight up at God, and it don't matter how much they loved Granny. They want her scary-looking, smelly, dead ass out of their house as fast as possible. So if you don't grab that phone on the first ring, they might hang up and call Jesup over in Dunedin. Then you've got to shower, shave, put on your suit, go get Granny and embalm her before she turns green on you, so you'd better get yourself some clean skivvies for tomorrow."

While Ray went on about Granny, Jerry entered the kitchen. He said, "Colton Albright sounded pleased. He wants to meet our Casey. Now let's have a look around."

We began where we were, in the kitchen. Jerry pointed out the stove, but said no cooking during business hours—nothing worse than the smell of fried onions or pork chops wafting into a visitation. This meant cereal for breakfast, sandwich for lunch, late dinner. Ray noted that the twins had taken to eating cereal at all three meals. "Open the cabinets," Ray said. "Nothing but Frankenberry and Count Chocula."

My new living room looked like the rest of the funeral home— mostly antiques—except this room was littered with the odd pieces that hadn't grown timeless, like the coffee table with the inlaid mother-of-pearl angel in its center. "Blatant reference to Angel Shores, as well as the afterlife," Ray said. "Tacky." I liked the coffee table, my eyes drawn to the fine detail of the inlay. The coffee table sat in front of a huge sofa. "Largest sofa in the Southeast," Ray commented, "and the only one in that particular shade of green. It's ugly as hell, but if it ain't the most comfortable couch you ever sat on, I'll wipe your damn hiney for a week. Go on, kid. Try it out." I sank a foot and a half into the cushion. On the wall next to the TV hung a picture of Jesus. Beneath Our Lord, a Florida license plate read Arrive Alive.

We had to walk through Morey and Lester's bedroom to get to mine. Their bedroom looked normal, except for the photo of a grinning Uncle Fester between the twin beds. At the end of the mortuary students' bedroom stood a dark wooden door. Jerry twisted the glass knob and allowed the door to swing open. "I lived here myself," Jerry said, "as did Colton Albright before me—but the first man to live here was John Morton himself. He and his father built this place together. We hope you like your new home."

A huge four-poster dominated John Morton's bedroom with colonial menace, its bedspread suited royalty—dark violet with golden tassels. The bed rested upon an Oriental rug. Next to the bed, a nightstand equipped with a black telephone, a black pen, and a white pad of forms. A hand-tooled dresser with an oval mirror occupied a corner. From the ceiling, a miniature chandelier swathed the room in dim yellow light. It was the most beautiful room I had ever seen. Now it was mine, and the Presence of Morton-Albright abided here stronger than any other place in the funeral home. Jerry said, "John Morton and Sara, his wife, lived here until she became pregnant with Jewell—now Jewell Albright—Colton's wife."

"*Cruel* Jewell," Carl whispered in my ear.

Jerry went on, "When Sara became pregnant, John Morton built her a new home. I live there now. Colton lives in Clearwater."

"*Jewell* lives in Clearwater," Ray said. "Colton lives at Skeeter's Barbecue."

I took a last look inside my new room before Jerry closed the door. I saw the bells, big enough for a fire alarm, on the wall, just above the headboard of John Morton's bed. "Only one man ever slept through the bells," Carl said. "Deformed guy. Ray's cousin."

"He was not *deformed*," Ray said. "I talked Jerry into hiring him because my poor old mama begged me to help the kid."

"He didn't make it," Jerry said. "Wasn't cut out for the work—unlike our new man here. Take a walk with me, Casey. I've got something to show you." Jerry led me to the Druid Road entrance. Folks rarely used this entrance anymore—no place to park on Druid. We entered the vestibule and paused before four picture frames, each haunted by an old face. "Founding fathers," Jerry said. "Don't let them scare you. People didn't smile for pictures back then. Colton's the only one left now. He's eighty-two years old."

I followed Jerry out the front door, the sun blinding me. Jerry led me to the corner of the property, at Druid and Mayfair. The traffic on Druid zoomed behind us. Towering behind Jerry, Morton-Albright gleamed white in the blazing sunshine. The most beautiful of all the old mansions in Angel Shores—now my home. I lowered my eyes to Jerry's smile. Behind him rested the black horse-drawn funeral carriage. Black lanterns hung at each corner of the carriage, the coffin space windowed with thick glass, gone purple from years in the sun. Jerry patted the side of the coach. I could see the pride in his eyes. "We Stiles were livery people. This carriage belonged to my great-granddaddy, O. M. Stiles. The carriage has been right here on this spot since 1931, when they put the old horse out to pasture and bought a LaSalle motorized funeral coach."

"My dad loved this carriage," I said.

"So does all of Angel Shores, Casey. It reminds folks of how long Morton-Albright has been around. It reminds those of us who work here that we serve our families under the Morton-Albright name." Jerry turned and pointed across Druid Road, to a low brick building of three shops: Druid Cleaners, Al's Barber Shop, and Cynthia's Flowers. "I own that building," Jerry said. "That's where you get your suits cleaned and your hair cut. Cynthia, of Cynthia's flowers, is my wife—she's one of Colton Albright's daughters. Ray's wife, Denise, is the other one. We're all family here, son."

Jerry started toward the porte cochere. He kept talking as we walked, but I didn't pay attention—too busy remembering Ray's words: *Jerry's got a daughter.* I began thinking of how I might bring it up in conversation, when I heard Jerry say, "Watch out!" Too late—I had stepped in dog shit. The collapsing of the pile released a stink between Jerry and me. Embarrassed, I looked up at him, expecting a laugh—at least a smirk. His face showed only concern, both for me, and the precious front lawn of Morton-Albright. He apologized— Mrs. Stinson sometimes walked her beagle over here at night. I rubbed my shoe on the grass, and we continued our walk into the porte cochere—a wooden tunnel like a covered bridge, attached to the side of the funeral home. Empty now, the porte cochere housed the three funeral cars just before a procession to the cemetery. Jerry asked me if Ray and Carl had given me the business about my black suit, then assured me that Meredith Talbert would have me looking like a Morton-Albright man in time for Mrs. Pfister's visitation this afternoon, but first, we had to make my employment legal with the state of Florida. That meant filling out forms.

At Jerry's office, the door across the hall opened and a silver-haired man stepped into the hallway. The man didn't look at me. He asked Jerry for a word in private. He only glanced at me when Jerry introduced us. The man's name was Lex Talbert, Meredith's brother. He looked dour and creepy, as though working up a frown. Jerry assured Lex he'd be right in, after he dropped me off. Lex returned to his office and shut the door. "Don't let Lex rattle you," Jerry said. "He doesn't socialize with the rest of us. You won't see him drinking coffee in your kitchen."

Jerry seated me in his own chair. Before me lay the forms, required by the state of Florida, allowing me to practice embalming as an apprentice. Jerry explained the forms, his voice now solemn: "When you sign these forms, it's more than just your name on paper—it's a promise that you will discharge your duties here with professionalism and discretion. You must never discuss what goes on in the back room with anyone outside the trade. Do I have your word?"

"You do."

"Good man. In return, we promise to provide you with everything you need in life: everything from the clothes you wear to the mortgage on your first home. We pay all your costs at the Taylor School. We require one year of apprenticeship before you matriculate—see how you work out. Sounds fair?"

It did. Jerry left me with his alabaster pen. All I had to do was read and sign—no hesitation there—but the family pictures on Jerry's desk distracted me. I guessed the strawberry blond woman to be Jerry's wife, Cynthia, who ran the flower shop across the street. Her freckles showed, even in the soft focus of the photograph. Next to

Cynthia's picture stood a larger picture—a girl, about my age—Jerry's daughter, no doubt. Her face was nearly white—as though it had never seen the sun—except for her mother's freckles, fewer and darker, splashed across her nose. Black hair framed her perfect face. Her eyes were paler than Jerry's—ghostly, they were—forlorn, but in a pretty way, peaked with hopeful brows. Her smile betrayed disarming sneakiness, canines a notch longer than her front teeth. It was her smile that drove my eyes back to her own—I expected a wink. It was only a picture, but her countenance exuded the same feel that haunted the funeral home itself. I signed the documents without reading them, fearing the girl would vanish from the frame if I looked away. I crossed the *t* in Kight, just as Jerry entered the office and patted my shoulder. "The boys need you in the embalming room," he said.

4

In the embalming room, Mrs. Pfister still lay naked on the table.

"Did Jerry tell you about Natalie?" Ray asked.

"The girl in the picture on Jerry's desk?"

"That's Natalie," Ray said, "Jerry's daughter."

"Jerry didn't mention her," I said.

"Don't worry, kid. Jerry will tell you all about Natalie. She's the reason he hired you."

"Make a cute couple, you and Natalie," Carl said.

"What's she like?" I asked.

Ray snickered. Carl joined him, then they both burst into laughter. When they finally calmed down, Ray wiped a tear from under his glasses. "Sorry, kid. I'd love to tell you about Natalie."

"College student," Carl said. "USF. Major in photographic arts."

"Likes to take pictures," Ray said.

"Needs a boyfriend," said Carl. "Bad."

"*Real* bad," Ray added, "and she *is* the reason Jerry hired you—no doubt about it. We knew, the minute your narrow ass came through the door in that black suit. Natalie has hated every apprentice we ever hired, but she'll love you."

"She'll think you're deathy," Carl said.

"Deathy," said Ray. "Natalie's favorite word. You'll meet her soon. She pops in from time to time.

"*Sneaks* in, you mean," Carl said.

"*Sneaks* is more accurate," Ray agreed. "Sneaks into the funeral home at night and takes pictures of dead people. Gotta watch yourself too. She will scare the living fuck out of you—pops up out of nowhere. Jerry told us to throw her out if we catch her, but we help her sometimes. We kinda feel sorry for Natalie, don't we, Carl?"

"Yep. Shame about Natalie," Carl said. "Uncle Jerry says the embalming room is no place for a girl—she might see something *bad,* like John Morton's wife saw."

"Hell, Natalie's already seen all there is to see," Ray said, "including a dead man with a penis the size of your forearm. Jerry was standing right here when she barged in. She saw Mr. Forearm lying there, snapped his picture, said, 'I'll bet someone's missing *him* back at the ranch,' then she lit out. Jerry claims he confiscated the film, but I bet Mr. Forearm is now part of Natalie's portfolio."

"She's no pervert," Carl assured me. "She mostly goes for the bloody stuff. Oh, and one more thing—I guess we might as well warn you. Tell him, Ray."

"She bites," Ray said.

I looked at Carl, who agreed with Ray in a slow nod. "Draw blood if she's of the mind," Carl said. "Ray took two stitches once. He commented on Natalie's training-bra-type figure."

"Do you really think she'll like me?" I asked.

"Hold up your fingers," Carl said.

I splayed them before him.

"Looks like ten to me. She'll like you. Our last apprentice, Ray's brother, had sixteen fingers."

"He did *not* have sixteen fingers," Ray said, "and he wasn't my brother. Now, quit lying to the kid, here. It's casket time."

. . .

In the dressing room, Ray opened the scissors gate of the elevator. He said, "Grab that church truck over there, kid." Ray pointed to a device that looked like a steel accordion on wheels. "We use it to move caskets around."

Ray operated the elevator by pulling, hand over hand, a loop of chain that dangled from the ceiling. The elevator inched upward. "This is *my* elevator," he said. "Pretty dam cool, huh?" When we reached the second floor, Ray stopped the elevator. Darkness lay beyond the scissors gate. Ray opened the gate and stepped into the room. I followed his footfalls in the dark. Without warning, Ray switched on the lights. Thirty open caskets leaped out of the dark. I sucked in a breath.

"Freaky, isn't it," Ray said. "Meredith did the same thing to me—just flipped on the lights. I nearly dropped one in my drawers."

"Doesn't it scare the families?"

"Light switch downstairs. Families never come up here in the dark. We also warn them they're about to see a room full of open caskets."

"But you don't warn the new guy."

"Nope. Come with me. I'll show you *my* casket first." Ray's casket: I had never seen a piece of furniture so finely crafted, so exquisitely polished. "The Marcellas Cherry," he said. "You put me in this when I die. We get our caskets free—employee benefit. Natalie's got this same casket in her living room. Don't look at me like that—won't be long before you pick yours out, too. We all do it," Ray said. He pointed out caskets around the room. "Colton Albright goes in the mahogany. Carl wants that ugly bronze over there. Jerry, the Promethean. Meredith's got dibs on the Toccoa oak. His brother, Lex, is going in that green Dumpster out back."

I pictured Ray lying dead in the cherry casket, his head resting on the pillow, eyelids blurry beneath his thick lenses. I looked up to comment, but he had already trotted to the other side of the room.

He motioned me over, to a narrow coffin, the color of a brand-new penny. Ray said, "Wood caskets don't seal, so put me in this first. It's a solid copper inner liner with a glass pane over the pillow. After I'm inside the inner liner, put me in the Marcellas and close the lid. Nobody looks at me in the casket. Give me your solemn word. I make everybody swear. Now follow me. Prepare yourself for a spiritual experience." Ray held himself erect and stepped across the display room to the grandest of all caskets, so distinctive that a separate array of ceiling lamps illuminated it. It could have been John F. Kennedy's casket, or Valentino's—pewter, dotted with shiny silver in small amoeba shapes. "The Millennium," Ray said. Solid copper. Deposit finish. Fifteen thousand dollars. It's here for show, like the old carriage out front. Folks expect to see a casket like this at Morton-Albright." I lingered over the Millennium, mouth open, until Ray grabbed my arm and took me to Mrs. Pfister's casket: The Primrose sealer. "Sealer means there's a rubber gasket between the lid and the body of the casket—protects the remains from outside elements—keeps the worms off Granny. When foul gases build up inside a sealer casket, the damn thing burps like Tupperware."

Ray let me work the elevator chain on the way back down. We wheeled the Primrose into the dressing room, where Ray and I interrupted Carl, working on a pimple in front of the mirror. Ray asked him, "Did you pack the orifices?"

"No, I did not pack the orifices," Carl said. "Casey needs to learn. You need to learn, too."

"That's not funny," Ray said. "You know I hate packing."

Carl picked up a huge pair of forceps and tweezed them together under Ray's nose. Carl said, "One of these days, I'll be packing your orifices."

"Cut that shit out, you pervert. You're scaring Casey and me."

In the embalming room was a roll of cotton, attached to the wall like paper towels. Carl tore off a couple of sheets, then tore the sheets into strips. With the forceps, he pushed the strips of cotton into Mrs. Pfister's nostrils. It sounded like baby knuckles cracking.

"Damn, I hate that." Ray winced. I asked the reason for this procedure. "Kid, packing the orifices is disgusting and absolutely necessary. It prevents human substances from leaking into that two-thousand dollar Primrose we brought down here for Mrs. Pfister. You get a leak, and you're in trouble—*big* trouble. Pretend Granny dies. Your priest drops by the funeral home, to say the Rosary with you and your friends and relatives. Pretend the funeral home did not pack Granny's orifices. Now, imagine a bowel movement in the middle of that Rosary service. There you are, saying Hail Marys and your poor old dead granny decides to take a dump in her brand-new casket. At first, you think maybe somebody farted, but before long, you're *praying* somebody farted. You peek over at the others— they smell it too. You can see it on their faces. It's bad. This is not you smelling yourself while you're reading the funny papers on the john. We're talking about fecal matter that has been inside a dead person for a couple of days. We're talking all four horsemen of the Apocalypse taking a shit in the middle of your service." Ray paused—gave me a moment to imagine the stink. "So what do you do then?" Ray asked. "Stop the Rosary and make an announcement? Hell, no. That announcement has already been *made*. The Rosary goes on. Nobody's going to stop praying, sniff the air, and ask out loud, 'What the fuck is that?' They already *know*. They know your granny crapped a death turd and broke up the party."

"Bad for business," Carl said, clanging the used forceps into a sterilizing tray.

"Why do you pack the nose?" I asked.

"So Granny can't smell the death turd and jump out of her casket."

"The Fly Factor," Carl said. "Only takes one fly to crawl up a nose and lay a thousand eggs—that's a thousand maggots you've got, squirming out of the nose."

"Distasteful tasks," Ray said. "Hell, kid, it's the reason we're here. Folks pay us to stick cotton up Granny's rectum because *they* don't want to stick cotton up Granny's rectum—and I sure as hell don't want to do it either. That's why we hired Carl. Carl's the packer man. Carl, tell Casey why Jerry calls you his Yankee nephew."

"I spent my teenage years in Green Bay, Wisconsin," Carl said.

"See there? Carl told his daddy he wanted to be a Packer when he grew up and his daddy sent him to Mortuary School. Looks like Carl got his wish."

Carl flipped Ray the finger. Ray flipped him back, then handed me a shopping bag full of clothing. Ray said, "Find Mrs. Pfister's panties." I had never touched such garments. It embarrassed me to handle them. Ray said I'd get used to it, but not enough to try them on.

Ray slipped Mrs. Pfister's big panties up to her knees. He and Carl lifted her legs, way up. Stiff with formaldehyde, her buttocks rose up from the table. Ray and Carl hiked her panties up and straightened them out. Next, the bra. Her breasts didn't actually go in the bra, because they sagged, so Ray put the bra where it was supposed to go and stuffed it with cotton. He said Natalie had once watched him stuff a bra. "I suggested she try it herself. That's when she bit me." Ray styled Mrs. Pfister's hair and sprayed it with Aqua-Net. Carl cut the flowered dress all the way up the back. They put the dead woman's arms in the sleeves and tucked the dress underneath her. Ray stippled translucent cream onto Mrs. Pfister's face, then a dust of powder. Ray misted her with the perfume that had been included in the bag of clothes. "Emeraude," he said.

Ray and Carl approached Mrs. Pfister on her right side. Together, they worked their hands underneath her, rolled her toward themselves, and picked her up off the embalming table. They carried her toward the casket like a battering ram. Ray adjusted her in the Primrose, then closed the lid. He said, "We can't roll her with the lid open. Someone might walk in on you while you're rolling through the lobby. It's not dignified—makes them look like they're going for a wagon ride." Ray opened the Quiet door. He spoke to me in a loud whisper. "Keep your hands on the sides of the casket as we roll. They'll act like cushions if we smash the casket into a doorjamb. That way, your hand takes the damage instead of the casket or the funeral home. Rule Number Three: Skin grows back."

The Blue Room looked elegant but small. Its walls were papered in faded white with dark blue designs. A powder blue love seat sat against a wall. Ray flipped a switch on a black telephone, sitting atop an end table. There was a telephone in every room of the funeral home, so you could always answer on the first ring. You had to remember to turn on the ringer when you entered any of the public rooms, then shut it off when you left—that way a family member wouldn't accidentally answer a death call.

Ray and I lifted the casket from the church truck and placed it upon a bier. The telephone rang. Carl picked it up. Ray said, "See what I mean? You never know when that phone will ring. Probably a lovey-dovey call from Carl's wife." Carl waved his hand at Ray, shushing him, then put down the phone. "Casket spray," he said. "Bernard's bringing it over now."

Ray ran out the door. Carl and I trotted to keep up. Bernard worked for Jerry's wife at Cynthia's Flowers, across the street. According to Carl, Ray loved to watch the guy run across the road. Ray stopped in front of the picture window, overlooking Druid Road. "Watch him, Casey. It's your first day. You don't want to miss the most exciting thing that ever happens around here."

Across Druid Road, I could just make out a baseball cap above the huge spray of roses Bernard carried, the kid's face obscured by the flowers. Bernard jogged toward the middle of the street. "Here he comes," Ray said. "Holy shit—you see that Impala swerve? Carl's going to be packing that kid's dumb ass this very afternoon. Ain't that right, Carl?" Bernard made it to the middle of the road. Now stuck there, he balanced himself upon the double yellow lines. Honking and swerving cars whizzed past him in front and behind. "Kid doesn't know whether to shit or wind his watch," Ray said.

Bernard beat it across the road. A honking Volkswagen flew past as Bernard's foot bounded onto the curb. Ray opened the door for the kid, then started in on him, "Shit fire and save matches. What is wrong with your brain, Bernard? Put those flowers in the van and drive them over like a citizen."

The lanky kid snickered at Ray's comment. Face full of freckles, grin full of braces, Bernard claimed it took too long to drive the van to the funeral home—he couldn't just drive straight across the street because of the unceasing traffic on Druid Road. Instead, he had to drive a two-mile square of right-hand turns to the Morton-Albright parking lot. "Takes two minutes to run across the street," Bernard said. "Takes twenty to drive."

"You'll be dead a lot longer than twenty minutes," Ray said. "Then you and Carl will have a date with a roll of cotton and a pair of forceps. Ain't that right, Carl?"

In the Blue Room, Mrs. Pfister looked better with her clothes on. Carl placed Bernard's spray atop the foot-end lid of the casket, then switched on the torchier lamps, one at each end of the casket. Ray played with the dimmer switch for the overheads, the recessed ceiling lamps directly above Mrs. Pfister. "Cosmetic lamps," Ray said. "Special tones of light that give the makeup a lifelike appearance. We do some damn fine work here at Morton-Albright. Look at Mrs. Pfister now, Casey."

I approached the casket and admired the result of all our work with Mrs. Pfister. She *did* look good. She *did* look peaceful, as though she were sleeping. I understood the art of embalming—it softens the family's confrontation with death. I also considered all we had done to achieve this setting. We had done things to Mrs. Pfister that would have killed her, had she been alive.

On the way back to my new apartment for lunch, Ray said he'd slap me if I ever said, "Granny's laid out in the Blue Room." According to Ray, Mrs. Pfister now lay *in repose.*

• • •

Carl went home for lunch. Ray tore into a brown paper bag. He set three sandwiches before himself, then peeked under each slice of bread. "Deviled ham, baloney, olive loaf." Ray gobbled up all three sandwiches with grunts and noisy swallows, then let out a ten-second belch, all before I had unwrapped the wax paper from my ham and cheese Margee had packed for me. Ray said, "Man, I love that olive loaf." Margee would have hit him with the flyswatter and made him leave the table, and Ray was now headed for *more* food—a crate of oranges in the corner of the kitchen. He picked out two and threw one to me. "Winstead oranges," he said, "from my daddy's grove." Until now, I hadn't made the connection with Ray's name. Everybody knew Winstead Groves, and their air-conditioned tourist stand on County Road 5. Their place was as famous as Skeeter's Barbecue. "Yep, I'm a Winstead—destined for a life of tractors and bee-stings. Then I laid eyes on Denise Albright." With a penknife, Ray went to work on the orange. He confessed a lifelong disinterest in citrus production. Since Ray hated working in the groves, his daddy had given him the delivery truck to take care of the commercial accounts that demanded fresh fruit, like the Angel Shores Country Club. "That's where I met Denise," Ray said. He had spotted Denise in her tennis outfit, walking toward him. Ray was carrying a crate of Winstead oranges. "When I saw her face, my legs got all wobbly. I had to stop her."

Ray stood in the middle of the sidewalk and blocked her path. Denise read the label on the box, "Winstead oranges. My daddy only buys Winstead oranges." Then, she took an orange out of the box and asked if she could keep it. Ray offered her the crate. He said, "My name is Ray Winstead, and I'd be pleased to meet your daddy. In fact, I'll personally deliver his oranges, right to his front door."

You already *do*—that's what Denise said. Said her daddy was Colton Albright, the Undertaker. Everybody in town knew his name. Denise told Ray, "Every week, *you* leave a box of oranges next to the refrigerator at Morton-Albright Funeral Home. Those are my daddy's oranges. I eat one every day. Wanna meet my daddy?"

Ray met her daddy at Skeeter's Barbecue. "There sat Colton Albright with Jerry Stiles and the mayor of Angel Shores. She introduced me, then took me to another table—said she only dated boys who worked for her daddy. I thought, how bad could it be? I started work the next Monday—puked every day for two weeks straight. Meredith called me Vomit Man." Ray slouched in the chair. He'd asked Denise to marry him as soon as the puking phase ended, but she had refused—no marriage license without a funeral director's license—family motto. Her daddy, Colton Albright, had failed to produce a male heir to the business (not that the old man hadn't tried—Cynthia and Denise were separated by twenty years). Jerry and Cynthia had borne Natalie, another female. The responsibility for the baby boy that would inherit Morton-Albright now fell to Denise. "Problem is, Denise *can't* have babies," Ray said. "Morton-Albright is without a male heir, and this is where *you* come in, kid. Jerry hired you for Natalie, who happens to be of childbearing age. You've got to marry her and have babies—*boys*, to be exact. Now it's time for my nap."

"That's it?" I asked.

"That's it." Ray said. He sat down on the largest couch in the Southeast, dropped his head to one side, and began snoring. I sat down on the other end of the couch.

The two men woke me up with their talk. Jerry, and an older man with a big smile and a striking shock of white hair. I jumped off the couch and apologized for falling asleep. Jerry assured me that naps were allowed—especially when you've been up half the night worrying about your first day at work. Ray snored on. Jerry introduced me to the man with the white hair: "Meet Meredith Talbert."

"Welcome aboard, Cap'n," Meredith said. "You'll look fine, once we get you out of that black suit."

I could see why Jerry had chosen Meredith to help me with my new wardrobe. The light gray suit he wore accentuated his white hair. The red in his tie brought color to his face. Black oxfords shone like patent leather. He looked professional, but not in a distant way—more like he'd be your best friend, if it weren't for the suit. Tiny crow's feet around Meredith's eyes gave him a wise look; his smile broadcast sympathy. He drove me to Sammy's Men's Store. We hadn't been in the car five minutes when Meredith said, "Yessir, Cap'n, that Natalie is a fine girl, but I'm sure Jerry's told you all about her by now."

Jerry hadn't mentioned her, I said. "He will, Cap'n," Meredith said through a chuckle. "We're all family here. My brother, Lex, and I are on the Morton side of the family—cousins, removed several times, this way and that. Morton-Albright wasn't always a funeral home, you know. It started out as a furniture store. That's where you went to buy your coffin way back then." Meredith's ancestors had bought that furniture store from the Mortons. The place burned down when Meredith and Lex had been in their twenties. The fire department blamed it on bad wiring and a closet full of solvents and stains. "Our parents died in that fire," Meredith said. "Old John Morton felt so bad, he insisted that Lex and I work here, at the funeral home. Even put it in his will—a job for life, and retirement at full pay."

After John hired the two brothers, Lex "got marrying eyes for Cynthia," according to Meredith. "Lex wanted in on the funeral home—he blamed old John for the bad wiring and the fire." Lex saw the fire as negligence on John's part. Meredith saw it as an accident. He said, "I'm just happy for a job to go to every day, and grateful for John's kindness. Jerry ended up with Cynthia. Lex never married." Meredith pointed beyond the windshield. Along the southern horizon, nine buildings, under construction, rose above the treetops—Sunset Towers. "My God," said Meredith. "They're going to ruin our pretty little town, aren't they, Cap'n?"

Sammy Ford, the tailor, greeted us at the door of his shop. He scanned me, top to bottom and said, "My God, would you look at that black suit—wouldn't even pass for midnight charcoal in the dark. That suit is *black,* son. Let's get you out of it, put you into something that'll impress Natalie." Sammy paused to wink at me. "I'm sure Jerry's told you all about Natalie, nice-looking boy such as yourself."

Jerry hadn't told me anything, I said.

"He will, and she's a pretty one, too—took pictures of me and my store. She put that one up on the wall over there—said I was part of the Morton-Albright story. That girl knows all that's gone on in Angel Shores for the last hundred years."

Sammy looked like a tailor from an old movie—short-statured, tie loosened, sleeves rolled up, vest unbuttoned. Tape measure around his neck, he wore half-specs way down his nose and a marking pencil behind his ear—rumpled, for a man who made sure that well-to-do people looked their best. Sammy suggested a gray chalk-stripe for now. He'd send six more over to the funeral home by late evening, plus a dozen shirts, ties, socks, and two pairs of shoes. Sammy measured me, then disappeared with Meredith into a back room, to arrange my wardrobe. I headed for Natalie's photograph on the wall—a picture of Sammy, bent over his sewing machine, his head encircled by a cloud of smoke from a carved meerschaum pipe, clenched between his teeth. The store smelled of the woody chocolate tobacco from that pipe, as did everything you bought from Sammy Ford.

Dressed in my new clothes, I stepped into the lobby of Morton-Albright. Jerry, Ray, and Carl were waiting for me. They patted my back, tugged on my sleeves, and made more jokes about my black suit. Their attention embarrassed me, until I realized what they meant: I belonged with them. My dream had come true. I was an Undertaker. Actually, by law, I was an embalmer's apprentice, but it meant the same to me.

Meredith taught me how to make the sign for Mrs. Pfister's

repose. I stepped back and admired it, now affixed to the wall next to the door of the Blue Room.

Alice Pfister
Calling Hours—Tuesday 2:00–4:00 P.M., 7:00–9:00 P.M.
Service—Wednesday 10:00 A.M.

Meredith commented on the lack of flowers in the Blue Room— small service, he said. "They keep getting smaller, too, Cap'n. Old folks move down here from up North, families spread out all over the country—not like it used to be—lots more cremations now. The trade is changing every day, except among our own—still plenty of crackers around. They still take pride in a full-service funeral. Let's check on Mrs. Pfister."

As we entered the Blue Room Meredith warned me about allowing visitors to view the remains. "Never let anyone in a repose room for a first viewing without checking the body yourself. Make them wait in the reception area." Meredith approached the casket, leaned over Mrs. Pfister, and smelled deeply. "Always smell the body," Meredith said. "If you smell anything besides the decedent's cologne, tell someone right away." He pinched the skin up on the back of her hand and let go. The skin moved back, slowly. "Not too hard, not too soft," he said. "Ray's work. Carl's a good embalmer too, but Ray is perfection. Carl gets his license next month—he won't be embalming forever. Ray's stuck in the back room for life. Did Jerry tell you about Ray, Cap'n?"

He hadn't, I said.

"Of course not," Meredith said. "I keep forgetting it's your first day. Seems like you've been around here a long time. I guess that means you've got the gift, Cap'n."

"I'm not squeamish, if that's what you mean."

"Takes more than that to make a good man. Ray didn't do so well in the back room when he first started, but the families loved him when he became a director. Ray's not as ornery as he lets on. He knew how to comfort a family. That's what this place is all about, Cap'n—comfort. Ray still provides comfort—just take a look at Mrs. Pfister here—but Ray doesn't wait on families anymore. It's a tragedy, and a damn shame."

It happened a year into Ray and Denise's marriage. Ray was the most gifted man since John Morton himself. There was talk of Ray succeeding Jerry as manager and senior director. Then came the news everybody had been waiting for: Denise announced that she was pregnant. "We all thought the Golden Child was on his way," Meredith said. All of Morton-Albright prayed for a boy—an heir to the business. Ray passed cigars around every Friday for seven months. They didn't even bother with girl names. They'd name their son after John Morton, with the middle name, Raymond—call the boy Johnny Ray.

In the eighth month of Denise's pregnancy, the trouble began. She felt bad. The doctor found an irregular heartbeat in the unborn child. Six weeks before the due date, the baby came—a premature boy with multiple birth defects: Hydrocephalus, spina bifida, undersized lungs, heart problems, and jaundice. Johnny Ray died while Ray held the baby's tiny fingers. "Our hearts were broken," Meredith said, "but none as bad as Ray's. He acted strong for a while, but we all knew better." A month after the baby died, Ray met with a family who had lost a child to crib death. He broke down and sobbed, right in front of the family. Jerry made Ray take a few weeks off. He came back in better spirits, until he met with a family who had lost a four-year-old girl to a swimming pool. Ray broke down again. He walked around the funeral home with the shakes, yelling at everyone. Before long, Ray was crying over nursing home deaths. Everyone feared he'd quit the business altogether. "Ray seemed fine, as long as he stayed out of the arrangement office. My own brother, Lex, urged Jerry to fire Ray. Jerry wouldn't hear it. He loves Ray, you know." Instead of banishing Ray from Morton-Albright, Jerry created a new position for him—embalming room supervisor. Ray took on all the jobs that were not related to making arrangements—jobs that the funeral directors had formerly shared.

"Ray's the one irreplaceable man on staff," Meredith said. "He handles everything from embalming to ordering caskets—works the funeral, too—sees to the sealing of the vault at the graveside. Ray will teach you everything you need to know about working in a funeral home, except waiting on families, and one other thing: Ray doesn't embalm children."

I felt stricken inside for Ray—not simply because his son had died but that after all these years, Ray had remained uncomforted. I began to feel strange inside, as though I were on the verge of another episode. I didn't want to have it in front of Meredith, on my first day of work. Tension pulled at the muscles of my shoulders as I braced myself, ready for the crash that killed my parents. Instead, I went straight to the path, the uncanny state of calm I normally experienced *after* an episode. My attention now drawn to Mrs. Pfister, lying in her casket, I noticed that her dress was wrinkled in places. Her collar just slightly off-center. I leaned into the casket and began tugging at her sleeves, adjusting her collar. Her hands were folded at her waist. Her wedding ring was tilted. I corrected it. As I worked, I noticed other tiny imperfections in her appearance— the tilt of her head on the pillow, a bit of lipstick just below her lip line. I remembered a box of Kleenex on an end table. I turned around. There stood Meredith, Jerry, Ray and Carl, all looking at me, astonishment on their faces. I figured I was in trouble with Ray—more eager shit. They'd all tease me, I thought, but they didn't. Jerry was the first to speak. He said, "Son, it was my understanding that you had never worked in a funeral home before. Is there something you'd like to tell us?"

"She was wrinkled," I said. "I fixed her. I've never even been in another funeral home in my whole life. What did I do wrong?"

"Nothing," Ray said. "That's the point. You did everything right. How did you know what to do?"

"I didn't know what to do. It just seemed the logical thing. —it seemed like instinct."

"He's got the gift," Carl said.

FINAL ARRANGEMENTS • 45

"There ain't no gift," Ray answered. "Casey watched me doing the same thing earlier today. He catches on quick, but there ain't no gift."

Jerry said, "Gift or no gift, our Casey is a talented young man."

At 2:00 P.M., Meredith posted me at the door of the main entrance, to greet callers for the Pfister visitation. I stood there for two hours. Nobody showed. Meredith came for me at 4:00 P.M. He glanced at the empty register book. "See what I mean?" He said. "Mrs. Pfister's got a daughter in a hospital in Maryland—same cancer that killed Mrs. Pfister. She's also got a sister here, local—in a nursing home—might make the service tomorrow. Meantime, you can walk with me to my home, just down the street. You can meet my wife, and try some of her fried chicken."

Meredith's wife, Teresa, was talking on the phone when we walked in. I smelled the chicken—I was famished. Teresa waved at us, then spoke to the person on the other end of the line, "I've got to go now, sweetheart. Meredith just came in with a handsome young fellow. They look hungry." Teresa hung up the phone and untied her apron. She wore a sweet face with a friendly smile. "Natalie on the phone," Teresa said. "That girl is the sweetest thing. She made us a family album for our fortieth, bless her heart. I'm sure you've heard all about her by now."

Between mouthfuls of fried chicken, I explained to Teresa that I hadn't heard much about Natalie. Teresa had been at the hospital when Natalie was born, and claimed to have been the first person Natalie had ever bitten. "When she was teething—drew blood, the little devil."

"Don't let that girl get hold of your arm, Cap'n. She's *still* teething."

"We love Natalie," Teresa said. "She's her own girl though—modern—but there's a part of her that's old, too—those clothes she wears. She likes rummaging through what folks leave behind. I ran into her at the Winn-Dixie not long ago, all dressed up in black lace, like a young widow from one of those old movies. She drove away in that black car of hers."

Meredith cleared his throat at Teresa. She said, "I'm rambling, but Natalie will be awful glad to meet you after that other boy. Land sakes, but he was a mess—something wrong with his hand. I met him at a service for a friend of mine. He scratched himself the whole time, right in the chapel—made me itch all over—a Mr. Beecham, I believe."

"Ball," Meredith said. "Mr. Ball."

I took my place at the main entrance at 7:00 P.M., waiting for nobody to show up. Meredith called me away from the door, said I had a phone call. "Your aunt," Meredith said. "She sounds worried."

Margee. I had forgotten all about her. As soon as I picked up the phone, she started the interrogation: Was I all right? Did I see anything bad? How come I didn't come home at five, like everybody else? I let her talk until she tired herself out. Then I told her—*I live here now.* I had to hold the phone away from my ear until she stopped her stream of worried jabbering. When the phone went silent, I pressed it against my ear and whispered to Margee, "*I need underwear. Now.*" Margee was sure I'd had an accident in my pants from seeing something horrible. When I finally calmed her down, she promised to drop off a suitcase. "I'll leave it at the door," she said. "Don't expect me to come inside. God only knows what y'all are up to in there. Whatever it is, I don't want to see it."

Nobody showed for Mrs. Pfister's evening hours. At nine o'clock, Meredith turned off the lights and locked the place up. We stepped onto the veranda and sniffed the warm night air, sweet with the gardenias that surrounded the funeral home. Beneath the canopy of cypresses, a large, black car motored across the parking lot toward the exit. Meredith pointed at the car. "There goes Natalie now," he said. Even in the dimness, I knew the make and model of Natalie's car—a 1966 Chrysler Imperial: the Green Hornet's car.

5

In my apartment I met the mortuary students. Identical twins. A pair of black-rimmed glasses sat upon each of their noses. One of them stood at the kitchen sink, putting a Band-Aid on his hand. A bottle of Bactine sat on the counter.

"I guess you're Casey," said the uninjured twin. "I'm Jeff Carothers. You just missed Natalie. She bit Randy."

"Again," Randy said.

"Ray told me your names were More and Less," I said.

"That's because we don't have twin names, like Robby and Bobby. Ray makes up a new set of names for us every time he forgets our real names, which is most of the time. He said you were hot stuff with Jerry Stiles, and Natalie didn't waste any time getting here. She pretended she'd left a roll of film in the refrigerator."

"She didn't even look in the refrigerator," Randy said. "She just started asking questions about Casey Kight—probably wanted to make sure you had the right number of fingers—last guy they hired was a polydactyl."

"Poly-what?"

"Polydactyl. Ray's kin. Guy had eleven fingers, no shit."

"It wasn't a proper finger," Jeff explained, "more like a withered stem, growing out the side of his hand—no fingernail on it or anything. I don't know why he never had that damn thing cut off. Disgusting—not to mention his skin problems—squeezed-out tubes of Lanacane all over the apartment, scratching all the time—allergies too. Guy never even blew his nose. He'd just suck it up and swallow it. Ray fucked up when he brought that guy here. Beecher Bell. Fuck of a name, huh?"

"We called him Belcher Beech," Randy said.

"We had a few other names for him, too," Jeff said. "Beecher Meat, Beecher Balls, the Beecher Creature."

"Terry Dactyl," Randy added. "That one pissed him off the most."

"Randy told Natalie that you were a poly-dick-tyl—told her you had an extra dong. Natalie bit him, then she started going through your suitcase, holding up your underwear and stuff. I pretended to call Jerry. She lit out of here quick."

"She's not allowed on the premises after dark," Randy said. "Jerry's orders."

"Jerry's a great guy," Jeff said. "Unfortunately, we hardly ever work with Jerry."

"We work with Lex," Randy said.

"Creepy fellow," Jeff allowed.

"He's an asshole," Randy said. "He glorifies JFT."

"Jacob Funeral Trust," Jeff said. "Huge conglomerate of funeral homes. Lex says they're the wave of the future. They buy out funeral homes when the chain of family ownership becomes extinct. If you can't pass your business on, you have to sell it. JFT waits like a vulture."

According to the twins, JFT paid cash on the spot—full asking price, plus a stipend, if the owner agreed to serve a few years in a public relations capacity. That way, it appeared to the public that the funeral home was still being run by the original family, not some big corporation. When word of JFT got around, sellers began inflating their prices, and JFT paid. A private individual looking for an opportunity now found himself priced out of the market. "And that ain't all," Randy said. "I've heard scary shit about JFT. They do weird things to the bodies."

"Now, you don't know that, Randy," Jeff chided. "Casey, you'll have to excuse my brother. He's the excitable one. I'm the smart one—that's the best way to tell us apart."

"Fuck you, Jeff."

"Fuck you back, Randy."

They both took a swig of Coke and gave each other the finger.

"How well do you guys know Natalie?" I asked.

"We never dated her, if that's what you mean," Randy said. "She's off-limits. Jeff and I have to go back to our own funeral home in Sebring. Morton-Albright needs Natalie here—for bait."

"Randy means that Natalie should marry someone who can take over the business someday. We can't do that. Natalie's cool with everything. She loves this old place. She'd never let Morton-Albright slip out of family hands. Of course, Natalie won't be happy until she's in the embalming room with a trocar in her hand. Don't worry. You'll meet her soon."

"Police rotation," Randy said. "It starts Thursday at midnight. Think of it as a Natalie-magnet. Our county morgue doesn't have a refrigerator like Hillsborough, so the medical examiner's office pays the funeral homes in the area to remove the bodies and embalm them."

"Police rotation is cool." Jeff said. "You get to see all the legendary stuff—hellacious accidents, murders, suicides—you never know what you might see. Natalie never misses Police rotation—you know, *click click*?" Jeff pretended a camera in front of his face.

The twins agreed to swap weekends off. I'd take the coming weekend to get the rest of my belongings.

In John Morton's bedroom, I opened my closet and smelled the tailor's pipe tobacco. All six suits hung there, along with a dozen white shirts and an assortment of ties, just as Sammy had promised. The ties had been hung around the hangers of the suits they matched. On the floor of the closet, two new pairs of black shoes—wingtips and penny loafers.

I unpacked my suitcase, full of new underwear and tee shirts, and a new pair of blue pajamas, still in the wrapper—Margee's final expression of motherhood. I put them on and lay down on John Morton's bed, soft and slept-in. The Presence that abided here wrapped itself around me like a blanket of calm, and just before I fell asleep, I remembered Jerry's last announcement at my parents' graveside: "You may retire at your leisure." So many times, I had worked on that phrase in my mind. At the age of nine, the words had sounded cryptic, indecipherable, but when I saw the Morton-Albright employees leading my relatives to their cars, I realized that, "You may retire at your leisure," was a polite way—a *respectful* way—of telling everybody to go home. That's where I was now—home, and I longed for the day when I would utter that phrase myself.

I jumped out of bed like Christmas morning—my first funeral service. I hummed in the shower. I smiled and chuckled to myself as I slipped into the smell of wool, starched cotton, and Sammy's chocolate smoke. I worked a dimple into my tie, just beneath the four-in-hand I had knotted for the third time. I admired myself in the mirror, standing tall, working my face into a variety of Undertaker expressions. No matter how hard I tried, I still looked like a kid in a nice suit. I had become a man, but only in the legal sense of the word.

Margee had taken me to the doctor when I was sixteen. The DMV had refused to give me a driver's license, even after I showed them my birth certificate. They made Margee sign a paper. The doctor described my condition, right in front of Margee: "Both of his testicles are descended and slightly enlarged. There is a slight amount of hair on his scrotum. If you look closely, you can see a little bit of peach fuzz on his upper lip. He's on his way to puberty, but your boy is a late bloomer."

"How late?" Margee asked the doctor.

"He's sixteen—couple years or so behind his peers."

"That explains a lot," Margee said with embarrassingly obvious relief. I knew what Margee meant. She wanted to know why I displayed no interest in girls. Now a girl in a picture frame on Jerry's desk had *all* of my attention, and we hadn't even met.

I caught myself smiling again in the mirror. I worried that glee would overtake my Morton-Albright demeanor during Mrs. Pfister's service. In the TV voice of the man who announces, "We now conclude our broadcast day," I enunciated phrases like, "Good morning," and "Right this way, please." Then I remembered the mortuary students, Jeff and Randy. Embarrassed that they might have heard me, I peeked out the door of my bedroom into theirs. They had already left for school. I shut the door and resumed my place at the mirror. Ray walked into my bedroom without knocking—he just walked right in. "I was the last Morton-Albright man to live in these quarters," he said. "I am now your official embalming instructor as specified in your apprenticeship documentation. Carl can assist—he's a licensed embalmer. I'm a licensed funeral director. The difference is a year of apprenticeship after mortuary school. That's when you learn how to wait on families. It's four years from where you are to where I am, and it's my job to make sure you get there. I will continue to barge in, without knocking, unless I know for a fact that you are in here with a female of the opposite sex. That means if you want privacy, you'd better hook up with Natalie, real quick-like."

Out in the parking lot we all washed the cars in our shirts and ties—first duty on any funeral day. "Nobody's exempt from car-washing detail," Ray said. "Nobody but Lex." Lex Talbert arrived twenty minutes into our project. He didn't even look at us when he got out of his car and headed for the building. I wondered who would answer the telephone on the first ring when we were all outside at the same time. Ray showed me the telephone, inside the wooden three-car garage. "This used to be the stable for the horse that pulled the old carriage out front," Ray said. Now the stable housed the three funeral cars: Hearse, limousine, lead car—all brand-new Miller-Meteor Cadillacs, in stunning midnight blue. It thrilled me to touch the automobiles with the soaping mitt.

Each man took a turn with the rinsing hose. We played a game of squirting each other, then pretending it was an accident—you had to bounce the stream of water off some part of the car. You couldn't spray the other guy directly, and you had to look in some other direction when you sprayed—no obvious aiming allowed. It was a mundane task, so everybody used the opportunity to goof around with each other. Washing the cars became one of my favorite activities—nobody had ever wanted to goof around with me before. I was now among my own kind, relaxed and having fun. I stayed calm, even when the military jet whizzed overhead. When I looked upward toward the east, I saw the mechanical arm of an enormous crane—the biggest crane I had ever seen, and I wasn't the only one marveling at the thing. We all stopped washing and spraying to look at it. "Sunset Towers," Meredith said. "I hear they're going to pack sixty thousand people into that place."

The morning too warm for seven o'clock, a red sun made everything glow, heating up the town like an electric burner. Sweat popped up in the recessions where Ray's hair used to grow. "Hot one today," he said. "Everybody stick a lump of dough in your pocket. By the time Dr. Hamilton says Amen, we'll all have a biscuit to eat." Ray's joke made me sad for him—I pictured him holding the tiny fingers of his dying son. It was my turn with the rinsing hose—I wasn't paying attention for thinking of Ray—the hose lodged itself under a tire. When I sprayed, I soaked my new penny loafers right through to the skin. Everybody laughed, but it didn't embarrass me at all, it made me feel like one of the guys. I squished all the way to my room to change my shoes. Ray followed me inside, his face a blank. In silence, he watched me change into my wingtips. I glanced up at him as I tied my laces, seeking remnants of grief for his lost son.

"Come with me," he said. "I've got a surprise for you."

I followed Ray down the hallway. As we walked, Ray looked straight ahead when he spoke to me. "It was Meredith." Ray said. "He told you about the baby. I can always tell when somebody finds out. You've been giving me the poor-Ray look all morning. Stop looking at me like you're the guy who had to shoot Old Yeller. I've had my troubles, but I ain't Old Yeller." Ray stopped in the middle of the hallway, then turned to face me. "Rule Number Three: Forget Ray's tragedy. It's part of being a good man. I know this from personal experience. You've got to stay just this side of the heartbreaking part of the job. You *will* go crazy if you fail to detach yourself slightly—starting with me." He took a step toward me and folded his arms across his chest. I still pitied him inside, but I worked the pity from my face. "That's better," Ray said. "You've earned your surprise."

Ray took me to the bat cave, to the door marked Supply. "Here's your big chance, kid. Take out that magic key of yours and open the supply room."

I inserted the skeleton key into the door and turned it, feeling the click of the mechanism. It made me so happy, I was on the verge of tears, at least until I twisted the doorknob. It turned, but the door was stuck fast. "We never lock this door," Ray said, "but I knew you were dying to use that key of yours. Now unlock it and let us in."

I had expected the supply room to be the size of a large closet—it was half the size of the lobby, its back wall ended at my apartment. Wooden racks on both sides held caskets, stacked three high. Extra church trucks, folded accordion style, stood parked by the door. A collection of wheelchairs occupied a corner. "Where's my surprise" I asked.

"Over there, against the wall."

"The vacuum cleaner?"

"Not just *any* vacuum cleaner," Ray said. "Allow me to introduce you to the Luxor 9000, the most advanced vacuuming device ever created. It's too heavy to push—the damn thing's self-propelled— take you all the way to Georgia if you had enough cord. Even has a headlight. Just remember to let go of the trigger when you want to stop—break a chair leg if you're not careful. Don't even think about putting your hand anywhere near the cleaning head, not unless you've got fingers to spare, like the last guy."

It was the biggest vacuum cleaner I had ever seen—as big as a lawn mower. I still failed to grasp the honor of operating a vacuum cleaner. Ray explained, "Vacuuming the funeral home is more than a job—it's a privilege—takes you to every room in the place. By the time you've vacuumed a hundred times, you'll know more about nooks and crannies than those English-muffin people. It's how the apprentice gets to know the funeral home. You start with the display room, every morning."

"If it's so heavy, how do we get it upstairs?" I asked.

"How many damn questions can you ask in one day? I can't wait to teach you embalming. The body will decompose on us before you stop asking questions, and I like talking, too. One of us is going to have to shut up and watch. That means you. We'll tip the Luxor backward and roll it on the rear wheels. You do understand the concept of leverage, don't you? Don't answer. Just follow me to the people elevator in the lobby. You need to see that too."

The people elevator was in the lobby, next to the staircase. Ray flipped the light switches for the casket display room. He winked at me, then pressed the elevator call button. The door slid open, revealing an elevator car the size of my closet. Ray and I squeezed inside, close enough to smell each other's toothpaste. Because of the smallness of the elevator, most families were encouraged to take the staircase to the display room. The people elevator was for old folks and lazy employees.

In the display room, Ray switched on the Luxor. The motor roared like a garbage truck. Ray demonstrated a few swipes, then clicked off the machine. I was to vacuum the display room, then use the people elevator to bring the Luxor into the lobby. It seemed like an easy job, until Ray left me alone with the Luxor—the thing looked angry. I took hold of the handle and clicked the switch. The motor roared.

The bag billowed out. I lowered the handle and squeezed the self-propulsion trigger. The Luxor bolted forward, entangling my leg in the cord. I fell down, but the Luxor kept on going. It clipped the Plexiglas stand displaying a Toccoa maple. The maple tottered, then fell to the floor. I heard the wood split, then watched the Luxor crash into the Millennium's stand. The fourteen thousand-dollar casket rolled over, fell off its base, and crashed onto the maple, destroying the wooden casket. The impact sent a shudder through the floor and into the walls. The Luxor's rubber guards bounced the machine off the Millennium. The cord, wrapped around my leg, steered the machine in a circular path that ended at a rack of burial garments. The Luxor toppled the rack, then devoured a peach burial gown. I scrambled for the machine, but tripped again because of the cord around my leg. My lurch pulled the plug from the wall. The motor died. I heard footsteps running up the stairs. I didn't even try to get up, I lay where I had fallen, which worked to my advantage. Jerry, Carl, and Meredith rushed over and knelt beside me. Ray plodded up the staircase last. He just stood there, arms folded, shaking his head. "My fault," he said. "Shoulda warned you about that damn trigger—it sticks. I'll get a table ready. The Luxor's gone and killed the new kid."

Jerry looked me over, then surveyed the damage. I was certain my funeral career had ended, until Jerry started laughing. His reaction surprised me, but the others joined in too—not howling, slapping their knees or anything. Just chuckling at my misfortune. They helped me off the floor and dusted me off. Meredith said I looked great in the navy suit. Jerry would call the insurance company to replace the Toccoa—not a scratch on the Millennium. Ray yanked the burial gown out of the Luxor. "Try vacuuming the lobby now, kid. The lobby antiques are all insured, but they're also irreplaceable—some of them handcrafted by John Morton's granddaddy."

I raced through the task, not wanting to miss any funereal activity. When I took the Luxor back upstairs, I tried not to look at the Millennium, now on its side atop the pile of splintered maple. I ran downstairs to meet Carl and Ray in the chapel. Just as I hit the middle of the lobby, the main entrance door opened. A blond woman in sunglasses and high heels stepped into the lobby. She looked racy in the sunglasses. The act of her taking them off stopped time, like a scene from an old movie when the private detective meets his heartstopping client, the gorgeous one with all the money. I could almost hear the saxophone playing in the background. Her chummy smile invited my eyes to link with her own. She belonged on a magazine cover. Margee's worries were over. I was interested in girls. I felt my heartbeat move in behind my larynx as I attempted to greet her, but she already knew my name: "Casey Kight," she said. I remained silent, knowing I'd first need to gulp my heart back to where it belonged. She said, "I'm Denise Winstead, Ray's wife." She extended a hand, nails manicured but unpainted. I could barely feel her skin for the sweat of my palm. From her hand, I followed the line of her sleeve to her breasts, but I wrested my eyes from them as soon as I understood the meaning of the words, "Ray's wife." I'd never feel sorry for Ray again. I just stood there, the gulp hanging behind my voice box.

"I heard about your little accident in the casket room this morning," Denise said. Her voice sounded playful and southern. "Ray called me right after it happened. He said I had to see it for myself to believe it. Is Ray in the chapel?"

I executed the gulp. "Nice to meet you," I said.

"I'm here for the Pfister service—they're my family," Denise said.

I opened the chapel door and followed her down the center aisle, struggling to keep my eyes from her behind. Ray called out to her, "Hey, Booger."

"Ray Winstead, you call me Booger one more time and you'll find a real one at the bottom of your coffee cup tomorrow morning."

Ray ignored her comment. "I see you've met Casey, our apprentice casket destroyer."

Denise kept her eyes on Ray but spoke to me. "Casey, I've got stories about Ray if you'd care to hear them—like the time he removed the wrong body from—"

"Okay, Sugarpie, you've made your point. Are you going to help us or just stand around looking good?"

"I'll show Casey how to fold the memorial records," she said.

Denise took me by the arm and led me to Jerry's office. She chatted with me along the way, never releasing my arm. She asked about my family, where I went to school. Here eyes met mine at the end of each sentence. I didn't want to look dopey staring at her face, but each time I peeled my eyes from her features, they wandered to a more forbidden body part.

Denise sat on Jerry's desktop. I took the leather chair. She showed me how to fold the memorial records and helped me with all fifty of them. We always ordered at least fifty, even for a small service like Mrs. Pfister's. The families liked to send memorial records to relatives and friends who couldn't make the funeral.

"Do you work for Morton-Albright?" I asked.

She declared her official title with a shrug: Funeral Director's Wife. The world wasn't ready for women funeral directors. Neither was Morton-Albright. "I do work for the funeral home, but not for money. You've met Jerry Stiles, my brother-in-law. He and the others work the Newcomers. A Newcomer is anyone who has lived in Angel Shores for less than thirty years. Jerry and the others make contact through the fraternals—strictly guy stuff: Jerry's the Rotary man. Ray's a Lion—the eye-donation thing. Meredith's an Elk and Lex just grunts when you ask him about his marketing activities. Have you met my daddy?"

"Colton Albright? No, I haven't"

"I see you're putting the family names together. We're all family here. Daddy handles the old guard of Angel Shores—politicians, bankers, judges. When the mayor dies, he comes here. Then, you've got the Crackers—our main source of revenue. Nobody handles the Crackers. They're loyal. We provide their churches with those hand-held cardboard fans with the big, curvy Popsicle sticks for handles. There's a painting of Morton-Albright on the fans."

Denise handled the last category of prospective clientele, retirees from up North who came south to die in the heat. "Old people," Denise said. "*Real* old, like Mrs. Pfister. Ever play canasta with a group of octogenarians? They forget whose turn it is; serve you boiling water in a cup with no tea bag."

"How do you talk them into coming here?"

"I find an old retiree on the street and knock him in the head. Then I put one of my business cards in his hand and call the police." Denise smiled and gave me a wink. "You can close your mouth, Casey. I'm sure you've noticed all the joking by now." Denise said it was normal—the joking. We spent our time in the middle of grief and sorrow. If we shared the sadness of our families, we'd stop being professional, or end up in Chattahoochee. The joking helped the sanity factor. Denise explained how the funeral home built clientele: we couldn't say, "Mrs. Jones, we heard you're dying. Please let us handle your final arrangements." According to Denise, we couldn't say *anything*, not even a hint. "I never use business cards," she said. "I'm a licensed social worker. I'm in demand for high-level volunteer work. I'm just there—everybody knows what my family does. Fifteen percent of our business comes from my contacts. I met Alice Pfister through the visiting ministry of First United Methodist. She requested my visit. I turned her over to Meredith."

I could see why people trusted Denise with serious matters. Her eyes warmed you; gestures invited you into her space. I found myself sliding toward her, across Jerry's desk. She whacked me on the shoulder. "Let's go upstairs and see that mess you made."

I walked toward the staircase, but Denise pressed the call button for the people elevator. With Ray, I felt uncomfortable in the elevator's tight dimensions—now, I headed for panic. Denise faced me. Her breasts nearly touched my lapels. She smiled at me all the way up to the second floor. She smelled great, too. I stopped breathing when she fingered my lapel. "Wait till I tell Natalie how handsome you are," she said. Her comment sent blood rushing into my cheeks—other places, too. The elevator door slid open. Denise placed her hand over her mouth at the sight of the splintered maple. "Oh, my, Casey. You did this all by yourself?"

I told her about the Luxor.

"Daddy's machine," she said. "He made Ray order it from Germany. Everybody hates it, except Natalie, of course. She claims the Luxor has murderous intent not found in American machinery." Denise kept talking. I had no idea what she said. I could not listen to her and look at her at the same time. I'd hear the beginning of one of her sentences, then realize I was only watching Denise move her mouth. I pictured myself kissing her, eating all the lipstick from her mouth, uncovering her breasts, sucking her nipples, smelling her fragrance. Bad enough that my first look at a naked woman had been the one we were about to bury, now my first flaming desires of lust were aimed at Ray's wife. I endured the elevator ride downstairs, certain that Denise could hear my pounding heart. When the door opened, she kissed the corner of my mouth. "Welcome to the family," she said. "Natalie will adore you." Denise's kiss lingered warm on my face. She called over her shoulder, "Keep it light, Casey. The first three letters in 'funeral' are *f-u-n*. We all need a little of that around here."

I let my heart slow down and straightened my jacket before I went back into the lobby. I got there just in time to watch Denise let herself into the chapel, but not before she sent me a wink and a smirk. I followed her inside, expecting a small crowd, as Meredith had predicted. I found only our own staff. Nobody showed for Alice Pfister. I focused on Denise and that walk of hers. She headed down the aisle toward the front pews. The tap on my shoulder startled me—Ray. "She's a sight, ain't she, kid?" He had caught me leering at his wife. "Don't worry, kid. Everybody looks at Denise that way—it can't be helped."

"What if nobody shows up?" I asked.

"We hold the service anyway,"

Dr. Hamilton walked onto the dais and sat down in an old high-backed chair. That's what I needed—a strong dose of Christian conviction to cure my adulterous heart. The minister mounted the podium and spoke: "Alice Pfister has laid down a life she could never keep, to take up a life she can never lose."

"I love it when he says that," Ray said. "When I'm dead, call Dr. Hamilton."

A chime rang from the lobby.

"Main entrance," Ray said. "Looks like we'll have a real funeral after all."

I followed Ray into the lobby. Two men in white uniforms stood on either side of a walker. Gripping the walker was the oldest woman I had ever seen. Her white hair matched the whiskers on her chin. "We're from the Palms Nursing Home," one of the men said. "This is Lillian. She's here for her sister. Do you need us to stay and help?"

Ray assured the men we had plenty of staff. We'd drive Lillian home in the limousine.

"She's a hundred and two," the man said in a low voice. "Try not to break her."

Ray took Lillian's elbow to help her along. She released her grip on the walker and whacked Ray in the arm. He raised his hands in surrender. He told Lillian to wait a moment, then left us. He came back with a wheelchair. Lillian refused. Ray stood in front of the walker, then leaned over and whispered in Lillian's ear. Lillian whacked Ray again, then sat down in the wheelchair. Ray rolled her down the aisle to the casket, for the first viewing. He helped her out of the wheelchair and stood right behind her—you never know how people will react at a first viewing. Meredith had told me that. "They may look all right when they first come in, then go to pieces when they view the body. Some of them are nervous in the car, voicing dread, nearly in a panic, then they immediately calmed down—it hadn't been as bad as they had expected." Every first viewing was different. Lillian could drop dead on us, I thought—but then I realized, at a hundred and two, Lillian had seen a lot more dead bodies than I had. She leaned into the casket, patted her sister's hand, kissed her on the cheek, and sat back down in the wheelchair.

Under the porte cochere, Ray dangled keys in front of me. "The hearse," he said. "I hope to God you drive better than you vacuum." I slid into the driver's seat and looked up at the headliner—much higher than a normal car. It had to be that way to accommodate the casket. The windshield was huge. The car made me feel even smaller than I was. I switched on the engine and felt the smooth V-8. The car smelled deliciously new. I turned around and saw the cryptlike space in the back. Meredith opened the rear door of the hearse and stuck his head in. "Hey, Cap'n," he said, smiling. He disappeared, then Alice Pfister's casket thudded against the rubber casket stop, just behind my seat. I felt the compression from the closing of the rear door. Ray said, "Headlights on high beams." I pulled out the headlight switch and clicked the high-beam button on the floorboard. I put my foot on the brake and shifted into drive. Out of the window of the lead car in front of me, Meredith waved his hand in a circle. Ray said, "Let's roll, kid." The two motorcycle escorts took off to stop traffic at Druid and Mayfair. Following Meredith, I eased the hearse out of the porte cochere. I was doing it. I was driving a casket to the cemetery in a brand-new hearse. I was an Undertaker.

On the way to the cemetery, I asked Ray what he had whispered into Lillian's ear to make her use the wheelchair. "I told her that if she didn't get her three-hundred-year-old Methuselah ass into the wheelchair, we'd leave *two* bodies at Fairview."

"Really?"

"Kid, you scare the hell out of me. I told her it was a long walk to the front of the chapel. I told her to save her energy for viewing her sister. Then I told her to whack me like I had said something bad, so she wouldn't feel embarrassed about the wheelchair."

We motored through Fairview's front gate at ten miles per hour, past the old part of the cemetery first. Under cypresses were headstones and private mausoleums, some mottled green and gray. They bore the names of Angel Shores' oldest families. The trees gave way to the memorial gardens—no headstones anywhere—just flat bronze markers imbedded in rolling grass. Somewhere out there, my parents lay buried. We parked near the Pfister grave site. Ray grabbed the handle of the hearse's rear door, then let go quick. "Ouch. Must be a thousand degrees today." Ray pulled his hand into the sleeve of his suit jacket, and used the material as a glove for opening the door. Carl trotted up from behind. Ray asked him, "How's Granny?"

"I think Granny left a lung on the floorboard. She's been hacking since we left the funeral home. She's got the death farts too. I'm surprised she didn't pass out from the displacement of oxygen in the car. I almost did. She's comfy, though—it's about sixty-five degrees in the limousine. We bring her out in this heat, her skull might crack from the rapid change in temperature."

"Thanks for the medical update," Ray said. "Let's make her watch the service from the car window. It's not likely her view will be obscured by the throng of spectators here."

"Granny wants to go to the graveside—she tried to whack me when I said she should stay in the car."

Meredith and Dr. Hamilton walked up beside us. Ray and Carl informed them of the situation. They reckoned a twenty-yard walk from the limousine to the graveside. Together, we carried Alice Pfister's casket to the lowering device set atop her grave, under the green tent. We walked back to the limousine. Ray got the wheelchair out of the trunk and set it next to the car. He helped Lillian into the wheelchair—it didn't roll well over the St. Augustine sod, even with three of us pushing. At Ray's command, we picked up Lillian, wheelchair and all, and trotted her to the graveside. Dr. Hamilton read a Scripture and said a prayer, shorter than a blessing over dinner. Meredith said the magic words, "You may retire at your leisure," and the three of us picked up Granny and ran her back to the limousine as fast as we could. She screamed and hacked and cussed the entire way. Ray tucked her in and shut the door. Carl already had his hand on the shift lever. Ray and I stopped by Carl's window. "Don't let her die on you until she's back on nursing home property," Ray said. Meredith waved as he peeled out in the lead car.

Ray and I walked back to the tent. He tore off his jacket, loosened his tie, lit a cigarette, and signaled for the cemetery crew. "That's Kip walking toward us with the clipboard—senior groundskeeper. Henry's driving the backhoe. Henry's ass stays in that seat all day long—eats his lunch on that machine. He turns off the engine if you talk to him, but his ass stays in that seat. Imagine Henry's ass after fifteen years of mechanical vibration. You could sneak up on him and whack him with a paddle and he wouldn't even feel it. Those two other boys headed this way—couple of parolees, no doubt."

Henry roared up on the backhoe. The parolees arrived with two shovels and a dozen teeth between them. They threw down their implements, then rolled the tent away from the grave, Ray and I walked in the tent as it moved, keeping ourselves in the shade. Kip scribbled on the clipboard, then flipped a switch on the lowering device. Mrs. Pfister's casket descended into the vault. With chains, the two parolees connected the vault lid to the bucket of the backhoe. Henry gunned the engine and lifted the gold-painted vault lid, swinging it over the grave. Ray yelled at me over the noise, "Make sure the vault seals." The lid made a scraping sound, followed by *chunk*. I said a quiet good-bye to Mrs. Pfister, my first case, then turned to speak to Ray. He was already halfway to the car.

"I'm taking you to meet the owner of Morton-Albright Funeral Home and Memorial Chapel," Ray said, cranking the hearse.

"We're going to meet Colton Albright?" I asked.

"Hell, no, kid. We're going to meet John Morton."

"Isn't he dead?"

"As a doornail."

The Morton-Albright plot presided over the far corner of the old cemetery, an area shaded by giant cypresses. Their roots vaulted up from the ground in places, threatening the odd headstone. In the center of the plot, an obelisk of white marble rose fifteen feet above the headstones surrounding it. Beneath the chiseled name, Morton, was a patinaed bronze plaque:

Show me the manner in which a nation cares for its dead and I will measure with mathematical exactness the tender mercies of its people—their loyalty to high ideals—and their regard for the laws of the land.
—Gladstone

As yet, only the Morton and Stiles families rested in the plot, but the Albright headstones were there, the names of Colton and Jewell inscribed in the marble, along with their dates of birth. A warm breeze rustled the Spanish moss overhead. Ray walked me around the square of the plot, to John Morton's headstone. "Kid, meet John Morton," he said. "The man is dead, but he might as well be signing your paycheck, if you stay around long enough to get one."

"I plan on staying," I said.

"I'm sure you do, but you haven't seen the Circle of Willis yet—it's the ultimate initiation. But for now, you need to know the most important thing about Morton-Albright: John Morton's will."

According to Ray, Colton Albright was all set to inherit the funeral home. Then, he went and knocked up Jewell, John Morton's daughter. John got pissed at Colton and wrote him out of the will. John bequeathed Morton-Albright to the next male descendent. So far, it's girls, girls, and girls. Colton and Jewell had two girls, Cynthia and Denise. "You already know what happened to Denise and me, childwise. Cynthia gave birth to Natalie, your future wife. That makes you, Casey Kight, our last hope of keeping Morton-Albright in the family. You knock Natalie up with a boy and bang—this whole thing ends in the delivery room." If Colton died before a male heir was born, Morton-Albright would become the property of his estate—Colton wouldn't own the funeral home until after he died, leaving Jewell as the executor of his estate. "Here's the catch—it's a big one, so pay attention: In the state of Florida, you must be a licensed funeral director to own a funeral home. Jewell doesn't have a funeral director's license, and I doubt she'll be signing apprenticeship papers anytime soon. Since she can't own the funeral home, she has no choice but to sell it to a licensed funeral director, under the supervision of the State Board of Funeral Directors and Embalmers."

"I don't see what any of this has to do with me," I said. "It seems that Jewell would want to keep the funeral home in the family. You and Jerry are licensed. It makes sense that she would sell the funeral home to her own family."

"Kid, this ain't altogether about family. It's about money—*big* money. Millions—all because of Sunset Towers. That place will quadruple our business—we're talking tens of thousands of dying oldsters—make millionaires out of whoever ends up with Morton-Albright. Ever watch *The Beverly Hillbillies*? Think of Jewell as Jed Clampett. Now think of Sunset Towers as the oil Jed finds on his property. Nothing against Jed, but he didn't sell that ten-million-dollar shack to Aunt Pearl, he sold it to the oil company. Now think of the oil company as—"

"Jacob Funeral Trust," I said.

"Damn, kid. How the hell did you figure that one out on your second day, if you don't mind my asking?"

"Jeff and Randy told me."

"Who?"

"The twins—the mortuary students."

"Oh, yeah, Morey and Lester, and you're absolutely right about JFT. Jerry and I have saved a wheelbarrow full of money for a down payment to Jewell, but JFT will write a check for millions. Jewell doesn't know dick about the funeral business—probably never heard of JFT. My guess is that Lex Talbert is in on this whole thing."

Ray's suspicions began two years ago, when Lex's behavior changed, right after the announcement about Sunset Towers. Lex had always been a crank, but lately, the man had turned smug. "Like he knows a secret," Ray said. "He stopped washing the cars, started coming in late; reads the trades when there's work to be done. Maybe I'm just paranoid—our whole future is at stake here. The problem is this: Cruel Jewell has never promised to sell to the family. Jerry keeps after her for something in writing, she keeps putting him off, and there's lots of subterranean family shit going on I haven't even told you about, so it's possible that Cruel Jewell is holding out on us until the last minute, just to keep our sphincters puckered right up until the end."

"So things could work out, but there's a fly in the ointment," I said.

"More like a green turd in a pickle jar, but you get the idea." It all depended on how long Colton remained alive—eighty-two years old, bad health. "Wait till you see him. The man looks like Death eating Lifesavers." Ray checked his watch. "Let's go meet Colton before he dies," Ray said. "He's old as hell, but the man loves to talk. If you want to say something, you've got to wait until he breathes. You'd think his jaws would feel thankful when he sleeps, but they don't—Colton keeps right on talking. He used to nap on the big couch in the apartment, back when he kept hours at the funeral home—talked the whole time he slept—say things like, "Get them horses hitched up," or, "Start baling that hay," and you know damn well Colton's never been on a farm in his life. Now he hangs out at Skeeter's. Don't you dare sit down with him. He'll keep us there all day."

Skeeter's Barbecue declared a salivation war on me with noise and the smell of smoked pork. Off to one side of the arena of picnic tables, Skeeter had preserved the original dining room, all open booths and a quieter atmosphere. Until now, I never knew this room existed, its entrance a plain white door with no markings. The dining room remained in late '50s decor—red vinyl upholstery and laminated tabletops, swirled in soothing patterns. I could still smell the famous barbecue, but in this room, the aroma of Skeeter's fare competed with cigars and pipe smoke. Ray leaned and whispered to me, "There's Colton Albright, in the corner with Vernon Davis—district attorney." Ray signaled to Albright, got the man's attention. A big smile crossed the old man's face. He motioned us over. "Join us for lunch," he said in that gravelly voice of the elderly. Mr. Davis nodded hello, then used our entrance to wipe his mouth and leave. Ray said we couldn't stay. Albright gave him the eye. Ray said, "I wanted you to meet the new kid. He's got a mess to clean up, back at the store."

"So I hear," Albright said. "Jerry stopped in for a bite, then took off on me. He told me about the woodpile upstairs." Albright cocked a wrinkled eye at me. "You must be the casket wrassler," he said. "I'm the rich old bastard who used to run the funeral home."

"I'm Casey."

Albright smiled. His face, sprayed with freckles and age spots, sagged pallid; a slight tremor ran through his jowls. "My shaking arm doesn't shake the right way anymore," he said. "You'll pardon the left hand." He grasped my hand with his fingers and shook my hand sideways.

"How's the Brunswick stew today?" Ray asked.

"I didn't have any stew," Albright said, "but I'm fixing to have your ass sent out here on a blue plate if you don't sit down and order lunch." We both slid into the booth while Colton told us about his lunch. "Skeeter made me a rabbit pie. Yesterday he fried up two squirrels. Casey, you a squirrel eater?"

"Never tried it, Mr. Albright."

"Don't call me mister. You call me Colton or the old bastard, like everybody else. You like possum? Skeeter's fond of possum. I told him, don't try to sneak any possum on me. It's too greasy for my gall bladder. Truth is, I ain't had a gall bladder for years. It's in a jar of formaldehyde somewhere in my kitchen, next to my appendix. Terrapin, now, that's a different story. Skeeter makes a fine terrapin stew. It's got yellow tomatoes, okra, and some kind of greens. Now, you're probably wondering how an Albright like me got mixed up with a bunch of Mortons."

"He probably isn't wondering that at all," Ray said. "He's probably wondering when you'll stop talking long enough for him to order lunch." As soon as Ray uttered the words, his eyes opened wide and he sucked in a breath. He looked down at his crotch. I looked too. I saw the end of Albright's cane pressed against Ray's pants in the area of his privates. Albright told Ray his shaking arm didn't work so well, but his pushing arm still worked fine. The old man chuckled, then continued talking. "Now, as I was telling Casey, the Albrights—"

"Excuse me, Colton, but would you mind removing your cane from my scrotum?"

"You gonna hush?"

"I'm going to eat."

"As long as you've got something to do with your mouth besides disrespecting an elder. Now, Casey, my daddy was Barron Albright."

"Your father was a baron?"

Colton chortled. "Ray, where did you find this boy? Never mind. Keep your mouth shut. Casey, my daddy's first name was Barron— that's *two* R's. He was a banker—Albright Mortgage Association. He financed the building of John Morton's funeral home. I never cared much for the mortgage business. Since my daddy held the note on Morton Funeral Home, he gave old John a call, talked him into hiring me for a week. My daddy figured I'd see a dead body and come a-running back to the bank. Instead, I moved right into that apartment of yours. John Morton taught me the trade—treated me like his own son." Colton took a breath. Ray said we had to get back to the store. We'd take our sandwiches to go. Albright said, "Oh, all right. I'll just sit here and get old, all by myself."

"You're already old," Ray said. "Casey and I were just out at Fairview admiring your headstone."

"Nice one, ain't it. I'm more partial to granite, but marble goes with the rest of the plot. How about you, Casey? You a marble man? If you are, you'd better watch out for that Natalie of mine—she takes after her grampaw. Have y'all two set your wedding date?"

"The kid's only been here two days," Ray said. "He hasn't even met the girl."

"Well, now, there ain't nothing wrong with short engagements. Jewell and I eloped to Key West. That was back in nineteen and . . . let me see."

6

I was hot and tired and sweaty by the time Ray and I locked the hearse in the garage. Ray said, "You don't look so perky now, kid. Nothing wears you out like working a funeral in the Sunshine State, except for lunch with Colton Albright. You did them both in the same day. Go take it easy in the chapel. You can clean up from Mrs. Pfister's service. Probably a few flower petals on the floor, stuff like that. You can pick them up by hand; relax in a pew. It's peaceful in there—lots of air-conditioning, too."

Jerry had been right about Ray Winstead—he wasn't as ornery as he pretended.

The chapel was as peaceful and air-conditioned as Ray had promised. The chapel was also the showplace of Morton-Albright's magnificence. It was perfectly round, like the Capitol Rotunda. The walls vaulted up into a high dome full of skylights of stained glass. At the front of the chapel, I bent down to pick up some fallen petals. When I stood up, I was nine years old—the beginning of an episode. Part of me felt the panic rising in my chest—a stronger force suppressed it—

gently, filling me with comfort. It was okay to remember now—that's why I was here—to remember.

I looked around the chapel, bursting with people and flowers. The sun, streaming in through the stained glass, splashed every petal with tinted light. Margee was holding my hand. Mom and Dad's caskets stood before us—the lids were shut. From a table between the caskets, Mom and Dad smiled at me from their wedding portrait. It wasn't enough. It bothered me that I couldn't see them in the caskets. Even though I had witnessed the plane crash, I still couldn't believe they were really dead. Something inside me had to know for sure. I found a latch under the lid of Mom's casket. I had lifted the lid an inch when Margee pressed it back down. "You can't do that," she whispered. "I know you want to see them, but you can't. You must trust me, Casey. Your mom and dad are in there. I know it for sure."

"You've seen them?" I asked. Margee nodded, tears running down her face. I opened my mouth to argue, then remembered the crash— my parents were all burned up. I didn't want to see them that way. Margee huddled me into a pew. Everybody got quiet. Our minister read a prayer from a book. He said Amen, and I heard the sounds of sniffles and coughs; the clicking of purses opening and closing. The minister began his sermon. I tried to pay attention, but a different voice was taking over, an old man's voice. It moved from my head into the aisle, as if calling me to follow. I resisted at first—it was my parents' funeral, but along with the voice came the urge to follow it. I told Margee I had to go pee. She dabbed her eyes with her hanky. "Come right back," she whispered. A moment later, I found myself in the lobby, staring at words in a picture frame, a Bible verse. I didn't know many Bible verses, but I memorized this one immediately:

Blessed be the God and Father of our Lord Jesus Christ, the Father of mercies and the God of all comfort, who comforts us in all our affliction, so that we may comfort those in any affliction, with the comfort with which we ourselves are comforted by God.

I wasn't sure who was comforting who, but there was a lot of comfort in that verse. I didn't expect to cry, but I did, until my shirt was wet with tears—not bad tears—good tears. Tears of comfort. I caught a passing shadow out of the corner of my right eye. I followed the shadow around the corner, one step at a time. We were on the right-hand side of the chapel, I could feel the curve of the wall, sliding my hand along it as I went. At the end of the hallway, a large space opened to my right. One wooden door stood open on each of the three walls. I chose the door on the right, the door marked Rose Room. On the wall next to the Rose Room door, a wooden placard read: In Repose, A. B. Seeley. I noticed that his name sounded like the alphabet.

The light dimmed inside the Rose Room, but not too darkly to see the open casket at the far end of the room. Inside the casket lay an old man. A kneeler in front of the casket provided a step for me. I peered in at the dead man. The feel of Morton-Albright played upon my spine, the verse on the wall running through my head.

The old man in the casket looked satisfied, like my grandpa after Sunday dinner. Through the dead man's spectacles, I examined his closed eyelids. Tiny wrinkles appeared through the magnification of the lenses. My fingers started at the knot of the old man's tie—a bit crooked. I straightened the knot, sliding it to the exact center of his buttoned collar. *That's right, son. You're doing fine. Unbutton his jacket. See how his tie is just lying there? Tuck it into his pants. That'll keep it straight. That's right, button the jacket. Let's show a little more cuff at the sleeve. Perfect.* The old man's voice guided me. I had heard it clearly at first, but soon it became my own thought, my own absorption into the work. I felt the dead man's hands—all bumpy at the knuckles. They felt cold. Hard, too. I looked at his face. He didn't seem to mind my touch. Then, his face began to shine—it became brighter, like Jesus' face in the Transfiguration. When the dead man's face turned radiant, I realized the light wasn't coming from his face at all, but from the overhead lamps—*they* were getting brighter. I heard a noise behind me and spun around to see Jerry with his hand on a switch by the door. The Undertaker. He looked right at me.

I misjudged my step from the kneeler and fell to the floor. The impact drove my breath from me. I gritted my teeth against crying in front of a stranger—he reached me in a few quick strides. I smelled his clean smell when he knelt beside me and rubbed my back. "Take it easy, son," he said. "Take one slow breath." He reached under my chest and rolled me over.

"I want to be an Undertaker," I said.

The next thing I knew, I was standing in Jerry's office, looking at the key in my palm. It shone like new brass. I looked up. Jerry sat there, filling in a form with his alabaster pen. How did his hair get so gray?

"What can I do for you, son?" he asked me. "You needn't be shy about walking into my office anytime, as long as the door is open. When it's closed, you mustn't even knock—it means I'm with a family."

"I'll remember that." I said.

Jerry was still looking at me as I gathered myself together. I fought for something to say. I said, "I wanted to thank you again for everything."

"That's an admirable gesture of gratitude, Casey—the kind of thing we look for in a new man. You've impressed us all."

"I was also wondering where the guys were—maybe some work to do."

"Glad you reminded me. They're in the display room, cleaning up what's left of that Toccoa casket. I promised to help out myself. Let's take a walk upstairs."

I told Jerry I'd meet him upstairs, after a trip to the restroom. I splashed my face with water from the sink, looked into the mirror and straightened my own tie. My event with memory frightened me. If I couldn't control it, what would keep me from doing something strange in the middle of a funeral? Or worse yet, what if I had barged into Jerry's office while he conducted arrangements with a family?

Instead of going directly upstairs, I walked back to the Rose Room and looked inside—empty.

On my way upstairs, I thought of resigning—my presence here could jeopardize the process, the rhythm of events, but as I neared the top of the stairs, I knew better. The comfort was upon me now, assuring me that I would not disturb the rhythm. I *was* the rhythm.

The other men had cleaned up most of the mess. It took the five of us to lift the Millennium back onto its steel bier. I endured another episode with the Luxor and vacuumed up the little pieces, then we set up a new Toccoa maple. Ray unwrapped it like a Christmas present. He opened the lid, and smelled deeply. He said, "Don't you just love that new-casket smell?" We all stopped what we were doing when we heard the chime of the Druid Road entrance (each entrance had its own distinct chime, so everybody knew which door was being opened). Footsteps hurried up the staircase. Bernard tromped into the casket room with an arrangement. "Late piece for Pfister," he said.

"From the late Bernard," Ray added. "You know damn well what 'late' means around this place. You ran those flowers across Druid again, and you know your ass is not supposed to be in this room."

"Nobody but Lex downstairs," the kid said. "He said y'all was up here."

Ray said, "As long as you're here, you might as well pick out your casket. Tell us what to put you in after we scrape you off the pavement."

Bernard pointed to the Millennium.

"Dammit, Bernard, you know your mama can't afford a fourteen-thousand-dollar casket. Check out that cloth-covered job over there. That's what you're going in. You'll get those damn braces off your teeth, too, when your head bounces down Druid Road."

Bernard ignored Ray and headed down the stairs. On the wall, a telephone rang. Ray shouted orders at me as fast as he could talk. "Line one—death call. Grab it quick, say, 'Morton-Albright Funeral

Home and Memorial Chapel, Mr. Kight speaking.' Try not to sound like Lurch from *The Addams Family*."

I ran to the wall and picked up the phone, following Ray's instructions as I spoke. I glanced at the others for confirmation that I had answered the phone correctly. Ray, Jerry, Meredith, and Carl all smiled back at me and nodded their heads. The caller identified herself as the nursing supervisor at Good Samaritan Hospital. Death call. I wrote down the information and tore the sheet from the pad of forms. I hung up and waved the paper in the air. Ray threw the removal car keys to me. "Bat cave," he said. "Let's roll."

The garage ramp wound downward and right, then left. Halfway into the left turn, Ray pressed the button of a device mounted on the dashboard. A horizontal slit of daylight appeared, then grew with a mechanical noise. I had never seen a remote-control garage door opener in my life. As I exited the garage, Ray pressed the button again. I watched the door close in the rearview. "Wow," I said. "That was cool!"

Clifford Moss had coded during heart surgery. He now lay naked on the embalming table, the skin of his chest divided in two by a fence of surgical staples. Ray rolled the instrument table toward the body, ready to embalm. The phone buzzed. Ray listened, said, "Aw, shit," then hung up. "Sorry, kid. Mr. Moss is a direct disposal—no embalming, no fancy casket, no funeral. Let's wrap him up in a sheet. I hate cremations."

We laid the body in the cloth-covered casket Ray had picked out for Bernard. The casket had not been required by law—the sheet would have sufficed, but Morton-Albright included a cloth-covered particle-board casket in the cost of cremation. The legal term for what we were about to do was *direct disposal*, but the Morton-Albright men abhorred the word *disposal*. "It sounds like you're taking out the trash," Ray said. "It's direct cremation, when you're talking to a family." We drove the body to a warehouse in an industrial park. Ray complained about cremation the whole way there. "It ain't right," he said. "Cremation is an India thing. It needs to *stay* in India, because we can't make any money on it here—not unless there's a viewing. The whole American funeral trade is based on the casket sale. We don't make much money on professional services—just enough to cover costs. Then you've got folks like Carl's wife, Suzy Pocahontas. She believes cremation protects the planet Earth from underground death vibrations. Her moon is in the seventh house, if you know what I mean—a hippie chick."

Jenner Cremation Services. Ray backed the hearse up to a garage door, then tapped the horn. The garage door opened behind us. We climbed out of the car to meet Myron Cheeves, Jenner's cremation-ist. A rash grew on Myron's bony face. A big scar cut a fishhook shape into his forehead. Spit flew out of his mouth as he talked. "I'm Cheeves—Myron Cheeves. Just remember, Lyin' Myron; Cheatin' Cheeves. You Natalie's feller? She come out here and took pictures of the retort—that's what we call the big oven. You can watch me sweep out Mr. Chilton."

The retort commanded the center of the warehouse like a giant science fiction machine. Myron pressed a big black button. The retort's heavy door slid upward with an electrical sound. I expected to see a pile of ashes—I did not. Upon the floor of the retort lay a human skeleton, bleached out, like one you might find in a desert. Myron stuck a long-handled broom into the retort. He let the brush end of the broom fall just beyond the skull of the cremated skeleton, then pulled the broom toward himself. The skeleton fell to pieces as Myron swept—some of the chunks of bone the size of my hand. The fragments rattled into a bucket on the floor. Myron dumped the cre-mated bones into a grinder. The machine screeched and moaned. Pulverized bone, resembling ashes, fell out of the bottom of the grinder into a brown plastic box shaped like a book. Myron threw the box to me. I caught it and dropped it. Besides the thing weighing like a bag of sugar, it had burned my fingers.

"Hot, ain't it?" Myron said. "Hot as hellfire in that retort." He snickered at his own remark. The snicker worked itself into a frenzied cough. Hacking and red-faced, Myron leaned against a counter. He finally managed to dislodge a wad from his lungs, which he spat into a trashcan.

"Cremation dust," Ray mumbled to me. "Myron just hocked up Granny."

"Hear the news?" Myron asked. "Jenner done sold out to Jake's Funeral Trunk, or some such thing. Feller come down here from Alabama—name o' Stork."

"Stark," Ray said. "Lewis Stark. I've heard of him. His picture made the trades."

"He's the one you want to watch out for, this Stork feller. I never believed in the Booger Man, not till I seen Stork."

"Bad news, kid," Ray said on the way back to the funeral home. "Jenner sold out. You believe that? I've heard some awful strange stories about JFT, but it's this Alabama thing that pisses me off. Ever been to Alabama? Alabama isn't exactly civilized. I went to Dothan for my uncle's funeral. I headed for the nearest barbecue joint and ordered a pork sandwich. Took a bite and spat it right back into my plate. I thought they'd poisoned me. Know what I found in the middle of my sandwich? Cole slaw. You believe that shit? I mean cabbage and mayonnaise, kid."

"Cole slaw?" I imagined the taste and winced.

"Cole slaw, and the bastards didn't even ask me if I wanted it. I took that sandwich up to the counter and said that somebody had put cole slaw on my barbecue. The waitress said, 'That's how it comes, honey—you should have ordered it plain.' JFT is headquartered in Mobile, and I can't imagine anyone who eats cole slaw on his barbecue having enough sense to run a funeral home."

In the supply room of Morton-Albright, Ray set Mr. Chilton's cremated remains—cremains, for short—on a shelf, next to a dozen identical boxes, each labeled with a decedent's name. A label on the shelf bore the initials S.A.S. "It means 'Scatter at Sea,' " Ray said. "It also means a fishing trip."

Ray owned a small fishing boat. On each trip, Ray motored his boat out into the Gulf of Mexico. Armed not only with fishing gear, Ray took the boxes of cremains with him as well. "I say a little prayer, open the boxes, and pour the cremains into the Gulf, then I toss a wreath of Cynthia's roses into the water to commemorate the event. Then, I fish."

7

The first time the giant phone bells woke me up, I understood Ray's saying, "Your first impulse is to get your narrow ass the fuck out of the building." I had fled past the sleeping mortuary students, all the way to the front door of the apartment before I realized it was the phone, not the Russians attacking with nuclear weapons. I picked up the receiver in the kitchen, my breath coming hard.

"Lex Talbert," the voice droned. "Death call. Meet me in the parking lot. Fifteen minutes." The phone clicked silent.

"You didn't make it in time," Lex said, driving the removal car.

"I'm two minutes early," I said.

"I don't mean today, young man. I mean, you didn't make it in time to save Morton-Albright. Colton Albright's diastolic pressure is triple digit, my friend. The man will stroke within the year. You'll never have time enough to impregnate and deliver the lovely Miss Natalie, not even illegitimately. That *is* the plan, isn't it?"

I had just started working for Morton-Albright, and by all

accounts, I had already fathered a bastard son, with a girl I hadn't even met.

Lex parked the removal car in the driveway of the Dillard residence. He reached into his valise and removed a first call book. I reached for the door handle.

"Stay right here," Lex said. "I'll come for you when I need you."

When Lex slammed the car door, his valise fell over toward me. I saw a brochure of some kind. At first, I looked away—it was Lex's personal stuff. It wasn't right for me to snoop—but I was pretty sure I had seen the word Jacob, so I snooped anyway. I pulled the brochure from the valise. It's banner read "Jacob Funeral Trust. An Investment in Distinction." I slid the brochure onto my lap and began to read. A heading in black print caught my eye: "Bold New Retiree-Focused Construction in the Florida Suncoast Region Assures Soaring Local Mortality Rates." The following paragraph mentioned Sunset Towers, then the words: "JFT plans to exploit . . ."

I heard Lex's footfalls on the driveway. I shoved the brochure back in place and propped up the valise with my elbow, then got out of the car. Lex pointed at my chest when he spoke, "Follow me inside. Do not say a word. Do only as I instruct you. Understand?"

I understood: Lex Talbert was involved in a plan to sell Morton-Albright to Jacob Funeral Trust, just as Ray had suspected.

"A brochure?" Ray asked, the body of Albert Dillard lying naked on the table. I nodded at Ray, reciting the phrases I remembered.

"Investment prospectus," Ray declared. "Sort of an advertisement to draw money from investors. I told you Lex works the middle between JFT and Cruel Jewell. Hell, Lex might have his own money in JFT stock—split three times in the last two years. Son of a bitch might be rich by now."

"How do you know this stuff?"

"I read the trades, kid. Mostly in the bathroom—which reminds me—no jerking off for you. Save that sperm for Natalie. Think of it as Emergency Fucking. Stop looking at your pants and let's embalm Mr. Dillard. Arterial embalming is the cornerstone of our trade."

The first step of embalming was to relieve rigor mortis. Mr. Dillard was stiff, and bent in all the wrong places. The dead man's fingers curved inward, nearly into a fist. Ray worked the index finger until it became pliable. I took hold of the other hand, as I did, I felt inside my brain, the halo of another episode that never came—no plane crash, just a calm voice that I assumed was Ray's. *That's it. Work the fingers. Now the arm—move it back and forth—easy, now. Do the whole arm like that all the way to the shoulder. Twist the head left and right, up and down. See how loose he is now? Gotta make the whole body like that, so you can shape it the way you want it. Legs are the hardest—big muscles there. You're doing fine.*

"Thanks," I said. Ray didn't answer. I looked up. Everyone but Lex stood in the embalming room, staring at me. Ray said, "I don't know what you're trying to pull here, kid, but it ain't *even* fucking funny. Tell us where you worked before."

Jerry said, "Easy, Ray. My office. Now. Everybody."

I sat in the chair across the desk from Jerry. The others sat around the room, silent, their arms folded. Carl was the first to speak: "He's got the gift, Uncle Jerry."

"There ain't no fucking gift," Ray said.

Jerry shushed the two of them. He had been playing with his alabaster pen, turning it in circles with his fingers. He tossed it onto his desk. "What else do you know about embalming?" Jerry asked me.

"I don't know anything about embalming. I just did what Ray told me to do."

"I didn't tell you shit," Ray said. "You were mumbling—working the rigor out of Mr. Dillard, like you'd been doing it your whole life."

"Ray Winstead, I told you to hush," Jerry said. "You're upsetting Casey. We've got ourselves something here—a situation—that's what we've got. Casey, if I promise to make Ray keep his mouth shut, will you take us back into the embalming room?"

I slipped back into my apron, snapped on a pair of gloves, and stood over the body of Mr. Dillard, now relieved of his rigor. "What do I do next?" I asked.

"You oughta know, kid. You're the expert." Ray said.

Every man shushed Ray with a finger to his lips. Jerry said, "Wash his hair next. There's a hose attached to the flushable sink."

"Not the trocar hose," Carl said. "The gum-rubber hose."

I found the gum hose and turned on the water. I used it to wet Mr. Dillard's hair. I looked in a cabinet for a bottle of liquid soap. "Soap's on the second shelf of the instrument tray," Carl said.

"Carl's right, Cap'n," Meredith said, "but John Morton used to keep the soap bottle in that cabinet where you just looked for it."

"Lucky guess," Ray said. "I know, I know, keep my fucking mouth shut. I ain't saying a goddamn word."

I took the soap bottle, squirted some into Mr. Dillard's hair, and began massaging. I noticed his body odor—probably hadn't had a proper bath in a while. I squirted soap all over the body, then took a brush near the sink. As I scrubbed Mr. Dillard, the Presence of Morton-Albright fell upon me strong. *Wash him up real good—don't want him smelling up the casket. Scrub those fingernails—save you a lot of work later. That's right. Now rinse him—rinse and rub—get all that soap off him. Where's the magnet?*

"Where's the magnet?" I asked.

"It's stuck to the side of the instrument cart—so we don't misplace it."

I set the magnet near Mr. Dillard's head. It stuck to the enameled table. I thought it odd and stepped back to observe it.

"Table's made of steel—the ceramic is a coating."

The gum hose fit into a slot atop the magnet base. I stood there and watched the water run down the side of the table, listening to its sound as it poured through a drain at the foot-end of the table, into the flushable sink. The sound of the water calmed me even more. I stood there, listening. I felt a hand on my shoulder and looked up—Jerry smiled at me. "Set the features next," he said. "Put this rubber head block under the back of his head first."

Right. The features.

Wrong—get you into trouble that way. Get that thing out from under his head. Good man. Raise the vessels first. Use the wheel under the embalming table. Tilt the table so the head is lower than the feet. That's right, not too steep, now—you'll get water all over the floor.

"Okay, that's it. This kid doesn't know what the fuck he's doing." Ray.

I looked up at Ray, untied my apron and threw it down on the floor. I felt tears filling my eyes, but I wasn't going to let Ray see me cry. "See what I mean?" I said. "I don't know anything about embalming. I just do the logical thing, that's all. I do have a feel for it, but I'm ignorant. I don't even know how to set the features—whatever that means. I was going to—now I forgot."

Jerry spoke to Ray, still in his calm voice. He said, "If you don't shut up, you'll walk out of here with a trocar sticking out of your ass. We clear on that?"

"I'll be glad to help with that, Uncle Jerry," Carl said.

Jerry gave Carl the eye, then turned to me. "Take it easy, son. You were about to say something. You said you were going to—"

"Raise the vessels first," I said.

"Why would you do that, son?"

"It only makes sense. Let's say you tack the mouth shut while Mr. Dillard's head is on the headblock. Then you start looking for the jugular vein, only you can't find it because Mr. Dillard is tilted the wrong way—all the blood is in his lower extremities. If you tilt his head down, the blood will run into the vein so you can see it. If you set the features first, then lose the vein, you have to take Mr. Dillard's head off the headblock. His mouth will pop open." A shiver ran

through my body as the Presence pulled away. "What did I just say?"
I asked.

"Jesus Christ," Ray said.

"My God in heaven," Meredith said.

"He's got the gift," Carl said.

"There ain't no goddamn—never mind," Ray said.

"John Morton's old trick," Jerry said. "We don't teach it anymore.
You'll flunk your practical examination before the State Board if you
use that trick. They demand you follow a certain order of things
when you embalm. If you make a habit of John's old trick, you might
forget authorized procedure in front of your examiner. Everybody
back in my office."

Jerry spoke, slow and deliberate, "Gentlemen, I can't figure this any
better than you can. We've got ourselves a situation, like I said. Keep
it to yourselves—not a word. Everybody with me on this? Good. Now
clear out—everyone but Casey and Ray."

Nobody had ever stuck up for me before—not that I could
remember—except Margee. I was accustomed to ridicule by my
peers. In school, I had always been the weird kid. Now that I was
among my own, Jerry became my advocate; my protector. I felt hum-
bled that Jerry took my part with Ray, a man of the trade who had
worked by Jerry's side for thirteen years. At first, I worried that our
meeting would cause Ray to turn bitter toward me, but as Jerry
spoke, I realized that every man on staff was as dedicated to Morton-
Albright, and the honor of the trade itself, as I was. When the other
men left the room, Ray dropped his bravado in the presence of Jerry
Stiles. Even though I was the new man, I could see that everyone
deferred to Jerry's command. He didn't lord his power over us. He
didn't need to. His strength came from an obvious inner quietude
that emanated from his pale blue eyes. I watched Ray relax as Jerry
spoke to him.

"I have entrusted our Casey into your care, and that's what I expect you to do. I expect you to care for him, the same way you have been cared for here at Morton-Albright."

Ray immediately apologized to me. "Sorry, kid. You'll have to forgive me. I've never seen the likes of you before. You are one weird kid—but you're *my* weird kid for the next four years. Working for me ain't easy, but it ain't supposed to be easy. That's what made me suspicious. This job is too damn easy for you. Most men, you've got to bring them along slow—and here you are, ready to stick the trocar in the whole damn town. I don't buy this business about the gift—probably because I don't have it. Most of us puke our way to getting licensed."

Jerry explained Ray's concerns. For most men, getting licensed meant getting the hell out of the embalming room and into an arrangement office. That was the natural progression, and the reason why most embalming in any store was done by the apprentice. The time you spend in the embalming room is meant to desensitize you, but most men retained their natural revulsion for the handiwork of death. "When there's no revulsion left, you've gone over to the other side," Jerry said. "Ray seems to feel you're already there. I take a different view." According to Jerry, some men were believed to have the gift—an artistic feel for embalming. "Such men bring comfort to families by the work itself. Their compassion exudes from the presentation of the body. John Morton was such a man. If there is a gift, he had it. Some folks around this place think you've got it, too. Be careful, Casey. There's an invisible line between this side and the other. Ray will be watching. So will the rest of us."

Ray turned to me and said, "The first order of business is to take some of that eager shit out of you. Don't worry, kid. I've got plans."

In the emergency room of Angel Shores Hospital, I lay on my stomach while the doctor sewed four stitches into the back of my head. I looked at my bloody clothing hung over a chair. "That dead guy snored," I said. "*Snored*. What did you expect me to do? I thought I killed him with the trocar when I stuck it into his heart."

"Mr. Dillard was already dead, kid," Ray said, now seated on a swivel stool inside the curtained emergency suite. "If anyone killed him, it was me, when I shot him."

"Sounds like murder to me," the doctor said.

Dr. Keith and Ray had known each other for years. Ray told him about my accident—I had been aspirating Mr. Dillard with the trocar. Ray had guided me through the process—loudly, and with eye contact, to prevent me from wandering into the state of trance I had been experiencing. Gift or no, Ray was making sure I was learning the craft from *him*. "I *am* the embalming room supervisor," he'd said. I was sure I had punctured Mr. Dillard's heart—I had seen the dark blood charge through the hose. Ray had told me there was more blood. He kept telling me to force the trocar higher. It perturbed me—I knew the spearpoint of the trocar had gone beyond the heart—nothing was coming out of Mr. Dillard at all. Ray kept telling me to aim higher. I forced the trocar one last time, and punctured the trachea—the trocar sucked air in through Mr. Dillard's nose. It made the dead man *snore*. Snoring was the last thing I expected from a dead person. I yanked the trocar out of the body with such force, it sent me flying backward, into the glass pane of the fluid cabinet. My head broke the glass, imbedding a shard in my scalp. Dr. Keith must have thought it was funny—I felt my head jiggle under his hand, a silent laugh running down the doctor's arm. Ray kept going, "Carl once made a man fart backwards with the trocar—same technique. Talk about an odd noise."

"You'd better quit, Ray," Dr. Keith said. "You'll make me injure your friend."

"The guy *snored*," I said. I picked up my bloody shirt and walked to the removal car in my bloody undershirt. Nothing bleeds like a scalp wound. I touched the back of my head, feeling the stitches through the surgical tape. I took Ray by the arm and stopped him in the middle of the parking lot. I said, "Hey, wait a minute. You made me do that. You knew the guy would snore. It scared the hell out of me. I hope you're happy."

"I *am* happy," Ray said. "You don't spook so easy, kid. Now that I know you're spookable, I'm satisfied that you and I can have the proper relationship." Ray checked his watch. "Mr. Dillard's a shipper—looks like we've still got time to get him to the airport. Fly him back to Saint Louie."

The airport. I had never figured the job would take me to the airport. The pain began in my head. I felt dizzy, and fell trembling against a car. Ray studied my face. "You don't look so good, kid," he said.

I started shaking all over. I cried in front of Ray; my anger rose up against him. "If you're trying to take my eagerness away, you've done it," I said. "I might as well quit now—I can't go to the airport—can't even go near the place."

Ray went white faced. His eyes widened. He put his hand on my shoulder. I jerked back. "I'm sorry, kid," he said. "That was a cruel thing I did. I didn't mean it. I swear to God Almighty, it wasn't part of my plan to shake you up like that. I had forgotten about your parents."

I didn't need to search Ray's face for sincerity. I heard it in his voice—he had nearly choked on his own words.

"Kid, every man here has got a weakness—a job he can't handle. Nobody will ever make you do what you can't do. We all help each other with this stuff. I can't embalm kids—can't even make the removal. I'll send Morey and Lester to the airport."

"Jeff and Randy."

"Frick and Frack."

At 4:00 P.M., Ray sat me down in my living room. "Tonight's a special night," he said. "Police rotation. It starts at midnight, so everybody goes home early, except you, seeing as how you're already home." Ray told me not to bother Jerry tonight—monthly Rotary dinner, always on a Thursday, always with his wife. "That means Natalie's on the loose, and police rotation is her main gig. I suggest you introduce yourself to her, then immediately fertilize one of her ova with your semen."

I yakked with Jeff and Randy till midnight. It felt good to be with guys my own age who were dedicated to the trade. Like me, they had suffered ridicule from other kids, just because they had wanted a career in the mortuary business. "It's in our family," they said. "Our father is the most respected man in Sebring. It's an honorable trade, meant for honorable men. You hear stories all the time about Undertakers stealing the gold fillings out of people's teeth, weird shit like that. People don't realize that nobody has more respect for the dead than a funeral man."

I seized out of my sleep and rubbed my eyes, trying to make out the human form in the doorway of my bedroom. I suspected Natalie— she had snuck up on me, as I had been warned, but the voice that came out of the darkness was Ray's: "Wake up, kid," he said. "You don't want to miss your first murder."

On the way to the crime scene I told Ray I hadn't heard the giant bells. "Sheriff called me at home," Ray said. "I'm the official funeral director for police rotation." He commented on the dark skies, said it would rain all day. "Seems like it always rains on murder days. Domestic homicide. That means you get to see the Circle of Willis. That'll cut down the eager factor a notch or two." Ray drove us to a neighborhood of cinder-block houses. We spotted the police cars in the driveway of an aqua blue house. In the front yard, a weathered plastic flamingo bent halfway over. A tricycle lay overturned beneath a sapling.

A few steps with the stretcher put me into a scene from a detective movie: Plainclothes guy leaning against a doorjamb with a cup of coffee and a cigarette; Gray-uniformed sheriff's deputies mumbling about the Braves and quail hunting. None of them looked at *her*, unless they had direct business with the body. I could not take my eyes from her.

Not much older than myself, the dead woman lay on her back on the living room floor. A bloody kitchen knife lay a few inches from her hand, but she did not appear cut. Dr. Kendall, a youngish blond man with wire-frame glasses, hovered over the body. He lifted the dead woman's tee shirt. "Gunshot wound to the abdomen," he declared.

Detective Jones explained the case: The dead woman's husband had admitted to the shooting, but hadn't called for help until three hours after he had shot her. He admitted he was drunk, claimed the victim had been drunk, too. He also claimed that she had tried to kill him with the kitchen knife, so he shot her. "He's got a possible defense wound on his forearm," Jones said. "Their little girl was sleeping over Grandma's, thank God. If we get the dead woman's prints off that knife and find alcohol in her blood, the husband walks, unless we can prove that his waiting to call for help caused her death—then self-defense becomes manslaughter. Husband claims she died the instant he shot her. Get her done and over to Kendall's morgue, pronto."

Her name was Marianne Blessing, twenty-three years old. We laid her on the table and cut her clothes off her. She wore only jeans and a tee shirt—no shoes, no panties, no bra. The bullet hole in her abdomen looked like a trocar puncture. The sound of small thunder rolled above. Rain tapped against the frosted window of the embalming room. "Okay, kid," Ray said. "Follow my orders and work your magic gift."

The calm settled in on me, as did the voice in my head. I took the scalpel and made my first incision on the woman's neck, just above the clavicle. With two hooks shaped like dentistry instruments, I separated the muscle tissue protecting the main embalming vessels: The jugular vein, and the carotid artery. The concept of arterial embalming was simple—the injection of embalming chemical into the carotid artery forced the body's blood out of the jugular vein. I slipped a stainless steel tube, equipped with a plunger, down the jugular and into the heart. I pulled the plunger, and Mrs. Blessing's blood flowed from a fitting on the side of the drainage tube. The gum hose sent a constant stream of water down the gutter of the table, to dilute the normal stickiness of the blood, which ran down the gutter of the table and into the flushable sink.

"We have established drainage," Ray said. "Now, we shoot her."

An embalming machine is nothing more than a pump—like a heart without a beat. A glass tank, shaped like a cylinder, sat atop the embalming machine. I filled it with water and added a bottle and a half of embalming fluid. The fluid contained more than just formaldehyde. It also contained a pinkish dye, and emollients. The dye worked like makeup from the inside out. As soon as I clicked on the machine, the color of Mrs. Blessing's fingernails changed instantly from dark purple to lifelike pink. The transformation of color also let you know what parts of the body were getting fluid—a blood clot or some other problem often prevented flow—the unembalmed parts remained deathly purple. Such was the case with Mrs. Blessing's legs—they refused the flush of pink. Something was wrong—a mixture of blood and embalming fluid poured from her mouth. Ray switched off the machine. "Purge." He said. "Bullet must've whacked a major vessel. Her abdomen is filling with embalming fluid—the pressure forces everything out of her mouth. By the way, nice incision, Casey. Like you've been doing it all your life. Looks like you'll get to make another one. We'll have to shoot the legs separately." Ray and I stood on opposite sides of the table. Together, we incised the inner thighs, searching for the femoral arteries. I found mine first.

When Mrs. Blessing's feet went pink, Ray was satisfied. "Close her up," Ray said. "You've seen stitches on a baseball—same thing." I stitched her closed, then took the trocar from the wall. Ray told me to put it back. "No cavity work," he said. "She goes to Dr. Kendall now. Then, the Circle of Willis. After that, your initiation is complete."

Mrs. Blessing's family bore her maiden name—Campbell. Nine Campbells showed up at two o'clock in the afternoon ("Cracker family," Ray had said). The Campbells demanded that we have their Marianne ready to view by five—they'd wait in the lobby while we readied her. Meredith explained that her body was still with the medical examiner. They didn't care. They'd wait.

Dr. Kendall called at four o'clock. Marianne Blessing had been shot through the vena cava—bled to death within moments. Nobody could have saved her. Her blood tested alcohol-positive, too. The husband would go free. Ray sent Carl out in the rain to the office of the medical examiner.

When Carl returned, he rolled Mrs. Blessing into the embalming room and slid her onto the table, her body wrapped in a plastic shroud. Ray prepared me for what I was about to see: "Kid, when your friends and neighbors find out what you do for a living, some of them will ask you what's the worst thing you've ever seen. I've been in the trade thirteen years. I've seen it all—but there is nothing more hideous than what a medical examiner does to a human body in the course of his daily routine."

Carl removed the plastic shroud. A flash of lightning brightened the room. The young Mrs. Blessing looked like a deer, gutted in the woods. Dr. Kendall's Y-incision began at the sockets of both shoulders. The two incisions joined at the breastbone and continued down to the pubic crest. Ray peeled back the large, thick flaps of skin, muscle and a layer of yellow fat. A bulging trash bag sat in the middle of the cavity. Ray said the bag contained her organs. He lifted the bag out of her body and set it on the table, between her legs. He opened the bag and rolled it down, revealing a pool of innards and blood. The smell of puke and shit filled the embalming room. Ray slapped a pair of scissors into my palm. "Start snipping the viscera," he said.

"Small snips. Helps the embalming fluid permeate the organs. Do not snip pieces *off* the organs—that's considered excessive mutilation. Can you believe it? Kendall disembowels people like a Spanish Inquisitor and nobody says a word. We make an embalming incision half an inch too long, and it's 'excessive mutilation'—and that's the *law*, kid, so be careful when you snip."

With gloved hands, I sorted through the mess in the bag and started snipping to the sound of thunder and rain. Carl threw me a bottle of cavity embalming fluid and told me to pour it all over the viscera. The chemical fumes watered my eyes; burned my lungs. Carl retied the bag. I realized that during the entire operation, I had not once heard the guiding old voice. Inside Mrs. Blessing, two dark pools of blood lay on either side of the spinal column. Carl sucked the blood out with the aspirator hose, then dried the cavity with a towel. Ray positioned himself behind Mrs. Blessing's head. "Moment of truth." He announced.

Over the top of Mrs. Blessing's head, an incision ran ear-to-ear. Ray snipped stitches, then grasped a tuft of her hair. Like peeling off a mask, Ray pulled the woman's scalp down over her face. Her forehead covered her eyes, the hair of her head askew on her chest. Ray peeled the other half of her scalp backward, revealing the entire top of her skull. From the side, the head now looked like a giant protruding eye—the skull was the eyeball, the two peeled-back flaps of hairy, red scalp were the eyelids and lashes. The cranium itself had been sawn through into a lid of sorts, shaped like a skullcap with earflaps. Ray removed the cranium. The inside of her skull was empty.

"Where's the brain?" I asked.

"You snipped it up with the viscera. Now look here, kid." Ray pointed to the middle of the empty cranium, to a circular collection of arteries. "*That*, kid, is the Circle of Willis."

Compared to all I had seen and done with Mrs. Blessing's viscera, along with the unflapping of the young woman's scalp, not to mention the removal of her skull, the Circle of Willis seemed decidedly ungruesome. I asked Ray, "What's the big deal?"

"What does the top of Mount Everest look like?" Ray asked. "It looks like a *rock*—like the whole rest of the goddamn mountain, but people kill themselves all the time trying to get there. It's not the summit, kid—it's the *climb*. You've just made that climb, because you will never see anything more revolting than this. Worse than the fucking Mansons. *And*, you've just mutilated the organs of a human being, simply because it's your *job*. Once you've seen the Circle of Willis, you know what it means to work in a funeral home. Consider yourself initiated."

"Tell Casey the rest," Carl said. He winked at me when Ray started talking. I could tell why: The Circle of Willis was one of Ray's favorite subjects—second only to my semen and Natalie's eggs. He gestured like a professor as he talked, "The Circle of Willis causes the phenomenon of colateral circulation. Thomas Willis discovered his circle in the seventeenth century. He wrote a book about it called *The Soul of Brutes*—cool title. In that book, Willis said that the soul of man flows through the nervous and circulatory systems. He said that when things go wrong in the Circle of Willis, the result is melancholy—a distemper of the brain that can lead to stupidity, as in Carl over there, or foolishness, or even madness. Circle of Willis goes bad, you go koo-koo in the head."

"C'mon, Ray. Tell Casey everything."

"Carl, you ought not to make sport of a man's spiritual beliefs, especially when your own wife, Suzy Pocahontas, believes a multitude of weird shit."

"Then tell him, Ray. Make a convert." Carl winked at me again, as soon as Ray turned to face me. His face got all serious, as though he were about to pronounce a benediction. Solemnity rang in his tone: "Kid," Ray said, "The Circle of Willis is the seat of the human soul." Ray almost caught Carl in midsnicker when he turned around. Carl put on his Undertaker face, and said, "Now, tell Casey what a human soul looks like."

"I will, as soon as you shut the fuck up. The human soul is spherical, glowing white—about the size of a shooter marble."

"Like that one there?" I said, pointing to the inside of Mrs. Blessing's skull.

"Jesus, kid, you're giving me the willies."

"Look!" I said. "There it goes. Can't you see it? It's floating toward the window, hovering there now. My God, Ray. I think it wants to get out."

Ray ran for the window. "No shit? See there Carl, I told you. Casey can see it. It's like you said. He's got the gift. Holy mother-fuck-me."

"Quick! Open the window," I said.

Ray obeyed me.

"It's gone now," I said. "It flew right out the window."

"Jesus God," Ray said. "I never would have figured. Carl's right, kid. You've got the gift."

Carl said, "Yep, Ray. He's got the gift all right—and you taught it to him. You've been fucking with Casey ever since he got here. You've just been fucked back. How's it feel, fucker?"

An odd look of bewilderment crossed Ray's features. He looked at Carl, then at me. We kept our faces blank as long as we could stand it. Carl started laughing first, then headed toward the door. "Shooter marble, my ass," he said. "C'mon, Casey, pork sandwich on me." We left Ray standing in the middle of the embalming room, his mouth wide open.

8

The family of Marianne Blessing watched Ray and me roll the pink casket through the lobby. The way they aimed their eyes at us made me feel like we were passing before a firing squad. In the Iris Room, Ray and I placed Mrs. Blessing in repose. Meredith walked in. "Trouble," he said, pointing a thumb toward the lobby. "These folks are upset, and not in the usual way. They know the husband's out of jail now. His name is Jimmie Blessing. The Campbells out there say they'll kill him if he comes here. I called the police. They'll park on Mayfair until the Campbells leave tonight. You two stay in this room until they've seen the body. No telling how they'll react—they're sort of taking it out on us." Meredith went to fetch the Campbells. He stopped at the door and gave us the okay sign. "Nice job, fellows. She looks real good."

The leader of the clan, Sophie Campbell, led the family into the Iris Room. A short tank of a woman, Mrs. Campbell strode toward the casket with her mouth turned down and her nose in the air. The others, including the dead woman's five-year-old daughter, waited in a semicircle while Mrs. Campbell viewed her grandniece's remains. "Hair's wrong," she snapped. Meredith whipped out his comb. Sophie Campbell snatched it from his hand and reworked the hair. She took a step back and said, "Too much makeup." Meredith pulled out his hanky and dabbed at Mrs. Blessing's face. Sophie still wasn't satisfied. "We want the kneeler too, so as we can pray to the Good Lord for vengeance upon the bastard dog what done this to our poor Marianne."

Ray motioned me to follow him to a small storage closet in the repose reception area. The closet contained three kneelers, one for each repose room. "These folks are getting on my nerves," Ray said. "We'll give them the antique kneeler—it'll impress them. They'll think they're getting the royal treatment they deserve, but this thing is hell on the knees—no padding. It hurts—and speaking of hurting, don't think I've forgotten your little trick in the embalming room, kid. I'm just being nice to you so you'll forget I'm out for revenge."

Ray and I lugged the antique into the Iris Room and placed it in front of the casket. The thing weighed like a spinet piano. Sophie Campbell gestured her family toward the body of Marianne Blessing. They approached one by one, knelt for a moment, then returned to their semicircle. Ray and I were watching from behind. You could actually see the surprise of pain wiggle up their backs. Ray whispered, "That kneeler's torture." Meredith shot us both a quick wink—he knew Ray's motivation with the kneeler, and covered his mouth like he was rubbing his face, to hide the smirk. When he got himself under control, Meredith introduced Ray and me to the Campbells. Except for the slightest nod, none of them acknowledged us. The little girl broke ranks and marched up to me. Bottom lip sticking out, she rared back her fist and plowed it into my groin. I gritted my teeth and followed Ray out the door, where I leaned against a wall from pain. Ray said, "Kid, you'd better hope that little girl didn't kill any tadpoles. You'll need them for Natalie."

• • •

A throng of Campbells murmured into the lobby at 7:00 P.M. They all wore grim faces and discount-store clothing. Sophie Campbell posted two sentries at the main entrance. "We don't want no Blessings here," she said.

Every man of Morton-Albright worked the visitation, in case of trouble, even Lex and the twins. When calling hours ended at nine o'clock, Sophie led the guests like a platoon to the parking lot. Meredith sent everyone home. He dismissed the twins, who complained about having missed a half night of drinking on their supposed day off.

From the veranda, Meredith and I watched as the Campbells chatted around their cars, then began piling into them. Most of the cars drove off at once. The rain had slowed to a drizzle. Thunder and heat lightning played in the distant sky. Meredith placed his hand on my shoulder. "Let's lock this place up, Cap'n. We always start in the back, so we don't end up in the dark."

Beginning in the Iris Room, we headed toward the lobby, turning off lights, checking doors. In the minister's room of the chapel, Meredith found the clergy door unlocked—it opened to the outside, to allow the minister a quiet entrance. He opened the door and frowned when the doorchime didn't sound. He flipped the switch, made sure of the *ching*, and locked the door. When we returned to the lobby, we found Sophie and six other Campbells, each holding a blanket and a pillow. "We'll sleep on the floor," Sophie announced, "in the room with our Marianne."

"I'm sorry folks, but y'all can't sleep here. I know vigilance is an old tradition, but our insurance doesn't allow it anymore. You'll have to leave now."

"We don't want no Blessings here!" Sophie Campbell spat. "We aim to make sure that murderin' trash, Jimmie Blessing, stays away from our Marianne."

"Police car parked down the street," Meredith said. "I'll call him if y'all don't leave. Besides, we'll have a man here in the building, all night long."

Sophie backed down at the mention of the police—the Campbells were no lawbreakers. "Who's the man watching over our baby?" She asked.

Meredith gestured toward me. "This is Mr. Kight," he said.

Sophie stepped close to me and sniffed in my direction. "This boy ain't no man. He's just a kid. What's a kid going to do against a murderin' pissant dog?"

Meredith took my part. He said, "Mr. Kight might be young, but he is a young *man*. He's responsible, and he'll take good care of Mrs. Blessing."

"Don't you call Marianne by that name. When she died, she got divorced, too. Her name is Campbell, and you can by-God go in there and change her nameplate to Marianne Campbell, and we'll have it engraved into her headstone, too." When Sophie finished with Meredith, she stuck a finger in my face. "As for *you*, Mr. Kight, just see that you do your job, because if that murderin' dog-shit bastard comes a-knockin', and you let him in, I swear to God on high, I'll kill ye."

I looked down at her face, now wet with tears. I pitied her, but Meredith had explained to me that we could not stop Jimmie Blessing from seeing his dead wife. When Marianne Blessing died, her body became the legal property of her next of kin: her husband, Jimmie Blessing, now at large.

Meredith locked the door behind the Campbells. He walked me to my apartment. "You scared, Cap'n?"

"Not at all," I lied. I figured Jeff and Randy could help me out if things went bad.

"If Jimmie Blessing shows up, tell him we're closed. He can see his wife tomorrow, during normal business hours. If he gives you any trouble, call the police."

The twins had left me a note: "Getting drunk at the County Line. Be home late. We'll try not to wake you."

Damn. I consoled myself with the idea that Jimmie Blessing would probably expect Morton-Albright to be full of bloodthirsty

Campbells, especially if he knew anything of Sophie. I headed for John Morton's bed. The rain picked up again. I lay there in the dark, listening to the approaching thunder. The rain tapping on the window reminded me of the snipping sound of the scissors on Mrs. Blessing's intestines. The rainy night set me to worrying: Ray was busy at home, thinking up new ways to scare the hell out of me. It seemed like years since I had spoken to Margee—she'd be up all night, worrying about me. I was worried about worrying her. Natalie, a girl with black hair and sharp teeth, awaited her first bite of my flesh, and the cops down the street were probably asleep in their squad car. For the first time in my life, I was all alone in the middle of the night. I had pulled the covers up to my neck, trying to forget the smell of rancid viscera, when I realized that I wasn't alone at all—the Presence swirled into the room. I felt it all over me, like being wrapped in my mother's arms. It didn't frighten me when her face appeared before me in the air. She was beautiful, my mother, and I remembered—she *had* wrapped me in her arms. I remembered her kisses all over my face, Dad rubbing my head, telling me I was a good boy, like I had done something extraordinary for them. Then we were dancing around the Victrola, all of us. Mom, Dad, Margee and me—celebrating. What were we celebrating?

Ching.

The clergy entrance—the door Meredith had locked. If Jimmie Blessing could shoot his own wife, he could damn sure break in through a locked door. I stripped off my pajamas and yanked on my pants. I hurried to the lobby, buttoning my shirt as I ran. I flipped on the chandelier. The lobby stood empty, the chapel doors closed. Maybe the intruder was hiding in the chapel. I headed for the phone to call the police, then stopped. What if the wind had blown the clergy door open? What if the door was so old, it just didn't lock right anymore? I hadn't heard any other sounds. If I called the police for nothing, I'd look like an idiot—plenty of ammunition for Ray. Besides, there was a telephone in every room of the funeral home. I'd take the hallway to the chapel door that opened near the porte cochere entrance. There, I could spot Jimmie Blessing on his way to his late wife's repose room, *then* run and call the police. And the murderer had more to contend with than me—the Presence was on me strong.

I heard the wind of the storm rushing through the porte cochere as I crept to the rear door of the chapel. I opened the door just enough to stick my hand inside and feel around for the light switches on the wall—none within reach. I slid inside the chapel and flattened myself against the wall. In the dark now, I slid along the wall, still feeling for the switches, then remembered that I had never seen any switches in the chapel—none besides the dimmers just inside the main chapel doors, clear at the other end. A stupid move—I had left myself in the dark. Now I was scared. Presence or no, I was getting the hell out of the chapel. I began sliding back the way I came. A noise stopped me—a weak cough. I stood still and let my eyes adjust to the dark, my pulse pounding behind them. Slowly, the shadowy rows of the pews appeared. I lifted my eyes toward the opposite side of the chapel. The silhouette of a human figure appeared against the opposite wall.

We opposed each other like 3 and 9 on a clock face. I fought the urge to flee, sliding instead toward the front of the chapel, and the light switches. I kept my eye on the figure against the far wall. As I moved clockwise in the rotunda, the figure moved with me, step for step. I stopped. The figure stopped. I cleared my throat for my funeral voice. It came out squeaky with fear: "Mr. Blessing?" I called out. "I'm Mr. Kight. I know why you're here. I'll turn on the lights."

No answer. I slid along the wall, heading for the lights. The figure moved the same distance, the same speed. I took my eyes off the silhouette and ran the six strides to the switches. I flipped them on, bathing the pews in bright light. The chapel stood empty. I walked a circuit around the chapel, finding no one. I even checked behind the podium, then the organ—no one there. I made a stop in the minister's room—the clergy door remained locked tight. As I dimmed down the chapel lights, I noticed the moon through the stained glass skylights. I convinced myself that the silhouette had been my own shadow—an illusion of moonlight. Perhaps I hadn't heard the doorchime at all. I had been nervous anyway. The wind sometimes made musical sounds on its way through an old window.

In my bedroom, I left my pajamas in a pile on the floor and lay on John Morton's bed, this time in my underwear in case I had to dress quickly again. I worried that I'd lay awake worrying all night, but the rain against the window put me away, and I was celebrating with my parents again.

The flash woke me up—lightning, I guessed—but it was as though the lightning had flashed *inside* my room. I saw orange spots before my eyes, but heard no thunder. What I *did* hear sent me yanking on my pants again—the apartment door clicking shut. Struggling to get my pants up, I fell into Jeff and Randy's bedroom. They had not yet returned. When I reached the apartment door, I heard the sound of footfalls running in the hallway. I opened the door—the hallway was empty. I buttoned my shirt and started down the hall toward the lobby, following the sound of the footsteps. From behind me, a loud rapping noise jerked me around. I stood there, staring at the jalousie door of the employee entrance. I walked toward it, slowly, my eyes and ears on alert. Through the frosted glass of the jalousie, the figure took on a more definable shape. The knocking came hard this time. I opened the door. A man stood on the veranda.

The man's hair, wet with drizzle, hung down over his face. He slicked it back with his hand and spoke in a drunken slur. "I'm Jimmie Blessing. I come to see my wife."

I choked down my fear and explained to the admitted killer that the funeral home was closed, as Meredith had suggested. I told him to return during normal business hours. He pulled a revolver out of the back of his pants, closed one eye, squinted the other, and leveled the gun at my face.

"I'll take you to your wife," I said. "Just let me finish getting dressed—this way, in my apartment."

Jimmie cocked the gun. "You think I'm stupid?"

"No, I don't think you're stupid. Look at me. I'm barefoot, my shirt's unbuttoned and I'm not wearing my tie and jacket. It would be disrespectful for me to take you to see your wife like this. Besides, Mr. Blessing, the law is on your side in this situation."

"No shit?"

I repeated what Meredith had told me, that his wife's body was his legal property and he had every right to see her. "Wouldn't you prefer to do this the right way? You don't need your gun. You have my word. You can watch me finish dressing."

"No—you're a right honorable man. You go on and dress. I'll wait, like you say."

I slipped into a fresh shirt, knotted my tie, and chose the penny loafers. "Right this way," I said to Jimmie Blessing, and led him to the Iris Room. He was still carrying the gun, but was now pointing it downward, instead of at me. When we arrived at the Iris Room, I asked him to wait outside the door for a moment, remembering Meredith's instruction—never allow anyone inside to view a body until I had first checked it out myself. Jimmie nodded—he'd wait.

In the Iris Room, I left the overhead lights turned off, picturing Sophie Campbell down the street with a pair of binoculars and a gun of her own. I turned on a couple of table lamps, then went to the casket, where I lit the torchiers. The Iris Room now dim with shaded light, I dragged the antique kneeler out of the way to get at the casket. I checked the young Mrs. Blessing. Perfect—just a few tugs here and there and a quick brush of her hair with my fingertips. I backed away from the casket and adjusted some flowers, then gripped the kneeler to replace it, but Jimmie moaned from the reception area, and I heard a noise like he had fallen to the floor—he was obviously intoxicated. I ran to the door. Jimmie stood in the reception area, bent over a potted ficus tree he had knocked down. "I am so sorry," he said.

"It's okay," I said, "Come this way, please."

Jimmie sobbed louder as we walked toward his dead wife. "Oh, Lordy, Lordy, Lordy," he wailed. As we passed by the middle window, a bright flash from outside startled us both. As we both turned to look toward the window, Jimmie's leg became entangled with mine and he fell, striking his head on the corner of the misplaced kneeler. The impact knocked him around so that he fell onto his back. His gun fired. The bullet smashed through the windowpane. From outside the window, I heard a squeal, then a flopping sound. Running to the porte cochere entrance, I pictured Sophie Campbell lying dead on the ground. She had come to kill me for letting Jimmie into the funeral home, only to be murdered by the murdering pissant she had so despised. I ran through the tunnel of the porte cochere to the patch of bushes under the window of the Iris Room, the area bathed yellow under the lamp of the Morton-Albright sign.

I stood over her in the drizzling rain. She lay among the bushes— black trench coat, bow tie. Blood ran from her forehead. Natalie. I knew her face from the picture on Jerry's desk. I had finally met Natalie, only to have her die in my arms. She moaned. I sat down cross-legged in the wet cypress mulch, placed her head in my lap, then brushed her black hair from her face. I got blood on my hand— *her* blood. Her eyes flickered open. She looked up at me through dreamy eyes, then jumped to her feet. "Aw, shit—my camera!" she said. Natalie wobbled through the bushes, pawing through the leaves, cussing as she went. "Found it!" she announced, "And my hat, too." She placed the fedora cocked upward upon her head and popped a flashbulb into her camera. She aimed the thing at me and shot. Orange spots peppered my vision.

"Still works," she said.

Because of the flash, I could barely make out the hand she extended to me. I touched paper, not skin. "My card," she said. "Natalie Stiles. You're Casey Kight, no doubt. You saw your parents die in a plane crash. Is that true?"

My vision clearing, I looked at the business card—no address, no title, no phone number—just two words in open block letters: Natalie Stiles. "My phone number's on the back," she said. "I have my own private line." I looked her over as the orange spots faded. She stood an inch shorter than I did. Incredibly thin, dressed like a cub reporter, she looked like a marionette. Blood ran down her face in a long trickle. She seemed not to notice. I told Natalie it was true. I had watched my parents die. "You're bleeding," I said.

"Cool. Let's check it out in the mirror. The bullet hit the flash reflector. See the crease? It jammed the camera into my head. Daddy keeps a first-aid kit in his office. You can doctor me. Sorry about your mom and dad. I heard about your trocar accident today. Get any stitches?"

"Four."

"Cool. Did the dead guy really snore? Did Ray tell you about the man who farted backwards? I heard about how you smashed the casket upstairs. Sorry I missed it—Denise said total devastation. Daddy said you stepped in dog shit on your first day. Can you believe that? Dog shit on Morton-Albright property, for godssake. Daddy said you wore a black suit to your job interview. Now, that's deathy."

Denise had made my heart pound—Natalie stole it right out of my chest. Denise radiated feminine sex, the kind that made your knees wobble. Natalie delighted me with her boyish manner, making me unafraid to engage her pretty face. Without a thought, I put my arm around her as we walked together through the porte cochere. I spoke to her without a stutter. "What else do you know about me?"

"Your middle name is James," she said. "I have *two* middle names: Morton and Albright."

"Your name is Natalie Morton Albright Stiles?"

"Mm-hm."

"Are you going to bite me now?"

"No, silly. You're expecting it."

Natalie checked herself out in the mirror that hung in Jerry's office. Blood had run from the cut in her forehead, through her eye, all the way down to her neck. "I look deathy as hell," she said. "Take my picture." She popped a bulb into the camera and handed it to me. "Just aim and shoot—the button's on the top."

I peered through the viewfinder. One of her high-top black sneakers was untied. She wore dark gabardines and a white shirt. Her open trench coat revealed a brown tweed jacket. The bow tie was real—no clip-on. A camera bag hung from her shoulder. I searched for the outline of her breasts, but the shirt hung large on her.

"My *face*," she said. I aimed the camera and took her picture. "Now try one of me on the floor. I'll advance the film for you so you don't screw it up." Natalie lay down on the floor and played dead. She lolled her head to one side and opened her mouth slightly. I snapped her picture. She asked, "Did I look shot in the head?"

"Yes—just like a cover from one of those true crime magazines."

Natalie turned onto her side and propped her head up with her palm. She took her time looking me over, a smile at the corner of her mouth. She stood up and headed for the rest room. "First-aid kit is in that cabinet," she said, pointing. "I'll go clean up. You can get ready for surgery, Dr. Kight."

Natalie returned looking better, pressing on her cut with a folded paper towel. The cut was no larger than an embalming incision, but a black bruise was on its way. I sprayed the cut with Bactine and covered it with a square Band-Aid.

"That was me in the chapel tonight," Natalie confessed. "I came in through the clergy entrance, like always, only someone had locked the door and set the chime. You seemed so cute, following me around the chapel and introducing yourself as Mr. Kight, I sneaked into your bedroom later and took a picture of you sleeping in your underwear—really, Casey—briefs? The way Daddy talks about you all the time, I never would have figured you for the Fruit of the Loom type."

My face burned red. I had always worn whatever underwear Margee bought for me. I changed the subject. "You disappeared when I turned on the chapel lights," I said.

"I ducked under a pew. You walked right past me. I thought about grabbing your ankle, but I couldn't have you fibrillating right there in the chapel. We may never have met." She smiled and raised her eyebrows. "By the way," she said, "isn't there a guy in the Iris Room with a gun?"

"Jimmie!" I said. I had forgotten all about him.

"Jimmie? You two know each other?"

Jimmie Blessing lay on the floor of the Iris Room, still grasping the gun. I approached him slowly, then kicked at the gun to knock it from his hand. The gun fired, putting a hole in the side of his wife's casket. Jimmie ignored the blast. Natalie flinched. "Easy, tiger," she said.

"Sorry. Looks like Jimmie's out cold." I pried the gun from Jimmie's hand and slid it away from him, just in case he regained consciousness in a bad mood. Natalie knelt beside him, checking his pulse with her fingers at his jugular. "He's not out cold, Casey—he's dead." She stood up.

"Are you sure?"

"*You're* the one who works in a funeral home. I take it you've actually seen dead people. Back away for a second." She aimed the camera at Jimmie. "Wait." She said. "Put the gun back in his hand. It looked better that way."

"What about the cops? I don't think we should disturb the scene."

"You already disturbed the scene. You kicked his hand and touched the gun. Put the gun back in his hand. They'll never know." Natalie took a dozen pictures. Spent flashbulbs littered the floor. Still shooting, she asked me, "How do you think he died?"

"He hit his head on the corner of that kneeler."

"Subdural hematoma," Natalie said, "and by the smell of him, I'd guess ethanol intoxication played a role in his demise. How did he fall into the kneeler?"

"He tripped over my feet."

"You killed him?"

"It was an accident."

"You killed him accidentally?"

"I didn't kill him."

"Your feet killed him. Your feet are attached to the rest of you. What do you think? They'll try your feet for involuntary manslaughter?"

"The kneeler was Ray's idea," I said.

"Blame it on Ray," Natalie said, peering through her camera toward Jimmie, "but you killed the guy." She raised the camera and flashed the bulb in my face again, blinding me. "Gotcha," she said. "I love this camera. I would have died if it had been ruined. It's a newsman's camera from the forties. Every picture looks like the one of Oswald getting shot." Natalie walked toward the body of Marianne Blessing. "Girlfriend?" she asked.

"No. I'm not seeing anyone right now."

"Not you, ya dope. Her. Dead girl. Was she his girlfriend?"

"Wife."

"How did she die?"

"He shot her."

"Was he going to shoot her again?"

"No. He was going to shoot me."

"Really? Call Daddy. He'll be impressed. Give me twenty minutes to get home before you call. I'm not supposed to be here. Don't rat me out."

I followed her to the parking lot. She climbed into the Imperial and shut the door. She spoke to me through the open window. "This was the funeral home's lead car, back in the Chrysler era. Green Hornet drove one just like it on TV.

"I know."

"You know? How big is your stack?"

"My stack?"

"Your stack of comic books."

"I've got fourteen Harvey issues of Green Hornet. I keep them in protective sleeves. The stack of other comics is next to my bed—a foot high, maybe more."

"I'd love to get a look at your Harveys. I used to pretend Daddy was the Green Hornet. He looked great in his suit, driving this car. Are you a Marvel man, Casey?"

At first, I thought she had said "marble man," as Colton had. I told her I preferred granite, trying to impress her.

"I said Marvel, not marble. Do you like Marvel comics?"

"I have a few Spider Man."

"You mean the *Amazing* Spider Man."

"Yeah, and Thor, god of Thunder."

"Loki is *my* man. He's evil, but he gets to wear that purple cape."

"Yeah, but Thor throws lightning bolts."

"Speaking of lightning, I'd better flash back to the house. You have a death to report. Barbecue at my house on Sunday. Daddy will invite you. Say yes." Natalie put the car in gear and started backing up. I called out to her, "What should I wear?"

"Boxers."

Jerry called Colton from the funeral home. Albright called the police and asked them to dispatch from the station instead of using the radio—keep the reporters away. The police called Kendall, the medical examiner. Jimmie Blessing was dead, all right. Dr. Kendall said so. "I'm ruling this death an accident, pending a postmortem exam. Probably a subdural hematoma, exacerbated by ethanol intoxication."

Jerry and the cops tried to make me out a hero. I kept telling them I took the gun away from Jimmie *after* he died. After the cops took pictures, (half as many as Natalie had taken), Dr. Kendall suggested we let Jesup Funeral Home handle the case, even though we were on police rotation. "The man died in your funeral home. It wouldn't look good for you to bury him, too."

Jerry agreed, and soon, two men from Jesup had Jimmie Blessing strapped onto their stretcher. Jerry bent down to pick something up from the floor—a flashbulb. He lifted an eyebrow at me and stuck the bulb in his pocket. I looked up at the ceiling. Jerry said, "Take tomorrow off. Have yourself a quiet weekend. I'm having a barbecue at my house on Sunday—someone I'd like you to meet."

At 5:25 A.M., I awoke to the presence of a man in my room—something strange in his hands. A shotgun. I jerked myself upright. "Get your ass out of bed," Ray said. "We're going hunting." I tried to refuse, but Ray turned on the light and started throwing clothes at me. "Barbecue on Sunday," he said. "We need a pig—you can't show up to meet Natalie empty-handed. You *will* kill a pig this morning."

The Winsteads were all up and eating breakfast. Ray's mother fixed bacon, sausage, grits, biscuits, two dozen eggs, and a loaf of toast. Ray's father told us where the pigs had been rooting, said Jerry had barbecued nothing but Winstead pigs for thirteen years, ever since Ray had gone off to work with the stiffs. He said nothing tasted like a wild pig, shot in an orange grove. "Whatever they eat goes right to the meat," he said. "Them pigs don't eat nothing 'cept fallen oranges. When an orange rots, it gets sweeter. All that sugar goes right into the pig meat. Tourists stop by my stand—they all swear by Indian River citrus—until they taste a Winstead Valencia—ain't no sweeter orange in the world. It's my own hybrid. Took eight seasons to develop it. We grow navels too—Northerners don't like to bother with seeds, but—"

"Daddy, Casey doesn't care shit about oranges, and we ain't got much time."

I said, "Let him talk, Ray. This is interesting."

Ray's father said, "It's about time you brought home somebody that's got some manners, boy—and you watch your mouth around your mama. Nobody says shit around here unless they step in it."

Ray whispered in my ear as he strapped on a pistol in a shoulder holster, "Don't get my daddy going on about citrus. He talks more than Colton Albright, you get him going. Now grab the shotgun. I'll show you how to load it. I'm assuming you've never fired a gun in your life."

I hadn't. Ray slid three red casings into the shotgun, then worked the pump. "Aim and shoot, kid. Nothing to it."

Ray expected to shoot a pig, drop it off at Halloran's Butcher Shop, get to work an hour late. As we walked through the groves, Ray finally shut up long enough for me to tell him that Jimmie Blessing had died in the Iris Room last night. I told him the whole story, except for the Natalie part.

"You went and killed Jimmie Blessing. Damn, kid. I never figured you for a killer."

"He hit his head on *your* kneeler."

"True, but *you* tripped him, killer." From that day forward, Ray stopped calling me kid and started calling me killer.

The hunting expedition turned into a mere assassination. I had expected gigantic boars with bloodstained tusks. The wild pigs looked mean enough, but they had grown accustomed to Ray's family working the groves. They just stood around, snorting and eating, like normal pigs in a barnyard. They didn't even look at us. I raised the shotgun and took aim at one of them, but I couldn't do it. I couldn't pull the trigger and take the life of an animal who was just minding his own business. Ray would call me chickenshit. I aimed off to the side of the biggest pig of the bunch. I figured if I missed enough times, Ray would grab the shotgun and kill the pig himself. I yanked on the trigger. The recoil of the twelve-gauge against my shoulder sent me to the ground.

"Damn, killer—you got one!" Ray yelled.

"What?" I couldn't believe it. I stood up and walked with Ray, toward the stricken animal—I had shot the damn thing trying to miss it. The boar flinched with our approach. Its eye darted around in the socket. Ray pulled his revolver from the shoulder holster and delivered the kill shot to the head. The pig made Ray only fifteen minutes late for work. I called Margee and told her I was coming home.

"Were you fired?" She asked. "Did you quit? Did you see something awful?"

"I'm just tired," I answered. "Short on sleep."

Margee kissed me and hugged me when I got home. She asked me a hundred times if I was okay. I entered my bedroom—a kid's room. The headboard of my bed was a wagon wheel. Now I lived in a mansion and slept in John Morton's bed. I had hoped to sleep until dark, but Margee woke me at three in the afternoon. The copy of the *Herald* in her hand and the look on her face told me I'd spend the rest of the afternoon explaining.

The article in the *Herald* was kind to Morton-Albright. None of the funeral home staff were named. Colton Albright had handled the police and the press. The news hadn't even made the front page, Margee stumbled across the article looking for Winn-Dixie coupons. She figured the death had something to do with my coming home early. I tried acting surprised. She said, "Don't treat me like I'm stupid, Casey James Kight," then she just sat there waiting with that Aunt Margee squint on her face until I told her the whole story about Jimmie Blessing. I left nothing out, except the part about Natalie.

"You killed this Jimmie Blessing."

"No, but I did kill a wild boar with a shotgun at six o'clock this morning." I aimed a make-believe shotgun at Margee and yelled *"Bang!"*

Margee jumped. "That's not funny," she said.

The next morning, I slurped black coffee and headed for Sammy's Men's Store. Sammy asked me right away if I had met Natalie. I said "Tomorrow." Sammy guessed that I needed something to wear to Jerry's barbecue.

"How did you know about the barbecue?"

"Jerry loves that old brick barbecue of his. Ray took you out boar hunting? I'll bet you never fired a gun in your life. That shotgun knock you on your behind? Always does the first time you fire one. What kind of clothes you need?"

"Underwear. Boxer shorts."

Sammy laughed. "You're going to need more than underwear, son—most important day of your life, meeting Natalie and all. I'll fix you up. Dignified, but casual." Sammy only carried the best of everything in his store. He warned me to wash the underwear before I wore them. "Hand-dyed Madras cotton," he said. "They bleed."

Margee was crying when I got back home. She had something to tell me, she said. She paced around the kitchen, wringing her hands, making me nervous. She said, "Oh, hell," then held out her left hand. The diamond on her finger sparkled in the sunlight coming in through the window.

"Jesus, that was fast," I said. "I go out and buy some clothes, come back home, and you're engaged?"

"It didn't happen that fast," she said. "It took twelve years. That's how old this diamond is."

I fell into my chair. Margee told me about Chet Armstrong. He lived in Valdosta, and had asked Margee to marry him the day before she came here to watch me while my parents were away in Hawaii. "I told him I'd think it over while I was gone. Of course, none of us knew I'd be gone so long. I wrote him—told him to forget about me. I had a child to raise. He said he'd wait, and that's exactly what the damn fool did." Margee set a box on the table. She spread out twelve pictures of Chet, twelve birthday cards and several stacks of love letters, each tied up in a ribbon. I looked through the pictures—handsome face, mostly streaked with grease. He had started out as a mechanic and now owned his own shop. "I never met a man like Chet," Margee said. "He was so understanding—asked about you in every letter he wrote to me. He and I both had people to care for—his mother's got multiple sclerosis. Most of what he makes goes to her care. He couldn't leave his mother, and I couldn't leave you."

"You can leave me now," I said. "I've got everything I need. Sell the house, take the money and go marry Chet."

I knew what was coming next. I braced myself for it. Margee hugged me and cried all over me. Every time I thought she was finished crying, she'd start up again. It seemed to go on forever. While Margee wept, an odd thought entered my mind. Margee hadn't worked a day in her life. How had we been living all these years?

"Insurance money," Margee said. "Your daddy put a pocketful of quarters into a vending machine at the airport. His last thoughts were to provide for you, in case something happened to him." There was more money too. The airline had sent us a settlement. Margee had put all the money into an annuity. She got a check every month.

"Then, there's your college money," she said, "from the Betty Beeson Home Permanent Company." They had sponsored the Hawaiian Getaway Sweepstakes. My parents had won the grand prize—six days and seven nights in Waikiki.

"You mean we're loaded, and we live out here in the county?"

Margee nodded. "I wanted to be careful with the money. After the accident, I was afraid something might happen to *me*. You'd be left all alone. I kept that money back, in case you needed it."

"How much is left?"

"About a hundred thousand in the annuity. Fifteen thousand went into your college fund. It's been sitting in the bank for twelve years."

"I've got fifteen thousand dollars?"

"No. You've got a hundred and fifteen thousand dollars, plus interest."

Margee took convincing, but we finally settled—I'd keep the fifteen grand; she'd take the rest. I'd know who to call if I ever needed a loan. I asked her when she was leaving. She said, "As soon as you're settled in. You're still happy with your job?"

"I am."

"You aren't in any trouble for killing that man, are you?"

Sunday—the day of Jerry's barbecue. On my way out the door, Margee presented me with the family treasure—Dad's old Victrola and his entire record collection. I kissed Margee good-bye, then tore out of the driveway before she started crying on me again. I lugged my stuff into John Morton's bedroom, all but the Victrola. I set it up in the living room, so everyone could enjoy it. From my new collection of boxer shorts, I chose a red plaid. I slipped them on and admired myself in the mirror—definitely more adult. I clothed myself in white, as Sammy had suggested for a warm spring day: poplin trousers with a brass-buckled blue belt, white short-sleeved oxford with a gold anchor embroidered on the pocket and a pair of white canvas shoes with labels that read Sperry. "Gives you sort of a yacht club look," Sammy had said. "Impress Natalie for sure." I checked the mirror to make sure the red boxers didn't show through my white pants. I unfolded the blue ascot Sammy had insisted upon, but I had no idea how to tie the damn thing. I threw it onto the bed and roared off for the barbecue, and Natalie.

9

I rang the Stiles's doorbell, wondering what costume Natalie had chosen for our first official meeting. I pictured the two of us, strolling together, linked by extraordinary wardrobe. I recalled her reporter's outfit, the one she had worn on the night we met, and the mourning clothes described to me by Meredith's wife, Teresa. Now I wore my own costume, sophisticated and expensive.

Natalie answered the door in cutoff jeans and a tee shirt. Except for the black high-top sneakers and black socks, she looked like a normal girl dressed for a steamy Florida Sunday. She shielded her eyes against me, pretending blindness from my white clothing. "You can't go into the backyard dressed like that," she said. "Ray's been referring to you as the Killer since he got here. Step outside, he'll call you Commodore."

"I'll go home and change," I said.

"I'll fix you. Take off your shoes—nothing dorkier than a brand-new pair of boat shoes." In the Stileses' living room, I removed my

shoes. Natalie ran to the garage and returned with a hammer. She
started beating my new shoes. "The blue socks," she said. "Take them
off—dorky as hell."

I took them off.

"Take off your pants," she said. "I'll cut them off like mine. You'll
look cool. Come on, ya dope. Your shirttail will cover you."

I stood up and dropped my pants to my ankles.

"I said *off*, not down. Throw them here."

I kicked out of my pants. Natalie picked them up and yanked
open a drawer. She withdrew a pair of scissors and snipped them in
the air, then put a hand to her chin. "Hmm," she said, eyeing me.
"Better give me the shirt. It's got that emblem thing on it. I'll cut the
pocket off."

"Give me back my pants and I'll take off my shirt."

"Come on, Casey. For godssake—we don't have time. Daddy's got
a big surprise for you. Hurry up."

I took off my shirt and gave it to Natalie. She smiled, then threw
the shirt back at me. "Put your clothes back on," she said. "I just
wanted to see if you wore boxer shorts for me. Was that the reddest
shade of red they had, or were there redder ones?" Natalie giggled
and came after me with the scissors, snipping them at the air. I ran
backward in a circle, trying to dodge her.

Cynthia Stiles opened the door and stepped into the living room.
I recognized her from the picture on Jerry's desk. She said, "I see you
two have introduced yourselves."

"Oh, Mother, I was just teasing him."

"Your father says that Casey is a fine young man. Now, the fine
young man walks in the door and I declare if you don't talk him into
taking off his clothes."

"Not *all* of them. I just wanted to see his underwear. For godssake,
Mother, I'm twenty-two years old, and I've never seen a man in his
underwear. Besides, Casey wore dorky clothes. I didn't want Ray to
hurt his feelings. See? I'm cutting off his pants now." Natalie cut my

pants, turning the scissors in various directions as she went. She gave them back to me and smiled.

"That's better," Cynthia said. "Now apologize to Casey for making him take his clothes off."

"Sorry, darling," she said.

"You two run along now," Cynthia said. "Natalie, behave yourself." Natalie got all excited, like a kid. "C'mon, Casey. Upstairs. My room."

Cynthia grabbed Natalie by the shirtsleeve and whispered in her ear. Natalie rolled her eyes and grabbed my hand. We ran up the stairs together. When we entered Natalie's bedroom, she slammed the door behind her and leaned against it. "Mother says I have to wear a bra—that's what she whispered to me." She slipped out of her tee shirt, tousling her black hair into her face. "Do you think I need a bra? For *these*? Mother's afraid some pervert will see them and go crazy. He'd *have* to be a pervert—they haven't grown an inch since I was twelve. How many perverts can there possibly be in a town the size of Angel Shores? I'm sure I've met them both by now." Natalie rummaged for a bra in her wardrobe. When she bent down, her movement revealed a poster-sized photograph on the inside of her wardrobe door: A dead man with a shockingly gigantic penis—Mr. Forearm, no doubt. Natalie stood up, facing me with her nipples. A bra dangled from her finger. "It's my only one. I never wear it unless Mother insists."

I followed the centerline of her abdomen to her navel—an outie— it protruded like the end of my pinkie. The thing seemed designed for sucking. The sucking urge fell upon me. I felt like one of the perverts her mother had warned her about. Natalie just stood there smiling, her thumbs stuck into her cutoffs. "We've gone this far," she said. "Wanna see the rest?"

"You mean right now?"

"We've got plenty of time. The rest of my apartment is deathy as hell. This is just the bedroom." Natalie hooked up her bra and slipped back into her tee shirt. She threw one at me. "Wear this, Commodore." She took hold of the wardrobe door to close it. She looked at Mr. Forearm, bugged her eyes at me, then slammed the door shut. "Oops. You weren't supposed to see that. Don't freak on me. It's just my wardrobe, not my hope chest. Do you like the bed?" Natalie's bed surpassed John Morton's in elegance, canopied above and on every side with some ancient gossamer fabric. On the floor next to the bed lay Natalie's stack of comic books. On a wall hung the Oswald photo, the alleged assassin frozen in pain as he clutched his abdomen. "I want you to come, now. Come see the rest." Natalie opened a sliding door and led me into her quarters. At the end of the long room, the Marcellas Cherry casket rested upon a bier, the remaining living space decorated like a repose room.

"Why does your apartment look like a funeral home?" I asked.

"Why does yours?"

"I live in a funeral home."

"So do I—Natalie's Funeral Home. Daddy won't let me work in the real funeral home, so I fixed my place up to look like one. He pretends it doesn't bother him, but you'll never catch him showing his Rotary friends around upstairs."

"So why are you a photography major?"

"Since Daddy won't make me an apprentice, I appointed myself Morton-Albright's official historian. First, I collected all the old pictures, then I started taking new ones—sneaking, taking pictures in the embalming room. I realized what a dope I was—I mean, shit, where would I take the film for developing? Eckerd Drugs? I couldn't risk freaking some Eckerd guy. I went to college to learn how to develop my own pictures. I go into the darkroom. Inside the darkroom, there's an even *darker* room. Deathy dark. You go in there to develop. It's so dark, you do everything by *feel*. The darkness enhances your sense of touch. If you're nice to me, I'll take you there. We can go for coffee after."

"You mean like a date?"

"No way, cowboy. People like you and me don't date—we mate. We stay with our own kind—forever."

"I've never been on a date before."

"I have. Daddy made Carl take me to the prom. He even made us pose for pictures, just to prove we went. Daddy couldn't stand the idea of his only daughter not going to the prom."

"All the girls at school thought I was creepy."

"Why? Were you wearing your Commodore outfit?"

"No. I went to school in my black suit."

"How deathy of you."

"You think so? How about you? How do you get along at college? Why don't you live in a dorm?"

"A dorm? I can't live in a dorm. I hate smelling other people who aren't my own family. You know, that other-people smell? I can barely stand to visit other people's houses. There's always some icky smell, like ripe bananas, or feet. Daddy knocked out two walls and gave me the whole side of the house."

Natalie took my arm and led me to the casket. The Marcellas had been lined with quilts. "I begged Daddy for this casket—he likes it when I grovel like a little southern girl. He took out the casket bed so I wouldn't sleep in it. I talked my grandmother Stiles out of a dozen quilts. I told Daddy I was *storing* them, but he took the latch out of the casket lid anyway, so I wouldn't lock myself in. Try it out."

"You mean, lie down in it?"

"I'll help you." Natalie placed a wooden step in front of the casket, then opened the foot-end. She steadied me as I climbed in. She said, "It's tricky at first—narrower than you think."

I lay down in the casket. Natalie closed the foot-end, then backed away. "You look great. How does it feel?"

Before I could answer, a knock came at the door. Over the edge of the casket, I saw Jerry walk in. I tried to raise the foot-end of the casket—locked shut. Jerry had removed only the latch from the head-end. He smiled when he saw me in the casket. "Don't get up, Casey," he said.

"Doesn't he look great, Daddy?"

"He does, and you look good too, sugar." Jerry kissed his daughter on the cheek. "Your mother sent me up. Dinner's in half an hour. Don't make us wait for you."

"We won't."

"I'll get back to that fine little pig that Casey bagged for us. You kids enjoy yourselves."

"Daddy, we're not kids."

"You're right, sugar." Jerry winked at me, then stepped out the door. "Play nice, now," he said.

Natalie helped me out of the Marcellas. "You killed that pig we're going to eat?"

"It was an accident. I didn't mean to kill it. I aimed the gun off to the side. I missed."

"If you missed, then why am I smelling barbecue? Let me get this straight: first, you kill a man by tripping him, then you kill a pig by missing it? I'll be careful around you. You're a dangerous man, Casey James Kight. Come with me, check this out." Natalie took my arm again. She took me to the long wall of her apartment. Three family crests hung in frames. "Morton, Albright, Stiles," she said. Above the frames, two trocars crossed like swords. "The implements of our family tradition." She said. "Trocars are phallic, don't you think? Come to my kitchen. I'll show you something *really* cool." An embalming machine, filled with red liquid, sat on Natalie's kitchen counter. She took two metal tumblers from the cabinet, then turned on the machine. She filled each of the tumblers from the embalming machine's hose, threw in some ice cubes, then handed one to me. She raised her tumbler in a toast; clinked hers against mine. I looked into my tumbler and smelled. She said, "Don't be afraid. It's only Rootin' Tootin' Raspberry. The machine is brand-new. Ray ordered it for me. He and Carl lugged it up here when my parents were away."

I sipped, then spat the stuff into the sink.

"I forgot," Natalie said. "You've got to add your own sugar. Can't run sugar through an embalming machine. Gums up the seals." Natalie plopped a bag of sugar onto the counter. She hefted it, and poured half a cup of sugar into my tumbler. On the back of the bag of sugar, Natalie found a coupon. She said, "Aw, shit—twenty cents off the next bag. I have to do something. This will only take a minute." She rummaged through a drawer and found a pair of scissors. "Don't worry," she said, "I'm not going to chase you around with them again." She poured the bag of sugar into an empty pickle jar, then cut out the coupon. She then opened a drawer full of coupons and tossed the new one into the drawer. "I have to cut them out," she said. "I never use them, but when I see those dotted lines around the coupon, I have a compulsion to cut them." She leaned back against the counter, smiling at me. I loved her face; her dark freckles. I took a drink. She said, "I've never had sex, you know."

I sucked my soft drink down the wrong pipe and coughed the red stuff all over the counter. Natalie gave me some paper towels. I changed the subject. "Why does your father keep you out of the embalming room? He's such a nice man. He lets you do all this stuff up here. He knows you want to work the family trade. Why does he keep you out?"

Natalie took my hand and led me back to the wall. There hung an aged picture of a young woman, lovely in that old-fashioned way, her hair put up loosely, stray wisps of it curling near her cheeks. Natalie sighed at the photograph. "Daddy won't let me embalm because of *her*. Sara Morton, John Morton's wife. Sara was the first woman to work in Morton-Albright's embalming room. She was also the last. Sara freaked out—went koo-koo on everybody." Sara Morton had been pregnant with Jewell. She went into the embalming room and saw a child, violated beyond anything human. Sara ran screaming out into the middle of Druid Road and collapsed there. No woman had ever been allowed in the embalming room since.

"That doesn't sound fair," I said. "You don't strike me as the fainting type."

"Never fainted in my life. The men all believe a myth—that Sara Morton freaked out because she was a woman. The truth is, most *men* can't handle the embalming room either, and it's not just

Morton-Albright. The entire funeral profession belongs to men. No girls at the Taylor School."

"Denise works for the funeral home."

"I'm not Denise. I don't want to do what Denise does. Try to imagine her with a trocar in her hand, blood on her apron. Imagine her pretty little fingers in a bag full of viscera. She inherited the business genes. I got the deathy ones. I belong in the embalming room. Ray says I should have been born a man. He says I almost made it—my lack of endowments. I don't want a dick, just a trocar."

I sat there, speechless—not from Natalie's ambition for embalming. It was just that I had never heard a girl say "dick," at least, not to my face.

"I lost track of myself—what was I talking about? Oh, yes—Sara Morton. She went koo-koo, like I said, *and* she was pregnant. John Morton sent her off to a sanitarium in Georgia. That means my grandmother, Cruel Jewell, was born in an insane asylum. You can bet Granddaddy Colton brings *that* one up whenever he gets the chance. Jewell despises the funeral business—Sara scared the hell out of her—wouldn't let her near the funeral home. That's how Jewell ended up in our furniture store. That's where she met Colton—John Morton had sent him there to pick up some coffins. The Talberts were running the furniture store by then, but Jewell wanted the furniture store for herself. We specialized in handcrafted furniture and English antiques, so all the wealthy people bought from us. Jewell wanted to be high society—as high as it gets in Angel Shores, but she knew damn well that John Morton would never give her the store, because she was a woman. That's why she went after Colton. She knew how much John loved him. If she married Colton, John would give him the furniture store. But John had other plans for Colton—Morton Funeral Home. When Colton and Jewell announced their engagement, John drew up papers making Colton a full partner, to be signed on the wedding day. He ordered a new sign and changed the name of the place to Morton-Albright. John promised the furniture store to the Talberts. Jewell was pissed as hell. That's why she knocked herself up with Colton—for revenge against her own father. A bastard child would drive John Morton back to the furniture store. Undertakers were revered as clergy back then—a scandal would ruin him forever. Jewell told her father that Colton had forced himself on her, making her pregnant. John nearly *killed* Colton. He tore up the partnership papers and wrote him out of the will. Colton and Jewell eloped to Key West. When they returned, Jewell expected to find Morton-Albright out of business. She hadn't figured on love—everybody loved John Morton. The women even gave her a baby shower. They treated her and Colton like two newlyweds in love, unable to bear a long engagement. John reconciled with Colton, then sold the furniture store to the Talberts. He saw his daughter for who she was—Cruel Jewell—and she wasn't finished yet. She killed Lex and Meredith's parents. She lit the match that burned down the furniture store, but that wasn't her final act of revenge—that won't come until Granddaddy dies. She'll have the power to sell Morton-Albright to an outsider. She knows that. We don't believe she'll go outside the family—we all believe she's torturing Colton. When he dies, there's no one left to torture. She has nothing against her two daughters—my mother and Denise. She has never treated Daddy with anything but respect. She just wants to send Colton to his grave a worried man."

"What about Lex Talbert?"

"He's an asshole. What else is there to know about him?"

I told Natalie about Lex's JFT prospectus.

"JFT will die before Granddaddy," Natalie said. "They're already under investigation in three states for improprieties. I read the trades, you know."

"Like Ray," I said.

"Not like Ray. I am *not* a bathroom reader. How disgusting. I'd rather find a dead rat in someone's bathroom than a magazine rack. Now look at this last picture. It's the only formal photograph ever taken of the deathiest man who ever lived—John Beresford Morton.

Look at him. So deathy. Takes your breath away to look at him."

Even as a young man, John Morton's face belonged to a ghost. I fought back a gasp. I heard his words in my head, as if they were coming from the picture: *You've got the gift, Casey.*

"Are you listening to me?" Natalie asked.

"I'm sorry. Wandered off. What were you saying?"

"You've got the gift, Casey. That's the word around Morton-Albright, anyway—John Morton's gift. It's legendary. People would fall down in a faint when they saw his work. I've only heard stories. John put his soul into his art. The bodies—they gave off Presence. You could see it. You could feel it. Some say he was a genius with makeup and lighting. Others say he possessed supernatural talent. I can see it in his face. I can see it in *your* face, Casey."

"This is getting spooky," I said.

"It hasn't even begun to get spooky. You've been with us less than a week, and everybody is talking about you. It's too bad John's wife went koo-koo on him—they say it affected his work, and not for the better. This is the house John built for Sara. John Morton died here, in my bedroom. Still, there's one thing that doesn't fit. John Morton loved Colton like a son. The two of them spent all their time together, since both of their wives were crazy as hell. Why didn't John change his will and leave the funeral home to Granddaddy? That's the biggest mystery to me."

"How do you know all these things? How do you know Jewell set the fire?"

"I don't know everything. I suspect everything. I know the people involved. I put everything together in a way that makes sense. Like you, Casey. You make sense—your coming here in our final hour—out of nowhere, you walk into the most beautiful funeral home in the world, a place built with all the love that John Morton had, and you come here with his gift."

"I didn't exactly come out of nowhere, and I'm not sure about any gift. I first met your father at my mom and dad's funeral. I was all torn apart. I found comfort at Morton-Albright. It's the only place

I've ever felt comfort. I can't remember much of my childhood. Margee says it's probably for the best. I don't believe that. I want to remember. I had a mom and a dad, and I want to remember them—I couldn't do that until I came back to the place of comfort, where I felt safe."

"Are your parents buried at Fairview?"

"Yes. Somewhere in the memorial gardens."

"Somewhere? You've never visited your parents' grave?"

"Never. Not since the day we buried them. Margee and I could never make ourselves go and look."

"How sad," she said. Natalie touched my cheek. I looked straight into her eyes, pale and ghostly. She said, "I've got one more picture to show you." She sat me down on the sofa and pulled out a big, black photo album from a drawer in the coffee table. As she opened the book, I envied Natalie's family history, but envy gave way to fascination as I realized that I had entered the story, that my own picture could find its way into this book someday. Someday turned out to be *today*. When Natalie turned the page, there I lay on John Morton's bed in my briefs—the picture Natalie had taken when she sneaked into my bedroom.

"This is my favorite picture," she said. "Some dead guy in his underwear."

"Nataleee!" Cynthia called out from downstairs.

"Uh-oh, we're late, and Daddy's got a big surprise for you."

When Natalie and I stepped into the backyard, everybody applauded our entrance: Jerry and Cynthia, Ray and Denise, Carl and Suzy. (Lex and the twins were minding the store). I could see why Ray called Carl's wife Suzy Pocahontas—she looked like a Cherokee princess with her long hair and leather headband. Ray stood up and raised his can of Pabst. A twenty-dollar bill dangled from his other hand. "I won twenty bucks from Jerry," he announced. "I bet him that Natalie would get Casey into the Marcellas." More applause—laughter, too.

Denise stood up. She said, "I won the bet with Cynthia about Natalie getting Casey out of his clothes."

Natalie took a bow, then took hold of my pinkie. Facing me, right in front of everybody, Natalie put my finger in her mouth and bit me—*hard*. I yowled to more applause.

"Welcome to the family, son," Jerry said, raising his own can of Pabst. He stood up and assumed his funeral director pose, hands folded at his waist. He had an announcement. "Casey has only been with us a few days, but I know a good man when I see one. He's diligent, professional, and he risked his life during the Jimmie Blessing affair. I've decided to waive his year of required service, and allow him to matriculate at the Taylor School in the fall, assuming he continues his excellent deportment."

Everyone applauded, especially Natalie. I had spent my whole life being ridiculed for my black suit, and my morbid fascinations about becoming an Undertaker. Now, all these wonderful people were affirming me for the same reasons that others had rejected me. I said, "Thank you all for having me. This is the best moment of my life. I'll never let you down—any of you."

"Try not to kill anyone else in the funeral home," Ray said. "You'll do fine."

We all dined on the boar I had killed by accident—Undertakers, just having a good time on a Sunday afternoon. Jerry sprayed down the brick barbecue pit with one of those trigger hoses. I went to offer help and to thank him for his kindness. On the way, I watched Ray reach into the cooler for a final Pabst. He stopped. He stared— toward the back porch of Jerry's home. The other picnickers froze. They stared in the same direction as Ray. I saw her too—the woman, standing on the back porch. She looked seventy, and wore a black dress—not a streak of gray tainted her black hair. It fell in long tresses, framing the face of a fallen angel, at once comely and granite. It was her: Cruel Jewell. Panting next to her stood the biggest dog I had ever seen, a giant Great Dane. Jewell Albright descended the five steps to the yard. "Sit, Talus," she commanded the dog.

Natalie choked, "Grandma?"

"Mother?" Cynthia squeaked.

Ray muttered the Lord's name. The woman so unnerved Jerry that when he turned to view his mother-in-law, he failed to release the trigger on the hose. The spray hit my crotch as he turned. Though narrow, the stream from the hose hit me with force. Soaked to my privates, Sammy Ford's words about my new underwear tumbled into my mind: *Make sure you wash them first. They bleed.* They were bleeding, all right. I looked fatally emasculated, the red infusing into the front of my white pants. I took my place next to Natalie, standing before her grandmother. Natalie took hold of my wet hand. Cruel Jewell looked at me, and said, "I'm here to meet this new man I've heard about."

I approached her to identify myself. Talus bared his teeth and growled. Jewell said, "Talus doesn't take to strangers. You'd better let me come to you." She stood taller than I had expected—nearly my height. She stood closer to me than I expected, too. She seemed interested in my eyes—she didn't look at them, as in a normal greeting. She looked into them, tilting her head, as though she were trying to look inside me. All I could think about was my red-stained crotch, so when she said, "I'm sorry about your parents," I thought she said, "I'm sorry about your *pants*." I told her not to worry, it was just my underwear bleeding, not me. Natalie whispered in my ear, "Pa-rents, not pants."

"Sorry, Mrs. Albright," I said. "It happened a long time ago, but thank you."

She said, "I see you've met my granddaughter. I'll be on my way now." As she turned to walk away, Cynthia tried to squeak out a remark, but Jewell cut her off with a look, then let Talus and herself out through the back gate. A sigh rippled through the party. The sigh lapsed into murmur. The Morton-Albright associates packed up and left—no jokes from Ray. He just shook his head and went for his car. My embarrassment finally caught up with my bleeding underwear. I figured it a good time to disappear, myself. I thanked

Jerry and Cynthia for the barbecue, then took Natalie's hand to say good-bye. They refused to let me leave. Cynthia made me undress in the downstairs bathroom. She washed and dried my pants and underwear while I waited in the bathroom. Natalie kept knocking on the door, asking me, "Are you peeing?" She rattled the doorknob. "Can I watch?" She asked. "I've never watched a man pee. We can take turns."

"Natalie! Get away from that door," I heard Cynthia snap. "He's a nice young man. Talk to him nice."

Natalie taunted me again, "Caaasey, it's Nataleee. You don't have any pants on and I'm thinking about it."

"Natalie!" Cynthia's voice came louder this time. "Leave that boy alone!"

Most of the red washed out of my pants. My underwear was two shades lighter. After a bowl of fresh, sugared peaches in heavy cream, Natalie walked me to the garden behind her home. The first orange clouds of sunset tinged the horizon. Two key-lime trees grew among the hibiscus and jasmine. In the center of the garden, a small granite tombstone inscribed with a name: Caesar.

"Dog?" I asked.

"Cat. He suffered from convulsions. His real name was Seizure. I named him, but Daddy said Caesar sounded better around company. We buried him next to the bird feeder because the cat liked to stalk the birds."

The evening breeze blew in from the Gulf. It blew Natalie's hair deliciously, revealing the blue-green bruise on her head from our first meeting. I remembered her blood on my hand after finding her in the bushes. Natalie stepped closer and rested her palm on my chest. I gazed into her eyes, so pale the sunset illuminated them with red and violet fire. There, before Caesar's headstone in the evening garden, I took Natalie into my arms, and kissed her. I held her close, and promised upon my own soul to help her dreams come true. "I won't give up until I watch you embalm," I said.

I headed out front toward the driveway, my insides still brimming

with Natalie's kiss. I spotted Jerry with a shovel near the side of the
house. He was looking at the pile left by Talus, the Great Dane. I went
to say good-bye. Jerry looked up from his task. "Damn dog shits
mud, like a cow," he said. "Look at this shovel."

I offered my help, but Jerry said I had suffered enough for one day.
He said, "Looks like you and Natalie . . . well—you know."

"Yes, sir. She's different than I had expected."

"She's different, all right. No argument there, son."

"No, sir. I mean, she's wonderful."

Jerry stood up and smiled at me. He said, "I'm sure she feels the
same way about you, son. We all do." He put his hand on my shoulder. "Just keep Natalie out of the embalming room," he said.

In John Morton's bed, I lay on my back, looking up at the miniature
chandelier. The window was open, and an occasional breeze whispered through the prisms. All I could think about was Natalie's kiss. I
could still taste her. I pictured the dark freckles across her nose and
into her cheeks. How she had chased me around with the scissors.
How she had smiled at me after cutting out the coupon on the bag of
sugar. *My mother had cut out coupons too, only she didn't just throw*
them away. She had used them at the grocery store. I had remembered
something about my mother, a part of my life before the crash. Up
above me, a new breeze ran through the prisms of the chandelier,
and the rhythmic noise of scissors snipping played in my head—the
scissors now in my hand, snipping the viscera of Marianne Blessing,
then Natalie snipping the coupon, then my mother doing the same,
like a triangular thought that never ended. I felt the halo of an
episode coming on. A thousand scissors filled my head. I put my
hands over my ears, shut my eyes, and watched my parents board the
airplane. I watched the men begin to roll away the silver staircase my
mom and dad had climbed. I ran to the men, begging them to stop. I
ran up the staircase, and banged on the closed door of the jetliner. It
sounded like knocking on wood.

It *was* knocking on wood. Someone was knocking on wood, the wooden door of John Morton's bedroom. I opened my eyes and saw the glass doorknob turning. The Presence of Morton-Albright fell upon me strong. The door eased open without a creak. Blackness lay beyond the threshold. Clothed in black, Natalie stepped into the bedroom. "I want another kiss," she said. "Nice jammies. Your aunt Margee picked them out?"

I looked down and saw my pajamas. I didn't remember putting them on. I sat there for a moment, blank minded, feeling the Presence. Natalie smiled, and said, "Well, do I get my kiss, or do I have to beg?" She walked across the room, sat next to me on John Morton's bed, and took her kiss.

"What time is it?" I asked.

"Time is for the mortals," she said.

I looked over her shoulder at the alarm clock. It was nearly midnight. I had arrived at the funeral home at seven-twenty.

"You shouldn't be here," I whispered, remembering the mortuary twins. "You'll get into trouble with Jerry."

She whispered back, "You're the one who's in trouble," then she kissed me again, pressing against me. Natalie giggled, then rolled over to the other side of the bed, put her head on the pillow, and went to sleep. I poked at her shoulder and whispered her name. She did not awaken. I nudged her harder, and whispered in her ear, 'Wake up, Natalie. You should go home.' She lay there, eyes open in slits, mouth ajar. I shook her and called her name—nothing. I should call Jerry, I thought—explain the situation: Natalie asleep in my bed, the first day we had met. Jesus. What about Cynthia? She'd think I was the pervert, looking at her daughter's breasts. Besides, I was in trouble already: I had promised Natalie I'd get her into the embalming room. I had promised her father to keep her out. I had to get Natalie home. I tried standing her up. I'd walk her to the Chrysler and drive her home.

A rag doll in my arms, Natalie couldn't stand up. I dragged her toward the door, trying not to wake the twins. What if I dropped her in the parking lot? I put Natalie back into bed and sat down, trying to calm myself down enough to think.

The stretcher.

I ran to the bat cave and yanked the stretcher from the removal car. Sliding her onto the stretcher would be easy, just like a dead person. In John Morton's bedroom, I got Natalie onto the stretcher and fastened the three safety belts around her. I rolled her down the hallway to the removal car. I fished around in her pocket for her house keys. Now I could take her off the stretcher and put her into the front seat with me, but sliding her into the back of the removal car seemed easier. I locked the stretcher into place, and tore off for Jerry's house.

I unlocked Natalie's front door and rolled her into the living room. A light came on at the top of the stairs.

"Natalie? That you, sugar?" Jerry.

"It's Casey." I called up the staircase.

"Is Natalie with you, son?"

"Yes, but she can't hear you."

I heard him bounding down the staircase. He turned on the lights and looked at his daughter, seat-belted onto the stretcher. Jerry stood there in his pajamas and robe. He didn't look angry. He didn't look anything. His face was absent of expression. I told him that Natalie had come to the funeral home about an hour earlier. We had been talking. She fell asleep.

Cynthia called out, "Jerry, what's going on down there?"

"Come down and have a look," Jerry answered.

Cynthia stepped into the living room. She put her hand over her mouth. "Oh, for heaven's sake," she said.

"Sleep disorder," Jerry said. "Sometimes you can wake her, sometimes you can't. She's a sleepwalker, too."

"I wish I could sleep like that," Cynthia said. "Natalie scared me to death when she was a little girl. I used to bang pots and pans over her head, trying to wake her up." Cynthia giggled and elbowed Jerry in the arm. Jerry chuckled. Behind them, the grandfather clock gonged midnight. The two of them laughed through all twelve gongs, knocking into each other. Natalie never moved. Jerry said, "Let's talk over a cup of tea, son. We'll put Natalie on the couch."

"Good night, Casey," Cynthia said. "What an honorable young man." She hugged me and gave me a kiss on the cheek, then giggled all the way up the stairs.

In the kitchen, Jerry snickered as he dipped his tea bag. He said, "Natalie's never had a fellow in her life, until now. Don't take offense, but you don't strike me as a girl chaser."

"Natalie's my first."

"If you two were a couple of crazy teenagers, I'd worry. You're both in your twenties, over the age of consent—marrying age. Next time Natalie falls asleep while you two are *talking*, let her sleep."

Lying in John Morton's bed, I puzzled over Jerry's words—age of consent and all that. It could only mean one thing: Jerry wanted an heir to the funeral home. If I made Natalie pregnant with a male child, I would save the funeral home, unless Colton Albright died first.

10

"Okay, killer, where's Natalie?" Ray asked, the moment he stepped into the kitchen the next morning. I told him Natalie was at home.

"Bullshit. That *is* her 1966 Chrysler Imperial sitting in the parking lot. Let's hope you caught her on the right day of the month. We'll have a party when the rabbit dies."

Carl walked in. He called Natalie's name aloud.

"She's not here," I said.

"Right. Black Beauty's in the parking lot and Natalie's not here. Let's go wake her up, Ray—ask her if she's with child."

Jerry strolled into the kitchen. Ray and Carl cleared their throats and whistled tunes. Jerry gave them a sideways glance as he poured himself a cup of coffee. When Jerry headed for his chair at the table, Ray stood in front of him, blocking his path. Ray said, "You didn't happen to notice a certain *car* in the parking lot this morning, did you?"

"I *did* notice that car," Jerry answered. "I also noticed my daughter at her own breakfast table this morning."

"I told you guys she wasn't here," I said.

The doorchime for the Druid Road entrance sounded. "I'll get it," Ray said. "Could be a walk-in." When Ray left, Jerry explained that when deaths occurred among the Crackers, they often drove straight to the funeral home, instead of calling first. They always walked around to the Druid Road entrance, because it used to be the front door, back when you could actually park on Druid. So when the doorchime sounded for the Druid Road entrance, it could only mean one of two things: Either a Cracker had just died, or, Bernard had just run across Druid Road. Ray came back with flowers in a blue vase. "Bernard," Ray said.

"Late piece for Blessing?" Carl asked.

"Nope. This envelope says 'Mr. Casey J. Kight, Apprentice Embalmer.' Let's see what the card says."

I tried grabbing the card from Ray, but he had already plucked it from the envelope, holding it high above my reach. He read the card aloud: "You crazy, deathy man. Love, Natalie." Ray set the flowers in the middle of the table. "Kinda pretty, aren't they? Natalie might not be here *now*, but *something* happened last night." Ray folded his arms across his chest, waiting for an explanation. I could feel my cheeks flushing. Jerry smiled at me; gave me a wink. He said, "Mind if I tell them, son? It's a damn funny story." Jerry left out no detail about how I had brought his daughter home last night.

"In the removal car," Ray said, lighting a Marlboro. He snapped the lighter shut. "Killer, you are one weird fucking kid."

Jerry added that when Natalie had sat down for breakfast this morning, she asked if anybody knew how she had gotten home last night. "I told her the story," Jerry said. "The only thing that upset her was not remembering the ride home on a death cot. I won't tell you boys what else she said about Casey."

"The flowers say it all," Carl said.

We settled in for coffee and doughnuts. No one mentioned the appearance of Cruel Jewell at the barbecue. I sat there, remembering how she had searched my eyes, then turned my attention to Natalie's flowers. As I relived my first kiss, the other men divided the morning paper between themselves, and set to making body noises—mostly snot sniffling and throat clearing, but too much Pabst at the barbecue had afflicted Carl with the farts, and he was letting us all know it with the kind of flatulence that begins on one pitch, and ends on another. Ray rattled his newspaper and scolded Carl, "You're playing the trombone with your ass. You're purposely adjusting your anal sphincter to make those sounds. Meanwhile, you sit there turning the pages like you're reading that damn newspaper. Either play us a song we can all sing to, or read your paper. Just don't try and bullshit me that you can do both at the same time."

"The Exorcist is playing in Clearwater and there's a coupon for Skippy peanut butter—fifteen cents off the regular price." Carl spoke and squeezed out a new fart simultaneously. Ray wasted a look on Carl, who ignored him. Now the doorchime of the main entrance rang. Ray didn't take his eyes off the paper. "Killer, do your apprentice job and get me another cup of coffee. While you're up, go see who walked in the door."

I greeted Sophie Campbell, who stood in the middle of the lobby. She said, "Mr. Kight, we Campbells are grateful for what ye done." She took a step toward me and lowered her head. "Jimmie Blessing won't never kill nobody no more. I heared he pulled a gun on ye. You will be rewarded someday. Lord bless ye, Mr. Kight."

She left me there to wonder what reward I deserved for killing a man with my feet. The phone rang—police rotation call. Howard Christmas Tree Farm, Highway 12. Ray and I ran the call. Ray drove, smoked cigarettes, and worried out loud. "What in the hell kind of unnatural death could happen on a Christmas tree farm?" Somebody fall out of a Christmas tree? Hanged himself from a Christmas tree? Hell, no. A Christmas tree is too small for that shit. This is something *else*. Get ready for some weird shit, killer. Are you sure the dispatcher didn't say anything about this case?"

"No information on the cause of death, or on the condition of the body—no name, no age, no sex."

"This is a bad one, killer. They *always* tell you something about the case, unless it's bad. Then they clam up tighter than my anal sphincter is right now. They use *chain saws* on Christmas tree farms, don't they? Maybe a chain-saw accident. Maybe a chain-saw *murder*. Whatever it is, it's too damn early in the morning for this shit."

Two police cars blocked the entrance to Howard Christmas Tree Farm. Dr. Kendall's sedan sat parked on the shoulder. Ray parked the removal car in the middle of the road. Detective Jones raised his hand over his head and pointed toward the waist-high Christmas trees that dotted a field. The detective pinched his nose as he pointed.

"Aw, shit," Ray said. "Get the stretcher and the body bag. Looks like a floater."

"Drowning?" I asked.

"On a Christmas tree farm? Floater means dead for more than three days. The body bloats up with gas from decomposition. If it's in the water, it floats, like a bar of Ivory soap."

Fifty yards of Christmas trees separated us from our target: A yellow station wagon with fake wood panels. A swath of downed trees led to the car. We couldn't drive the removal car on the soft soil, we'd risk getting stuck—not professional. Ray and I walked with the wheeled stretcher. It bounced as we rolled it over the dirt. We met Dr. Kendall's assistant as he returned from the car. The first whiff of stench crawled up my nose. "It's a bad one, fellas," the assistant said.

"No shit. I can smell it from here." Ray said.

Kendall had looked at it through the car's rear window. "He'll try and post it, if y'all can get it out of the car. Dead about a week. Maybe longer. Hard to tell with this heat."

Ray said, "Aw, criminy shit."

A hum emanated from the car, as though someone had left it running. Ray swore and shook his head. He gagged every few steps. He stopped and puked, thirty feet from the station wagon. I looked at the car. The windows had been painted black—not just the rear window, every window I could see. I wondered how Kendall had managed to view the body through the black windows. What kind of crazy person would drive a car with the windows painted black? We continued forward. The humming intensified. It became more nasal in tone—not like a car's engine, more like an electric motor. At ten feet, the reek clung to my whole face. It seeped through my clothes and into my skin. At arm's length from the wagon, I saw what had blackened the windows—the black was moving, and not with paint.

Flies.

The electric-motor sound I heard was their buzzing.

With the heel of his fist, Ray banged once upon the side window of the wagon's deck. A clump of flies fell off, creating a porthole. Ray put an eye to the glass. "I am not *even* believing this shit. Have a look, killer." Ray banged off a few more clumps, I looked through the glass. The backseat had been folded down to make a bed. The body lay on its back in the middle of a sea of squirming maggots. The torso had filled with gas and exploded in the Florida heat. Entrails hung from the headboard. Writhing maggots filled the cavity. A giant blackened tongue protruded three inches beyond the teeth. Maggots wormed in and out of the ears, nose, and empty eye sockets. Ray said, "We've got to let those flies out of there." He grabbed the handle at the bottom of the wagon's rear door, lifted the door, and stepped back, as quick as he could. It didn't matter. The flies were so many, they pelted us with their bodies as they fled. Ray snapped on a pair of gloves, then tossed the box to me. He stuck his head in through the rear door of the car, then turned and puked again. "Most of the flies are gone, except for a few hundred on *him*. I'm assuming it's a him—women around here don't die this way. Bring the stretcher up close. Open that body bag. I'll pull him out." Ray grabbed a mottled foot and pulled on it with his gloved hand. All he got was a layer of skin that sloughed off the foot. Ray flapped his hand until the skin flew onto the car. He grabbed onto the leg and pulled harder. Ray said, "He's stuck to the metal floor, sun baked him right into it." Ray squeezed the leg and pulled harder. The leg came out. The rest of the body stayed in the car. Ray's face went crawly. He held the leg away from his suit and dropped it. "Like boiled chicken," he said.

"You told me there was nothing worse than the Circle of Willis," I said.

"Lord have mercy on me, killer. I have led you astray."

We pulled the body out in pieces, brushing off flies and maggots as best we could. The pieces went into the body bag. My initial revulsion faded more quickly than I had expected—there were greater powers working in me: I used my ability to place myself into the calm of shock, which I had practiced for so many years. Though I pitied the dead man, I was able to detach myself with little effort. It didn't mean I was without feeling. I felt the skin slip under my glove. I beheld the sight of mottled, decaying flesh. The stink of death gnawed at my stomach—yet I thought only of Natalie, her kiss; the way she felt in my arms. I longed to see her again.

It took Kendall less than an hour to gather enough information for the death certificate: male Caucasian, between fifty and sixty years of age. Cause of death: acute ethanol and carbon monoxide poisoning. "In other words, he got real drunk and left the car running," Ray said. We drove the bag of body parts to Morton-Albright. Ray unzipped the bag and poured fifteen pounds of embalming powder all over the remains. We placed the bag in a metal case that sealed with a hundred screws.

"This is how you embalmed my parents, after the crash, isn't it?"

"That's none of your goddam business. It happened before you came to work here, which makes it a private matter. I am bound to secrecy by the Code of Ethics. Don't ever ask about your parents again. Understand?"

I understood: I would never find out about my mom and dad. I helped Ray fit the metal case into a cloth-covered casket, like the ones we used for cremations. Ray said we both now smelled like Mr. X. He told me to take a shower and change into a fresh suit—air out my old one outside the garage door of the bat cave. Ray grabbed a fresh suit from his own rack in the supply room. He called Dr. Hamilton and asked him to meet us in the indigent section of Fairview Cemetery. Ray drove us there with Mr. X in the back of the hearse (Ray didn't like the John Doe designation, he called all John Does Mr. X.)

Dr. Hamilton stood in the blazing sun. Mr. X had laid down a life he could never keep, to take up a life he could never lose. Ray gave the minister a check for fifty dollars. Henry roared up on the backhoe. Ray said, "Rich or poor, everyone gets a decent burial. The county pays us only a hundred dollars. The cemetery takes a loss, too, but we make a fortune in goodwill."

"Colton Albright is here to see you, Casey." Jerry said. "He's in my office. I'm waiting on a new family—Carl made a removal while you and Ray buried John Doe."

Colton Albright sat in Jerry's chair. He wore a tan seersucker suit and a narrow tie with a crooked knot. He said, "Casey, when I was your age, we had to wash those cars in our shirts and ties."

"We still do that, Mr. Albright."

"Good. Just checking. Don't call me Mr. Albright."

"I'm sorry, Colton." I stumbled over his first name. "My aunt Margee raised me to show respect."

He interrupted, "For old bastards like me. I know we met at Skeeter's, but this is my formal hello. You handled that Jimmie Blessing fellow in a manner befitting our trade. It's a crude way to say thank you, but young folks like yourself can always use some extra cash, so we'll double your pay this week. Take that Natalie of mine out to a nice place for dinner. She might go cheeseburger on you, but there's nothing wrong with a girl who's not interested in f-f-fineries." Albright's eyes glazed. He began to rock, back and forth. He reached into the air for something that wasn't there, then his face hit the desk. I called an ambulance, then ran for Ray. He redialed the ambulance company and commanded them: No siren within two blocks of the funeral home. Ray shushed the paramedics as they wheeled the stretcher into the office. "There's a family making arrangements in the next room," he whispered. Under the porte cochere, Ray boarded the ambulance with the unconscious Colton Albright. Ray assured me that I had done the right thing by not disturbing Jerry. "The families always come first," he said. "Tell Jerry what happened when his family leaves."

After hearing about Colton, Jerry started for the Druid Road entrance. He would walk across the street to the flower shop, and to Cynthia. On his way out the door, the phone rang as he passed it. He stopped and picked it up: nursing home death. Jerry scribbled, tore the first-call sheet from the pad, and gave it to me. He said, "Let Carl run this call. You get the phone—if Natalie calls, I don't want her hearing about her granddaddy from Lex."

In the embalming room, I told Carl about Albright, then gave him the information for the nursing home death. Carl agreed to run the call. "I'll go get the body. You embalm it. I'd like to be at the hospital if Colton . . . if he checks out."

What if he *did* check out? It made me realize how much I stood to lose—a selfish thought, but it had been a very long time since there had been anything for me to lose. *Welcome to the family*, Jerry had said. Would they still be my family if they lost the funeral home? Would Natalie still want me when Morton-Albright no longer needed an heir? I didn't have time to think about it. The doorchime sounded for the Druid Road entrance: Bernard. Flowers had already begun to arrive for Jerry's new case. I was about to place the flowers in the repose reception area when Lex Talbert stepped into the lobby. He wore a strangely satisfied look. Lex summoned me into Jerry's office, where he paced before the window with his hands behind his back. He asked me to sit down. He said, "Remember what I told you? You're too late. Colton won't make it through the night. I know you don't like me, but I've done you a favor. I've noticed your zeal for the work. I've mentioned your name to others—people who appreciate your talents. It's not often that men like you come along. You and I have more in common than you imagine. I'll still be here when your friends abandon you."

The telephone rang on Jerry's desk. Lex snatched it before I could answer: Natalie. Lex covered the receiver with his hand and spoke to me in a low voice, "We'll talk more about this later. For now, I'm sure Natalie would rather hear about her grandfather from you. I'll give you some privacy." Lex left the office and closed the door behind him.

Natalie didn't want to go to the hospital. She loved her grandfather, but she was phobic about hospitals: "The whole place will reek of other-people sickness," she said. "I could get sick-germs. Just in case you're wondering, I'm here alone, all by myself. There's nobody else here. Just me. Alone."

I promised her I'd come as soon as Jeff and Randy arrived from their day at school. As I went to the embalming room, I wondered if Natalie was capable of handling the smells and sick-germs of the job—especially a stinky job like Mr. X—not to mention the maggots. Her revulsions might overwhelm her desire for the embalming room. If I allowed her to see a decomposed body, and Natalie vomited, she'd abandon her pursuit of an embalmer's career. I would fulfill my promises, both to Natalie and Jerry: I'd let Natalie in, she'd change her mind, and stay out of the embalming room forever—unless Colton died tonight. Change everything, forever.

"Pfister sister," Carl said, removing the sheet from the body he'd removed from the nursing home. It was Lillian on the embalming table, the ancient woman from Mrs. Pfister's service. "You take it from here," Carl said. "You'll do fine without me." Carl left me with the body, and the presence.

I'm here to help you, son. Make your incision. I began on Lillian like a priest performing Mass, like a never-forgotten ritual. I loved the smell of the embalming chemical as I poured it into the machine. I froze when Lex entered the room—the Presence had departed. Lex said, "Set the pressure for three and a half pounds. Turn the flow control a quarter turn to the right. Flip the switch to Mix for half a minute, then click it to Run." The fluid pumped into Lillian. Her nails turned pink. "I used to do this, you know. The next body on that table will be Colton Albright's. I'm not trying to be cruel, just preparing you for the future. Come see me when you finish here."

"I was doing fine before you came in. I'm going to see Natalie when I finish."

"Then go to her. We'll talk later. Morton-Albright is lost to Jerry and Ray and Carl. It doesn't have to be that way with you."

Natalie answered her front door in a long black dress. She smiled. I followed her black sneakers up the staircase. She had dimmed the lights in her apartment. We embraced. I searched her face for grief. I saw only her usual look—somber eyes, brows expecting some happy event. I hadn't known what to expect from Natalie during a time of personal tragedy, so it didn't surprise me when she asked me to dance with her. "We'll dance to sad music," she said. "Hold me close to you. I'd like that." Natalie had never danced before; neither had I. We danced in a realm of shadow and light. The warmth of her body sent light into my inward parts. Our dance had aroused me. Natalie kissed my cheek, then led me to the sofa. She asked, "May I have one of your Lifesavers? I like the pineapple ones."

"I don't have any Lifesavers," I said.

"Certs?" She asked. "Rolaids? Tums? You're holding out on me, Casey. I felt the roll in your pocket against me while we were dancing." Natalie looked at my pants and giggled. She wagged a finger at me. "It's not polite not to share," she said. "I'll show you what Granddaddy will look like when he's dead." She opened the family album to a picture of Colton Albright, lying in a casket. I gasped at the photograph.

"He's not dead, Casey. He's pretending."

"I know he's pretending. *Why* is he pretending?"

Natalie flipped page after page. Jerry lay in the Promethean, Carl in the bronze. Next, Meredith in the Toccoa oak. Natalie asked, "Isn't that the casket you smashed?"

"No. I smashed the maple. I can't believe they let you take these pictures."

"Let me? They were like little boys— 'Me first', they kept saying. I made them all lie down in the caskets at once, instead of taking turns. Then I walked around the room and took their pictures. Look. Here's Ray. You can't see him. Closed casket. He makes everybody swear. I've got the Marcellas cherry. Have you picked out your casket, darling?"

"No."

Natalie put her arms around my neck. She said, "You belong in the Millennium." She closed her eyes and kissed me, then stood up straight. "I've got to go to bed, right now," she said. "I've got a sleeping problem, you know. It's coming on me now. I'll take the cherry. You take the bed."

"Maybe I should go."

"All right, I'm being selfish. You take the cherry. It's all yours."

"I don't want the cherry."

"I know you want it. You're just being polite. How sweet. Don't say I didn't offer." Natalie climbed into the Marcellas. She laid herself down and folded her hands at her waist. "Kiss me," she said.

I leaned over her. The phone rang.

"Get that, please?" she asked.

It was Ray on the phone. "Hi, killer. Lex said you'd be with Natalie. I'm damn proud of you. Colton suffered a mild stroke. He can't pick his nose with his right hand, and he has no idea in hell what my name is. Tell Natalie her granddaddy's okay, at least for now. Doc told us all to go home and let Colton rest. Cruel Jewell went home first. I'll stay the night if I can fit my fat ass on the waiting room couch. Jerry and Cynthia left ten minutes ago. Get your pants on."

I went to the casket. Natalie lay there in her black dress, her eyes half-closed. Her mouth hung open slightly. I nudged her to tell her the news about Colton. She didn't move. I heard her parents' car in the driveway, then Jerry calling out her name as he climbed the stairs. He knocked on the door, then came in.

"I can't wake her," I said.

"Again?"

Cynthia entered the room. Jerry motioned her over. He said,

"Come look at your daughter." Cynthia peered into the casket. She lifted Natalie's hand, then let it fall. "I declare. She is so precious."

I slipped into my suit jacket to leave. Jerry said, "It's late. Stay with us tonight. Jeff and Randy can handle the phones." I opened my mouth to resist, but Jerry stopped me. He said, "Take Natalie's bed. She won't mind, and we don't either. We're all family here, and there's a door between you two. Strawberry pancakes for breakfast."

Some small sound she made startled me out of my sleep. Natalie pulled aside the gossamer canopy and swayed at the end of the bed, naked. Her eyes and mouth were partly open. She breathed, in the rhythm of deep slumber. I whispered her name. Her hand moved downward to her sex, where her fingers played. She turned sideways. I leered at her profile, the delicate protrusion of her nipples. "Natalie," I whispered.

On hands and knees, she glided through the canopy onto the foot of the bed, creeping toward me in the dark. She laid herself down on her back, her head tilted toward me, eyes aglaze. Breath sighed out of her body. Maybe her sleep disorder was dangerous. I placed my head on her chest for a heartbeat, its pulse was steady and slow. I kissed her on the spot where I had listened, then moved my mouth to her nipple. She drew a breath. I raised my head to look. Her mouth remained slack; her eyes fixed. I saw her navel from the corner of my eye—a magical thing, designed for sucking. I felt a tremor in her body as I sucked, but when I looked up, she appeared the same—completely unconscious. I slipped out of my shorts, and lay upon her stillness, longing for her kiss. When I took her virginity, she groaned. Her eyes, now alive, met mine. "I was pretending for you," she whispered. "Was I sweet?" After a tender kiss, we tore each other to pieces. When we settled in for slumber, I whispered in her ear, "Your grandfather's okay." She smiled, then fell away, into sleep.

• • •

The dream woke me up—a *bad* dream—ejaculation snapped me into consciousness from my dream of sex, delirious and carnal—and it hadn't been the face of my angel, Natalie, beneath me, but the face of another. Ray's wife, Denise. She had taunted me in the dream, "Natalie only wants you for a baby. She wants you for a funeral home. I can't have babies. I just want you."

I felt sick, as though the dream had been my own fault. I knew better, but I didn't feel that way. I switched on the small lamp of the nightstand and noticed my arm, covered with Natalie's teeth marks. The rest of me looked pretty much the same. Natalie lay naked with her mouth open, drooling onto her pillow. I rubbed my face in my hands; saw blood on my fingers. I touched my sore mouth, my lower lip bleeding. The girl loved to bite. There was blood on the bed, too—Natalie's virginity spilled onto the sheet. I covered her up to her neck with the sheet, got up, and dressed myself. I went to the kitchen for a glass of water, wondering what I should do.

Jerry and Cynthia were liberal-minded parents, but there was no way I'd risk them actually catching us in bed together, strawberry pancakes or no. The predicament left me without a bed. The couch wasn't much bigger than a love seat—and the Marcellas—I could only imagine Jerry's puzzlement when he discovered that Natalie and I had exchanged beds in the middle of the night. I needed to go home, put on my pajamas, and sleep in John Morton's bed.

11

The removal car's clock read 2:10 A.M. I regretted leaving Natalie, but
now I couldn't go back. I had locked Jerry's door behind me when I
left. I drove past the mortuary on Druid, to make the left turn onto
Mayfair. The light in Jerry's office shone through the picture window.

Shit, I muttered to myself. *Lex left the fucking light on, and the goddam mortuary students didn't bother to turn it off.* I usually didn't
think in swears, but I felt worn, still disturbed by my sex dream of
Denise.

In my apartment, Jeff and Randy snored from their bedroom. I
took off my shoes, then went to turn off the lights in Jerry's office.
When I hit the lobby, I heard two voices, male and female. The voices
didn't sound like two people making funeral arrangements—an
argument, it seemed. I flattened my back against the elevator. Hidden
within the recess of the elevator door, I could hear everything. I recognized the voices, too: Lex Talbert, and Cruel Jewell. Lex was insist-
ing that Colton would not live to see the dawn. He demanded they
call Lewis Stark, the JFT man who had made the trades. Jewell dis-

agreed: Dr. Prichett had ensured Colton's survival. Lex argued, "Doctors are known for that kind of talk. Colton Albright is a ghost."

Jewell commanded Lex to shut up. At a time like this, someone in the family might happen upon John Morton's will—the *real* one. "John Morton gave me that will himself," Jewell declared. She recollected how she had taken the new will from John. She had promised to deliver it to a man named Percy, the family attorney. Signed in John Morton's own hand, his signature had been witnessed by their housekeeper, a young woman named Wilma Ritchey. Jewell had read the will herself, instead of taking it to Mr. Percy. John had left her nothing—everything went to Colton—John's final gesture of forgiveness toward the man he had treated as a son, and judgment against his own daughter. Jewell had burned the will in the kitchen—washed the ashes down the sink. John Morton died the next day.

"That means John Morton's will is gone, forever," Lex said.

"I know it's gone, imbecile!" Jewell snapped. "I'm talking about the copy he made for Colton. I hoped we'd find it here. It must be at Cynthia's house."

"That copy is a myth," Lex said. "John went senile. You said he babbled through his last day."

Jewell admitted the babbling, but John had seemed lucid about the copy of his rewritten will. John had beseeched Jewell to deliver the copy to Colton, forthwith—a token of everlasting peace between the two men. Jewell found no document after searching John's desk. The old man faded into babbling again. Jewell pleaded and demanded, then shook her dying father by the shoulders, commanding him to reveal the location of the copy. She slapped him once across the face, then left him to die. As she reached the doorway, she heard his scratchy voice, "It's here." Jewell turned to see a smiling John Morton patting himself on the chest. "I've got it right here, in my pocket."

Jewell's voice drifted from Jerry's office now, "But Father, you don't *have* a pocket. You're wearing your—" She was about to say the word "pajamas," but John Morton had already exhaled his last breath.

"Colton left you everything in his own will," Lex said. "If he dies, John Morton's will won't matter."

"Dr. Pritchett says he'll live. You know Natalie. The little packrat will start going through all the old things, now that Colton's sick. She'll scour the attic. My father died in her room. She'll find that will and I'll get nothing—*again*."

"Natalie's got other things on her mind," Lex said.

"That boy, you mean. The one with the bleeding underwear. I saw the look in his eyes. It was John's look I saw—like my own father looking right at me. That boy is a strange one. We've got enough problems with Natalie. She's all the strange we need right now."

"The girl is distracted," Lex said. "Her mind is on the delivery room—not scouring the attic for a document that doesn't exist. Even if she's pregnant tonight, it's already too late. Your husband's brain is bleeding—not Casey Kight's underwear. Besides, I've got plans for him. I've already told Stark about the boy. Stark is losing his supervisor. He wants Casey for JFT."

Jewell said, "All these years I've made them wait. I just wanted Colton to die in anything but peace. I never imagined this awful place was worth four million dollars."

"Three million," Lex corrected Jewell. "You're forgetting my fee—and the law. You've got to sell this place to a licensed director, not to a corporation. I do the selling. I've already made the deal. We'll have a big funeral for Colton, then you can buy all the antiques you want—open that fancy store. Now go home."

I pressed myself flatter into the recess, my back against the elevator door. Jewell rushed past me. I moved to sneak back to my apartment, but my elbow depressed the elevator's call button. I heard the whirr of the motor, the elevator now on its way down. Maybe I could sneak up the stairs before the elevator went *ding*. Lex hadn't needed to wait for the bell, he had already heard the motor. He stood before me now, arms folded across his chest.

Ding.

The elevator door opened. I fell backward, into the elevator, onto my butt.

"You ought to be more careful, young man. Step into my office. It's time for our talk."

I got up and brushed myself off, terrified of Lex. He sat in Jerry's chair. I sat across the desk from him. I calmed down as I studied him: his craggy face was without decipherable expression. He seemed neither menacing nor benign—just creepy, for his lack of presence. The more I studied him, the more my fear gave way to *real* Presence—the feel of Morton-Albright was upon me; an anointing, from the very timbers and stained glass of the mansion itself. I spoke to Lex in my well-practiced funeral voice, "I heard everything about John Morton's will, and your plans to sell Morton-Albright to Jacob Funeral Trust. I will stop you if I can. The sanctity of this place is against you."

"Why would a smart young man display such ignorance? You belong with JFT. You're just their type. They reward men like you. Ray Winstead and I agree on one thing: there is no gift. What you possess is the ability to detach yourself completely from the revulsion of naked death in its most hideous forms. You're all blood and guts, and without remorse for it. JFT needs a new supervisor for its centralized embalming facility. They need a man like you—strong enough to withstand an eternity in the embalming room. They'll pay, too—quadruple your salary. I have it all arranged."

"You only think you understand me," I said. "I'm here to comfort people on the worst day of their lives. Ray Winstead is my best friend. Jerry's like a father to me. I'm in love with Natalie."

"I can smell her on you." Lex said. "You've known these people for what—a week? Jerry is your father? Ray is your best friend? These people are using you—for your *sperm*, of all things. You're blinded by pride, young man. These people compliment you, and you take them seriously. All they want is to keep Morton-Albright in the family. You'll mean nothing to them if they lose this place—and they *will* lose it. Colton Albright is a doomed man."

Lex's words shook me. It was as though he knew my own doubts— he had taken them a step further. I was sure my new family hoped I'd produce an heir before Colton Albright's death. Even now, my seed swam in Natalie's body, searching for a ripe ovum. Her family showed me respect and affection, but I wondered if their affections would continue, should the business fall out of family hands. I also had to face my own truth—that I had come to Morton-Albright in search of my own soul, not to wait on families. I had come here for the Presence, and the Presence was teaching me the trade. *That* was worth saving—the Presence of comfort.

I told Lex, "We start looking for John Morton's will tomorrow morning, whether Colton dies or not. I'm going to bed."

"Before you go to bed, let me tell you a bedtime story. It will give you nightmares, and you will change your mind about Morton-Albright. The story begins with an unusual name." Lex paused for effect, which annoyed me. He pronounced the name: Waldo Shipper.

"Only two people know where Waldo Shipper is buried: Ray Winstead and myself. Ray buried Waldo Shipper's casket at Fairview Cemetery. However, Mr. Shipper is not *in* that casket. Waldo Shipper is buried in the woods, near Angel Shores Beach." Lex's face reddened as he chuckled. "Sorry," he said, wiping his eyes. He guessed that Ray had confused the dead man's name with a term we used for shipping a body to another town: A *shipper*. Ray thought the dead man was headed for the airport, not Fairview Cemetery. The incident had occurred during the time of Ray's tragedy. On the day of Mr. Shipper's service, Ray had six bodies to care for. He refused help from anyone, trying to make up for his phobia of waiting on families.

The Shippers had planned a service for that day. Ray wouldn't have found that unusual—it was customary for a shipper family to hold a local service before they shipped the body elsewhere—but the family of Waldo Shipper had no intention of shipping the body *anywhere*, except to Fairview Cemetery, six blocks away. On the morning of the service, Lex had checked in with Ray to see about Mr. Shipper's body. He found Ray in the embalming room, snipping the viscera of another case. Ray directed Lex to the dressing room. "I found Waldo Shipper. He was embalmed, but naked and uncasketed. His service would begin within the hour. When I asked Ray to hurry, he told me to go fuck myself." Lex figured that Ray had already devised a plan for Waldo Shipper—the family had requested a closed casket. Since nobody would view the remains, Ray had rolled Mr. Shipper's empty casket into the chapel, thinking he'd dress and casket the remains after the service, then drive the body to the airport—only Mr. Shipper wasn't *going* to the airport. Lex asked Ray why he had failed to line up the funeral cars under the porte cochere, for the procession to the cemetery. Ray answered him, "I thought this case was a shipper."

"You should have seen the look on your best friend's face when I told him that Shipper was the dead man's *name*, and that he was a local burial. I did not yet know that the casket was empty, but I knew *something* was wrong. I had seen Ray with the fidgets before, but never like this."

"He didn't tell you?" I asked. "He didn't go to Jerry?"

"Stop the funeral and embarrass Morton-Albright? Ray was already worried about losing his job—he could no longer bear to wait on families. If Ray lost his job, he'd lose Denise—she is the only reason Ray suffers the embalming room. So Ray played along, and for the first and only time in the history of Morton-Albright, we held a service for an empty casket—*my* family. My own revelation came at the cemetery. A shortage of pallbearers forced me to help with the lifting of the casket. The casket seemed light, but Ray's face told me a lot more than the weight of the casket."

After the graveside, Lex had secretly watched Ray load a cloth-covered casket into the hearse, then screech out of the parking lot. Lex had followed him in the lead car, to the woods near Angel Shores Beach. Ray must have feared being noticed—he took this road and that, to a dirt road, no wider than a path. Lex parked on the shoulder of the pavement and followed Ray on foot, into a forest of pines and scrub. "In a clearing, I saw Ray dig a hole with a shovel. Believe what you will, but I pitied him then. I never said a word to anyone. I will keep my silence, as long as you keep yours, regarding JFT and this business of a second will."

"And if I don't?"

"I tell your bedtime story to the State Board, the police, and the press. Your best friend loses his funeral director's license, spends some time in jail, and the name of Morton-Albright is destroyed forever. Illegal burial is a criminal offense. Family ownership of the funeral home is pointless without the Morton-Albright reputation."

"And you're doing this for a million dollars? For money, you'd ruin this beautiful place?"

"See what I mean, Casey Kight? You prefer the place of the dead to justice. Wait until Lewis Stark hears of this. JFT will love you. Have you forgotten how it feels to lose your own parents in an accident? They call them accidents, but there's no such thing. Suppose a lazy mechanic caused your parents' plane crash? How would you feel toward that person? How have you been living all these years? I'll bet the airline paid you off. John Morton was a well-respected man. That's how his furniture store passed the fire inspector. John knew the building wasn't up to code. He gave me a job for life, in the house of the dead, to ease his guilt. I've spent every working day of my life thinking about my mother lying on the embalming table in the back room. You're goddamn right I want the million dollars."

Lex Talbert had no idea that his own co-conspirator, Cruel Jewell, may have set the fire that killed his parents. I nearly blurted it out, but my tongue locked tight. Natalie had no proof—only a feeling. Despair rolled into my bones.

"Are we finished?" I asked Lex.

"You keep your silence, I keep mine. I have no quarrel with you, Casey. I'm trying to ensure your future in your chosen career, and I'm very, very sorry about your folks."

I arose from my chair and walked into the lobby, fighting tears. I felt pity for Lex. I could not fault him for what tragedy had done to him. Look what it had done to me, to Ray. I never had wished more for someone to talk to. But I could talk to no one—not without endangering Ray, and Morton-Albright itself. I was desperate enough to talk to Margee, only I knew what she would say: "I knew you'd get into trouble, working in that creepy place." Lex had been right about my new family—I loved them, but I did not know them, not well enough to confide in them. If I told about John Morton's will, Lex would ruin the place with scandal. If I said nothing, Morton-Albright would fall into the hands of Jacob Funeral Trust. Either way, Morton-Albright would cease to be what it was: the abode of the Presence of comfort. Nothing else mattered. Fate had made me the guardian of the Presence, and a poor one, sure enough. I made my way through the lobby. The doors of the chapel beckoned my eye. It seemed the right place to think things over. I padded down the center aisle and sat in the front pew. Starlight illuminated the lilies in the stained glass, and the outline of the pulpit on the dais. The chapel looked like a church, but a different kind of sanctity haunted this place. When it came to church, many were called, but few were chosen. When it came to death, *everybody* was chosen. There were no sinners, or saints—not in the Morton-Albright chapel. The mercy of comfort here was for everyone.

My thoughts were disturbed by the sound of slippered feet, shuffling through the chapel toward me. Natalie, I suspected. She had awakened to find me gone. Now she was upset with me for leaving her. I whispered her name into the dark. No answer returned. Instead, I heard a sigh, then someone sat down next to me—I could feel the depression in the cushion of the pew. I was tired beyond reaction, except for my eyes, bugging to make out the person sitting next to me; and my heart, racing the hell out of my chest. But the calm overwhelmed me, like morphine shot into a wounded soldier— irresistible calm. Then came the Presence. I had felt it before, but never with such power. It grew as it swirled around me, filling the chapel with the fragrance of a thousand flowers. Its sweetness flowed through me, up my spine and into my brain, raising the hair on me in places where I was pretty sure I didn't have any hair at all. Words entered my mind, carried upon an old voice. *You know why you're here. You feel the comfort, but you'll never understand it until you pass it along. That's what you've got to do. Pass it along. Don't worry about this old place. You've got the gift, son. Pass it along.* I heard the words, but I did not understand their meaning. My eyelids began closing on their own. On my way into sleep, I saw him sitting next to me: the old man himself.

I woke myself up with my own snoring, my head leaning over the back of the pew. I had dreamed the whole thing. It would take a week to work the crick out of my neck. I staggered into John Morton's bedroom. The dial on the clock said I'd get two hours of sleep.

Natalie burst into my bedroom at 6:00 A.M. and switched on the light, starting me awake. The look on her face demanded my attention. Her clothing demanded it too. In striped men's pajamas and a maroon silk robe, hair slicked back behind her ears, she looked like Nick Charles, the Thin Man, dressed for morning cocktails and a murder to solve. Her footwear changed her back into Natalie Stiles— black high-tops, black socks. From the pocket of her robe, she withdrew a pack of cigarettes. She tapped one out of the pack and hung it from the corner of her mouth. She lit it with a match and took a puff, blowing the smoke upward before she spoke, "You popped my cherry and ran. Not quite what I expected from a man who knows how to handle a trocar." She tapped her ash onto the floor. "We had a religious experience, you and me. Have you ever said God's name that many times in church?"

"Did you drive over here dressed like that?"

"Don't change the subject," she said. "I don't smoke. It's making me dizzy." Natalie opened the bathroom door and flipped the cigarette, barely glancing for aim. I heard the hiss in the toilet water. She said, "Now, where were we? Oh, yes. My virginity. Your virginity. *Our* virginity."

"Natalie, I woke up naked with you, *Naked,* for godssake. What was I supposed to do—wait for your dad to wake us with strawberry pancakes?"

"Look, death man, I'm twenty-two years old. Do you know what that means? It means I'm old enough for sex, and I've never wanted sex with anyone but you. Now, I've got to ask you a question. This is hard for me, so keep your mouth shut until I ask it." Natalie began to sniffle. She wiped tears from the corners of her eyes with the sleeve of her Thin Man robe. "Jesus, look at me. I can't believe I'm doing this."

"Natalie, I—"

"I told you to shut up until I ask you the question. Now, I've got to know something. Do you want me or not?"

"I—"

"Don't answer yet! I'm not finished. I don't mean, do you want to fuck me for a while. I mean, do you want *me,* the way I want you? Okay. You can talk now."

"I want you, Natalie. I want you forever."

She sat down beside me on the bed. "Then help me out of my jammies," she said.

Ten minutes later, the giant phone bells above John Morton's bed blasted me out of Natalie. "We tried to call Ray Winstead," the police dispatcher said. "His wife told us he was at the hospital. We've got an apparent suicide at Gulfside Motel, Beach Road. Gunshot wound to the head. Officers on the scene say bring a bag."

I drove to the hospital for Ray. I found him sleeping in the waiting room. I nudged him awake. He had fallen asleep wearing his glasses, now hooked behind one ear and dangling off the other. How could a man who had just spent a night of uncomfortable vigilance for his father-in-law have buried a man in the woods? It didn't make sense. There was more to that story than Lex had let on.

Ray hocked his throat clear. "Is Colton dead?" He asked.

"No, but some guy in a motel shot himself in the head last night. Let's roll."

• • •

Ray said the Gulfside Motel was exactly the kind of place where a man would drink a bottle of Jim Beam, then blow his brains out. The empty bottle of whiskey lay on the floor, next to the bed. Detective Jones handled the shotgun with a towel. The suicide note was pinned to the dead man's shirt: "Dear Francine, can't take the pain anymore. Love, Robert."

"This is some weird shit here," Ray said, looking at the dead man's head.

Dr. Kendall explained the physics behind the death of Robert Cooley. "He stuck the shotgun in his mouth and pulled the trigger with his toe—he's missing one shoe and one sock. He must have been a quail hunter—birdshot in the shotgun shell. The shot pellets were so small, the discharge of the weapon disintegrated the skull—vaporized it. Without a skull to contain the force of the blast, the head blew up like a balloon, then deflated. The blood and brain spewed out of his nose."

Robert Cooley's head looked like a flat, rotten pumpkin with a gourd for a nose. Mr. Cooley's eyeballs dangled out of their sockets by the optic nerves. Broken, blackened teeth were surrounded by lips, nearly burned off.

"No rush on this one," Kendall said.

Back at the funeral home, Jerry, Carl, and Natalie sat at the kitchen table, Natalie still dressed in her Thin Man pajamas. Ray headed for the doughnuts.

"You missed some fine pancakes this morning, son," Jerry said to me.

I apologized, "It's hard for me to sleep in a strange bed. Good thing I came back in time for the police rotation call, especially with Ray at the hospital."

"Good man," Jerry said. He patted Natalie's hand. "See there, sugar? Casey didn't run off on you last night. He's a good man, trying to do a good job."

Natalie fired me a squint. I had lied to her father. Natalie didn't like it. Jerry told her to go home and change her clothes for school. Natalie stuffed half a doughnut into her mouth, got up, and threw the rest of it in the trash. "I'm wearing my bathamas to thcool today," she mumbled while chewing.

Denise popped in just as Natalie walked out the door. They bumped into each other. "Morning, Natty," Denise said, smiling.

"Mfonin," Natalie grumbled through her doughnut. She slammed the door on her way out.

"What's with her?" Denise asked.

"Lover's quarrel," Ray said, casting his eyes at me.

Denise giggled. "So soon?"

Carl said, "Casey banged Natalie last night, then he ran off on her."

"Carl, there's no need for that kind of talk," Jerry said. "Casey felt he needed to get back to the funeral home. Natalie needs to learn about sharing her life with a funeral man."

These people kept secrets from each other, yet my sexual relationship with Natalie had already become family knowledge, freely discussed over coffee and doughnuts.

"Aw, poor Casey," Denise said. She walked over and kissed me on the mouth. She whispered in my ear, "Was Natalie sweet for you?"

"Hey, Booger," Ray called to Denise, "ain't you got no sugar for Daddy?"

"Not if you don't cut it out with that Booger shit, Ray Winstead. I'll bet Casey didn't call Natalie Booger last night." Denise announced the reason for her visit. "Lillian Keller—the nursing home death. No service—just a delivery to the cemetery. Nice casket—Windemere sealer. You can put her in a burial gown. Kip says, drop her off at Fairview anytime."

"Nice work, Denise," Jerry said. "By the way, Robert Cooley's family called while you boys were making the removal. Any hope for an open casket?"

"Not without a basketball pump," Ray answered. "Bad head."

"The family wants to see him. I'll look at him later."

"I stopped by the hospital," Denise said. "Daddy knew me, but he asked when Ray and I were getting married."

"I'll take old Lillian to Fairview," Ray said. "Mr. Cooley's head requires subcutaneous embalming. I hate that shit. Carl, show Casey the sub-q procedure."

"We'll do the head first," Carl told me in the embalming room. He selected a short trocar of small caliber, a steel button on the trocar's handle. He connected the instrument to the embalming machine hose and pressed the trocar's button. Embalming fluid sprayed out of the spearpoint. Carl pierced Mr. Cooley's face and head, injecting fluid. After the procedure, white trocar buttons dotted the head.

Meredith stepped into the embalming room, said we got a new call at Kennedy Hospital—a little boy. "Drop Mr. Cooley off at the morgue, then go get the child. I'll tell Ray about the boy when he gets back from Fairview."

Jody Christian, four years old, now lay on the embalming table, dead of leukemia. Purple spots covered his body. Carl let out a breath and shook his head. "Same as embalming an adult, except the instruments are smaller. Think you can raise the vessels in his neck? Go easy on the pressure and flow of the embalming machine. I'll call Western right away. They specialize in smaller caskets." Carl went for the door. He opened it, then turned to me. "Trick is, just focus on the job. Keep your mind on the vessels and instruments. Make it easy on yourself. Understand?

I understood: Carl didn't want to embalm the child either. I could see why—the feelings were on me already—how Jody Christian must have suffered, not understanding why he was so sick; why Mommy couldn't make him better. His brokenhearted parents—all their hopes and wishes for their beautiful son—gone, blown away. How they must have adored him, so precious in their sight. Was that how my mom and dad had thought of me? What were they thinking when they saw the ground rushing toward them from the little windows of the airplane? Fear for their own lives? Impossible. I knew what they were thinking. Their last thoughts were of me. I felt the worry in their hearts as they entrusted my safekeeping to Margee, and to God. How they must have prayed for me. I untied my apron, folded it neatly, and placed it back into the drawer. I could not bear to mar the child's flesh with the scalpel. All I could do was look at him and weep. What could any of us do to comfort Jody's parents?

You can start by doing your job, son. Sometimes doing your job is the best you can do. You've got the gift. It's time to pass it along. When you comfort others, the comfort comes back to you. Don't be afraid, son. I'm right here with you. Now put on your apron, and put your love into your work.

Mr. and Mrs. Christian decided against prolonging their son's repose: One night of visitation tonight, burial tomorrow in Saint Pete, near their home. "Plenty of good funeral homes down that way, Cap'n," Meredith said, "but there's only one Morton-Albright."

Over a hundred people signed the register for Jody Christian that evening. Except for the absence of Ray Winstead, we were prepared: We had placed dozens of boxes of Kleenex in the lobby and the Iris Room, where Jody Christian lay in repose. All of us were given ammonia inhalants to use on the guests, if necessary. When calling hours involved a child in an open casket, anything could happen. Jerry reminded us to expect uncontrollable emotions—this was going to be tough on all of us.

The reaction of the crowd surprised us all. There were tears, but not the kind of hopelessness Jerry had warned us about. Most of what I witnessed was a kind of reserved grief—sad and necessary, but as I watched people leave, I noticed an odd look about their faces. Toward the end of Jody Christian's calling hours, Meredith came up from behind and placed his hand on my shoulder. "Come with me,

Cap'n. Meet the family." Meredith took me by the arm and led me to the Iris Room, now occupied by a dozen callers. He walked me to the young woman, standing next to the tiny casket. "Mrs. Christian," Meredith said, "This is Mr. Kight. He's the man who prepared your son."

I extended my hand to Mrs. Christian, but she threw her arms around me and hugged me close, weeping on my neck. I patted her back, not knowing what else to do. She kept hugging me, sobbing, unable to speak. Long moments passed before she released me. She wiped her eyes. "Jody looks so good," she said. "He was sick for so long. Now he looks like he's sleeping, like when I used to check in on him at night. I was expecting this to be so awful. I feel like he's here, in this room, saying, "I'm okay, Mommy." I know my son is out of pain, in some peaceful place. God bless you." She embraced me again, sobbing, "God bless you," over and over again. I felt a hand on my shoulder, gently pulling me away from Mrs. Christian. I turned to meet Jody's dad, a tall man with his son's blond hair. He gave me his hand. "Bob Christian," he said. "I'm sure there aren't many your age willing to take on this kind of work. It's nice to know there are young men who still care about people." Meredith put his arm around my shoulder and walked me to the Iris Room door. He said, "Nice job, Cap'n. You're a good man. You've got the gift, son."

I hurried to the main entrance, fighting back tears. Jerry intercepted me. "Casey, I have never seen anything like this since old John himself. You should be proud of yourself."

I stepped onto the veranda, where the sweetness of the gardenias awaited me. *Great feeling, being a good funeral man, isn't it, son? You passed it along—the comfort. Don't you worry. The comfort will come back to you.*

I needed a long night's rest, but I didn't get one. A thud against my chest started me out of my sleep. I switched on the lamp of the nightstand—that's when I saw the amputated hand, drenched in blood, lying upon my chest. I flung it against the wall and jumped out of bed.

Natalie emerged from the bathroom, a smile on her face. "That's for lying to Daddy this morning. Fuck with me again, you'll get another scare." She picked up the hand from the floor and wiggled it at me, still smiling. "It's rubber," she said, placing the thing in my hand. "Halloween thing. Looks real with the blood candy—my own recipe: sugar water and red food coloring—deathy as hell. We're even now. Let's have sex."

I pointed the rubber hand at her, then opened my mouth to yell, but Natalie started undressing. "You have something to say?" she asked. I dropped the hand to the floor.

At dawn, Natalie invited me into the shower with her. "Don't you just love getting wet?" she said. She stood there smiling, slicking the palm of her hand with a layer of soap. With the soap on her hand, and her hand on me, she spoke in her teasing voice, "You left on a police rotation call yesterday morning, didn't you? I know all about the dead man's head. I want to see it. They'll close the casket, you know."

I told Natalie she was too late. The body would be casketed within a couple hours.

"Pleeeze? Let Natty see the head. If you say yes, I'll keep doing what I'm doing."

"Oh, yeah? What if I say no?"

"I'll keep doing what I'm doing, anyway. I like what I'm doing."

"I like it too. I'll do what I can." I held her close to me, under the spray of hot water, kissing her like crazy. Afterward, we dried each other. We took our time, so it wasn't long before we needed another shower. I had never imagined myself being smitten in love, and being so corny about it. Even Natalie said, "This is so not-deathy." She giggled day and night—sometimes, for no apparent reason.

When I had finally knotted my four-in-hand knot for the third time, I wondered how she had found out about Mr. Cooley's head. She said the cops told her everything: "Police scanners," she said. "One in my apartment, one in the Chrysler. The cops talked about the Cooley head all day."

. . .

We returned from Jody Christian's graveside service to find Ray at the kitchen table, reading the newspaper—back at work, now that the little boy had been put to rest. I understood his absence, not as a weakness but as proof of heart. I could not have embalmed the child myself had it not been for the guiding hand of the Presence. It made Ray seem even less capable of burying a human being in the woods—it didn't fit his character. His ornery exterior protected his gentle nature. I was growing more suspicious of Lex's accusation, but I had to be sure before I exposed his plan to sell Morton-Albright to Jacob Funeral Trust. Still, even if I told the family about John Morton's second will, what were the chances of our finding it? The telling of my secret would only cause the others to suffer through the days that would end in the death of Colton Albright. It seemed best not to tell them, to preserve the Presence of Morton-Albright, up to its final moment.

Now something that Natalie had said put a new possibility into my mind: what if JFT ceased its operation in Florida? "They're under investigation in three states, for improprieties," Natalie had said. Without JFT's millions, Jewell had no reason to sell the funeral home to an outsider. Her revenge was for Colton, not for her daughters and their families. She had said so herself, and it would be easy to find out if JFT was under investigation in Florida—easy enough for Natalie, anyway. Ray looked up from his newspaper. "Natalie's in your bedroom," he said. "Get to work."

"I found your Harveys," Natalie said. Lying on the bed in her panties, reading a comic book—I had never seen anything sexier in my life. I forgot about JFT, and went to work.

12

Jerry asked the men into his office to discuss Mr. Cooley: the family wanted to see him. Jerry argued, "We must prevent them, even though they have every legal right. They want to know for sure that it's him, and that he's dead."

Ray said, "There's no restorative artist in the world who could fix that poor man's head. It's as round as the moon, almost as big, and as flat as one of Cynthia's strawberry pancakes, with a couple dozen trocar buttons—which reminds me, I'd better order some more. What Mr. Cooley needs is a new head, and we don't have any lying around at the moment."

"We could use yours," Carl said. "Nobody would notice."

"That's okay. Your wife wouldn't notice if your dick was missing, either. So shut up. This is important—how about the family album speech, Jerry?

"I already tried it. I told them Mr. Cooley was in no condition for viewing. I told them to find some nice photos of him, sit down as a family, and go through the pictures together—pick one out for the table next to his casket. They wouldn't hear it. They want to see him."

I remembered the funeral of my own parents—their caskets had been closed as well. Margee had identified their remains. I knew how the Cooleys felt. They wanted one last look, just as I had. When I saw my parents' caskets, they may as well have been empty. I remembered their wedding portrait on the table in the chapel—not proof enough, but it set me to a plan that might satisfy the Cooleys, and Natalie, too. I blurted it out, "Is there a leader of the family? A spokesperson, like Sophie Campbell?"

"Calvin Cooley," Jerry said. "Decedent's brother. He's the one making the noise."

"Let's take a picture of Mr. Cooley's head and show it to his brother. It might change his mind about the rest of the family viewing the remains. Natalie's a photographer. She could take the picture."

"Forget it," Jerry said. "You know how I feel about my daughter in that blasted embalming room—especially with Mr. Cooley's head."

"The killer may have a point," Ray said.

"Might as well admit it, Uncle Jerry," Carl agreed. "We all know Natalie's previous work."

Jerry looked at me. His face reddened, then faded into a smirk. "Son, my daughter has gotten hold of you but good. I like your picture idea, but Natalie will not take that picture. *You* can talk her into letting us use her camera."

"Fuck, no!" Natalie declared, when I asked for her camera. "It's my camera. I take the picture." She fumed and sputtered around John Morton's bedroom, reminding me of my promise in the shower.

"I tried, Natalie. We've got to keep the family from seeing this man."

"Put the guy in the casket backward. Open the head-end. They can look at his feet."

"I promised you a look at his head. When I take the picture, your dad will realize that he can't send the film to the Eckerd guy. You're the only person with a darkroom. You get to develop the picture of Mr. Cooley's head."

"Oh, all right. But I'm only doing this because we're tricking Daddy." She gave me her Nikon and showed me how to work it. She followed me to the embalming room door. She folded her arms and looked at the ceiling, tapping her foot. Jerry, Ray, and I entered the embalming room. Mr. Cooley waited on the table.

"Shoot the fingers first," Ray said. "Masonic ring on his finger. There's an old, curved scar on the inside of his right calf—right there. Shoot that, too. Those two items might convince the brother. Shoot the head last."

I took the three pictures, then gave the camera to Jerry. He looked at the thing, working his face into different expressions. He cocked an eyebrow at me. "Now I get it," he said. "We can't send this film to Eckerd's."

Natalie looked like a kid waiting to open a birthday present when Jerry handed over the camera. He sent me along with her to USF to warn Natalie if anyone tried to enter the darkroom while she developed the pictures.

In the Morton-Albright parking lot, Natalie threw me the keys to the Green Hornet's car. "You drive," she said. "I'll play with your dick."

USF darkroom: the sound of running water and the glow of the safety light. I could see why Natalie liked it here—I felt immediately relaxed. It was like being in a large embalming room, only without the bright lights. Natalie led me into a room the size of a closet. "The deathy-dark darkroom," she said, then shut the door. I had never stood in the complete absence of light. After a brief spell of claustrophobia, the darkness expanded beyond limits. "There's a bench, right behind you," Natalie whispered. "Feel for it and sit down."

"Found it," I whispered back. "Why are we whispering?"

"People whisper in the dark. In the deathy-dark room, it's better that you don't even whisper. Be still. Be quiet."

There, in the dark, I heard the sound of Natalie unzipping her pants.

The picture of the scar did it for Calvin Cooley. He had put his face down on Jerry's desk and wept. "I cut Robert's leg," he'd admitted. "Kids, playing with a knife. Twelve stitches. I'll tell the others it's him."

At the visitation, a portrait of Mr. Cooley sat on a table near the casket. Afterward, Jerry helped me lock the place up for the night. He chatted with me as we turned off the lights. At the main entrance, he tapped my shoulder. "You tricked me into letting Natalie develop that film. I thought, why would a smart young man like Casey go against his employer like that? Then it hit me—he's in love with Natalie."

"I'm crazy about her, Jerry."

"Young and in love. That's nice, son. Keep her out of the back room."

A note from Jeff and Randy read "Back late." Now that I had come to work for Morton-Alright, the twins *always* came home late. I rarely saw them. I figured they were avoiding Lex. Either that or they were avoiding the sounds Natalie and I made when we were together. No Natalie tonight, though—she had to study (two weeks behind in all her classes), and although sex with her was becoming an addiction, I welcomed the night alone. It was one of those evenings after a long day's work that was suited for doing something that required hardly any thought, and even less energy. My Green Hornet comics would make it a perfect evening. I got into my pajamas, pulled an issue from the middle of the stack, and began to read. Mostly, I looked at the pictures. There's nothing like comic-book art. You can tell the whole story by looking at the pictures, frame by frame. At first, I thought I had slipped into a dream.

I was still turning the pages of the comic, but the pictures were changing: Britt Reid, the Green Hornet's alter-ego, became Jerry Stiles—a much younger Jerry Stiles, with black hair and an unwrinkled face. Kato, the oriental sidekick and chauffeur, became Ray Winstead—he was younger too, and twenty pounds lighter. The car they drove was no longer Black Beauty but a black Morton-Albright hearse. They were racing toward the funeral home, away from the scene of the plane crash that killed my parents. A plume of fiery smoke filled the background and I was reading like it was just a normal comic book, only there was a spinning inside my head and then Jerry and Ray were in the embalming room standing over my mother's body and she was all burned up. The next frame was a close-up of my mother's charred, skeletal face and she grabbed Jerry's lapel with her two remaining fingers and yanked him close to her and there was a comic-book dialogue balloon coming from her mouth and the words said, "Please, in God's name, don't let my boy see me like this! Tell him it's not his fault. You hear me? It's not his fault!" The dream-state spell I was under vanished. I jumped out of the bed, shaking all over. I paced the room, trying to calm myself. That's when the Presence swirled into the room, its voice no longer in my head—it came to me through my ears. "Being a good funeral man means protecting your families. Sometimes you've got to deny them the very thing they want the most—one last look. Your Margee took that last look for you, but you weren't satisfied. You handled that Cooley case well, son— saved them a lot of heartache. Now lie back and feel the comfort."

"No!" I shouted. "I don't want to feel the comfort. I want to know what the fuck you want with me!" There wasn't much echo in John Morton's bedroom. My words vanished into the air. So did the Presence. I found Natalie's card, the one she had given me on the night we first met. I dialed her private line.

"Natalie Stiles," she answered, as if from an arrangement office.

She entered John Morton's bedroom wearing khakis and a white button-down oxford, shirttail out, Unbuttoned cuffs dangled to her fingertips. A tie, striped blue and red, hung loosened to her waist.

"I'm going crazy," I said.

"Me too. I can't stand to be away from you for more than five minutes."

"I don't mean it that way. I'm hearing voices. I feel a Presence. I saw an old man in the chapel. Tonight, the pictures in my comic book changed. Maybe it's all this death around me—you know—getting to me. I feel like I belong in Chattahoochee."

"Wow," Natalie said, clapping her hands together excitedly. "It's him. It's John Morton. Isn't he cool?"

"No! He is not cool. He's scaring the hell out of me. What do you mean, it's John Morton?

She nodded her head, smiling.

"Oh, Jesus," I said, flopping back onto the bed. Natalie flopped beside me. She lay on her side, her head propped up in her hand. She started jabbering, "When I was a little girl, Daddy let me hang around the funeral home on Sundays—they're quiet. Daddy kept the books on Sundays. Mother did the gardening. I sat in the lobby, reading comic books, stuff like that. Granddaddy Colton would show up around noon. He'd sit with me and tell me stories—everything about this place. After Granddaddy's stories, I'd follow him, sneaking, of course, always to the Rose Room. I'd hear him yakking away in there. I thought he was praying, or going daffy. One day, I couldn't stand it anymore. I stepped into the room and demanded that he tell me who he was talking to. Scared the shit out of him, being caught like that. He laughed, and said, "I'm just talking to old John." I said "Oh" like it was no big deal, then I ran to tell Daddy. He laughed. He said it was normal to talk to loved ones you've lost. Lots of people do it. The dead don't answer you, but you knew them so well in life, you could imagine what they would have said. Granddaddy and John were like father and son. Daddy said that Colton's mind still worked the right way, and that John Morton lived in heaven, not at Morton-Albright."

Natalie sat up, giggled, and cast her hands into the air. "Daddy was *wrong*," she said. "John Morton lives here, at Morton-Albright Funeral Home and Memorial Chapel."

"How are you so sure it's John Morton?"

"I *knew* him, ya goof, when he was alive." She lay back down and propped up her head, jabbering again, "John Morton died right after my birthday, which is the twelfth day of September, by the way—and don't worry, I'll tell you what to buy for me. Anyway, I had just turned five when my great-grandfather died. We kept chairs and gliders out on the front porch then, back when you could actually park on Druid Road. John would sit on the porch in a suit and a straw hat. The townspeople all came to visit John. They'd talk, play checkers, share a drink from John's flask. Everybody loved him. He'd let me sit in his lap. He'd grizzle my face with his whiskers, ask my advice on his next checkers move—but eventually, he'd ask me, "What time is it, Natty?" I'd pull his watch out of his vest pocket and press the button that popped the cover open. I couldn't tell time, of course, but I'd say, "It's time for my treat." He'd pat himself on the chest and look surprised. He'd say, "I've got it right here in my pocket." I'd squirm my fingers around in there until I found my prize—a piece of butterscotch, stick of Juicy Fruit, a few dimes—things like that.

"After John died, nobody sat on the front porch anymore. It had been John's special place. We removed the furniture when it started getting rusty. When I turned thirteen—that's when I saw him."

"You saw him?"

"Saw him. Daddy and Mother and I came here on a Sunday. I saw all of the furniture back on the front porch, all of it empty, except John's old rocking chair. He waved to me as we drove by. I bit a hole in my tongue to stop myself from yelling, "Look! It's Grandpa John!" We parked the car and I ran to the porch. It was empty. Back inside the funeral home, I felt him everywhere—chills all over. I still feel him, every time I walk through the door. That's why I started taking pictures all over the funeral home. I once saw a movie where a dead kid showed up in a photograph. I kept hoping John would appear in one of my pictures. I wanted to tell you about him that first day in my apartment, but I was afraid you'd think I was wacko."

"He doesn't come in here when we—"

"Screw each other's brains out? No, John wasn't the pervert type. Listen to me, Casey. John Morton is real. He won't hurt you. He was the sweetest man who ever lived—well, *almost* the sweetest."

After making love, while Natalie slept her sleep of death, I sat on the edge of the bed. Our lovemaking had distracted me from my comic book terror, but hadn't relieved any doubts about my sanity. The episode of seeing my mother, burned to the bone, still pierced my brain. The whole experience of losing my parents, and my childhood memories had always seemed like a benign disease—always there, but with little suffering. Margee had seen to that, but why? I was beginning to learn the necessity of grief, but Margee had never allowed it. She had spent years evading my questions, squelching my curiosity. Part of her reluctance to talk came from her own experience of having identified the remains of my mother, and my father—her own brother. I knew that. But what about the harmless things I had asked about? Had I ever owned a tricycle? A box of Tinkertoys? Why had she hidden all those pictures from me? I knew she hadn't thrown them away. She had always told me the same thing: "It will make you sad—very, very sad." But now that I was older, I *wanted* to feel the sadness. I wanted to feel everything you were supposed to feel. And what about the words my mother had spoken in my waking nightmare? *Tell him it's not his fault,* she had said through skeletal jaws. How could a plane crash be the fault of a nine-year-old kid? Why would I even think such a thing? Then there was Natalie. I wasn't sure which was crazier: my experiences with the Presence, or Natalie's explanation—that John Morton *was* the Presence.

Nothing had made sense in my life before Morton-Albright. Nothing made sense now, either. The only difference was the multitude of distractions and worries available to me now: falling in love with Natalie, embalming with Ray and Carl, the mystery of John

Morton's will, and Waldo Shipper—not to mention the biggest insanity of all: knowing that I was exactly where I was supposed to be. I remembered the verse from Ecclesiastes: "The heart of the wise is in the house of mourning." But where was the wisdom? And most of all, where was my heart?

Next morning, Jerry announced that the hospital would discharge Colton in a day or two. In the middle of his announcement, Meredith burst into the kitchen with a frighted look on his face. He paced the floor and ran his hand through his white hair, then spoke his trembling words, "Jacob Funeral Trust has gone and bought up Jesup's place."

"This shit is getting too close to home," Ray said. "Jesup won't be the last, either."

Jerry wondered why JFT would bother with a smaller operation like Jesup. They handled only seventy-five calls a year, and JFT had probably overpaid for the place. It didn't make sense, profit-wise. "James Jesup and I have been friends for years," Jerry said. "I'm surprised he didn't call me."

"He called me this morning," Meredith said. "That's how I found out. His voice was shaky-like—told me JFT had left him no choice. He told me to pass the news along, and that we shouldn't contact him for a while—let things settle down—tell Jerry to stay out of this and watch our own backsides. He mentioned something about Jenner Cremations, too, but he wasn't making much sense by that time."

Ray said, "We can pick up Clifford Moss from Jenner today. Myron Cheeves will talk. JFT's had their place for a week or so. I'll take the killer with me, see what we can find out."

At Jenner's, Myron fidgeted and snorted. He wouldn't even let us in the door. He said, "Sorry, fellers. I cain't let y'all inside no more—not unless you're JFT. That Stork feller pops in once and again—the Devil from 'Bammy, I call him. He don't talk like no devil—smooth as chocolate pie—but he'd slap a hoodoo curse on his own mama, that one."

"Ain't that some shit?" Ray said, driving back to the mortuary. "Lewis Stark is in town. He buys Jenner, then Jesup. Jesup is strictly Cracker business. When the Crackers find out about Jesup selling out, they'll all run to Morton-Albright. JFT won't make a dime from Jesup's business. Go figure that one."

By Friday, Ray had it figured. Our place had emptied of bodies. When the doorchime of the main entrance sounded, I got up from the kitchen table to see who was in the lobby. Ray told me not to bother with the door. "Jerry, Lex, and Meredith get the door on Fridays. Friday is payday. It's the day all the Crackers come in to pay on their funeral bills."

"They don't pay for it when they make the arrangements?" I asked. I had never seen Margee pay for anything more than once.

"Crackers can't pay like that. Their funerals tend to be expensive."

"Copper and bronze," Carl said.

"Carl's right. Crackers buy the most expensive caskets—not the rich folks, like you'd think. Every Cracker gets a fancy casket, three full days of visitation, tons of flowers, and a service in our chapel. It takes them six to ten years to pay for a funeral. At the arrangement, the family takes up a collection in cash—a few hundred dollars. After that, it's ten dollars a week, with no interest. John Morton set things that way. He built this place on Cracker business. We respect their ways."

"What if they don't pay?" I asked.

"Some don't. The Shelbys haven't paid us for generations, and the Shelbys are welcome here, anytime they need us."

"How do we stay in business?"

"Our good name keeps us in business. It's bad manners to send the family a funeral bill. It's like we're reminding them that Granny died and had a funeral. They *know* that Granny died and had a funeral. They stay with Morton-Albright because they know us. They visit this place every damn payday. Is this making sense to you, killer?"

Carl said, "First thing JFT changes when they take over a place. They make the family sign a retail installment contract at high interest. They've even got a collections department—assholes call you on the phone if you're late on your payments. They sue your ass if you don't pay up."

Ray folded his arms and said, "This Jesup thing is starting to make sense now. JFT doesn't care about their current business—they're going after the bad money Jesup's got hanging out there—a ton of it. They'll suck the place dry, for investment capital, and that can only mean one thing: they're not after Jesup. They're out for Morton-Albright. They're running Jesup's Cracker families here on purpose. There's still one thing that doesn't fit: why did old man Jesup sell out?"

"I think I can answer that question." We all turned our heads to see Jerry, who had just stepped into the kitchen. He had called James Jesup himself. All he would say was that he had brought shame upon his family. JFT had taken advantage of that shame and forced him to sell. Mr. Jesup would say no more. "Blackmail," Jerry said. "Every funeral home has a secret. It can't be helped. The funeral business is tightly regulated, but the State Board knows damn well that we all have to work in the gray, to serve our families—like the Cooley family. According to law, we should have let them see Mr. Cooley as he was, but it wasn't the proper thing to do. That's what I mean by working in the gray."

Ray added, "Let's say Granny comes in here with buck teeth and we can't close the mouth properly. We need the family's permission to do the required thing, but we don't tell them we knock those teeth back into her mouth with a rubber mallet. The law requires us to explain the exact procedure, but we don't—that's the kind of gray we're talking about."

"Ray's right about that," Jerry continued. "It's in the gray. The

Board never squawks, unless the gray turns to black, and the black is made known to them. In Jesup's case, I'd guess JFT found the black."

"Jesus." I couldn't help saying it. I pictured Ray burying Waldo Shipper in the woods. Lex had threatened to reveal it. That's how JFT would force us to sell, with or without John Morton's second will. I looked at Ray, examining his face for a reaction to Jerry's remarks. If Ray kept a black secret, he kept it off his face.

13

The summer of 1973 descended upon Angel Shores with murderous heat and bad news: One by one, the funeral homes of our environs fell to Jacob Funeral Trust. I supposed everyone knew the truth, but nobody would say it out loud: JFT was coming for Morton-Albright, and getting closer by the day.

Sunset Towers obscured views in all directions, except westward, toward the Gulf. Six of those towers already housed retirees, many of whom had died shortly after moving in, according to the obituary section of the newspaper. None of the Sunset Towers families had chosen us to care for their loved ones. Each case had gone to a JFT funeral home. Ray documented everything, from the addresses of the decedents, to the distribution of cases among the JFT chapels. He even recorded the daily high and low temperatures. Most of the Sunset Towers deaths occurred when the temperature topped a hundred degrees.

"Damn New Yorkers can't take the heat down here," Ray said. "Neither can I, for that matter. The mourners are going to start dying on us at the cemtary, this heat keeps up."

Meredith said, "They've got a whole city over there at Sunset Towers. Beauty parlors, pharmacy—even got a Winn-Dixie, right there on the property, and a movie house to boot. You'd think they'd be safe from the heat, with all that air-conditioning over there."

Good news abounded as well, at least among our own: Jerry received an announcement from Rotary—a dinner in his honor to commemorate Morton-Albright's service to the people of Angel Shores. Carl's funeral director's license arrived in the mail. He moved into Ray's long-vacated office, but not before his uncle Jerry sent him across the street for a haircut and mustache-removal. When Carl stomped in from the barbershop, Natalie and I were already giggling at Ray eating lunch; his growling swallows of olive loaf and white bread. Ray stopped chewing when he got a look at Carl. Although short hair suited Carl's tanned face, the mustache remained above his lip—not a mustache of hair, but of pure, white skin, untouched by the sun. He looked like a kid after a big glass of milk. Even though Ray couldn't speak for the half sandwich that filled his mouth, he found himself at the end of a finger, and a warning from Carl: "Don't say a fucking word." Carl stomped out of the apartment to take his place among his licensed brethren. Natalie and I beat Ray on his back to keep him from choking.

Jeff and Randy graduated from the Taylor School and went home to Sebring. Natalie emerged from the USF auditorium with a bachelor's in fine arts, an hour after an oven-baked quickie in the backseat of Black Beauty (her footprints remain embedded in the Chrysler's headliner to this day).

Colton Albright recovered from his stroke, at least, partially. Hands shakier, eyes glazy, voice as gravelly as a paving truck, Albright returned to Skeeter's, eating whatever experimental dish the barbecue man set before him.

Margee left for Valdosta with a big diamond on her finger. She stopped by the funeral home to say good-bye, but refused to come inside. In the parking lot, I introduced her to Natalie, who managed to behave herself like a normal person. Margee whispered in my ear,

"I knew you weren't spending all your time with dead people. Did you meet her at a funeral?"

"No." I whispered back. "I met her when I killed Jimmie Blessing."

Ray had assured me that Death took a vacation during the summer, just like everybody else. We could look forward to three months of puttering around the mortuary in the air-conditioning. JFT changed all that. It didn't matter that the retirees of Sunset Towers didn't know the name of Morton-Albright, the Cracker funeral became the craze of Morton-Albright's summer—the busiest summer in our long history. We drove farther and farther away from Angel Shores for removals. We buried in cemeteries clear down to the end of Saint Pete, graveyards unfamiliar to our staff. Our visitations hummed with soft drawls and southern-ese expressions, spoken by the descendants of ancestors who had settled the region back when malaria killed more people than car crashes. It was a phenomenon. According to Jerry, a Cracker switching funeral homes was something akin to a good Baptist converting to Catholicism—it just didn't happen. Each Cracker family had its own mortuary. If Great-great Granny had reposed here, at our place, Morton-Albright became that family's mortuary forever. And never mind the funeral home itself—some Crackers wouldn't even change *directors*, if they could help it. Seventeen years after John Morton's death, folks still asked for him. "And they know damn well he's dead," Jerry said. "They're just making a point of their loyalty." Abandoning one's Undertaker amounted to betrayal, until now. Jerry knew JFT's financial strategy: "They're driving the Crackers here, because Cracker money is delayed money." On the other hand, retirees from the North paid their bills within thirty days, usually with life insurance—all of the Sunset Towers deaths meant instant cash for JFT. Lex and I alone knew that JFT was in a hurry to raise the $4 million they needed to buy us out. Morton-Albright never even *asked* a Cracker family about life insurance—we left that money alone, for the family's survival.

Three weeks into the summer, an old man walked into our place. Jerry met him in the lobby. The man said, "My wife's passed, down in Pasadena. I called Benson's, just like we've been doing for years. I asked to speak to Joe Benson. The man told me nobody by that name worked there." The old man believed he might have dialed the wrong number in his grief, so he drove to Benson Funeral Home. He said, "The place didn't even look the same. All the old furniture was gone; looked like the waiting room at the doctor's office. Some young fellow come out and asked could he help me. 'Not unless there's a Benson here,' I told him. That young man said that most funeral homes weren't run by family anymore. I couldn't imagine my Edith lying in a place with plastic furniture, run by a bunch of kids. Then I remembered old John Morton's place. We'd drove here for the open house back when y'all built the new chapel. I come straight here. Nice to find a man here with some gray on his head. Are y'all still family?"

"We are," Jerry told the man, "and we intend to stay that way."

The increasing blasts of the giant bells sent me to hospitals and nursing homes so far away I had to scribble directions. Besides the night calls, (which required immediate embalming), I still arose every morning at six o'clock, washed cars, vacuumed and dusted every room in the funeral home, worked funeral services and calling hours, attended burials. The burials: I was now in charge of the funeral coach, the Miller-Meteor Cadillac hearse. The new responsibility also placed me in charge of the pallbearers.

Ray told me about pallbearers up North—they carry the casket on their *shoulders*. In the South, we did the more obvious thing—we carried it by the handles. I always had to ask if anyone had a bad arm, because most of the pallbearers were nearly as old as the decedents, and they all had one bad arm. They'd call out left or right, so I could place them all on the good-arm side of the casket. Ray accompanied me to the cemetery only if there was a shortage of pallbearers. I saw to the sealing of the vault. I loved working the graveside services—every one of them ended with the magic words, "You may retire at your leisure." Only a licensed director got to say those words, and I longed for the day when I would pronounce that final benediction.

While I was at the cemetery, Ray was embalming. Carl helped with removals. I worked evening visitations that lasted till nine. We often registered a couple hundred at visitation. We ran out of repose rooms, and opened the chapel for large visitations. After locking up at nine, then making love with Natalie, I'd fall asleep, only to jump out of bed to the emergency headache noise of the gigantic bells— the bells that Natalie never heard in her officially diagnosed state of "deep delta sleep, often prone to spontaneous manifestation." Then there was police rotation.

Ray said police rotation fell into two categories: weird shit, and weird shit. The weirdest was a man who committed suicide by locking himself in the deep freeze with a bottle of gin. He had wrapped himself in a blanket (presumably to slow down the chill factor, according to Dr. Kendall). The suicide note, taped to the freezer read, "Do not open this freezer. Call Morton-Albright." We thawed him on the embalming table for three days, until his blood melted. The other weirdest case involved a man and an airboat propeller. Ray had to order more body bags.

When Jeff and Randy moved out of Morton-Albright, Natalie moved in. At first, we blamed it on Natalie's sleep disorder when the men caught Natalie at the breakfast table. For a while, she always came to breakfast fully dressed. Before long, she was wearing pajamas and the maroon robe. She became fascinated with my dad's old Victrola and his record collection, which I had set up in the living room. I only knew that the music was mostly pretty and happy. Natalie knew that Django Reinhart had been born in a gypsy caravan, and I realized that Margee had left me a key to the identity of my father—his record collection.

There wasn't one sad song in the whole collection—sixty-three 78 rpm black lacquer records, which would break into pieces if you dropped one. I liked cranking the machine. Natalie and Jerry picked the songs, all from the '30s and '40s. Every morning, a new song sang a different memory in my head. It was the key to my remembering. Margee had taken away the pictures. She had forgotten the music— but then I realized how she had insisted that I keep the family treasure. She *knew* the music would make me remember, and she knew the music was happy. I *had* owned a tricycle—red and white, with fringe hanging out of the handgrips and a bell that my father said he needed to fix.

After he fixed it, the bell didn't ring anymore. When the bell rang, you couldn't hear the music. I remembered Margee telling me that Dad had taken the Victrola in trade for a wiring job. There was goodness in that. My father was a good and happy man. My mother was pretty, in the plain Cracker way.

Margee had told me about my mother's excitement when Dad brought the Victrola home. After Mom and Dad died, Margee never cranked the Victrola again, but when she spoke about my parents, it was always about the Victrola: my childhood had been a happy one.

Sometimes I would go into the bathroom and cry, remembering happiness. If we were happy, it meant we had love. I'd had a happy childhood, full of love. Why had Margee refused to let me remember for so many years, before finally giving me the Victrola? Regardless of her motives, I was remembering, and the memories were happy ones. But the memories were mingling with all of the strangeness of my new home, not to mention the chronic sleep-deprivation—the result of endless hours of lovemaking with Natalie, followed by endless hours of work. With Jeff and Randy gone, I zombied through the summer, neither fully awake nor asleep. I never would have made it without help—Natalie's help.

Within the first few weeks of summer, Natalie began accompanying me on night removals, on the nights when the phone bells could actually awaken her from the coma she knew as sleep. In the beginning, she waited in the removal car while I took care of business inside the place of death, but Natalie eventually talked me into sneaking her into Methodist Hospital. "For chrissake, Casey—here I am, deathy as hell, and I've never even seen a morgue," she'd said, and there was nothing that brought me more pleasure than watching Natalie get her way—like a kid with a new toy. At the hospital, I made her promise to stand still, keep quiet, and keep her hands in her pockets. She said nothing, but crossed her heart, and worked her most sincere look onto her face. Once inside, Natalie put her hands on everything in the morgue. She searched through cabinets and played with the autopsy instruments. She *was* quiet about one thing—lying down on the autopsy table. Scared the hell out of me when I turned around and saw her, lying there with that death look of hers. I whispered rebukes, but Natalie ignored me and kept probing.

At Morton-Albright, I performed all of the night embalming. Florida law required me to embalm under the direct supervision of a licensed man. Ray made up his own law: "Call me if you get into trouble." I was doing a good job. They trusted me.

After night removals, I let Natalie accompany me to the embalming room. She just wanted to watch—she promised. Then came the night she asked me to let her flip the switch on the embalming machine. I told her it was against the law, she wasn't a licensed apprentice. "I've got my own embalming machine at home," she said. "I know how to flip the goddamn switch." She did own an embalming machine. I let her flip the switch. Next time, she wanted to fill the embalming machine with water. She said, "It's just water. There aren't any laws against water. Four gallons. I'll get the fluid—bottle and a half of Perfecta 21 for a normal case like this one, if I'm not mistaken." She gave me the fluid and I poured it into the water. Next case, Natalie poured the chemical. She used each new case to take herself one step further into the embalming process: she washed the hair, closed the mouth, implanted eye caps, until she considered setting the features a single procedure. Finally, she asked for the scalpel.

"No." I said.

"If I screw up, I'll never ask again," she said, snapping on a pair of gloves. "I promise."

I tried to ignore the pleading look in her eyes, but Natalie had spent her entire life perfecting that look. I slapped the scalpel into her hand. Natalie made the embalming incision just above the clavicle as deftly as any man at Morton-Albright. When she looked up at me from the incision, a tear ran down her cheek. She wiped it away with her sleeve, and said, "Now look what you made me do, deathman," like her crying was my fault. When she thanked me, and hugged me tight, a single, astonishing realization entered my head: Natalie had the gift. The Presence swirled into the embalming room.

By the middle of the summer, Natalie had raised vessels, performed multipoint injections, operated the drain tube, worked on her baseball stitch. The night she plunged the spearpoint of the trocar into the heart of Edgar Holliday, I watched her face for squeamishness. Instead she giggled, and said, "Now, *this* is deathy." I thought of Jerry, at peace in his night's rest, while I was teaching his daughter to embalm the dead.

The men of Morton-Albright complimented me on Natalie's work—how incredibly serene the bodies looked, and the presence they affected. I passed the compliments along to Natalie. Our working together meant less time in the embalming room, and more time in bed, but the more time we spent in bed, the more I worried: we'd made love a hundred times, and Natalie wasn't pregnant. We were fulfilling our own desires, but we were not fulfilling the requirement of John Morton's will—an heir to the family business. I considered discussing it with Natalie, but I worried that doing so would quash her passion for me—I didn't want to turn her passion into a job. Besides, Colton Albright's health was improving, and Natalie and I were doing our best.

While Natalie and I were doing our best, JFT was busy acquiring Fairview Cemetery. Kip retired. Henry's ass stayed on the backhoe. He remained friendly with us, until Ray brought up JFT. Henry cranked the backhoe, pretended he couldn't hear a thing, then drove away.

14

"Beepers," Jerry said, scattering Motorolas onto the kitchen table. "You clip them onto your pants, over your belt."

Nowadays, every teenager in Angel Shores wears a beeper. Back in '73, you needed a reason. Jerry's reason: our busy summer—forty-six cases in July—a new record. Jerry said the beepers would give us more time off. "Especially Casey," he said. "We take turns forwarding the phone lines to our own homes. That way, Casey can leave the funeral home at night. I'm also taking him off evening visitation, except when we really need him. He's doing a great job, and I don't want to wear him out, so the rest of us will take turns working the smaller visitations. If you get a death call at night, beep Casey." Jerry passed the beepers around, each with our own code number.

"Where's mine?" Natalie asked.

"You don't work here, sugar."

"Yeah, but I want one. They're cool."

"You're with Casey all the time. You two can share." Jerry then explained the beeping process. At his command, Ray punched numbers into the telephone. My beeper sounded. Jerry showed me how to stop the beeping. Four numbers appeared on the little screen: 7734. "It works," I said. Ray came over to look. "Damn right, it works. Read the number upside-down." The numbers read "hell." Jerry said, "Now watch this." He flipped a switch on the top of the beeper, handed the thing to Natalie, then told Ray to dial again. A buzzing sound came from the beeper. Natalie squealed, juggled the thing in her hands, then dropped it onto the table, where it convulsed like a dying insect.

"Vibrator," Jerry said. "You can go to the movies, watch TV— whatever you like, without disturbing anyone."

Natalie said, "Hmm—a vibrating thing that hangs off your pants. No woman invented this thing. Some *man* thought it up." Natalie turned the beeper over in her hand, inspecting it. "Still, it's a deathy thing," she said. "Every time we hear that beep, it's announcing the death of a human being." She stood up and held the thing over her head, like the Statue of Liberty's torch. "And therefore, never send to know for whom the beeper beeps. It beeps for thee."

None of us men got the John Donne reference. Natalie spent half an hour explaining it to me later.

Jerry called me into the living room while everyone played with the new toys. He said, "It's Natalie I'm worried about. That's another reason for the beepers. She's spending too much time in the mortuary. I don't want her getting any ideas. I want you two to get the hell out of here. Go walk on the beach together. Take in a movie. Go out on a real date."

Shit. That's what I realized I was deep in, when I saw the look of concern on Jerry's face. Natalie had a lot more than ideas—she had the gift. I wondered how long we'd be able to contain *that* secret. I said okay to Jerry, then headed for the kitchen, where I snatched up the phone on the first ring. A woman sobbed into my ear. She uttered a single word: Carl.

"Carl Midkiff," he said into the phone. He turned toward the rest of us, rolling his eyes and making the koo-koo sign, twirling his finger at his temple. We all stopped talking and listened to Carl. He yelled into the telephone, "You did what? Tampa airport? Are you out of your fucking mind? I *know* the baby's crying. I can hear her. What did Mom and Dad say? Hell, no—you can't stay with Suzy and me. Because we live in a one-bedroom apartment, that's why. Uncle Jerry? He's right here. Ask him yourself."

"Veronica." Carl announced.

Natalie folded her arms on the table to cushion her head, as she let it drop. "Shit fuck piss," she mumbled at the tabletop. We heard little of Jerry's conversation with Veronica, only his soothing tone. Natalie sat up when I nudged her. She said, "Veronica is Carl's sister—my cousin. She's my age. You'll hate her."

Jerry hung up the phone. He spoke to Carl, "You come with me to the airport. Veronica and Gretchen can stay at my home until she straightens things out with her husband. We've got plenty of room."

"The hell we do," Natalie said. "She's got a baby. Where are you going to put them?"

"Guest room."

"Across the hall from my apartment? Can't we pay for a motel? She's got a baby. It'll cry. It'll stink. You know how I am about smells."

Jerry assured Natalie that Veronica would only stay a few days. She'd patch up things with her husband, then go home. "Besides," Jerry said, "you haven't been around the house much lately."

"It doesn't matter. I'll know there's a smell in the house. How long will it take for the smell to go away after they leave?"

"You've got to come home tonight," Jerry said. He reminded Natalie of his Rotary dinner. "You promised to take pictures of your mother and me before the dinner, in my study. It won't take long—fifteen minutes—then you'll come with us at the country club."

"I'll show," Natalie said. "Could you please lock them up somewhere, before I come home?"

Jerry pointed a finger at Natalie and opened his mouth to speak. Carl grabbed Jerry's arm, and said, "We'd better get to the airport. Veronica's half out of her mind."

. . .

Since Natalie was going to Jerry's dinner, I had no excuse to keep me from working the evening calling hours with Lex Talbert. I had been procrastinating a confrontation with him anyway. This time, it was I who invited him into Jerry's office for a talk. Lex said, "I hope you've changed your mind about working for JFT. Lewis Stark wants to meet you."

"I don't want to meet Lewis Stark, and I will never work for JFT. I know what you're doing. John Morton's second will is pointless. Lewis Stark will threaten Jerry and Ray with this Waldo Shipper thing. It's how they got Jesup to sell out—they found a secret."

"You misjudge me, young man," Lex said. "I promised my silence in exchange for yours. Lewis Stark doesn't know about Waldo Shipper, and neither does Jewell Albright. Things will stay that way, as long as you keep quiet. You may not agree with me, but I am a man of my word."

I was about to tell Lex that I didn't believe his story about Ray burying a man in the woods. The telephone stopped me: Natalie. She was in trouble. Big trouble. She needed me right away. From the hysteria in her voice, I believed her. I called Ray and asked him to cover the visitation.

"Work with Lex Talbert? You *are* shitting me, aren't you, killer? I'm in my underwear. The Braves are on."

"Natalie's in trouble," I said.

"That's how we want her—in trouble—the pregnancy kind of trouble." Ray agreed to work the visitation if I agreed to try and get Natalie into trouble after getting her out of it.

Natalie answered the door, radiating tension. Upstairs, Veronica's baby screamed. Gretchen. Natalie said, "Do you hear that? It's driving me crazy!" She paced the living room with her hands over her ears.

"Where's your cousin," I asked.

"Veronica? Who the fuck knows? Bitch."

Veronica had needed baby stuff from the store. She had taken Cynthia's car. When Natalie arrived to take the pictures, Veronica had not yet returned from her errand.

"I begged them not to leave me with the baby. I wanted to ask Mother to stay, but I didn't want to ruin Daddy's big night—the community service award is Rotary's greatest honor. Daddy deserves it. Mother expected Veronica home any minute. All I had to do was *be* here. As soon as they pulled out of the driveway, the kid started screaming. That's when I called you. I didn't know what to do."

"Why is the baby crying?"

"How the hell should I know? I don't know what makes babies cry. I don't *like* babies. They're gross."

"You didn't check on her?"

"Go into the room with the screaming kid? That's why I called *you*."

Until this moment, I had always assumed that all females had some kind of baby instincts built right into them. Apparently, I had been wrong. Natalie expected me to take charge of the situation, so I did. I told Natalie to calm herself. Whatever was wrong with Gretchen was probably normal baby stuff. We just needed to go upstairs and look at the kid.

"Okay," Natalie agreed, "but you go first."

In a crib in the guest room, baby Gretchen lay on her back, eyes shut tight, fists balled, legs kicking, screaming like she had a nail in her back. Natalie stayed behind my back, peering over my shoulder at the baby.

"She probably wants her mommy," I said. "Pick her up and hold her. That might work."

"Pick her up? Look at her. She's evil. *You* pick her up."

"I've never picked up a baby in my life, I might hurt her."

"Yeah? Well, I might *kill* the little snot."

"Jeez, Natalie, you're the *girl*—you know, maternal instinct and all that? Maybe it'll kick in if you hold her. I'll take her if you can't handle it." I backed away from the crib and placed Natalie between me and screaming Gretchen. Natalie gave me a look, then bent down and picked up the convulsing infant. She held the baby away from her, at arm's length. The kid screamed louder.

"Not like that," I said. "Hold her close, like a mommy."

Natalie brought the baby in closer to herself, almost to her breast. Her eyes bugged wide open, then came the scream—not from the baby, from Natalie. I had never heard anyone scream like that, so loud and high-pitched, it rattled the window. I couldn't even hear the baby crying anymore. Natalie stopped screaming only long enough to take a breath, then shrieked out a new one. This time, Natalie worked her screaming into words: "It stinks! It stinks! Take it, Casey! Take it now!" Natalie flipped the baby around; Gretchen's screams now aimed at my face, vibrating my eyeballs. I took the baby in my arms and held her close while Natalie ran to throw up. The kid had a load, all right—a bad one, worse than anything you'd ever smell in an embalming room.

With Natalie disabled, I was stuck with changing the kid's diaper. I spied a pile of cloth diapers on a chair next to the crib. A container of baby powder rested on top of them. I started to lay Gretchen back down in the crib, to change her, but I was prevented by a big splotch of yellow-brown goop, presumably the same stuff that now filled her diaper. Holding the screeching infant in one arm, I snatched a diaper and the powder with my free hand. I took Gretchen across the hall, into Natalie's apartment, where I placed the baby on Natalie's Oriental rug. The baby kept screaming and stinking. Natalie kept throwing up. Between the noises and the stench, I began feeling woozy myself.

Natalie wobbled out of the bathroom, her face dripping with water. "Oh, Jesus, not in my apartment," she pleaded, until I explained the goop in the crib. Natalie fled the room. She returned with a stack of newspapers. She spread them out thick in a five-foot square. "Put her on these," she said. I put Gretchen on the newspapers, unhooked the safety pins and spread the flaps of cloth away from the baby, revealing the mass in her diaper. Natalie sighed, "Oh, God. Baby shit." She heaved twice, but kept her place behind me. The mess was a mixture of solid and liquid stink. I slid the diaper from underneath the baby. I wadded up the thing and set it aside. The kid was still screaming, so I had to yell, "We've got to clean her."

"I'll get the toilet paper," Natalie yelled back. I sent her a look. Natalie shrugged. "That's what everyone else uses."

"We need something wet," I said. "It's all kind of stuck to her."

"I've got Fantastik under the sink. We can spray her."

"You can't spray a kid with Fantastik. Get a damp cloth. Make it warm—not too hot."

Within a few minutes, little Gretchen lay clean, powdered, and rediapered, but the kid kept on screaming, like someone had slapped the shit out of her.

"Great job, Daddy," Natalie said. "*Now* what do we do?"

"Is there a bottle somewhere?"

Natalie found the bottle in the crib. She brought it to me, full of brown, bubbly liquid. I looked at the bottle, then at Natalie. "Dr. Pepper," she said. "I don't drink milk. It comes out of cow nipples."

"Try water."

I sat down on the sofa holding Gretchen in my lap. Natalie brought the water. I stuck the bottle into the baby's mouth. She stopped crying and started sucking, then fell asleep. I asked Natalie where we could lay her down.

"Back on the newspapers," she said.

I told her the baby needed to feel cozy, but we couldn't put her back in the crib, because of the goop. The sofa was no good either, the baby might roll off onto the floor. "Let's put her in the Marcellas," I said.

"My bed? Are you crazy?"

"Line it with newspaper. Cover the newspaper with a blanket. The kid can't fall out of a casket, and she's already done her business."

We stood over the baby, now asleep in the casket. Natalie put her arm around my waist and pulled me close. She sighed, "Gretchen does look peaceful, lying there." She closed the casket lid and walked away.

"Jeez, Natalie, you can't do that."

"Just kidding," she said, reopening the lid.

Natalie and I sighed ourselves onto the sofa. For the very first time, my beeper went off. Morton-Albright's number appeared on the little screen. "Ray," I said. "He's pissed I'm taking so long."

On the phone, Ray sounded conciliatory. He knew things could get complicated with Natalie. "We've got a death call, killer. You've got the removal car. I'll finish visitation with Lex. He's a weird one. The son of a bitch knows I hate him, and he's been nice to me all night. Too nice. Something's up, killer, and it ain't good." As I jotted down the death call information, I heard a car pull into the driveway, followed by a thud against the house. Natalie ran to the window. "It's her. It's the bitch. Tell Ray to bring his shotgun. There's a pig in the driveway."

From all that Natalie had told me of Veronica, I expected to see a sloppy, unattractive woman, lacking intelligence, and prone to hysterics. When Veronica wobbled into Natalie's apartment, whining, reeking of beer, I could see that Natalie had been right.

"Where's my baby?" Veronica demanded, her voice slurred.

"Shhh," Natalie whispered through a finger at her lips. "The baby's sleeping."

Veronica hiccupped, then belched. "Where is Gretchen sleeping? She's not in her crib."

Natalie led Veronica to the casket. Veronica smiled. Gretchen appeared content, lost in some baby dream. Veronica then eyed the Marcellas. Trembling, she drew a deep breath, then screamed it out at such a frightened pitch, not only did it wake the baby but the cops dropped by, later on, to make sure everything was okay. Veronica and Gretchen now screamed at the same time, competing for volume. Natalie reared back her hand and slapped Veronica's face. "Now look what you've done," Natalie said. "You woke the fucking baby."

Veronica's face settled into distant shock as she picked up
Gretchen and stole out of the room. She kept saying, "My baby, my
poor baby. What have they done to you?" As if lying in the casket had
caused Gretchen some irreversible trauma. Hell, the kid didn't even
know what a casket *was*. Natalie took me by the crook of my arm. I
asked her if I could give her a ride to her father's dinner.

"Why would I go there? We've got a removal to make."

Together, we removed the body of Marshal Bender, then embalmed
him at the funeral home. A sweet night for both of us, we fawned
over each other, cheerful and affectionate, until we undressed for
lovemaking. I lay naked in bed, and Natalie was moving in close. My
desire for sex fled from me. All I could think about was Natalie and
Veronica's baby. I admired Natalie's loyalty to her family. The family
needed an heir, and Natalie was willing to give them one. The problem was simple: Natalie hated babies—they grossed her out to the
point of retching. She'd make a great funeral director, but a horrid
mother. Nerves overtook me. I could no longer risk pregnancy with
Natalie, and I had to tell her that she was not fit for motherhood. I
got out of bed and into my pajamas. Natalie asked me why I was getting dressed.

"I can't talk serious when I'm naked. We have to talk serious."

Natalie cleared her throat and nodded.

I said, "Natalie, I can't have a baby with you. I'm crazy about you,
but I can't get you pregnant—not after tonight with Gretchen."

"You're right, Casey. You can't get me pregnant." Natalie got out of
bed and slipped into one of my shirts. She opened her purse and
withdrew a circle of plastic. She gave it to me, and told me to open it.
Inside lay a circle of pills, each under a clear plastic blister. I said,
"This is some kind of medication. Are you sick? Is that why you can't
get pregnant?"

"I'm not sick. *You* are. It's the Pill."

"Birth control?"

"Jesus, Casey. Could you imagine me with a baby?"

"So all this sex hasn't been a race against Colton Albright's death to produce an heir to rescue the funeral home from the possibility of Cruel Jewell selling the place to Jacob Funeral Trust?"

Natalie looked at me as if I had lost my mind.

"Have you lost your mind?" She asked.

"Then why are we—?"

"Tearing each other's clothes off every time we're alone? Making love all night until the alarm goes off? Spending every morning in the shower together? I know damn well why I'm doing these things with you. Why are you doing them with me? Here's your big chance, death-man. You say it first, unless you're chickenshit."

"I'll say it. Just give me a minute."

She sang, "Casey's a chickenshit" to the tune of "Ring Around the Rosy."

"Okay, okay. I love you, Natalie."

"I love you too, Casey Kight."

We kissed long, sealing the words we had spoken. After the kiss, a look of puzzlement crossed Natalie's face. "Where in the hell did you get this heir-producing idea, ya goofball?"

"Ray," I said. I explained the other clues as well: John Morton's original will, Colton's health, Jerry's encouragement, Natalie's own sex drive. I left out my discussion with Lex Talbert. He had suspected the same. I told Natalie what Ray had said to me on my very first day—that Jerry had hired me for Natalie, to impregnate her with an heir to the business. All the other stuff seemed to support Ray's idea.

"Sad about Ray," Natalie said. "Don't hate him for it. Nobody demanded that Ray produce an heir, just a quiet hope. When you came along, Ray made you the heir to his own anxieties. Let them go, Casey. I'm not having a baby, not even for this place I love so much. Ray was right about one thing—Daddy did hire you for me. Not for an heir. Just for me."

"So Morton-Albright is doomed, and everybody knows it?"

"We still hope Grandma Jewell will sell to Daddy and Ray."

I knew that sale would never take place. I yearned to tell Natalie of the second will, but if we found it, Ray would make the papers for Waldo Shipper, as Lex had promised.

Natalie said, "My hope does not rest with Jewell Albright. It rests with John Morton, who is *not* at rest—not yet, anyway. Don't you see why he's hanging around? He still owns the funeral home, for godssake."

"I didn't believe in ghosts when I came here, and I'm trying like hell not to believe in them now—but if they do exist, I certainly wouldn't want to piss one off, even if it *is* John Morton. What if we lose Morton-Albright? This deathy-as-hell-John-Morton-Presence thing is going to be pissed."

"We won't lose this place, Casey. Don't you understand? John Morton didn't build this place because of some freakish desire to spend all his time with the dead. Okay, he *did* have the freakish desire, but more than anything, he was brave enough to comfort people on the worst day of their lives. He softened the blow of death, through his work, and through his way with people. That's why everybody loved him so much. When people saw him, they thought, *That's the man who comforted me when my mother died.* This whole place is built on love, and it's stronger than the hatred of a thousand Cruel Jewells. You can see it in people's faces when they leave this place. Everybody dies, but our families leave here knowing that love goes on forever. It's such a deathy thing. And what about you, Casey Kight? How did you feel on the day of your mom and dad's funeral? You don't have to answer. I already know. I know, because you came back. You came back to feel the comfort, didn't you?"

"The heart of the wise is in the house of mourning," I said. "I came here for wisdom. I came to remember my childhood before my parents died. I remember only the happy things, in the music we play on the Victrola. If my childhood was so happy, why have I blocked it out? It can only mean one thing: somewhere inside me, there is one horrible memory, waiting to be remembered. The comfort is here, but my memories are incomplete. Maybe I'm too far gone to remember."

Natalie put her arms around me and pulled me close. She kissed my cheek, then whispered in my ear, "You're not gone. You're distracted."

I was distracted, all right—distracted by all that was going on around me. I had been pulled into a *storm* of distraction: the work of my apprenticeship, John Morton's will, Waldo Shipper, Lex Talbert, my experiences with the Presence, and Natalie herself. I was never alone. I was always preoccupied, as though the old place itself made sure of it, protecting me, preventing me. It knew. I wasn't ready to remember.

15

September twelfth: Natalie's birthday. We celebrated the occasion under her command. Natalie hated surprises, unable to bear suspense. She passed out notes to each of us with a precise description of her desired present. From her father, Natalie asked for a Steinman spy camera, the one with the stainless steel finish, not the black one. Although she knew all of her gifts, she insisted that each present be wrapped, in the paper of her own choosing, which she herself supplied. From me, she asked but one thing: a picture of me reposed in the Millennium. She took the picture two days before her birthday, developed it herself, framed it, then gave me a square of silver paper for wrapping. No party, no birthday cake—just presents. When someone gave her a present, Natalie gave the giver a thank-you note, describing the present she had asked for, and how much she enjoyed receiving it. My note said, "Thank you for the wonderful picture of yourself. I shall treasure it always. How very thoughtful of you to remember my birthday. Yours, Natalie."

A week later, Natalie enrolled in a single graduate-level photography course. She had refused to enter the master's program. "They don't offer a Master of Suspense degree," she'd said, but she needed a photography class to retain access to the USF darkroom, and Jerry wanted her out of the funeral home as much as possible, especially during the day, because of her sleep disorder. He didn't want Natalie sleepwalking, possibly without clothing, into a funeral service. My own classes at Taylor were held in the afternoon, so Natalie had no excuse to enter the funeral home until after dinner—Jerry's orders. My hours with Natalie were now limited to evenings and weekends.

By the time I matriculated at Taylor, I had embalmed over a hundred cases. We were still busy. With me working part-time, we'd need a new apprentice soon. I worried about giving up John Morton's bedroom to some new guy.

The Taylor School accepted me the moment Jerry introduced me to Dr. Claude Taylor Singer, president of the institution—a lean, middle-aged gentleman with sunken cheeks and temples. "Good embalmer?" Dr. Singer asked Jerry of me.

"Ray Winstead taught him," Jerry answered.

Singer nodded, stood up, and extended his hand to me. "Welcome to the Taylor School of Mortuary Science, Mr. Kight. Why don't you walk around the campus and have yourself a look. I have business with Mr. Stiles."

The campus was small but adorned with lovely buildings that looked like funeral homes of different shapes and sizes. The smallness of the campus accounted for the staggered sessions—juniors, like me, attended classes in the mornings, seniors in the afternoons. Ray had already warned me that I wouldn't learn much embalming in mortuary school—it took two years to prepare for your State Board examination, and Taylor held a nearly perfect record of graduates passing their Boards on the first attempt.

• • •

"You've got a new roommate, Casey," Jerry told me in the car. "Daniel Coggin. He's a senior. JFT bought his host funeral home, and he feels uncomfortable with the situation. Family problems back home, too. I told Singer we'd take the young man on with us. We've had a long relationship with Taylor, so we owe them this courtesy. Natalie should spend more time at home now, until we see what this new fellow is like."

The day before school began, Natalie moved back home, grudgingly. She claimed there was still a smell in the house, left there by Veronica and her baby. I told Natalie she had done right by moving back home—it didn't take me long to realize that Daniel Coggin was unstable. Ray just said, "That boy ain't right." Daniel told me right away that his name was Daniel—not Dan, not Danny—Daniel. Daniel's father owned Coggin Funeral Home in Fort Myers. "For the time being, he owns it," Daniel said.

Daniel's constant frown reminded me of Lex. Late at night, I'd hear Daniel screaming into the telephone at his father. The walls that separated us muted Daniel's tirades, but I heard the words he emphasized, like "drinking" and "gambling" and "Jacob Funeral Trust" and "Don't be such a fucking asshole, Dad."

I tried to converse with Daniel whenever I found him in the living room. He answered me with grunts and nods. I felt sorry for him, but his aloofness pissed me off. Hell, I was just trying to be nice to the guy. One night, when I was particularly annoyed with his mood, I thought I'd try getting him into the Morton-Albright spirit. We had our own problems, but working in the Presence kept us happy employees. I found Daniel in the living room, and expressed my concern for him. I said, "It must have been tough working for JFT." Darkness rolled across Daniel's face. He said, "You people think you're untouchable here. You're not. They're coming for you. One day you'll wake up and find yourself working at JFT Central—it's their centralized embalming facility. They sent me there, the fucking bastards—they sent me to Central. I'm just a fucking mortuary student. Nobody works at Central but real JFT."

I tried to cheer him, "But that's all over now. You're working with us. Then you'll go back home. You'll never need to worry about JFT again."

"You don't understand, dipshit. I may not have a home when I go back. JFT is working my father hard. They're working him to sell out. My dad was the most respected man in Fort Myers. He's not perfect, and JFT is using that against him. When I found out about it, I went to Lewis Stark himself. He said, 'Face it, Coggin, your old man fucked up, and so did you, by coming here. Report tomorrow to Central Embalming.' You'll end up there too, with the animals. That's what you become at Central—an animal. It's not human, the way they act there. Get the picture, fuckface?"

I didn't get the picture at all, not until a week later, on Friday, when Taylor canceled their afternoon classes. They had called Morton-Albright to tell me. Two hours later, Daniel stomped into the apartment. His face and shirt were covered with chunks of muscle tissue embedded in slime. He smelled like formaldehyde. I kept my eye on him. He flung open the door to his bedroom and began throwing his things into a suitcase. I followed in behind him, watching. He turned around and looked at me, slime dripping from his face. He said, "My father sold our place to JFT. I'm a fucking ghost, man. I'm outta here for good."

"Where are you going?"

"Valhalla."

Short on Viking history, I had no idea that Valhalla meant heaven (Natalie told me later). I was short on Florida geography too, but Valhalla seemed a likely name for a Florida community—Osceola, Palatka, Tallahassee, Valhalla.

Daniel's lack of concern for his personal appearance made me suspect his rationality. I figured it best not to fool with the guy—just let him pack up and leave. "Good luck in Valhalla," I said.

"I'll leave through the garage," Daniel said, rushing past me with a shirtsleeve hanging out of his suitcase. "I left a box out there."

Jesus, but was I glad to see him go. Natalie could move back in with me now. I missed her, and with an unexpected day off from school, I could get back into the embalming room and help Ray with his backlog of cases. As I walked down the hallway to the embalming room, I heard the rumble of the garage door as it opened. Daniel was gone.

"You're late for school," Ray said, hovering over a new case.

"They canceled classes."

"Good. Get yourself into an apron. We've got more bodies here than Vincent Price had in *The House of Wax*."

I slipped into an apron, and told Ray, "Daniel left just now—for good, I think."

"For Chattahoochee, I hope," said Ray. "That boy ain't right."

"He left for Valhalla."

"I don't believe I ever heard of a Valhalla," Ray said. "Kid said he was from Fort Myers. Maybe it's one of those small towns down that way. He's probably got kin in Valhalla. Daniel left through the bat cave?"

"Yeah."

"I heard the garage door open. It never closed. Dumbass left it open. Go hit the remote in the removal car."

I slid into the removal car's front seat. When I pressed the remote button, I killed Daniel Coggin. That's how the cops figured it, anyway.

Using the garage door, Daniel had devised an electronic gallows for self-execution. He raised the door, then threw the knotted end of a nylon rope around the hook that connected the garage door with its mechanical opener. A horizontal beam ran the width of the garage. The beam stopped the rope from following the track of the closing door—it made the rope rise vertically when the garage door closed—simple, but ingenious. Daniel then fashioned a noose for his neck. The scuffmarks left by Daniel's shoes on the floor of the garage indicated two possible struggles: Either Daniel had not allowed himself enough slack to reach the button, or, he had changed his mind when I hit the remote.

After pressing the remote in the removal car, I went back to the embalming room. Ray pulled the trocar out of the body on the table and hung the implement on the wall. "This one's done," he said. "Help me get her onto the dressing table. We've got a removal at Mercy—big fella, and those bastards in the morgue always go to extra trouble to put the big guys in the top drawer. They think it's real funny."

Ray drove down the bat cave ramp. I pressed the remote to open the garage door. The hanging body of Daniel Coggin lowered into view. Ray slammed hard on the brakes. We hit Daniel with the removal car—not hard, just sort of bumped him with the grille, but the car kept creeping forward. Daniel's body, facedown on the hood of the car, slid toward us. When the removal car finally stopped, Daniel's face was smushed into the windshield, his features distorted by the sliding. Like the unfortunate Mr. Cooley, Daniel had pinned a note to his shirt, legible through the windshield: "Sold to JFT." I looked at Ray, his face still frozen in slamming-on-the-brakes position, arms braced for the collision that had already occurred. I touched his shoulder. Ray jerked then relaxed. "Fuck me and call me Agnes," he said, "I've gone and pissed myself."

We ran up the bat cave for Jerry. I heard Ray panting behind me. I burst into Jerry's office. He started when he got a look at me, breathing like a racehorse. He spoke into the phone, "Thanks for the call, Dr. Singer. We'll keep an eye out for Daniel."

I waited until Jerry placed the receiver into its cradle, then told him the news: "Daniel's dead," I said, panting. "Hanged himself in the garage."

Jerry bolted out of his chair and followed me out the door. On the carpet in the middle of the lobby we found Ray, lying on his back, clutching his chest.

"Call an ambulance!" Jerry shouted.

I summoned the ambulance. Meredith ran out of his office and tended to Ray. Jerry called Dr. Kendall for Daniel Coggin. He called Cynthia too. She entered the lobby out of breath, having just dodged the traffic as she ran, Bernard-like, across Druid Road.

"Denise will meet us at the hospital," Cynthia panted. "Natalie's on her way, too." Cynthia rode to the hospital in the ambulance. With Ray out of the building, Jerry took my arm and led me to the garage. He said, "The police were already on their way to pick up Daniel. He went berserk at Taylor this afternoon."

Detective Jones and two uniformed officers met us in the parking lot. Jones told us about Daniel. "He made a mess of the school." Daniel had entered the school auditorium, armed with two boxes of dissection materials and a baseball bat. Daniel then mounted the stage, where he would have received his diploma the following spring. From the boxes of dissection materials, Daniel tossed cow hearts into the air, then whacked them with the bat. They splattered all over the back wall of the auditorium, and all over Daniel as well. After the cow hearts, Daniel started in on a box of sheep fetuses. Screaming about JFT the whole time, Daniel had drawn a crowd of seniors. A few of the braver ones tackled him, but Daniel had gotten away. Singer called the Hillsborough County Sheriff, then Jerry.

"Hillsborough called us," Jones said. "Asked us to come pick up the kid."

Jerry told the three men, "Daniel Coggin is dead. Kendall is on his way." As Jerry spoke the words, Kendall pulled into the parking lot. The medical examiner had brought the police photographer with him. All of us went to the garage, where Daniel still lay upon the removal car's windshield. The photographer snapped his first picture. One of the cops cut the rope and turned Daniel faceup on the hood of the car. I admitted pressing the remote button. Kendall summed up the case: "Tough call, here," he said. "The young man clearly intended suicide from the outset, but may have changed his mind—the scuff marks indicate a struggle—he may have tried to free himself after Casey pressed the button. That would make this an accident. The note doesn't say, 'I'm killing myself for such and such a reason,' however 'Sold to JFT' is telling, nonetheless." Kendall said he'd call the family himself and explain the situation. Most families wouldn't want the word *suicide* on the death certificate—neither would Morton-Albright—a suicide on the premises would make the front page. "On the other hand, ruling this an accident exposes your funeral home to a lawsuit from the Coggin family. I'm sure you don't want that either."

Jerry placed his hand on Dr. Kendall's shoulder. "Let me call Mr. Coggin," Jerry said. "We're both funeral men. I'm more worried about who's on police rotation. If it's a JFT firm, they'll cause trouble for us—maybe call the papers themselves."

"Marston's is on call," Jones said. "They're JFT."

I blurted out an idea, "Maybe JFT *won't* call the papers, especially when they see the suicide note pinned to Daniel's shirt. It looks worse for JFT than for Morton-Albright. We could threaten to go to the papers ourselves, with a picture of the body and the note. Besides, Daniel Coggin's own father sold out to JFT, yesterday afternoon."

Our enemies arrived in a black Buick station wagon. The two men seemed amused with our predicament, until they saw the note. Jones nudged the photographer, who snapped a picture of the JFT men looking at the note. Jones placed the note in a baggie. "Evidence," Jones said, two inches from the JFT man's face.

"You boys can notify the decedent's father too," Jerry said. "Mr. Coggin is a JFT man."

Someone at Jacob Funeral Trust held more power over the press than Colton Albright. Not a word of the Coggin death appeared in any of the papers; not a word from the family either, not until we heard that Daniel's father put a bullet in his own brain.

At the hospital, we learned Ray's diagnosis: panic attack, caused by fright. We all snickered at Ray, who scanned our faces as we stood around his bedside in the emergency room. "Y'all go ahead and laugh," Ray said, groggy with drugs. "Hardee-fucking-har-har. Y'all

202 • Miles Keaton Andrew

would have pissed your britches too, if you'd seen that Coggin kid's face on the windshield."

"Casey didn't piss himself," Denise said, shooting me a wink.

"Killers like Casey don't scare. They stalk the earth without fear."

Natalie came back to the funeral home that night with a full suitcase. She made me tell her over and over again about Daniel Coggin whacking dissection materials in the auditorium. "Poor Daniel," she said. "He died with a broken heart, all over his face."

After lovemaking with Natalie, I sat on the edge of John Morton's bed, counting the teeth marks on my skin, pondering Morton-Albright's future. Natalie asked me what I was doing. We should be snuggling, she said.

"I'm thinking."

"Well, don't hurt yourself, death-man. Thinking is dangerous."

"So is rabies, from what I hear," I said. Natalie giggled at her teeth marks.

The incident with Daniel Coggin had convinced me: the sins of Daniel's father, whatever they had been, could not compare with Ray burying Waldo Shipper in the woods. I had my doubts about the event, but my doubts weren't proof enough. I had to know for sure. But even if Ray was innocent, we still needed John Morton's second will. Our chances of finding it seemed slim to none, and slim had boarded the bus for Valhalla. The only sure way to save Morton-Albright seemed impossible: we had to stop the operation of Jacob Funeral Trust in Florida. With JFT out of the picture, Jewell would sell to the family.

I asked Natalie, "What about JFT? You said they were under investigation in three states. Is Florida one of them?"

"Not yet, but they haven't been here that long. Besides, why worry about JFT? Jewell can't sell to them. They're a corporation. She can only sell to a licensed director, under supervision of the Board. Jewell hates the funeral business. She doesn't *know* any funeral directors—just Daddy and Ray, and Meredith, of course. He's a sweet man."

"He is," I said, "but his brother isn't so sweet."

"Lex Talbert? Ohhh, shit." Natalie started getting into her clothes. "We've got to tell Daddy, right away."

"Stop it, Natalie. We can't tell your father."

"The hell we can't."

"We can't. Listen to me. There is a problem. A big problem. You told me you love me. Do you trust me?"

Natalie stopped getting dressed. She said, "I trust you. What's the big problem?"

"I can't tell you. That's why you need to trust me. I know things. I can't tell them without hurting other people. There's only one way to save Morton-Albright for all time. We've got to stop JFT. You said they might have committed improprieties. What kind of improprieties?"

"The trades don't say when it's only an allegation. It could be money, mishandling of the bodies, or both. Why? What can we do? They're too big. We're too small. Get it?"

"I get it. I also have an idea—a dangerous idea."

"You're getting scary on me, death-man."

"I know. I'm scaring myself. Trust me?"

"Completely. By the way, this wouldn't have anything to do with a dead guy named Waldo Shipper, would it?"

"You know about Waldo Shipper?"

"Of course. It's been taken care of, but I can't tell you any more without hurting other people."

"I already know about Ray," I said.

"I don't mean Ray. I mean *other* people. We're sworn to secrecy. You said you love me. Do you trust me?"

"Completely."

"Good," Natalie said. "Let's figure this out. Ray will be pissed. We need to make sure he doesn't kill Lex. One family secret is enough. Anything else I should know?"

"Yes, but if I tell you now, you'll want to run right over and tell your father."

"No, I won't. I promise."

"I don't trust you."

"You said you did."

"Okay." I told Natalie about the conversation I had heard between Lex Talbert and Cruel Jewell about John Morton's second will. When I finished, she began to cry. "I knew it," she said. "John Morton was a good man. He loved my granddaddy Colton like his own son." Natalie started yanking on her clothes again.

"Stop it, Natalie," I said. "You promised you wouldn't run home and tell your father."

"I'm not running home," she said. "I'm calling Daddy and Mother here—Ray, too. It's time we all had a talk."

I tried to reason with Natalie, but she gave me that look just before she dialed the last number. She was right to call the meeting. I shrugged, and watched the telephone dial spin back to its normal position. Natalie didn't explain the reason for the meeting, but everyone came. Given the hour of Natalie's call, they arrived at Jerry's office within moments, looking sleepy and confused. I had expected Natalie to do the explaining. Instead, she announced, "Casey's got something to tell you."

"It better be good," Ray said. "I don't lie very well when it comes to Denise. I told her Casey was in trouble in the embalming room."

I rose from my chair, thinking of how to begin. It was more like my mouth just opened and the words came out, "The day before John Morton died, he wrote a new will, leaving all of his possessions, including the funeral home, to Colton Albright."

Jerry's face fell into his hands. Cynthia's mouth dropped to her chest. Ray smacked himself in the forehead.

"Tell them the rest," Natalie said. "The bad part."

"Jewell burned the will and washed the ashes down the sink."

With a collective "Aww," they slumped in their seats.

"There's more," I said. "John made a copy for Colton—a copy Jewell has never found."

"So how in the hell are we supposed to find it, and how long have you known about this?" Ray asked.

I looked Ray right in the eye. I said, "I've known since my first week of employment. I withheld the information because of you."

"What the fuck do I have to do with this?"

"You have Waldo Shipper to do with this," I said. "Lex knows all about it. He followed you to the woods that day." I told all that Lex had seen.

"Then he didn't see everything," Ray said.

"What did he miss?" I asked. Jerry answered my question, "It's all taken care of, son, but we can't say another word about it. There are other people involved."

"I only want to know one thing," I said. "If Lex tells Lewis Stark about Waldo Shipper, can he use it as blackmail, to force us to sell—assuming we find the will."

"He can try," Jerry said, "but Ray and I have already taken care of business. That's all we can tell you, Casey. Did Jewell mention anything that might be a clue as to where John put this second will?"

I recounted the conversation as best as I could remember. I finished the story by saying John Morton's last words: "I've got it right here, in my pocket."

Natalie jumped out of her chair, shaking. "He means his inside pocket, where he used to keep the candy. He owned about fifty suits. I kept every single one of them, upstairs in the attic. Let's go!"

Jerry forwarded the phone lines to his home. We locked the doors behind us and ran for our cars. For the first time in history, Morton-Albright stood empty of all persons, living or dead.

We dragged nine trunks of John Morton's things from the attic into Natalie's apartment. Four trunks contained personal items—cuff links, pipe lighters, fountain pens, straight razors—anything Natalie believed John Morton had touched. Five of the trunks contained the suits. We found candy, chewing gum, silver dimes, all of which

Natalie pocketed, certain that John had intended them for her. None of us found the will. The dawn was coming. Its first rays shone through Natalie's windows, overwhelming the lighting of the apartment. We wobbled from exhaustion where we stood or sat.

"Are you sure you kept *every* suit?" Jerry asked Natalie.

"All of them," Natalie said. She stood still, tapping her forefinger against her temple, her eyes shut tight. "All but *one*," she said, opening her eyes. "The one he's wearing now. The one we buried him in. John Morton's will is with him in his grave."

"Good God in heaven," Cynthia said.

"We can kiss that will good-bye," Ray said. "Even if we dig up John—he was buried in wood—been in the ground seventeen years. That will looks like a wet rag."

Jerry spoke up. "We embalmed John Morton for two weeks of repose. John's body was as hard as a sidewalk, and he was buried in more than just a wooden casket. We reposed him in a sealed crystal-and-copper inner liner, like the one in the display room, only John's was mostly crystal—thick lead crystal framed in copper—intricate etchings—like nothing you've ever seen. We placed the inner liner in the Marcellas. We buried the casket in the best sealer vault Wilbert made at that time. As long as those containers have suffered no damage, John Morton still looks the same as he did on the day we buried him, and so does that will, if indeed it exists."

"Jewell Albright believes it exists," I said.

Ray waved his hands in the air. "I hate to be the one with a quart of malt liquor while y'all are ready to uncork the Champagne, but we're talking about exhuming a body without legal cause."

"Ray's right," Jerry said, sticking his hands into his pockets. "Jewell Albright is John Morton's next of kin. She'd have to sign off on the exhumation. That will never happen, not if Jewell plans on selling to JFT, as Casey has warned us."

"But there *is* a second will," I said. "I heard her say it. I'll testify."

"That's the problem, Casey," Jerry said. "You *heard* her say it. In court, that's called hearsay evidence. It won't do. Jewell will deny the whole thing, and she's the only one who knows about the will."

"There's someone else," I said. "A housekeeper witnessed John's signature."

"Wilma Ritchey," Cynthia said. "She was about twenty years old— late thirties now. If we can find her, she would testify. She loved John more than she feared Jewell. Never left his bedside after he got sick."

Ray waved his hands in the air again. "Y'all are chomping on this thing way too hard. This Wilma gal can prove that she witnessed John's will. She can't prove it's in the ground with John."

"It's there," Natalie said. "I know it."

Ray shot Natalie a perturbed look. "Well, excuse me for asking, Natalie, but how in the hell do you know this for an absolute fact?"

Natalie raised her voice into a lilt, her eyes glistening, "Because John Morton is telling me so. Right now. I feel him."

I shook my head. All eyes were stuck on Natalie's trembling form. "Don't look at me like I belong in Chattahoochee," she said. "Casey hears him, too." Natalie pointed a shaky finger at me. I admitted the truth with a nod. Natalie crossed her arms. Her voice changed from the angelic lilt into Natalie, giving everyone the business: "I've got another hunch, too. Casey and I, along with Colton Albright himself, are not the only ones who know about John." Natalie took her time giving the squint to each person in the room. Each hung his head in turn. "Well?" Natalie demanded.

Cynthia began sniffling and went for a hanky in her purse. "He passed me in the lobby a number of times," she admitted. "I knew it was him. I felt his warmth, and I heard my name. He called me Cissy. Nobody but John ever called me that name."

Ray's eyes went leaky, too. "He talked to me on the veranda, after the baby. I felt his hand on my shoulder."

"Looks like everybody's fessing up," Jerry said. "Guess it's my turn, Remember that old adding machine? The one with the crank—used to be in Colton's office—my office now."

"I've got it up in the attic, Daddy." Natalie said.

"That was John's machine. When John was alive, I'd hear him tapping keys and working that crank while I locked up at night. I'd look in on him before I left, say good night. After John's death, Colton used that machine, too, but only in the daytime. One night I heard those keys tapping, just after a visitation. I wondered, "What in the hell is Colton doing here at this hour?" I looked into the office. Empty. I turned around to leave and heard that crank—no mistaking that sound. From behind, I heard John's old voice: 'Good night, Jerry. Take care of my babies.' He meant Cynthia and Natalie, always telling me that. It bothered me so much, I bought a brand-new electric machine the very next day—told Colton we had to keep up with the times. I stored the old one in the supply room. How did that old thing get into my attic?"

"Ray stole it for me," Natalie said.

"So what do we do now?" Ray asked.

"Find the Ritchey girl," Jerry said. "She might know more than we think. I've got friends at County Records."

"I'll ask Denise," Ray said. "Maybe she remembers something."

"Don't do it, Ray," Cynthia cautioned. "Denise loves her daddy. If my sister finds out that her own mother has done Colton wrong, she'll drive straight to Mother's house and strangle the truth out of her. I'm so mad right now, I could strangle it out of her myself. Even if Mother admitted to the will, she doesn't know where it is. Our only proof is what we all feel, with Natalie, that the will is buried with my grandfather. That means we might be crazy, but not crazy enough to tell a county judge that the ghost of John Morton told us the location of the will."

"So we're back to Wilma Ritchey," Jerry said.

"Or committing a crime," Natalie said.

We all looked at her. She spoke her plan, eyes set. "I say we exhume John Morton ourselves. In secret. We take the will out of his pocket and put him back in the ground. We'll say we found the will in the attic. That's where Jewell thinks it is, anyway, according to Casey."

"I'm not particularly opposed to that idea," Jerry said.

"Jerry!" Cynthia said, "You might get caught. I will not have my husband, the funeral director, going to Raiford for grave robbing. JFT owns Fairview now, anyway."

"Henry still works there," Ray said. "Think old John would mind getting himself grave robbed?"

Natalie said, "I think he'd mind if we failed to carry out his final wishes."

"Jerry's right about Wilma," Cynthia said. "She might well know more than we think. John was bedridden when he wrote that will. He wore only pajamas during his last month. Maybe he instructed Wilma to put the will in his suit pocket, thinking he'd wear it again before he died." Cynthia opened Natalie's closet, now containing a folded church truck and other funeral stuff. "John kept his suits in here," she said. Cynthia then explained John's habit of suit rotation: The suit he took off at night went to the left side of the closet. From the right side, John took the next suit and hung it on the door. Cynthia closed the door and showed us the hook, still in place. "The day John wrote his will, his next suit would have been hanging right here. Jewell wouldn't have bothered going through his wardrobe for a burial garment. She probably just took the suit off the door. The Ritchey girl would have put the will in the pocket of the same suit, knowing John's habits herself. If she can remember that suit, she can go before the judge. Even if she can't remember, she can damn well say she did, and she would do it if we told her our present circumstances. She loved John Morton."

"She'd be lying to a judge, Cynthia," Ray said.

"Damn right, she would," Cynthia agreed, "but which one is worse—lying to a judge, or digging up John Morton in the middle of the night?"

Natalie said, "Look at it this way—which one would be more fun? I vote for digging up John."

Jerry said he'd hunt down Wilma Ritchey until he found her, or reached a dead end. "In the latter case, let's wait until we're stuck with the latter case."

"I have another plan," I said. "It's dangerous. JFT is under investigation."

"We know. We read the trades," everybody said at once.

I continued, promising myself I'd start reading the goddamn trades. "Lex Talbert says that Lewis Stark is looking to hire me. Why he wants me, I don't know. If I accepted the job, I'd work at Central Embalming. Daniel Coggin hinted that JFT was in violation of the Code of Ethics, they way they handle the bodies. If I uncovered any violations, I could report them to the State Board. They'd shut down JFT for good."

Everybody told me I was crazy, except Jerry. He said, "Son, I'd never put you in a position like that. These people are ruthless, but we've got to remember, there's more at stake here than our little funeral home. We're talking about the entire industry, and we all know those words of Gladstone on the Morton-Albright obelisk." As Jerry recited the words, everyone joined in, as though they were saying the Apostle's Creed: " 'Show me the manner in which a nation cares for its dead, and I will measure with mathematical exactness the tender mercies of its people—their loyalty to high ideals—and their regard for the laws of the land.' "

Considering our options, I couldn't say how much regard we had for the laws of the land. It seemed to me that our tender mercies, and our loyalty to high ideals tainted our view of the law. If we followed my plan, if I accepted Lex's offer of a job at Central Embalming, we could avoid breaking the law. My new family was against it. They worried about what could happen to me in a place like Central. Mostly they worried about desensitization—that's what happens when you spend more time with the dead than with the living. Jerry explained it. "You'll be up to your eyeballs in blood and guts, day after day. Even though Ray is embalming room supervisor, he works visitations and services—keeps the human factor of death in perspective. Too much time in the back room can work on your mind, and not for the better."

I assured Jerry that I could handle it. He said, "That's exactly what I'm afraid of, son. Suppose it takes longer than you anticipate to gather enough evidence against JFT? I'll consider your plan as a last resort. You'll need to break ties with us to convince Lewis Stark you're for real. You'll be in there on your own. Lex was smart to recommend you. I can see why he did it. You're curious about what goes on at Central, aren't you, son?"

"I think we should all be curious about Central," I said.

"That's no kind of answer. We're talking about two different kinds of curiosity. The rest of us are curious about the illegalities that might be part of their routine. You're just plain curious. Let's you and me go for a ride; see what we can dig up—on Wilma Ritchey, I mean."

16

Jerry had found a family of Ritcheys in the Cracker part of town—my old neighborhood, the outer circle of Angel Shores. The house they had lived in was abandoned—no signs proclaiming the property for sale. Three houses away, a man rolled out a hose to water his lawn. Jerry and I approached him. He had that Cracker way about him—friendly, but obviously suspicious of our suits and ties. Jerry introduced the two of us; told the man we were from Morton-Albright. He scratched his head. "If y'all are looking for dead folks, there ain't none around here, not that I know of."

"We're looking for Wilma Ritchey," Jerry said.

"She finally up and die?"

"We hope not," Jerry said. "Wilma used to work for John Morton. She was his housekeeper."

"Then y'all should know that Wilma took sick, years back. Her family said the doctors here couldn't help her. They took her up North somewhere—said she'd be long in recovery. They left these parts some fifteen years ago—ain't come back since. Nice folks, the Ritcheys."

Catastrophic illness, long recovery. Left out most cancers, Jerry said. Sounded more like tuberculosis, a disease that required long recuperation. The neighbor man had said the Ritcheys went "up North," but Jerry doubted a Cracker family crossing the state line. He couldn't figure whether or not Wilma Ritchey had died—the abandoned house was a mystery. If she had died, the family would have returned home, unless finances had forced them to bury Wilma up North. In that case, the family might have stayed where she had been buried (a normal Cracker practice), until they had raised the money to have her body exhumed and brought back home. On the other hand, if Wilma had survived TB, the disease may have left her in a weakened condition, unable to travel. In either case, Tallahassee seemed the best place to look. The state capital would have had good hospitals and government money for long-term care. Jerry knew of a TB sanatorium there. He'd start with the death records of Tallahassee County.

As we drove away from the neighborhood of my youth, we passed the very street on which I had lived—Covington Place. I nearly asked Jerry to drive me past my old house. I bit my lip when I realized what I might find—an old, abandoned Cracker house, as dead as my parents. Margee had sold the place to a realtor, because the realtor hadn't been able to sell it—Crackers were superstitious about death houses. The realtor had paid her dimes on the dollar—on speculation, he had said. He'd need to wait until the memories of my parents' tragedy had faded, and even then, it would have been his duty to inform any prospective buyers of the crash, and the orphan child left behind.

September rolled into October, sending us relief from the hottest summer in ten years. Colton seemed invigorated by the cooler weather. The cadence of his speech returned to normal, as did his memory of Ray and Denise's wedding. He stopped asking when they would marry, and started asking about Natalie and the casket wrassler.

I knew that Natalie loved me, but she had never spoken a word about marriage. "We don't date," she'd said. "We mate." I knew we were young, but I couldn't imagine myself with anyone but Natalie, except for my occasional dreams about Denise. Since my first night with Natalie, I had dreamed often of Denise, always a dream of sex. My first dream had driven me into remorse—it felt as though I had lost my virginity with both women at the same time. Except for my dreaming, my heart belonged to Natalie, that is, unless Denise showed up at the funeral home. Now that Colton was getting better, Denise spent less time with him, and more time around the funeral home. Nobody who had ever seen Denise Winstead could deny her sexual presence. "She's dripping with it," Ray said about her. "I nearly shot off in my pants the first time I saw her. I see other men, the way they look at Denise. It doesn't make me jealous. It makes me the proudest damn redneck in the world."

Denise often joined us for breakfast in the mornings. She always kissed me first, always on the mouth, always with a sweet, "Good morning, Casey." Natalie didn't seem to mind. Neither did Ray. Nobody paid attention to Denise's habit of flirting with me. Every once in a while, she'd give me a little wink. It drove me crazy, but it also made me guilty. I wanted a lifetime with Natalie. I wanted about three hours with Denise, and although Natalie and I had spoken the words "I love you" to each other, our relationship was mostly unspoken, undefined—much like my shapeless childhood.

That was another thing to worry about—my childhood. I wanted to remember it completely. The security and comfort of Morton-Albright hadn't been enough, because my place here remained in jeopardy. Even though Colton Albright's health was steadily improving, we all knew the old man could drop dead whenever he felt like it. What would happen to Natalie and me, if we suddenly lost the funeral home? Would we survive it together? Natalie seemed so content with things as they were, I wondered if she would even consider marriage. I needed to know that I would have her for all time. I just didn't want to be the one to bring it up. If Natalie knew my heart, she would either fall into my arms, or tease me to death—maybe both.

I needed something permanent, and marrying Natalie seemed as permanent as things could get, so I tried hinting. I asked Natalie how long her parents had been *married*. I told her that Ray and Denise seemed to have a good *marriage*—endless stuff like that, all without a hint from Natalie.

Halloween. No visitations or services were ever held on Halloween—pranksters. "Worse than April Fool's Day around the funeral home," Ray said.

Natalie prepared for our Halloween adventure like a prom date. Our destination: the Halloween Horrorfest at the Seabreeze Drive-in Theater. A triple feature: *The House of Wax, The Bride of Franken-stein,* and *Psycho*—all classics, guaranteeing a full parking lot. The theater opened an hour before the movies began, giving everybody time to walk around the drive-in, showing off their costumes. When Natalie and I arrived as Kato and the Green Hornet, we drew a crowd the moment we stepped out of Black Beauty. Dad would have been proud of me—his son, the Green Hornet.

Natalie *knew* that *House of Wax* was my favorite movie—Vincent Price preserving the dead forever and all—but in the opening scene, as the carney barker hawked the morbid delights of the wax museum, Natalie snuggled up to me and started kissing behind my ear. I whispered, "Wait a minute. This is one of my favorite parts."

"Come on, Casey," she said. "Everybody knows you don't go to the drive-in to watch the movie." As if Natalie had ever been to the drive-in to do anything *but* watch the movie. I opened my mouth to argue, but Natalie had already wormed out of her chauffeur jacket, naked underneath. When she unzipped her pants, I started working on my own. We made love to the sounds of sinister voices, thunder and lightning, and the screams of those meeting their doom. We dressed, and took a walk to the concession stand during *The Bride of Franken-stein.* "Some bride," Natalie said. "She didn't even get a ring."

I seized Natalie's remark, hoping her words carried unspoken sentiment about marriage.

Psycho: Janet Leigh appeared on the screen in her underwear, in the room of a cheap hotel, with her lover. "What a slut," Natalie said, ripping off her own clothes, and tearing into mine. "She knows that jack-off boyfriend will never marry her. That's why she's so desperate." Natalie's message rang clear: Only a jack-off would postpone marriage to a woman he truly loved. Only a slut would stay with such a jack-off. Natalie now wrapping me in her naked skin, I deciphered her words like prophecy: Natalie was no slut, and I was no jack-off. The wedding was on.

At the Bates Motel, the boyish talk of Anthony Perkins excited Natalie. She started in on me with her biting thing when the actor spoke. With Hitchcock blaring from the speaker, Natalie postponed her final throes until the shower scene, her moans building as the sound of the running water filled the Chrysler. When the screechy violins announced the arrival of Norman Bates and his knife, Natalie announced her climax, her cries of pleasure blending with the final pleas of the woman in the shower.

We arose from our lovemaking for the eye scene. Hitchcock's camera pulled away from the dead woman's fixed pupil. Norman cleaned up his mess. Natalie fell into a snore. Tomorrow, I'd buy the ring.

Next morning, Sunset Towers made the front page: "Flu Strikes Retirement Community. Health Officials Fear Epidemic."

"All those old folks squeezed in together like that," Meredith said. "Age makes you more susceptible."

Ray said, "Imagine centralized embalming at JFT. The bastards want the whole suncoast. I'll bet they weren't expecting to get it all at one time. How many deaths so far?"

"Paper says fourteen," Meredith said. "Must be a bad bug. I feel sorry for those folks. We're the lucky ones—Sunset Towers is like a little town. I don't imagine the residents leave that place much. They've got everything right there on the premises."

Carl agreed, "Probably some New Yorker brought the bug down with him. As long as those people stay put that flu bug might burn itself out before it has a chance to spread."

Jerry was of a different mind. "It's still early in the year," he said, "and you boys are forgetting the people who work there, but live in the outlying communities. They could endanger the entire state, and with fourteen deaths already, this thing could go national."

"It's been many a year since the flu went deadly nationwide," Meredith said.

"My point exactly," Jerry said. "We might be at the peak of the flu cycle, worldwide. Probably nothing to worry about, though—all those old people in one place might be making it look worse than it is."

"Probably," everyone agreed.

At 10:00 A.M., I told the guys I needed a haircut. I headed straight for the bank and withdrew all the money I had saved while working at Morton-Albright, except for the ten dollars I needed to keep the account open. From the bank, I walked to Chamberlain Jewelers. I was about to enter the store when my beeper sounded. I ran back to Morton-Albright—death call, Angel Shores Hospital. I could run the call and buy the ring in less than an hour.

On my way to the hospital, I passed by my old street again, Covington Place. I decided to drive by my old house, just for a quick look. I was surprised by what I saw: Although the house was obviously vacated, it had been freshly painted, the same sky blue color I had remembered. The lawn had been recently mowed. A sign on the lawn read Offered by Campbell Realty. I had prepared myself for an old, run-down place. It looked brand-new. I stopped the car and got out. There were no window coverings of any kind, so I went to the living room window and looked inside, trying to place the missing furniture where it belonged. I could remember only the Victrola, against the wall opposite the TV. Yes, and there had been a sofa between them that looked straight out through the front window. If you sat on the sofa, you had to turn your head to watch the television. I usually lay on the floor. I went to the front door and tried the handle—unlocked—not that it would have mattered, there was nothing to steal. I entered my old home and stood in the living room. I heard a sound from the kitchen—a snipping sound, the sound of scissors. Someone was in the kitchen. Maybe the real estate guy. I called out a soft hello. Nobody answered. I crept to the kitchen. At the kitchen counter, I saw a boy with brown hair, lightened by the sun. He was working the scissors, snipping at a piece of cardboard. He couldn't have been more than ten. Some neighborhood kid had found himself an empty house to play in. I walked up behind him, making obvious noise with my footsteps to let him know I was there, so I wouldn't scare him, but he was involved in his task. I looked over his shoulder, to get a look at the thing he was cutting—a colorful cardboard box. He seemed to be enjoying himself. I couldn't help but chuckle, the kid was so cute with his tongue sticking out as he cut. He must have heard my laugh, because he turned around, looking perplexed. He asked, "What the hell are *you* doing here?" The deep voice didn't match the child's face, but it did match the face I was looking at now—the face of a man, early fifties, perhaps. Pain shot through my head. I felt my eyes crossing. I stumbled backward, into the wall. The man took hold of me and helped me stand erect. He asked, "Are you all right? Want me to go for a doctor? Who the hell are you anyway?"

I slowed down my breathing and let my eyes uncross before answering the man, "I'm Casey."

"Is that supposed to mean something to me?"

"This is my house," I said.

"The hell it is. I bought this here house over ten years ago. You might have noticed my name on the sign out there in the front lawn. I'm R. G. Campbell, realtor."

"This *was* my house," I corrected myself. "When I was a kid. I'm Casey Kight. I'm sorry I barged in on you. The door was unlocked."

"Did you say Kight?"

"Yes. Kight."

"You're the orphan boy, got left behind? Sorry, son. You gave me a fright. You shouldn't oughta go sneaking up on folks like that. Come back for a look, did ye?"

"Yes, sir. I was shocked at how beautiful the house looked—same color and everything. I was expecting to see it all run-down."

"It *was* run-down, until about a month ago. I figured it was time. Time to sell, that is. Lots of new folk moving into town. Of course, I still gotta tell 'em—you know, about your folks and all. You look like you done well for yourself."

I looked down at my suit. I told him yes, I had done well. I asked him if he would let me rent the house for a while. Not for long, maybe a month or so. I promised I wouldn't disturb anything. I just wanted to visit, every now and then. I offered to pay him up front, and pulled out the wad of bills I had withdrawn from the bank.

"You stick that money back in your pocket. I can't take no money from you. Wouldn't be right. I'm suspecting you've got some cobwebs to clean out of your attic. You take this here key."

It was an ordinary key that Mr. Campbell gave me, but I felt its power in my hand, as powerful as the key to Morton-Albright. I had been searching for memories in the wrong house. *This* house was the house of remembering. The house of mourning. I asked Mr. Campbell why he was cutting the cardboard. He said, "Yellowjacket nest in the bedroom. They come in through a hole in the window. You tear down the nest and they come right back. I'm patching the hole until I buy a new pane."

The realtor showed me to the front door. I shook his hand, and remembered his name—Campbell. I asked him if he was related to Sophie Campbell.

"She's my sister-in-law. How do you know her?"

"I work for Morton-Albright. I took care of Marianne."

"Good God Almighty," he said. "You're the boy what killed Jimmie Blessing."

• • •

I made the removal and embalmed the new case, my head still messy inside. I felt dizzy. My hands were sweaty inside the surgical gloves. I switched on the embalming machine. Its humming relaxed me. *That's right son, houses are queer things. This one and that one—each has its own story to tell. This one tells a story of comfort, and the comfort is yours. You stay close to home, now.* I wanted to stay close to home, but which home was mine? The Presence sent prickles all over my skin, then inward, washing me in comfort. I couldn't stop my tears—I knew the little boy in my old house. He was me.

My vision had made me afraid to ask for Natalie's hand, but it made me even more afraid to try to live without her. Something bigger than me had led me down my path of remembrance. It had led me to Morton-Albright. It had led me to Natalie. It had led me to my old house on Covington Place. Now it was leading me home.

I took the day off from classes at Taylor—funeral law. We were studying the specifics of what constituted excessive mutilation. I already knew the material from my hours with Ray. Besides, my powers of concentration had fled me. Ray gave me hell for cutting class, but admitted he'd done the same, after he quizzed me about the exact lengths of various incisions, and reminded me that the law helped prevent a man from falling too far into desensitization. "Funeral law is your conscience," Ray said.

At lunchtime, I took a walk to the courthouse square. I sat down on a bench across the street from Chamberlain Jewelers. I pulled the wad of bills from my pocket and riffled through them, then looked up at the jewelry store. I did this for a while, moving my eyes between the cash and the store, waiting for the courage to walk across the street and buy the ring. The courage didn't come. I got up off the bench and started back for Morton-Albright. I stopped when I remembered the words, *You stay close to home, now.* I ran across the street toward the store. I heard the blaring of a horn; the screeching of tires. I looked to my right. The car had stopped so close to me, I could feel the heat from its radiator. A man stuck his head out the window and yelled at me, "What's the matter with you, boy? Are you crazy?"

"Yes, sir," I said. "I hear voices. I see things that aren't there, and I'm getting married."

I ran into the jewelry store, full of adrenaline from near death in the middle of Main Street. I threw all of my money down on the counter in front of Mr. Chamberlain. He said, "From the look on your face, I'd guess you've got engagement on your mind. Local gal?"

"Natalie Stiles."

"Well, mercy me. That would make you Casey Kight, wouldn't it?"

"How did you know?"

"That gal of yours has already come in and picked out her stone, back when she was just a young girl. She came here about a week ago—asked me if I still had it, and I've already let it slip that she mentioned your name. I was supposed to have made a *suggestion* about the stone."

I wasn't sure I had enough money. If the diamond had been here that long, it must be expensive.

"It's not money that keeps it here—it's the cut. I'll show you what I mean."

The jeweler unfolded a green velvet cloth on the countertop, revealing an oblong diamond that radiated light like a prism. "Marquise cut," the jeweler said, "just shy of two carats. Folks around here don't care for the shape. When I bought it, I violated the first rule of jewelry: never buy a stone because you love it—it'll always be the one stone you never sell. Looks like we both got lucky today. Pick it up after lunch. I've already measured Natalie's finger for the setting."

After handing all my cash over to Mr. Chamberlain, I remembered Natalie's birthday—she hated surprises. She had known my mind all along. The thought unburdened me, and I wondered what other unspoken things she knew of me; the depth of her intuition—her lack of worry over the fate of Morton-Albright, her unwavering belief that John Morton's will lay with him in the ground. The heart of the wise was hers.

Ray told me the news when I returned to the funeral home: we'd meet at Jerry's house as quick as we could get there. Jerry had found a family of Ritcheys in the panhandle. At his home, early that afternoon, Jerry spread out a roadmap on the kitchen table. He said, "I located the death certificate of a woman named Pauline Ritchey." With his finger, Jerry made a circle around the Tallahassee area. Jerry said the Ritchey folks were Crackers. Predictable. Even if they needed a Tallahassee hospital, they would never live in a big town like the state capital. They'd have settled in a place like Angel Shores. Jerry placed his fingertip upon the star of Tallahassee, then ran his finger leftward, to the next county west—Gadsden County. Jerry had called the health department in Quincy, the Gadsden county seat. When Jerry introduced himself as a funeral director, the woman on the phone had agreed to help. "She wouldn't tell me anything but the name, but promised me a look at the death certificate if I showed up in person. I'll fly to Tallahassee tonight, rent a car, find a motel. I'll be standing at the front door of the Quincy Health Department when it opens tomorrow morning."

"I want to go," Natalie said.

"You'll miss school, sugar."

Natalie stood up and put her hands on her hips. "I spent the last four years of college on the Dean's List. Give me a freaking break for once, will ya?"

"Natalie!" Cynthia warned.

"I said 'freaking,' not 'fucking,' Mother. I'm doing better on my swearing—honest. Pleeeze, Daddy? Father-daughter thing?"

Jerry shrugged. Natalie bounced in her chair, smiling. Ray said, "Well, Jerry, you've proven yourself a funeral man. You looked for a death certificate. Normal folks would have tried the telephone directory first." Ray got up to leave. Natalie took him to the door. Jerry said, "Telephone directory. Should have thought of that."

I leaned over the table and whispered to Jerry and Cynthia. I asked them if we could talk alone, without Natalie. They looked at each other as Natalie reentered the kitchen. Jerry told his daughter he needed a private word with me. Natalie said, "Okay, but you'd better not leave me out of anything."

Cynthia ordered Natalie upstairs, away from the kitchen door. I cleared my throat. Cynthia said, "Good Lord, Jerry. Here it comes." Jerry shushed his wife. I tried to speak, but my intent was already apparent on their faces. I pulled out the ring box and opened it. Cynthia gasped, then said, "Oh, thank God. He picked the marquise."

"Good man," Jerry said.

"Then I have your permission?"

"And our blessing," Cynthia said. "We've never seen Natalie so happy. What have you done to her? She's even given up that biting thing of hers."

I could have opened my shirt and shown Cynthia her mistake about the biting thing. Jerry warned me of the long engagement ahead—no wedding date until I finished Taylor and passed my Boards. I shook hands with Jerry, hugged Cynthia, then went off to climb the stairs to Natalie's apartment—except she hadn't bothered to go upstairs. She stood in the living room with her arms folded across her chest. "Well?" She asked.

"Let's go for a walk."

Natalie walked beside me, whining. "Come on, Casey. You know I can't stand secrets. What were you talking about in there? It was about me, wasn't it? I know it was, or you would have let me stay. You better tell me. You're driving me nuts, you know. This had better be something good, or I'll brain ya."

While Natalie jabbered, I led her to the spot where I had taken my first kiss, before the headstone of the epileptic cat. "Close your eyes," I said.

"Forget it, death-man. I am *not* closing my eyes. If I do, I'll peek anyway. You can't trust me. You might as well give me the ring and get it over with."

"What?"

"Just pretend I didn't say anything. Look, I'm closing my eyes now. I'm not even peeking."

I opened the velveteen box, took out the ring, and slipped it onto the first joint of my pinkie. I closed the box, placed it in Natalie's outstretched hand and wrapped her fingers around it. I said, "Okay, you can look now."

"Oh, jeez," she said. "I wonder what could be in here. This is really such a surprise." She opened the lid, and saw the empty box. "All right, death-man, where is it?"

I took off running, toward Cynthia's shade house. I heard Natalie calling from behind, "I'm coming after you, Casey Kight. When I find you, I'm gonna brain ya. I'll say 'no', if you don't let me catch up."

I crept into Cynthia's shade house, where I hid beside the door. Natalie walked right past me. "I know you're in here. This isn't fair, you know." She spun around and saw me, but remained quiet. Maybe it was the shade house that affected her. The air was moist, earthy with potting soil. Tendrils of ivy surrounded us. Natalie took her time walking to me. She placed her hand on my chest, and said, "I'm a brat. You're trying to do something lovely, and it scares me. You've always let me have my way, until now. You ran away from me. I know you were teasing, but I also know you're *not* teasing. You're a good man, and it's time I let you be good to me, however you like, instead of the way I like."

I almost preferred Natalie's teasing to the look I now saw on her face. Her playful streak had often distracted me from her depth of feeling. I knew it better when we were apart, when I was in my private thoughts of her. Now she allowed it onto her face, and it scared me, too. We exchanged uncomfortable bursts of small laughter as I took her hand and slid the ring onto her finger. As she looked down at the diamond, I watched a tear splash onto the back of her hand. She wiped her eye, and said, "Now look what you made me do. You bought the marquise. You knew I wanted it. What do *you* want, Casey?"

"I want you to marry me."

"I will marry you, Casey."

I just stood there, looking at her, wondering how her joy of living had invaded my living nightmares. I knew then how different we were from each other: She played with death, for it had never touched her. Death played with me, for keeps. Somewhere in between, we had met.

"You can kiss me now," she said, and when I kissed her, I knew she was mine.

She said, "Wait. Weren't you supposed to be down on one knee? I think we should start over."

"Jesus, Natalie . . ."

"Sssh. I've got something for *your* finger, too."

We made love on top of the long table, Cynthia's potted plants strewn everywhere, the automatic sprinklers spraying us with dew. On our way back to the house, Natalie stopped to look at her ring in the sunlight. "Holy shit," she said. "Look at the size of that rock."

"How did you kids get all wet?" Cynthia asked.

"We ran through the sprinkler," Natalie said. "Casey's idea."

The next morning, Ray and I ran a police rotation call, our first case at Sunset Towers. After all I had heard, I was curious to get a look at the place. Ray asked me, "Is there *anything* you're not eager about?" The dispatcher had not known of the cause of death, only that it sounded "routine." All we knew was that Dr. Kendall and the police were there.

At the main gate of Sunset Towers, the concrete and glass structures obscured the sky. The uniformed man at the gate unfolded a map, traced a route for us in red marker, then handed the map to Ray. We drove the main road for two miles. I saw the swimming pools, tennis courts, old men playing shuffleboard—all kinds of amusements, all filled with elderly tenants. Golf carts hummed along the streets. Ray managed to get around the bus that kept stopping in front of us, only to find himself behind another. A gap between the towers opened into a shopping complex: Winn-Dixie, Eckerd Drugs,

Sunset Bowling, and a marquee listing six movie titles. A whole city, just like Meredith had said. At Tower Fourteen, Ray pulled the removal car into an empty parking space. A uniformed guard ran out of the building. "You can't park here," he said. Ray explained our business, but the guard said, "You still can't park here. I know who you are. We conduct all funeral business through the cafeteria loading dock. Follow me."

We backed in next to a Dumpster. Inside the building, clattering plates and the smell of dishwashers wafted from a door to our left. The guard pressed a button on the wall. "Service elevator," he said. "I'll escort you to the apartment, wait outside, then take you back down."

Inside the apartment, Dr. Kendall hovered over the new case. "What's the big deal?" Ray asked. "Looks like normal business from here."

"It *is* normal business," Kendall said. He apologized for bothering us. The old woman on the floor had been taking a lot of medication for a variety of illnesses—diabetes, hypertension, gout, phlebitis, and Parkinson's. The husband feared his wife had overdosed on medication—she'd been bedridden for two days prior, talking crazy and taking pills—possible evidence of high fever. She had also presented with symptoms of pneumonia. When the husband found her dead, he called the police. "I suspected flu," Kendall said. "I asked permission for an autopsy—any number of maladies afflicting the aged could end in pneumonia. I wanted a thorough rule-out and a blood sample for State Health. We need to get on this bug before it gets worse, and we can't declare an epidemic until we identify the virus. The widower gave me permission for a postmortem, until he called his own funeral home. Then he changed his mind. Carlyle's on their way over now. You boys can go home."

"How many flu deaths now?" Ray asked.

"Thirty-seven, we suspect. Most of them from here."

"The paper just said fourteen."

"Like I said, fellas—bad bug."

"And Carlyle is JFT," Ray said.

"Don't worry, Ray," Kendall said. "JFT may be big, but not big enough to invent a flu virus."

"That's not what I meant," Ray said. "*Everybody* from Sunset Towers goes JFT. Why?"

Later that day, in Gadsden County, Jerry and Natalie found Wilma Ritchey, the former housekeeper who had witnessed John Morton's will. They had found her near Quincy, in the next town over: Chattahoochee. Diagnosis: paranoid schizophrenia. Wilma Ritchey, incapable of rational speech, could not appear before the court, but samples of her handwriting abounded. Over the years, Wilma had written hundreds of letters to John Morton, her signature at the bottom of each one. The psychiatrist explained that John Morton was the object of Wilma Ritchey's delusion.

Natalie returned from Chattahoochee with her own bizarre report, which she had nudged out of Wilma's mother: Two months after his death, Wilma began conversing with John Morton, right in front of her own family. She'd clap her hands together and laugh; say things like, "Mr. John, you ought not to carry on about Miz Jewell thataway." Wilma began spending entire days nursing a nonexistent John Morton in her own bedroom. She stopped bathing for weeks. The housekeeper's family had thought Wilma's condition a temporary thing, that she was crazy with grief over John Morton's death, until the day she ran out of her bedroom, screaming, "Everyone out of the funeral home! Mr. John says the devils are coming!" Wilma guarded the bedroom door, whacking at devils with a broom, yelling, "Stay away from Mr. John, thou foul creatures of hell!"

When Natalie had found Wilma, the woman was *still* talking to John, seventeen years after his death. A nurse told Natalie that Wilma never spoke to anybody *except* John. That's how Natalie and Jerry had found her—in the middle of a conversation with John Morton.

"Wilma Ritchey talks to John Morton?" I asked Natalie.

"Not the *real* John Morton—a delusional John Morton."

"What's the difference? She's still talking to John Morton."

"True, but Wilma Ritchey is mentally ill."

"So, Wilma Ritchey talks to John Morton, and she's mentally ill. *We* talk to John Morton, and we're all perfectly sane."

"Exactly."

"This is insane."

"See? That proves you're *not* insane. As long as you *think* you're insane, you *can't* be insane, because you're thinking you *might* be insane. On the other hand, Wilma Ritchey believes she's *not* insane, and that's exactly what makes her insane. As long as you doubt your sanity, you can't be insane."

"Have you ever doubted your sanity?"

"Never."

17

The insanity of Wilma Ritchey left us with the insanity of our last resort: the secret exhumation of John Morton and his last will and testament. Carl and Denise had joined us. Jerry and Cynthia had informed them of the second will and our plan. They were finishing their story as I walked into the kitchen and took my seat at the table, next to Natalie. Carl's face spelled befuddlement. Denise paced, muttering curses against Cruel Jewell. Ray reminded us all of what we might find, if the old man's burial containers were compromised—a mixture of clothing and liquefied rot, resulting in a wet, illegible piece of paper—assuming the piece of paper even existed. Natalie stood firm in her belief. Jerry assured us of the integrity of the vault, the casket, and the inner liner. The consequences didn't matter. We all stood together as one. Jerry called for quiet. He said, "Before we begin this grim task which has befallen us, Casey and Natalie will bless us with some more cheerful news."

"You tell them," Natalie whispered in my ear.

"Just show them the ring."

Natalie splayed her fingers. The room burst into applause and big smiles. Carl and Ray took turns shaking my hand and slapping my back. Denise gave me a kiss, still on the mouth, but drier than usual.

"Time for business," Jerry said. "Henry's with us. He'll meet us at the gate. We exhume John Morton, check his inside pocket, put him back in the ground. If you feel you can't do this thing, you're free to leave now. Show me your hands—who's in?"

Every hand in the room went up. Jerry said, "I expected as much. Natalie, I have but one rule for you: no pictures."

"Aw, shit, Daddy. This is history."

"Natalie, bring me your cameras."

Natalie brought down the newsman's camera, and the Nikon as well.

Jerry said, "I want the spy camera too—your last birthday present."

"Damn," Natalie said, kneeling and reaching into her sock. She slapped the thing into Jerry's hand.

"When do we go?" Ray asked Jerry.

"Midnight. It seemed the appropriate hour."

We waited together in silence, save the ticking and chiming of Jerry's grandfather clock. When the clock gonged midnight, Jerry stood up and buttoned his suit. In the limousine, we cruised to the cemetery without conversation.

Henry stood inside the front gate of Fairview Cemetery, now JFT property. He covered his eyes against the headlights of the limousine. Jerry switched them off. In the dark, we followed Henry's golf cart to the old part of the cemetery, where John Morton lay beneath the cypresses. Henry said, "I hope y'all are ready for some hard work. The backhoe is too noisy and there's no clear path to the grave. We've got to do this the old-fashioned way." Together, we walked from the driveway to the far corner of the graveyard, toward the marble obelisk that marked the Morton-Albright plot.

Henry outlined the grave space with a spade, then passed out shovels. We dug as though driven by a whip. My shovel chinked against the burial vault.

Henry directed us, "Dig halfway down the sides of the vault. I've got to go down there and unseal it." As we dug, Henry jumped into the grave with a crowbar, where he groaned against the seal. "Seal's broken," he said, "and I don't smell a thing. Good sign, so far." He led us farther into the dark, to an ancient A-frame cranking device. The thing looked like a tall, yellow sawhorse made of iron. Together, we hauled the machine, snagging our dress shirts, cutting and pinching our hands in the mechanism. With a final heave, we set the device over John Morton's grave. Henry hung four chains from the machine, then attached the chains to the four corners of the vault lid. Henry strained at the crank of the apparatus, but couldn't budge the vault lid. "Need some more beef here, fellas," he said. Carl and I rushed to help. Groaning through clenched teeth, we cranked until the vault lid cleared the grave. Henry swung the lid over the grass. "Let 'er drop," he said. "Yank that handle stuck in the gear." Carl set his weight against the handle. The lid hit the ground.

Henry altered the workings of the swing arm of the machine, allowing the attachment of canvas straps. Henry jumped back into the grave and worked the straps under the Marcellas cherry. Carl and I started cranking again. John Morton's casket ascended from the grave. Henry swung the Marcellas over a casket cart. "Let 'er down easy this time—just lay off on the crank real slow-like." Within a few moments, John Morton's casket rested upon the cart.

"Now comes the hard part," Henry said. "Rolling this thing out of the old cemetery, down the driveway, then across the memorial gardens to the shed—all by hand. Nobody talks but me." Henry grabbed the steering handle of the cart. He beckoned Denise to help him pull. The woman lacking muscle, I could only guess at Henry's reasons for choosing Denise. Hell, the guy deserved it. "Let's get this thing moving," he said.

We struggled through the old cemetery in the dark. While Henry and Denise pulled, Ray and I pushed from the rear. Jerry and Cynthia steadied the casket on one side, Carl and Natalie on the other. The trip across the graveyard, bumpy with cypress roots, proved an unexpected burden. Henry misjudged our distance from a cypress tree. Its monster root tilted the cart toward Natalie and Carl. Natalie moaned against its weight, but the casket threatened to topple from the cart. Jerry and Cynthia pulled hard from their side. Henry ran up behind Natalie, propelling himself into the casket. I imagined John Morton inside, jostled this way and that. We righted the casket, then eased the rear tires of the cart over the root.

"Inner liner," Henry said. "Damn thing weighs more than I do."

Smelling of sweat, we rested at the limousine.

On rubber tires, the cart rolled easily along the asphalt drive. The drive ended fifty yards from the shed. Before us lay the memorial gardens, a field of bronze markers, the resting place of my mom and dad. We all took a breath and set out across the field. The resistance of the grass against the cart's tires called for renewed effort from our tired muscles. Avoiding the markers proved impossible—the cart bounced over them, hammering my joints. The absence of a moon left our surroundings unlit, with no visual distractions from our task. We labored in monotonous sound—the crush of the grass, the hum of cicadas, our own throaty breaths.

I measured our progress in single steps, disheartened with each glance at the shed, gray amid dark. Each time I dug my shoes into the grass for another push, the building seemed to move farther away. Headache pounded me into despair: we had all signed on for a round-trip—our journey back to John Morton's grave would be lightened only by the weight of a single sheet of paper, assuming the insane Wilma Ritchey had indeed tucked the will into John Morton's pocket. Now the ghost of John Morton had driven us all mad, like Wilma herself. Next we'd ward off the devils with brooms. Extending my body into another long push, I slipped on the grass, smacking my forehead against the casket on the way down. I rolled myself onto my back, pained and dizzy. My comrades encircled me, shadows in the dark. I felt their hands on me; heard their whispers. Natalie's fingers stroked my hair. I felt her kiss on my forehead. As they helped me up, my doubts of the invisible vanished. I *felt* them—their collective power—the power that had summoned good citizens of Angel Shores to a midnight walk with the dead: the power of hope—invisible, yet coursing through the hands that brought me to my feet. We'd gone crazy, all right. Crazy with hope. When I looked up, the shed loomed before me, not ten feet away.

Henry unlocked the door and switched on the light. Jerry and Ray rolled the casket cart next to a large worktable. Henry placed a pneumatic body-lifter next to the casket. He raised the lid. We all strained for a look inside, but the body-lifter and Henry's bulk left us without a view. Henry worked the straps of the body-lifter under the casket's inner liner. Out of the casket he raised the glass coffin, a thing beyond elegance. The etchings in the sides of the inner liner frosted the crystal, obscuring all but the shape of the man who lay inside. Henry lowered the burial case onto the table, unhooked the straps, and let them fall away.

The interior fabric of the casket lid had partially disintegrated over the years, covering the top of the inner liner with rose-colored dust. Ray wiped away the dust with a cloth, starting at the foot-end. Etchings of scrolls and flowers adorned the lid. Just above the waist, the etchings ceased, the glass now a window. John's charcoal jacket, vest, and striped tie appeared, his hands folded upon his waist. A gold watch fob arced into his vest pocket. Ray wiped faster now, to the white shirt collar and the tie's four-in-hand knot.

With a final sweep of the cloth, Ray revealed the face of John Beresford Morton. The shed itself breathed with our own gasps. The Presence seeped from the timbers of the building through my skin, clean into my marrow. I watched the expressions of the others: astonished, then smiling, then solemn.

Inside the glass coffin, John Morton glowed. His energy refracted through the prisms of the etchings. The Presence ebbed away. The glow of John Morton dimmed. Everyone stepped toward the coffin at once. Jerry intervened, "Let's do this the right way." We lined up as for a final viewing at the funeral home. Jerry stood at the head of the crystal encasement, placing his hand on the shoulder of each of us as we paid our respects. I went last, taking my place next to Natalie.

John Morton looked as though he had been embalmed that very morning. Without a mark or discoloration of the skin, John's face bore the look of a man who had died at peace with himself, his family, his God. Natalie touched the glass over her great-grandfather's face.

Henry went to work on the inner liner's seal with a flathead screwdriver. "I've seen my share of exhumations," he said. "Never like this. He looks good. *Too* good. Gives me the willies."

Carl, Ray, Jerry, and Henry lifted the lid from the inner liner and set it farther down the table upon a blanket of rags. We all encircled the coffin. Cynthia touched John's hands.

"Whatever else y'all need to do, I don't need to see," Henry announced. "I'll stand guard outside the door. Knock when you're done."

Jerry took Natalie's hand and led her to the coffin. He stood behind her and placed his big hands on her shoulders. "You're the reason we're all here," he said. "You have the honor." Natalie smiled at her father, then at me. She slipped her hand inside John Morton's inside pocket, as far as she could reach. She giggled, and withdrew a piece of butterscotch candy. "This is for me," she said, showing it off. "Don't worry, there's more." Natalie pulled out the envelope, held it aloft, then handed it to Jerry. "You read it, Daddy," she said.

Jerry unfolded the paper from the envelope. After a glance, he turned it around for all of us to see. He spoke with great solemnity. "Written on his own stationery with the imprint, 'John Morton, Angel Shores, Florida.' " Jerry cleared his throat. "Here's what follows:

"I, John Beresford Morton, of sound mind, hereby cancel, and cause to be invalid, my previous will. Upon what may very well be my deathbed, I take this opportunity to reclaim my peace of mind and soul, fully regretting that I have withheld the things I most dearly love from the man I love most dearly. With humble repentance, and hope of forgiveness, I hereby bequeath my entire estate; all money and property, including my residence, located at 33 Angelwoode Lane, and the business of Morton-Albright Funeral Home and Memorial Chapel, to my son-in-law, Colton Mallord Albright, to operate, disperse, or dispense with, in whatsoever manner he so chooses. To my darling great-granddaughter, Natalie Stiles, I bequeath my gold railroad watch, as well as any other trinkets of amusement I may have left unaccounted for. I have summoned my housekeeper, one Wilma Ritchey, to bear witness to my own signature.

"Signed, John Beresford Morton

"Witnessed, Wilma Ritchey"

Jerry folded the paper, reinserted it into the envelope and gave it to Cynthia, who placed it in her bag. Natalie reached into the crystal inner liner and grasped the chain of John Morton's railroad watch. Jerry placed his hand on her shoulder. "Don't touch it, sugar. Let's leave old John as he is. If Jewell suspects our actions of tonight, she might order her *own* exhumation. That missing watch chain might undo us." Natalie nodded her head, then turned away. Jerry looked at his watch. "It's two-thirty. We've endangered Henry enough. If we don't hurry, the sun may catch us at our deed."

Natalie and I met Jerry, Cynthia, Ray, and Denise in the parking lot of Skeeter's Barbecue. Ray didn't look so good—pale and worn out. He sniffed his nose, then coughed once—said he was just tired from last night's work. We had gathered at Skeeter's to tell Colton Albright the news—that he now owned Morton-Albright Funeral Home and Memorial Chapel. Denise said, "Let's be careful how we tell him. We want to make him happy, not give him another stroke."

Colton shooed away a local surgeon to make room for us at his booth. Jerry, Cynthia, and Denise sat across from the old man. Natalie slid in next to him, nudging him over with her hip. Ray and I pulled up chairs. Colton took his time looking us over.

"All right," he said. "Who died?"

"Nobody died, Daddy." Denise said.

"Then why the hell are all of you here at the same time? One of my medical tests come out bad?"

"Yeah, your mental test," Natalie said. "Aren't you happy to see us?"

"I ain't sure yet."

"Watcha eatin' there, Colt?" Ray asked.

"Skeeter claims it's gator tail. I think it's a big ol' rattlesnake. Skeeter said he killed one yesterday out back of the restaurant. He thinks I've gone a-wobble in the head." Colton offered us all a sample of the strange-looking meat on this plate. We all declined, ordering pork sandwiches when the waitress came.

"Folks say it all tastes like chicken," Albright said, "but it don't. Now, look here if I don't see a pretty ring on Natalie's finger. You trick some boy into marriage?'

Natalie pointed to me.

"The casket wrassler? Why, I heard he's killed another one over at the store. Garage, I believe. Isn't that what you told me, Ray? 'When the killer's around, bodies are found,' I believe that's how Ray put it."

"Daddy," Denise said, "we've got some other news, too. Wonderful news, but shocking. Before John Morton died, he changed his will. Natalie stumbled across it in the attic. We all thought you should read it."

"Changed his will? The devil you say. Let me put my glasses on." The paper trembled in Colton Albright's hand—just his normal tremor at first, but the tremor grew shaky. When Colton's eyes reached the bottom of the will, he hung his head and wept. He blew his nose into his hanky, then looked up and spoke. "Jerry, Ray, how would you two fellows like to buy yourselves a funeral home?"

"How much?" Ray asked.

"A dollar. I'll have Percy take this will before the judge tomorrow morning. We'll conduct business in the funeral home at noon. I'll tell Jewell. Just like all the kids say these days—I'm gonna blow her mind."

Next morning, Percy called at nine o'clock. Jewell had indeed shown up at the courthouse—with Lex Talbert at her side. She spat and fumed and yelled. The judge threatened her with contempt, then retired to his chambers. When the judge returned, he proclaimed the original will invalid—not because of the second will but because the first will had been illegal from the beginning. Jerry told us Percy's account of the judge's ruling. "It's against the law to pass on a business in perpetuity, holding it in an estate until some nonexistent heir shows up." The funeral home was ours, for a dollar.

When Lex Talbert called in sick, Jerry laughed into the phone and told him to get well soon. He hung up the phone and continued laughing, sending us all into a rollick. We toasted our success with the clink of coffee cups. "Here's to our new owners," Carl said. Ray reached into his pocket and withdrew two quarters. He gave them to Jerry. "Here's my half for the purchase of Morton-Albright," Ray said. "You'd better hang on to it so I don't spend it before we sign the papers." Meredith said, "You boys better watch yourselves. I might tempt Colton with a five-dollar bill."

Natalie slipped her arms around Meredith and kissed his cheek. "I'll give a twenty if you make me an apprentice."

Jerry interrupted her snuggle with Meredith, "You keep your money, sugar. I've been thinking. . . ."

"Daddy?" The word trembled from Natalie's mouth.

"I'm not as big a fool as you think," Jerry said. "I know damn good and well that not even Casey Kight, as fine a young man as I've ever known, could ever say 'no' to my lovely, spoiled, smart-aleck of a daughter. I don't blame Casey. The spoiling's my fault. There's a further complication as well, that set me to thinking: my Natalie's got the gift, a gift that no person can bestow or take away. To deny my daughter her rightful place among her fellows is to make her suffer. I've watched her suffering, hoping for a cure. She found it in Casey, who was man enough to go against my strictest rule. He taught my daughter the trade. I'm damn proud of him. Forgive me, Natalie."

Natalie ran into her father's arms, both of them crying all over each other. I felt my own tears coming. The other men looked at the floor, or any other convenient place to hide their own eyes. Ray finally said, "Is it my imagination, or did it just get wetter in here?" He coughed and blew his nose into a hanky.

The telephone rang: death call in the county. "Me and the killer," Ray said. "We run the call. Meredith can clean the toilets while we're gone. Carl can inspect the front lawn for beagle shit."

Carl said, "Don't get uppity on me. You haven't signed those ownership papers yet. Keep fucking with me. I'll pack your orifices alive."

"Just a preview of coming attractions, boys," Ray said. "My reign of terror over Morton-Albright begins at noon."

On our way to the home of the deceased Mr. Bentley, Ray rolled down the window of the removal car. He honked the horn and waved at everyone we passed. We laughed all the way to the decedent's home. We laughed *at* the decedent's home. The immediate family had left the body with an in-law, who kept her hand over her mouth throughout the removal. The woman watched from the doorway as we loaded Mr. Bentley into the removal car. Ray smiled at the woman, waved, and said, "Have a nice day." We both resumed our laughter the minute Ray tore out of the driveway. At the traffic light of Druid and Stapleton, Ray squealed the tires as he made the right-hand turn. He floored the accelerator, laughing as we whizzed along Druid Road. Ray said, "Looky there. It's Colton Albright, on the front porch with Jerry and Percy." That's when I saw Bernard, ready to step off the curb with two armloads of flowers. I screamed, "Stop the car, Ray! It's Bernard!"

Ray slammed on the brakes. When Bernard saw us stop, the kid beat it across the road—never saw the Cadillac speeding toward him from the opposite direction.

They say everything goes in slow motion when you witness a tragic event. With Bernard, it went frame by frame: When the Cadillac hit Bernard, I heard a sound like a hundred-pound bag of laundry dropped from a building onto a parking lot. Then came the steam, hissing from the Caddy's radiator, reminding me of that Fourth of July sound—the fuses of skyrockets launched into the air. At once, I understood why those skyrockets bore floral trade names: Exploding Daisies and Atomic Roses and Sparkling Lilies. From the floral arrangements Bernard had carried, red and white glads shot through the air in curved trajectories, followed by a profusion of orange birds-of-paradise, flipping sideways. Chrysanthemums and daisies burst into pieces and petals, fluttering down atop the Caddy's hood. Finally, a shower of sparkling vermiculite. Bernard sailed through the air, hit the pavement, and rolled.

Ray remained behind the wheel for a moment, shaking his head. He said, "Come on, killer. Let's go see if we can help that poor old man who hit him." Ray pulled the removal car sideways, blocking traffic on our side of the street. The driver of the Caddy had done the same, traffic now stopped in either direction. Ray and I got out of the car and trotted across the street to help the old man struggle out of his Cadillac. Ray kept telling him, "Don't worry, mister. It's not your fault." Bernard's approaching ambulance wailed in the near distance. I looked at the front porch of Morton-Albright. The three men were gone. I looked down the street, to see if they had gone for Bernard— no sign of them in the crowd. I peered over the top of the Cadillac. Colton Albright lay facedown on the front porch of the funeral home. Jerry and Percy knelt over him. I tapped Ray on the shoulder. We both ran to the front porch, where we gathered ourselves around our fallen gentleman. Denise ran out onto the porch and fell upon her father, crying, "Oh, Daddy, Daddy." She stroked his silver hair, hugging him as his limp body allowed. Natalie rushed out and pushed Denise away. She ripped open Colton's shirt and put her ear to his chest. She placed two fingers on his neck, feeling for a pulse. She jumped to her feet, and screamed, "He's alive!"

• • •

Dr. Pritchett told us of Colton's prognosis: Terminal. Massive stroke, no chance of recovery. "He might hang on a day or two," the doctor said, "but that's pushing it." We had left the funeral home unattended, save Meredith and the Bentley family. Natalie set off a chain of whispers: First to Jerry, who whispered to Cynthia, who whispered to Denise. Cruel Jewell had not yet arrived at the hospital, so her daughters took command. Denise told Dr. Pritchett, "Since my father is in his last hours, we'd rather you put him in a private room, so we can spend time alone with him. Please take him out of intensive care." Pritchett agreed. They wheeled Colton into his own room and hooked him up to monitors that hummed and beeped. Natalie shooed us all out of Colton's room. Denise whispered to Ray. Ray nodded his head, took hold of Carl and me, and drove us back to Morton-Albright. "What was all the whispering about?" I asked. Ray said, "You know as well as I do, there's a few people out there who want Colton dead—*now*. Certain visitors might succeed. We failed to conduct our business transaction. Natalie won't let anybody near Colton—that's the plan: No visitors. That means none of us but Natalie, and the rent-a-cop I'm about to hire for the door to Colton's room. I'll find the biggest, baddest, redneck bubba they've got. Meanwhile, we've got work to do. Bernard is on the embalming table, and his prognosis isn't nearly as good as Colton's. Good thing, too. If the kid was alive, I'd kill him for dying in front of Colton like that. Then we've got the Bentleys. They've got prearrangements for graveside only. Lucky us. Finally, we'll have Colton's funeral, and we're talking the biggest service in Morton-Albright history."

Jerry arrived at the funeral home late. He called me into his office and asked me to sit. He said, "I don't need to tell you the trouble we're in. Natalie will stay with Colton. Denise will keep Jewell *away* from Colton. I remembered your offer to go to JFT. Are you still willing?"

"I am."

"Good man. I've spoken to Bernard's family. They're in shock, as you can imagine. They're good folks, too, but not well off. They know Colton's death will draw a thousand people. They almost sent their boy to Jesup, just because of Colton. I told them we'd care for Bernard at no cost. I've also asked them for a favor. They've agreed to call Lex Talbert at home, and ask him to be their director. Lex is haughty enough to come in, if I'm any judge of character. He'll be happy to take on the family whose son's death caused Colton's stroke—rub our faces in it, so to speak. You'll need a good reason to defect to the other side, to avoid suspicion. I've got other plans, too. We'll take care of this tomorrow, after the Bentley graveside."

Jerry explained the ruse in detail. A knock came at the door—Ray. "I'm here for Casey," he said. "I'm taking him out tonight. Casey's going to get drunk with me, aren't you, Casey?"

"I don't think so," I said. "I've never been drunk before."

"There ain't nothing to it, and we need to talk. Turn on your beeper and let's go."

I had never been to a bar, but the County Line was exactly as I had expected—full of cigarette smoke and the faint smell of vomit. Ray led me to a table. He called the barmaid Sweet Thang and ordered two cans of Pabst and two shots of Jack Daniels. When our drinks arrived, Ray said, "Here's how you do it, killer." He swallowed the shot of whiskey in a single gulp, then guzzled the entire can of beer and crushed it in his hand, all in less than a minute. "Ahhh. Just what I needed. Your turn, killer."

I picked up the shot glass and smelled the liquor—ungodly foul. I tried a sip, and spat it onto the tablecloth. "I can't do it, Ray," I said.

"Don't worry, killer. You like Kool-Aid?"

"I don't think they serve it here."

"This is Florida. Every bar in Florida sells Kool-Aid. It's the official State Drink." Ray called Sweet Thang back over. He said, "Hit me again, and bring my friend here a planter's punch." Ray downed my drinks while we waited for the barmaid. He lit a cigarette, took a big drag, then coughed out the smoke. He couldn't talk for hacking, and went on until his face turned red. "Sorry, killer. I gotta quit these things. Ever seen cancer lungs after an autopsy? Black as hell. Every time I see them I say, "I gotta quit smoking," but I never do. Hell, there are worse ways to check out. Remember that man and the airboat propeller? Jesus. Half a dozen body bags, and we didn't even bother with the stuff hanging off the trees."

When my pinkish red drink arrived, Ray winked at me. I sipped at the straw—not Kool-Aid, but not bad, either. By the time I finished it, I was slurring profanity at JFT with Ray. He blew his nose into a napkin, then looked straight into my eyes, as serious as I had ever seen him. He said, "Killer, I brought you here because I've got something to say to you, and it ain't easy for me."

"Before you start, I want to say something first. Would you please stop calling me killer? I've got a name, you know."

"You're right, Casey. I've been busting your balls ever since you walked in the door with that black suit of yours. It's my nature. That's one of the things I wanted to talk to you about, and I ain't proud that it took liquor for me to tell you. You're a good man, Casey. You've got pride in your work, and feelings for other folks. I yelled at you when I caught you feeling sorry for me losing my son. I'm sorry I did that, but mostly, I'm sorry about your mom and dad. It must have been real tough, growing up without them. I'm telling you this, because once Colton dies, we might never work together again. I wanted to make sure we parted as friends." Ray extended his hand across the table. I let him take hold of mine. He squeezed it tight.

The last thing I wanted to do was cry in a bar full of rednecks. I loved Ray Winstead. I picked up my napkin and pretended to cough into it. Ray did the same, only he wasn't pretending. I asked him if he was okay. He said, "Nothing another cigarette won't fix." He tapped one out of his pack. "Casey, I know I'm not your daddy, and I'm not pretending to be, but you're fixing to marry Natalie Stiles, and I figured you could use some advice from an old hand at marriage."

Ray explained the secrets of married life, the stuff nobody tells you: how to get laid, right after an argument; how long you should wait before you fart in front of your wife; how to avoid household chores and go fishing instead (just do the chores as badly as possible, without being obvious).

"I'll sum it up in one word." Ray flipped his lighter open and lit his cigarette. "Domestication," he said, snapping his Zippo shut. "Domestication is the key to a successful marriage, and it starts in the bathroom, *not* the bedroom, like most men think—we're talking toilet training here. Don't look at me like that, Casey. You must comply with your spouse on bathroom issues. First, you get yelled at for pissing on the toilet seat. You raise it next time. Then you get yelled at for failing to return the toilet seat to the *down* position. That happens in the middle of the night, when your wife gets up to piss in the dark and sits her ass down in the cold toilet water. Then you get yelled at for pissing on the floor. The *floor*, Casey. Are you getting this?"

I nodded.

"You take your morning piss. It comes out in two streams because your dickhole is stuck together—one stream hits the wall, the other hits your foot. You think you've cleaned it up, but your wife says *she* cleaned it up. There's only one solution, and it ain't pretty: you've got to squat. I mean, you've got to sit your ass down on that toilet and piss like a woman. How many men do you know with stand-up urinals in their bathrooms? None. A man might be the meanest son of a bitch in the world, but I never met one with a urinal in his house. Know why? Because his wife would end up cleaning the damn thing, and women can't even stand to *look* at a urinal, much less clean one. That's why they don't sell houses with urinals—no woman would buy it. Golden rule of marriage: more squat, more twat. Get yourself domesticated. You'll spend more time on top of your wife than under her thumb."

Ray talked on, hacking, blowing his nose, and smoking cigarettes in between. My three glasses of planter's punch were empty, and my bladder was full. The liquor hit me when I stood up to go to the men's room. I wondered how the floor could be moving while I was standing still. Ray came along to help me, but stopped at the bar to order another drink. I went ahead. A woman screamed at me when I mistakenly entered the ladies' room. I wondered what the hell she was doing in the men's room, until I unzipped my pants in front of an empty wall. Ray came in and yanked me out the door. He took me to the men's room, said I'd taken his squatting advice too far. Ray stood at a urinal himself, pissing all over the place from trying to pee and cough at the same time. He managed to zip his pants, then put his hand against a wall and started hacking again, until his face went purple. He collapsed on the bathroom floor. I didn't waste time with the bartender. I called the ambulance from the pay phone.

The ambulance guys bitched about being called for a case of intoxication. "He's not drunk," I said. "He's sick. He's drunk *and* sick. He's not sick from drinking. Get him to the hospital. Take his temperature. He's on fire. I'll follow you."

I thanked God for the flashing lights and siren ahead of me. I had no idea where the road was. A team was waiting for us at the hospital. The ambulance crew had radioed in the fever: 106. Pneumonic influenza. I called Denise, then sucked down three cups of coffee while I waited for her. Even in a panic, she was gorgeous. I knew the alcohol was making me think that way. I left Denise in the emergency room with her husband. I took the elevator up to see Natalie, in Colton's private room.

Ray had picked the right security guard. The guy was as big as the door he guarded, and he wasn't about to let me pass. He didn't speak to me at all. He just stood there, bubba-like, pointing at the red sign next to the door: No Visitors. I told him my name, and where I worked. I showed him my driver's license. I told him that Natalie was my fiancée. Big as he was, I even tried pissing him off. I called him obscene names. I called his *mother* obscene names. Finally, I just reached by him and jiggled the door handle. He grabbed my wrist, then yelled for the nurse. When she arrived, he said, "Call security." Natalie must have heard my commotion. She opened the door, just a crack. She looked tired. I told her about Ray. I told her I just wanted to see her. She asked me, "Have you been drinking? Jesus, Casey, you're a mess. I love you, darling, but I can't let you in. Mr. Percy is here with me. This is critical. Don't make me cry. I want to see you, but I can't. Trust me. I'm trying to save our lives in here. I'll call you tomorrow. Go home, Casey. Go home now." Natalie shut the door. From behind, I heard the footsteps of the security guards. I turned around. Two guys in uniform, reaching for me. I backed up into Bubba. "I won't cause trouble," I said. "I'm leaving."

"We're here to make sure you do. We'll escort you to your car. Try to stay, and we'll call the cops. You're now officially trespassing."

I obeyed the two men. They slammed the door of the removal car, and waited as I cranked the engine. I obeyed Natalie too. I went home, drunk and tired, worried and alone. I fumbled with the key and let myself in. I never made it to John Morton's bed. In the dark, I tried for the couch. I didn't make that either. I passed out on the floor of the living room.

My beeper woke me up. I shut it off and opened my eyes. Daylight blinded me, stabbing my brain with headache—nausea too: My first hangover. I went for the drapes, to close them. They were gone. I looked out the window. The removal car sat in the middle of the front lawn. I grabbed the window sill to keep myself from falling down. '*Go home now,*' Natalie had said. I had gone home, all right— to 23 Covington Place.

The voice came from the bathroom, a woman's voice, "Don't bother with that, Casey."

"What?" I called out.

"I said, don't bother with that, sweetheart." My mother's voice. I felt myself shaking all over. I went for the kitchen. I saw the boy. The scissors were in his hand. I crept up behind him and looked over his shoulder. He was looking at the colorful cardboard box. A picture of a beautiful woman with curly hair adorned the box. The lettering read "Betty Beeson's Home Permanent." The child turned the box over. I read the big red letters: "Hawaiian Getaway Sweepstakes." Below the letters were palm trees and a sandy beach. The boy began cutting along the dotted lines. "Stop it," I said. He pretended not to hear me. I tried yanking the scissors away from him. My hand passed right through him. I tried to scream, but my throat locked tight. I tried to run, but my shoes might as well have been nailed to the floor. Panic raced through my nerves. I felt dizzy. I longed to pass out. Then came the voice in my head—my *own* voice, *This is what you wanted. You wanted to remember. You're remembering. Calm down and remember.* I looked down. The scissors were in my hand. I finished cutting out the entry form. I filled in the blanks with a ballpoint pen, the kind you click. I heard footsteps coming toward me. I looked up at the person coming toward me—a walking flame of fire. The fire sucked itself into the person, and I beheld my mother. She had just finished with the permanent. She looked beautiful with her new curls. She twirled around, and said, "How do you like it?"

"You look like a movie star."

"A movie star?" She giggled, and said, "Nobody ever wins those contests, Casey. See the words? Enter as many times as you like. It's a gimmick, a trick to keep you buying more."

"But you'll win. I *know* you will."

"Okay, let's put it in the mailbox, then it's off to Hawaii, then Hollywood. You can be my agent. A movie star needs a good agent."

My mother put the entry form inside an envelope. She let me lick the stamp. Together, we walked through the living room, full of furniture, then out the door to the mailbox. I opened it, placed the envelope inside, and raised the red flag. The sunlight scorched my eyes. I heard the music from the Victrola. In the living room, all our neighbors had gathered. Couples were taking turns, dancing the jitterbug to the scratchy records. We were celebrating. I was dancing with Mom. Dad scooped me up off the floor and put me on his shoulders. He announced: "Here's the reason we're going to Hawaii—our own good-luck charm. My sonny boy. Only a kid would ever believe such a thing." Everybody applauded me. Dad set me back on the floor. He looked me in the eyes and rubbed my head. He said, "Thanks, sonny," then turned me around to face the neighbors. He said, "Okay, now. Everybody gets to rub Casey's head, for good luck."

The brightness of the sun shot pain through my eyes and into my head. I looked out the front window at the removal car, sitting in the middle of the lawn. My beeper sounded. I turned it off, and lay down in the middle of the floor, shaking and trying to cry. I was all cried out. Only heaves and moans came from my mouth. I gritted my teeth and pounded the floor with my fists.

No wonder Margee had taken all the pictures away. No wonder she had taken me away from my childhood home. Our neighbors had avoided us after the crash—they knew that I had filled out the entry form. They had all rubbed my head for luck—now they feared their own doom, just as Margee feared my remembering: I had killed my own parents, with a pair of scissors and a ballpoint pen. I had killed Jimmie Blessing with my feet. I had killed Daniel Coggin with my index finger. I had killed a boar, trying like hell to miss it. Ray had named me killer. He had named me right. I scrunched myself up in fetal position, trying to kill the pain in my stomach. What black star had cursed my birth? I walked out into the cold sun, stepped across gray lawn, got into the removal car, and drove to Morton-Albright. I wobbled into my apartment. Carl was the first to greet me, "Good God, Casey. You look like hell."

"Thanks," I said, heading for the coffee.

"First hangover is the worst," Jerry said. "If Ray wasn't so sick, I'd strangle him for taking you out last night. Go take a shower and try to throw up. You'll feel better. We've got less than an hour before Bentley's graveside. Think you can make it?"

"I can make it."

I could barely feel the shower on my skin for numbness.

At the Bentley graveside, Meredith gave me a nudge. "You dismiss the mourners," he said. "Might be your last chance."

I took my stance in front of the crowd. I wanted to say, "You're all going to fucking die someday," but I didn't. I did like I was supposed to do. I said, "This concludes the services for Nathan Bentley. On behalf of the family, I'd like to thank you for your attendance and participation. You may retire at your leisure."

The graveside-only service meant no lead car or limousine—just me and Meredith in the hearse. He patted my knee as he drove. "You don't look so good, Cap'n. You ought to see the doctor, Could be that flu bug."

Meredith parked the car in the garage. I headed for Jerry's office, and plopped myself down in the chair. Jerry asked me twice if I was up for our plan. I was. He said, "Lex is across the hall with Bernard's family. As soon as they leave, I'm going to start yelling at you. We've got to make it look good for Lex, or he won't buy it. After that, you're on your own for a while. Are you sure you can do this?"

"I'm sure."

"Good man."

The doorchime rang for the main entrance, signaling the departure of Bernard's family. "Let's go," Jerry said. He pushed me into the lobby. I fell down onto my butt. I could tell by his face that he hadn't meant to push me so hard. The yelling wiped the sympathy from his features—they turned angry red. He yelled, "I trusted you, Casey! I trusted you with my only daughter. How dare you defy me like that? You kept her in that blasted embalming room all summer long, didn't you?"

I got up and brushed myself off. From the corner of my eye, I caught Lex's startled face.

"Fuck you, Jerry!" I said. "Fuck you and your goddamn funeral home. If you were any kind of father, you would have taught Natalie the trade yourself. You're an asshole! I hate you! You hear me? I fucking hate you! Go ahead, kick me out. Natalie loves me. She'll hate you, too."

Jerry took me by the lapels, and pushed me against the wall. "I want your ass out of here within the hour. Don't come back." Jerry released me, then turned to Lex. "Here's your boy, Lex. Casey tells me you've made him a better offer. He's all yours."

Lex stood there like a stone. Jerry hustled back to his office, then back into the lobby. He threw my apprenticeship papers at me. "You'll be needing these," he said, then walked away. Lex finally found the ability to move. He said, "Let's talk. My office."

"You look like hell," Lex said.

"I got drunk last night. I knew what was coming today. I misjudged you, Lex. You were right about Jerry and Ray. I grew up an orphan. They treated me like family. I had never been treated that way. I hope you understand."

"I do indeed. My parents died as well. John Morton gave me a job in exchange for their lives. He tried the fatherly role with me. I saw through him. He was only protecting himself from a lawsuit, which I would have filed had it not been for my brother. Now that Colton's funeral is being planned, they don't need you anymore, as you discovered this morning."

"Your offer still stands?"

"It does. Gather your things. I'll make arrangements with Mr. Stark. He'll see you today. I promise."

"Where do I meet him?"

"Central Embalming—the old Jenner building."

I hadn't cranked the green MG in months. It felt strange, driving my own car again, but the breeze picked up as I accelerated, blowing away my tears. I knew Jerry hadn't meant the things he'd said, but it hurt me just the same. I had finally remembered my worst memories, only to be cut off from the only real family I had ever known, banished from the house of comfort. I was on my way to meet Lewis Stark, the devil himself, by all accounts.

I pulled into Jenner's parking lot, full of cars. The sign over the door still read the same: Jenner Cremation Services, but when I entered the front door, everything was different: a lobby area, decorated with silver wallpaper and modern furnishings had replaced the spareness of the old crematory. A large, round gentleman introduced himself: Lester Boggs. "I'm Mr. Stark's personal assistant," he said. "You must be Mr. Kight. Mr. Stark is waiting."

Myron Cheeves, the old creationist, had been right. Stark didn't look like the devil. A handsome man with a friendly smile, he stood as tall as Jerry. His military posture exuded command. He greeted me with a manicured handshake. His suit must have cost more than my entire wardrobe. His office looked like Mr. Spaceley's office, from the Jetsons. His drawl was sweet—pure Alabama. His youth surprised me most—if Stark was over thirty, it didn't show. "Have a seat, Casey. Don't be shy. I don't like shyness in a man. It's cowardly."

"I'm not shy," I said. "This place has changed since I was last here."

"For the better. I hope we can be friends. You like guns? I love 'em. Check this one out." Stark opened a drawer, pulled out a black gun, and laid it in the center of his desk. "German Luger. I've got a passel of guns, but this one's my favorite. Go ahead, pick it up. It ain't loaded."

I picked up the gun, weighed it in my palm, and aimed it at an abstract painting on the wall. I laid it back down on Stark's desk.

"I don't like that painting either," he said. "My wife decorated the office. I can always tell a man by the way he handles a pistol. You've never shot one in your life, have you? But then, you wouldn't have had the chance, growing up without a daddy to show you how. I know a lot about you, Casey. You don't know jack shit about me. Lex says you got fired for teaching Jerry Stiles's daughter how to embalm. I don't believe him. I think you're a spy. All the smart ones try to send a spy in on us. It doesn't matter now. Colton Albright is dead."

"Colton is dead?"

"Died ten minutes ago. Lex called me, just before you got here. Morton-Albright is mine, son. Lex Talbert and Albright's widow are on their way to my attorney's office, right now."

I fought my impulse to run out the door. I just sat there, squeezing the arms of the chair until the impulse faded. I belonged in Central's back room, with my own kind, where I could do no more harm to the living. I sighed, audibly, and surrendered.

"I'm sorry to hear about Mr. Albright," I said. "But I still need a job. Do you have one for me or not?"

"I do, and you just passed your spy test. I figured you'd run when you heard about Colton. Run and comfort Natalie. You didn't even flinch. You're the man I need. I'll put some serious jingle in your pocket, too. I'm losing my best man, Ricky Van Wort. He's finished. Three years on the job burned him out. You don't strike me as the burnout type. Lex tells me you're all blood and guts."

"I'm not squeamish, if that's what you mean. When do I start?"

"Right now. We'll see what you're made of. Here's your key." He tossed it across the table to me. Another key. Another door. Another house. I remembered the voice: *That's right son, houses are queer things. This one and that one—each has it's own story to tell.* I understood it now. The houses were all mine. So were the stories they told. With Colton Albright dead, my story would end here, in this house. I handed my apprenticeship papers to Lewis Stark. He asked me if I had any questions.

"I am curious about one thing," I said. "At Morton-Albright, we kept track of all the deaths at Sunset Towers. They all went to JFT funeral homes. How did you manage that?"

Stark laughed, then wiped his eyes. "Sorry, Casey. I don't mean any disrespect, but, hell, we *built* Sunset Towers. We didn't build it *directly*. This company owns that company which owns another company, and so on—take years to trace the paper and the money. We filled Sunset Towers with old folks—people with one foot in the grave, and the other on a banana peel. Here's the good part: When folks buy a condominium at Sunset Towers, we require them to fill out a personal information form. At the bottom of that form, there's a box to fill in: funeral home to contact in case of death. Since none of those folks are from around here, they don't have a local funeral home. We insert a little pamphlet into their welcome packet. Check *this* out." Stark took a pamphlet from a drawer and laid it on his desk.

The wording on the pamphlet asked a question: "Have You Made Your Final Arrangements?" On the inside of the pamphlet, I read, "When would you rather make final arrangements? Before the inevitable happens, at a lower price, or on the worst day of your life?"

"These people don't know who to call, so we send a representative right to their door, with a book full of pictures of our funeral homes. They all have different names, so they never suspect that no matter which funeral home they pick, the body comes right here to Central. Right now, that happens to be our problem. This flu bug has got us swimming in bodies, and your job is to get them out of here as quick as you can kiss a duck."

"We also need to discuss my salary," I said.

"Bingo. Spies never ask about money. If you had walked into that back room without your money on the table, I would have turned your ass into cremation dust. How much do you want?"

"Whatever your present supervisor makes, plus twenty-five percent. He's underpaid, and probably doesn't know it, because I'd guess he's never worked for anyone but you."

"You're right, and you've got my attention. How did you figure that?"

"Because of Daniel Coggin. No man would leave a family operation to work in your Central facility, not unless he was a man like me. Are we clear on my salary?"

18

"Let the dead bury the dead." That's what Jesus told some man in the Bible. That man might as well have been me. I had spent most of my life without feeling. The Presence that indwelled Morton-Albright, and Natalie's touch, had brought me back to life. Now it had fled me as fast as it had quickened me, like some odd-shaped flower that had bloomed in the night, burned to a cinder by the morning sun. I slipped easily back into my self-imposed state of shock.

"Go ahead, Casey," Stark said. "I know you're dying to try out your new key." The door was black metal. I turned the key in the dead-bolt lock. The door was so heavy, it required the strength of my shoulder to push it open. It closed by itself with a pneumatic device. The clunk of the door reverberated through the cavern of Central Embalming— nothing more than a huge, open warehouse, compartmentalized into twelve embalming stations by movable walls, neck-high. I felt the heat from the two cremation retorts. Enclosed within high, rectangular walls, their stacks wormed up to the ceiling.

The whole place was a frenzy of activity and conversation. Reflective tape marked out a route for the forklift, its operator now removing a casket from the racks opposite the embalming stations. The caskets were stacked six high, and their racks hid most of the wall, half a football field in length. Stark led me to the last embalming station. "Farthest away from those damn retorts," Stark said. "One of the benefits of your job." Stark introduced me to Ricky Van Wort. Not much older than me, dressed in old clothing and a bloodstained apron, he smiled, and greeted me. "Boy, am I glad to see you."

Stark issued orders to Ricky. "Give Casey the full tour—and I mean *full*. He's cleared for complete access."

"Congratulations," Ricky said. "The juicers are going to hate you. Stark hired you from the outside. Word is, you're still an apprentice. Everybody here knows that Stark only hires licensed embalmers for supervisors. The only reason you're getting away with it is because you're not teaching anybody, so the licensed embalmers here are pee-issed at you already. If they fuck with you, fuck right back. Get their attention, you'll get their respect. Most of them are assholes, anyway, and you won't know them for long, so don't worry about it. They all quit after a few months, or switch to removals, then back again. The mean ones can't even take this shit day after day, so they'll never work in a real JFT funeral home. It's four years mandatory in a Central Facility before you sit behind a desk. I got a year off my sentence for good behavior, and her." Ricky cast his eyes to a picture of a young blond woman in a blood-splattered frame. "Wendy," he said. "She's back home in Montgomery. You got a girl?"

"Natalie," I said. "We're engaged, or at least we *were*—my former employer's daughter."

"Ouch."

"Yeah. It's a bad situation. Her grandfather died today."

"Jesus, and you're *here*? You *are* blood and guts, man."

"It's not like that. I'm not exactly welcome around her family anymore."

"You fucked up, huh?"

"I taught her embalming at night. Her father caught me and threw me out the door."

"Think she's still after you? Hell, Stark would hire her in a minute. We've got female embalmers all over the South. All you need is a pulse to work here, and after a while, it's better that you don't have the pulse. Let me get out of my apron. Time for the tour. Just follow the forklift."

We passed through a large opening in the end wall. Beyond it lay another fifty yards of work space, filled with vehicles: a dozen removal vans, seven Buick hearses, seven Buick limousines, three casket trucks. "The rolling stock," Ricky said. "The Buicks are JFT policy: Nobody in grief knows the difference between a Buick and a Cadillac, and the Buicks are a hell of a lot cheaper. Everything gets cheaper as we go along. A dollar here, a dollar there—it all adds up to more profit. It bothered me until I got my first profit-sharing check."

Ricky took me to a strange-looking machine. "From here to the front door, everything else is illegal. I'm telling you this because I know you're not for real. I don't know how you got past Stark, but you can't fool me. I work with juicers every day. You don't belong here. My advice is that you patch up things with your ex-boss and go home. I can see it in your eyes—you're not the JFT type. You're a nice guy. You're polite, you don't swear. I used to be just like you, until I got mixed up with these assholes. If you're a spy, I don't want to go down with JFT. I'll even *help* you, for chrissake. You don't have the killer inside."

I grabbed Ricky by the shirt and shoved him against the wall. I said, "Listen here, cocksucker. You don't know anything about me. I'm here because you're too pussy for this job. I'm here for the duration. Look into my eyes *now*. I was born for this place. You're just doing time. Go back home to Wendy, you sniveling little shit."

"Okay, man. Jesus. Just let me go."

I released him. He snatched a phone off the wall and punched two numbers. He spoke into the phone, "Lew, it's Ricky. The new man's with us. Yes, I'm sure. I laid it on thick. He's clear. The full tour."

"Sorry I had to do that, man. Spies are always ready for a guy like Stark. They're *never* ready for me. Welcome to Jacob Funeral Trust. This weird machine you're looking at is a casket crusher." Ricky pressed a button, raising the compactor lid. Inside the crusher was a block of wrinkled steel. "We keep this casket in here for the state inspectors. It's the only casket we've ever destroyed. Some cremations demand a viewing. We're supposed to cremate the casket, or destroy it, because reselling a used casket is illegal. We send the used ones to the workshop next door. They replace the old bedding and put the reconditioned casket back in inventory."

Ricky led me back to his embalming station. He took Wendy's picture off the countertop and dropped it into the trash. "Stark figured you were mushy over your girl, so he gave me one, too. We cut this picture out of a magazine. Nice touch, huh? Your job is to make sure that Stark doesn't need to get involved with day-to-day embalming operations. The man's got funeral homes to run, contracts to negotiate, stuff like that, okay? So the last thing he wants is a problem in Central Embalming that requires his attention. But he knows he's got more than he can say grace over with this flu epidemic, so things are moving in a weird direction around here, and Stark is spending more time back here. Apparently, he thinks you can get us out of this mess. He needs a man who can rapidly desensitize himself. You've got to do your full share of caseloads, directly oversee cremations, and keep these guys from going bugshit on you. The good part is that Central is built for speed. So you've got to shed that family-funeral-home skin of yours and enter the modern era of the funeral trade, and you've got to do it *fast*. You're gonna love the next part: juicing— embalming, if you want to call it that." Ricky explained JFT embalming procedure: Face and hands only, five-minute operation. The only parts that needed to look good were the parts that showed. No trocar either—a waste of time on local burials. JFT included a single day of visitation in their pricing. Extra days were a thousand dollars each. "Nobody packs asses with cotton around here, either," Ricky said. "We use plastic pants that zip all the way up to the armpits." JFT didn't dress the bodies, either. They sent them naked to the funeral homes, to avoid mixups with clothing. Autopsies were quick work too—no more snipping up bags full of viscera, just throw the bag into the cremation retort. The cavity got stuffed with excelsior straw. "In other words, there is no art of embalming. It's just taxidermy—human taxidermy."

A glob of mush splattered the side of my neck. Ricky said, "Get a towel and wipe yourself. I forgot to tell you about the Organ Wars. Some juicer's working an autopsy, a couple of stations away. He's introducing himself. Looks like brain. That's why the supervisor gets the end cubicle—you only get organs flying at you from one direction—keeps you out of the crossfire when things get messy. You'll never make it through the day in that suit. Never come to work without a spare set of clothes. These guys fill squirt guns with blood, then come up behind you and shoot. Stay away from anyone working a trocar—we do cavity work on shippers. You walk by the wrong station, and the guy will open fire on you with the reverse-flow switch."

A new pile of guts splattered me, this time on my face. "More brain," Ricky said. "I'll go tell him to cut it out."

"I'll go with you," I said. We found the autopsy case three cubicles away. A guy wearing a baseball cap stood over an open cavity. Ricky introduced us. "Greg, meet Casey."

"Hi, Greg," I said, the brain glop still hanging from my face. Greg laughed, and said, "Gotcha." I wiped off the glob and threw it at Greg, splattering him midface. "You need to work on your aim," I said. Ricky slapped me on the back, said, "Nice throw. Watch Greg close up the autopsy, and say good-bye to the baseball stitch."

Greg wiped his face, stuffed the cavity with excelsior straw from a barrel, then grabbed an electric staple gun. He shot thirty staples in less than a minute, the covered the Y-incision with clear packing tape. A caulking gun loaded with epoxy sealed the cranium onto the skull. Greg stapled the scalp together, then sealed it. "Three minutes," Greg said.

"Tag the bag," Ricky told Greg. "The Organ Wars are over." Greg signed his name on a tag, then twisted it onto the viscera bag. Ricky picked up the bag and told me to follow him to the sink—a long, deep trough with several spigots and drains. Ricky dropped the bag into the sink. "Every juicer must sign a tag before he brings the viscera to the sink. We had to start tagging because some of the guys were just twisting the tops of the bags. They'd put the bag upside-down in the sink. When the cremationist picked up the bag, the guts fell out into the sink, so the cremationist had to pick up the guts and put them back into the bag. Drove the guy crazy—the old guy from Jenner.

"Myron Cheeves?" I asked.

"Yeah, that was him. What a fucking goof. Stark fired him—the guy kept calling him Mr. Stork. Let's go see the fridge. It's a mess, and it's our main problem—the flu epidemic means we've got more bodies coming in that we do going out. We're getting a whole night crew of specialists coming in from all over the South. These guys are cold motherfuckers, and you will not be allowed in here after hours. That means apocalyptic illegalities; so don't bother trying to impress Stark by volunteering for overtime. We all work ten-hour days, just like in a normal funeral home, but it boils down to an average of minutes per body, from the fridge to the delivery van. Any questions?"

"The fridge?"

"Right. "

Ricky opened the refrigerator door—a huge walk-in. It had been designed to hold fifty bodies, stacked in stainless steel trays. The trays were full. All of the bodies on the floor wore red toe tags, or no toe tags. "Red tag means cremation," Ricky said. "No tag means cremation too—indigent. We don't waste tags on indigents, just an X on the foot with magic marker. Don't believe what you read in the papers about the flu—they only report confirmed cases. You're looking at the real numbers, right here, and it's getting worse by the hour." Colored toe tags dangled from the bodies on the shelves, too: White for local burial, blue for shippers. My first priority was to get the cremation bodies off the floor and into the retorts. The only way to get the bodies off the floor was to cremate more than one body at a time—illegal, without written consent, and nobody ever gave written consent. I realized now that Stark had trapped me. Accepting the job would make me a criminal, from the moment I tied my apron.

Ricky said, "Time to meet the sweeper. Actually, he's more like a shoveler. He's not even an apprentice, just a local jack-off—Derrick Lott. The guy is twitchy, too, and half a bubble off plumb, probably because he's a stoner. I smoke a little weed once in a while myself, but Derrick keeps a bag of it in his Popeye lunch box. He's going to hate you when he sees you in that suit, and you've got to get on his good side, fast. When he's pissed at you, he slows down, and you don't want that."

We found Derrick, shoveling bones out of a retort. The bones went into an aluminum garbage can. Derrick didn't look like a stoner—his hair was cut like an army recruit. "Hey, Ricky," he said politely. When he saw me, he stopped shoveling and leaned on his shovel. He asked Ricky, "Who's the fucking suit?"

"This is Casey. He's cool. He's not with Stark. He's the new head juicer. He needed the suit for the interview, that's all."

I told Derrick he could pick his own supervisor: me, or Stark. "And we both know that Stark's an asshole," I said.

"I hate the motherfucker," Derrick said. "My hair was past my shoulders when I started this job. I buzzed it after it caught fire a couple of times."

"Just do the same job for me as you did for Ricky, and I'll keep the motherfucker out of the hair you've got left."

Derrick said, "We're cool."

Ricky took me to the grinder. The old one had been replaced by the Luxor of grinders—huge, angry, ready to eat. "Grinds a canful of sweepings in ten seconds." Five trashcans of pulverized cremains stood next to the grinder, each with an ice scoop sticking out of it. "Commingled cremains," Ricky said. "Also illegal without written consent, but nobody can tell the difference between Uncle Fred and

Aunt Ethel. When the front office asks for cremains, Derrick fills the box and labels it with whatever name they ask for. End of tour. Stark wants you back in his office now."

Stark grinned at me from behind his desk. "Find anything interesting back there?"

"You mean besides your disregard for the Code of Ethics? If you meant it to bother me, you failed. Dead is dead—staples or baseball stitch, it's all the same to me. Double Ricky's salary and I'll clean up the floor in the refrigerator."

"I'll do it, but get one thing straight: if you report me to the Board, it'll take them three days to process your complaint. After that, the Board is required to give me twenty-four hours notice before an unscheduled inspection. I can have this place as clean as a preacher's ass in a day. Then I file against you for making a false complaint. I need that floor cleaned up, starting at seven A.M. tomorrow."

"You're letting me off early today?"

"I am. You need the rest. You're kicked out of Morton-Albright, too. Where will you sleep tonight?"

"Since you own Morton-Albright now, I'd like to keep my apartment there—throw it back in Jerry's face. Besides, Mr. Albright is now in repose. Jerry will have to deal with my signature in Colton's register."

"Hell, Casey. Colton Albright ain't dead. I was lying—waiting for you to run back. If you'd been spying, you would have left. The old bastard is still hanging on. As for your apartment, I'd be surprised if Jerry let you stay there tonight."

"I have my own place."

"I know. Twenty-three Covington Place. That's what I like about you, Casey. You're not just blood and guts. You've got spooky shit going on, too. Take a lot of walks down memory lane in that old house, do you? You give me the willies, boy. You're perfect for the job."

• • •

I drove straight to a pay phone and called Jerry—he'd meet me at the hospital: It was the only place we could be seen together without suspicion. We met in Ray's waiting area. "I'm in," I said. "You were right. They threw two men at me, a mean one, and a nice one. I was terrified. I've never acted that way before in my life. Stark told me Colton was dead, as soon as I walked in the door."

I explained all the violations I had seen. Stark had told the truth about the inspection process. Jerry said, "If we can get Ray out of here for a few hours tomorrow, you can drop the bomb, as soon as you walk in the door. You'll risk your license if you perform any work."

Ray's condition: His pneumonia was bacterial, not the viral type seen in children and the elderly. Ray was responding quickly to intravenous antibiotics, but his fever was still high. "The hospital won't release him unless his fever goes down—not even for a few minutes."

"Is he talking?"

"Hasn't shut up for hours. He keeps asking for the killer."

"Natalie?"

"She's still with Colton, under security. We lost Percy." The family lawyer had been waiting with Natalie. If Colton became lucid, Percy was to stick a pen in his hand and have him sign the documents for the sale of Morton-Albright. Colton's speech remained incoherent. Percy refused to accept Colton's signature—the law required a sound mind for signing the documents.

Natalie had her own project under way—no visitors, not even me. Even after remembering my hand in the death of my parents, when I thought of Natalie, I believed in her touch. Jerry suggested I call her. For now, Natalie was untouchable, and it seemed as though fate had designed it that way—that I would not have her when the memories came.

Denise was not untouchable. I met her as she walked out of Ray's room as Jerry left for home. She hugged me close and kissed me. When our lips parted, I felt the tip of her tongue. "You look tired," she said. "Hungry, too. I've got cold fried chicken in the fridge."

Denise had more than cold chicken; she had peaches and brandy, too, but mostly brandy. The sweetness of the peaches helped me tolerate the brandy fumes. Denise ate her peaches, drank the brandy, and poured herself another glass. She drank that one, too. On her way to the sofa, she took my fingers, and took me with her. She sat close to me on the sofa, brushing the back of my hair with her fingertips. It felt like years since I had been touched, and with Denise doing the touching, not to mention the gazing, it wasn't long before I found the hope of comfort behind her blue eyes. "Hold me, Casey," she said. I wrapped my arms around Denise, and reveled in her womanly squishiness. "It's been so long," she whispered in my ear. "I love your hands on me. You're gentle. I like that. Kiss me, Casey." It was then that I knew I could have her—the object of my dream lust. Her body was warm against me. It sent me into a confused state of arousal; the heat of her body belied the coldness in her kiss. In her mouth, I tasted the same emptiness of my own heart. When we parted, my quickened breath abated. I beheld her face: her perfect features waned into a mirror of my own desperate abandonment—two mirrors, reflecting only the dark. There was no comfort here, no deep affection—just two injured souls, grasping for what we had lost. I pulled myself slowly away from her, and stood up. "I can't do this," I said. "I love Natalie."

Denise began to cry, apologizing as she wept, "I'm so sorry, Casey. I've dragged you into my loneliness. I knew you were lonely, too. Ray—ever since the baby—he's been lost to me. I know he's hurt, but I'm hurt, too."

I told Denise that I could not fix her hurt. I couldn't even fix my own. I told her to trust in Ray's goodness, not mine. There was nothing good in me to trust. Denise said, "Then why did you turn me down?"

"I can only bring you more harm," I said. "In case you haven't noticed, being around me can get you killed. I am a mistake. I should have died with my parents. Death has attached itself to me, and it will not let me go. I've got to meet Death, face-to-face, to find out its business with me. If it wants me, it can have me, but I won't let it cling to me any longer."

The phone rang: Jerry. Natalie wanted us at the hospital, quick.

Bubba stepped out of the way when Jerry, Denise, and I approached Albright's private room. We found Natalie at his side. He was either sleeping or unconscious. Natalie held up a sheet of paper. "It's Granddaddy's new will," she said, "in his own handwriting. Percy can't argue with this. I got it out of Granddaddy a word at a time. He kept waking up, talking about horses and cows. Every time he woke up, I got a new word out of him. All it needs is his signature, and a witness. I've had it. I need to go home and sleep. Hell, I might be sleeping now. Am I sleeping?" Natalie stopped talking. Sitting straight up in the chair, eyes wide open, she began to snore. Denise offered to stay the night. She'd call if Colton woke up again. Jerry and I went to check on Ray. He was sitting up in bed. "I hope one of you has a pack of cigarettes," he said.

"Are you well enough to get yourself in trouble with the police tomorrow?" Jerry asked.

In the parking lot of the hospital, I cranked the MG. I didn't drive home, as I had told the others. I drove to Central Embalming. On the way, I realized I also knew I might leave this world at the end of Stark's pistol, but not before I had atoned for my sins. I prayed for the strength of Samson—how he had used the chains that bound him to break the pillars of the house of evil, even though he himself was destroyed when the building fell upon him. I had to do this without help; without the Presence; without Natalie; without comfort. With this in mind, I pulled into Central's property, and parked my car behind an adjacent warehouse. The secret labors of the night crew meant evil business.

I snuck into Central through the motor pool, dodging between hearses and removal vans. Once inside the main warehouse, I crawled on my belly beneath the casket racks until I reached the end rack. I stood up and flattened myself against the wall in the dark, facing the embalming stations. Stark himself stood at the head of an embalming table. A body lay upon it. Two dozen steel bins, like laundry bins on wheels, sat parked in a line. The smell of rotting corpses crawled up my nose.

The twelve-man crew had squeezed themselves into the cubicle with Stark. I couldn't see much, but I heard Stark's voice: "We're in trouble," he said. "We're out of room in the fridge. We've got bodies stacked in the retort areas, too, and the heat is causing rapid decomposition. The whole fucking place stinks. We've got to optimize the space in the retorts. That's why you gentlemen are here. Bodies don't stack like timber—limbs are sticking out, wasting space in the retorts. We can fill that space by changing the shape of the bodies. I'll show you how. Give me some room." The men parted as best they could, giving me a clear view. Stark gave a stopwatch to one of the men. "Time me," he said, then got to work. With a long knife, Stark made two quick slices at the thigh of the body, making a circular cut around the limb. He dropped a knife, grabbed a bone saw, and cut off the limb with four quick thrusts of the saw. He threw the limb into one of the bins. The timekeeper announced: "Thirty-three seconds." Stark calculated the time. "Two and a half minutes per body." He amputated the other three limbs, then scanned the group. He picked a young blond man, gave him the bone saw. Stark commanded him: "Take off the head."

The guy just stood there with the saw in his hand.

Stark said, "You've got to stop thinking 'human body' and remember your trigonometry. We've got a nice rectangular, stackable torso with a ball on top. That ball has got to go. Take off the fucking head."

The guy still couldn't move himself. Stark snatched the saw from his hand, said, "I *hate* pussies!" The men all took a step backward. Stark grabbed the body by the hair and jerked the amputated torso toward himself, then placed the edge of the bone saw beneath the Adam's apple. I didn't want to watch the rest, but I couldn't testify against Stark's action unless I actually witnessed it. I already knew it would remain in my mind forever: Stark sawed through the throat, then through the bones in the neck. Stark held the head aloft by the hair, then flung it toward the bin. The head hit the corner of the bin, then hit the floor. It bounced once, then rolled toward *me*. I ducked under the casket rack. Stark came after the head, swearing. "I'll work Station One," he said. "Y'all get busy."

I had seen enough. I lay under the casket rack, my mind so engorged with what I had seen, there was barely room for thought. Only the numbness of not knowing what to do prevailed inside me. When the thoughts began to creep into my brain, they were thoughts of judgment, thoughts that distinguished one thing from the other, right from wrong. Ray had said that I would never see anything more hideous than what a medical examiner does in the course of his daily routine, that there was no violation of the dead more excessive than autopsy. I had told Stark myself that dead is dead—there was no difference between a staple gun and the baseball stitch. I remembered the conversations of old Cracker men I had overheard during visitations. They said things, like, "When it's my turn to go, dig a hole and throw me in the dirt. I don't need no fancy funeral. When I'm gone, I'm gone." If the old men were right, then Stark's disregard for the flesh was only illegal, not immoral. And what of Ray? Where had he lain the body of Waldo Shipper? Did it matter? What of my new family? They had disturbed the grave of John Morton for a piece of paper. I had helped. Had we done right or wrong?

I peered out of my hiding place and watched Stark's men at work. If the flesh didn't matter, once its spirit had fled, why was I shocked to tears as I watched the mutilations? "All blood and guts." That's what some men said of me, but as I lay in my hiding place, watching, weeping, I wondered: who was I weeping for? The dead, who could neither feel nor think, nor react in any way to the violence done to them? My question answered itself for me: I remembered the young boy, Jody Christian, how his parents had been comforted in the Iris Room, how they had thanked me for providing that comfort. I imagined them lying there with me, under the casket racks, their son on one of Stark's tables. I remembered my mother, in the comic-book page, pleading, "Don't let my boy see me like this." That was when the words came to me, Gladstone's words, from the obelisk of the Morton plot: "Show me the manner in which a nation cares for its dead . . . the tender mercies of its people . . ." Like a church bell, the words rang in my head.

I drove to a pay phone and called Jerry. I told him what I had seen. The phone went silent, except for Jerry's breathing. I asked him, "Are we ready for tomorrow?"

Jerry cleared his throat several times, then worked at his answer. "Detective—Detective Jones," he said. "Jones came to the hospital after you left. When we run our play tomorrow, Lex Talbert must say the name. Do you understand? He must say the name Waldo Shipper, or we're finished. Colton hasn't signed the will, and I don't think he's coming back. Jones worked everything out with the hospital staff."

At 7:00 A.M., I strode past Stark's office. The door was open. He called me in. I sat down. "Colton's dead again," he said. "I just got off the phone with the hospital. At ten A.M., Jacob Funeral Trust will acquire Morton-Albright Funeral Home and Memorial Chapel."

"Four million?" I said.

"Lex told you. It's a fair price. We're in an equity situation with that place."

"Why didn't you use the family secret?" I asked. "I always wondered that. It's how you got Jesup. It's how you got Coggin. Why didn't you just threaten Jerry and Ray with the family secret?"

"Are you stupid, Casey? That's the first thing I went after. I had men scour back issues of newspapers, county records. I listened for rumors of sex scandal. Morton-Albright is the cleanest store I've seen. That's why it took us so long to get it. Even Lex Talbert told me the place was clean. There *is* no family secret."

"Then Lex didn't tell you," I said, "and now I know *why*. If he gave up the secret, you wouldn't need him anymore—the secret would have been enough for blackmail. That *is* how you normally work, isn't it? But Lex bragged to me about how he told you, so it didn't make sense to me, until now."

"Listen to me, you little shit!" Stark arose from his chair, breathing hard, hands on the desk, eyes on me. "I say you're a lying mother-fucker. Do you know what I do with lying motherfuckers?"

"Turn their asses into cremation dust?"

"I've seen spies before, but you're on a suicide mission, son. You'd better start talking, and you'd better make me believe your ass."

I told Stark everything Lex Talbert had told me about Waldo Shipper. When I finished, he said, "Fuck!" and picked up the phone. He yelled into it, "Glenn, wake your ass up. Call Jewell Albright and withdraw our offer, now!" He slammed down the phone, picked it up again, and told Lex Talbert to get his ass to Central.

I asked Stark, "Should I get started on the fridge?"

"You keep your ass right where it is. Where I can see it." He called in his assistant, Lester Boggs. Stark told him, "Call Derrick Lott. Tell him to get his ass in here, quick—I'll pay him a thousand dollars for an eighteen-hour shift."

Lex entered Stark's office in a cower, absent his usual smugness. Stark asked him a single question: "Who the fuck is Waldo Shipper?"

Lex eyed me, his face now burning red. I realized the man's weakness: he lacked self-control. He could have sat there, stone-faced, and called me a liar. Stark would have believed him. Instead, Lex Talbert betrayed himself to Lewis Stark, just by the way he looked at me, never mind the words. "You ungrateful bastard child. I helped you get this job. This is how you pay me back?"

"I was just trying to help," I said. "I didn't realize you were trying to fuck Mr. Stark, here. Whose side are you on, anyway?"

Stark grabbed the phone and dialed a number. "This is Lewis Stark at Jacob Funeral Trust," He said. "I want to report an illegal burial." He pulled the Luger from his drawer and laid it on the desk, then he gave the phone to Lex, and said, "Tell them everything you know about Waldo Shipper." White-faced, Lex studied the pistol, swallowed hard, and took the phone. When he finished talking, he slowly returned the phone to its cradle and said, "We're to meet Detective Jones and Dr. Kendall at the police department, now."

"Should I get started on the fridge?" I asked.

"Will you shut up about the goddamn fridge? The three of us are taking a ride."

At the police department, Detective Jones left Stark and me in the waiting area while he took Lex's complaint and deposition. Afterward, Jones put the three of us into an unmarked car. A cruiser drove behind us, followed by Dr. Kendall, the county medical examiner. On the way, Jones dropped a note into my lap; "Make sure Lex says the name." The word *name* was underlined three times. Jones pulled the car into the porte cochere of Morton-Albright. Jerry and Ray were waiting for us in the office. Ray looked like hell. I wondered if he'd last the ordeal. Jones explained the charges, then asked Ray, "What do you know about this?"

Ray said between coughs, "Can't we postpone this until after Colton's funeral? It's not like the body you're looking for is going to get any deader."

Jones apologized, but said we needed to take care of the matter now. Jones repeated his question—he asked Ray about the illegal burial.

Ray said, "You can believe what you like. I believe Lex has gone crazy from having geriatric sex with Cruel Jewell Albright. She's seventy-five, which pretty much makes Lex a necrophiliac."

Lex's face changed colors like a chameleon—mostly purple, though. He said, "You son of a bitch," and dove for Ray. Jones held Lex back and told him, "You're here to make an accusation, not to end up in the pokey for battery. We all know Ray's a smart-ass. Take it easy."

Lex stood up straight and tugged his jacket down. Jones gave Ray a last chance to defend himself. Jerry spoke up, "Ray, you don't have to say a word. Let me call an attorney."

Ray said, "I don't need an attorney. Lex needs an attorney. If he's banging Cruel Jewell, he might be stalking the nursing homes, too."

Jones fended off another attack by Lex. He said, "You move on Ray one more time, and I'll cuff your ass and take you to jail." Jones also told Ray to shut up and get into the back of the police cruiser. Jerry rode with Kendall. I grabbed hold of the armrest when I realized where we were going: Angel Shores Beach—the approach to Tampa airport. I now had more to worry about than our business—I feared the onset of an episode, right in front of everybody. My anxiety soared when I saw the county backhoe, rolling off the back of a flatbed truck, right in front of the clearing; the giant coquina rock; the place where I had stood after my job interview with Jerry. Panic sent me trembling. There was no way I could coax a name out of Lex in my condition. I couldn't even speak.

The backhoe roared up the incline to the clearing. We all followed its racket. The driver parked the backhoe at Lex's command, then let the engine idle. We arranged ourselves into four groups: Stark, Lex, and myself on one side of the backhoe's arm; Jerry and Ray on the other; the law in between. Two guys with shovels stood next to the backhoe. Kendall spoke first, "I'm here strictly as an observer for the moment. If we find a body here, it's my job to identify it."

Off in the distance, I heard the noise of an approaching jet. Jones looked at me, as if to ask for help with getting Lex to say the name. I shook my head as imperceptibly as possible. Ray must have heard the airplane too—he looked up into the sky, then at me. He kicked at the soil, then nodded his head. The roar of the jet grew louder. I looked up and watched the sky disappear, leaving only the airliner and its scream. I put my hands over my ears. I gritted my teeth until the shaking subsided—I had warded off the episode, but the shaking had made my bones hurt. Stark asked me if I was okay. It took everything I had inside me to say the word yes. Jones spoke next, "Ray Winstead, did you bury a body on these premises?"

"How the fuck should I know, Jonesy? I've been a funeral man for thirteen years. I've got bodies buried all over the county. Do you expect me to remember where I put them all? Lex Talbert seems to remember. Ask him."

Lex said, "I stand by my word. I know what I saw. I saw Ray bury the casket, right here."

"Let me get this straight," Detective Jones said. "First, you tell me that Ray buried a body, then you say he buried a casket. Which was it, a body or a casket?"

"It was both—the body was *in* the casket," Lex said.

"Did you see Ray Winstead put the body in the casket?"

Ray interjected, "Jonesy, I might as well confess." Ray waited until everyone got quiet, then said, "I confess that Lex Talbert is the perverted butt-spanker of the elderly."

"Goddamn it!" Lex screamed, his face twisted and scarlet-purple. "What the fuck is wrong with you people? Dig! The body of Waldo Shipper lies here, and Ray Winstead put him there."

"Excuse me," Jones said to Lex. "I'm not sure I heard you correctly. Did you say Waldo Shipper?"

"You're goddamn right I did. With my own eyes, I watched Ray Winstead bury Waldo Shipper on this spot!"

Jones turned to Ray. "Do you recall burying Waldo Shipper here?" he asked.

Ray said, "Waldo Shipper? Hell, he's buried at Fairview Cemetery. I saw to the sealing of the vault. I thought you were talking about some other body I might have buried and forgot about."

"Sorry, Mr. Talbert," Jones said. "We can't dig here."

"I stand by my word," Lex said. "Dig, goddamn it! Dig!"

"We *can't* dig. You specified a name, dumbass. There's no probable cause, now that it's your word against Ray's. According to police procedure, that requires us to dig in the most likely place first, at Fairview Cemetery."

Kendall said, "I'm the only person in the county who can recommend an exhumation at Fairview. I take the case before the judge. He'll decide against you, unless the family gives written permission, testifying that they have been informed of Lex Talbert's accusation of illegal burial."

Lex said, "I stand by my word. You'll find a casket buried in Waldo Shipper's grave. Make sure you look inside it. It's empty. I know. I know. I was there. The casket was far too light to contain a human body."

Jones summed it up: "Lex Talbert has just confessed that he knowingly buried an empty casket at Fairview Cemetery. Everybody clear on that?"

At that moment, my panic from the jet fled me, and I fainted.

I woke up in bed, coughing. Natalie's bed. She came in from her apartment, a cup in her hand. "I made coffee for you," she said. "It's only Folger's Crystals and hot tap water, but I let the water run a long time, so it got really hot. Denise told me what happened between you two. She told me everything. I love you, Casey."

"You can't love me," I said. "I remembered everything. I killed my own parents." I told Natalie how I had cut out the sweepstakes entry form, how I had filled it out with my own hand, then licked the stamp and put it in the mailbox. She listened patiently as I went on, "Then I killed Jimmie Blessing; then I killed Daniel Coggin. I've got some kind of death curse on me. Nobody's safe around the killer."

Natalie set the coffee cup down on the nightstand and kissed me. She said, "Then go ahead and kill me, because I'm not taking this ring off my finger, death-man." She placed my hand on her belly button. I ran my hand up to her breast. She said, "Wait a minute," then opened her bedroom door and leaned into the hallway. She called out to her parents, "Mother, Daddy; Casey and I are going to bed now. We're going to be having sex, so don't knock on the door or anything. If you hear me screaming, I'm just having an orgasm."

The blood ran out of my face. Natalie turned around, giggling into her hand. She said, "My parents aren't home, ya dope. They just left

272 • Miles Keaton Andrew

for the hospital. Come here, look in the driveway for yourself."
Natalie walked to the window that overlooked the driveway. I got up
and walked toward her. As I approached, she looked out the window
and sucked in a gasp through the back of her hand. Her eyes wide,
she backed away from the window. "Omigod!" she cried. I ran toward
Natalie, feeling my heart in the arteries of my brain. I looked out the
window. Black Beauty sat in the driveway, alone. "That's twice I got
ya," Natalie said.

"Now, let's start with Jimmie Blessing. You didn't kill Jimmie
Blessing. I killed him. I did it with my flashbulb. The flash made the
guy trip over your feet. No—wait—it was Jimmie's fault, because if
he hadn't killed his wife in the first place, he wouldn't have tripped
over your feet. Maybe it's his mother's fault, for having sex with his
father.

"Now, on to Daniel Coggin. First of all, the guy had a rope around
his neck. He was too chickenshit to press the button himself. He
wanted someone else to do it for him."

"But there were scuff marks on the garage floor," I said. "He
changed his mind after I pressed the button."

"See? He *was* chickenshit. Besides, he never would have been there
if his father hadn't sold out to JFT. Are you seeing a pattern here?"

"Yes. I keep killing people."

"That's *not* the pattern. The pattern is that these events keep
occurring in your life. Your life is trying to tell you something—that
you're not guilty. You're taking the message the wrong way."

Natalie started throwing magazines on the floor, naming them as
she went: "*Casket and Sunnyside, The Dodge Magazine, Southern
Funeral Director, The Taylor Quarterly*—the *trades*, Casey. This thing
that's happening to you—the trades call it survivor guilt. You feel
guilty because you survived and your parents didn't, so you connected yourself to their deaths. It keeps repeating itself over and over
again, waiting for you to resolve it. Suzy Pocahontas calls it karma. I
understand your guilt, but it's an excuse, Casey. Holding on to your
guilt keeps you from grieving. You've never even visited your parents'

graves. You've been procrastinating long enough. Grow up and start grieving, like a normal person—you're *supposed* to miss your mom and dad."

Natalie put her arms around my neck. She said, "By the way, Daddy says you did great with Stark. You're a brave man, Casey, and you're brave enough for grieving. I'm here to help you, death-man. Tell me what you want me to do."

"Help me destroy JFT. If we don't bring them down, they'll keep coming back. If we succeed, I'll visit my parents at Fairview."

"If we *don't* succeed?"

"We'll be dead."

"How do I fit in?"

"You take the most gruesome pictures of your life."

"Deal. Now, let's get back to the part where your hand was on my breast."

The phone rang—Jerry. Colton was awake. Natalie and I took off for the hospital. I coughed most of the way there. I asked Natalie if she knew what had happened after I passed out at the beach.

"Fainted, you mean," Natalie said. "Lex grabbed a shovel from a guy and started digging while he screamed profanities at Ray. As far as I know, he's still digging. Lex, Jewell, and Stark all think that Colton is dead at Morton-Albright. Stark and Jewell are negotiating. With no family secret and Lex gone koo-koo, Ray says Stark is sitting there with a fountain pen in one hand, and his dick in the other. Eventually, he'll have to let go of one of them—probably the fountain pen. Dr. Kendall got you out of going back to work—he said you've got the flu. That cough of yours makes me believe him. Now I've got sick-germs in my car."

The No Visitors sign still hung next to Colton's door. Inside the room were Mr. Percy, Jerry and Cynthia, Ray and Denise, Carl and Suzy, Meredith and Teresa. Natalie and I made it *eleven* visitors in Colton's room, some us in chairs, or seated on the windowsill, the others standing. Colton was unconscious again, and his heart monitor beeped erratically. Ray said, "We had him for a few minutes, but

274 · Miles Keaton Andrew

he didn't know what the hell his name *was*, so he did not sign the will." Ray showed us the unsigned will. Natalie snatched it from his hand. She shooed Ray from his bedside seat and sat next to her grandfather. Natalie stroked Colton's hair and spoke softly into his ear, "Granddaddy, it's Natty. You'd better wake up and go milk the cows." Natalie put her hand over her mouth, then looked up at the rest of us. She dropped her hand and giggled. "Granddaddy's been recalling his days on the farm." Percy shook his head. Like everybody else in the room, he knew damn good and well that Colton had never been on a farm in his life. Natalie kept talking to the old man, "It's time to feed the horses," she said. "Start baling that hay."

Colton stirred, then went limp. His heart monitor sounded a steady beeeeep. Natalie screamed in his ear. "Granddaddy! Wake up!" Colton Albright sat straight up in the bed and said, "Huh? That's right, Natty. Bale them horses. Feed that hay."

"That's right, Granddaddy!" Natalie said, clapping her hands together. Percy stood up and started for the door. He said, "I can't witness this. The man is not sound."

"He sounds fine to me," Ray said.

"Perfectly normal," Carl said.

Jerry said, "Sit down, Percy. It's absolutely clear—we all agree that Colton Albright is as sane as you are. Take that however you like. Just sit down."

Percy sat down. Natalie placed the will in Colton's lap. She worked his fingers around a pen, and said, "Now, Granddaddy, do you know who you are?"

"Of course I know who I am. I'm Colton Mallord Albright, and I *own* this here farm."

"We all know that, Granddaddy. We just need you to sign this paper."

"I don't sign nothing without my lawyer."

Percy said, "I'm here, Mr. Albright. We need you to sign your last will and testament."

"This don't give anything to Jewell does it? If it does, I'll be damned if I'll sign it. The farm goes to Jerry and Ray—all of it. Where do I sign?"

"Right here, Granddaddy, on the line next to your name."

Colton set the pen to the paper. He started to write, then looked up toward the window. He laughed and said, "Hello, John. I'll be with you in a minute. Gotta put my name down." Colton looked at us, and said, "John wants us to play checkers on the front porch." He smiled. Natalie said, "Granddaddy, you've got to sign your name."

"I know, I know. Just hang on to your britches. I'm a-writin' "

Colton said each letter aloud as he wrote, with unbearable slowness. He paused at the first L. He had three more to go—two in his middle name. Everyone sat frozen—eyes wide, no breathing. I stifled my coughing. Colton paused again at the D in Mallord. "Just like them ducks," he said. Natalie said, "A—come on, Granddaddy—A."

"A," Colton said. "L."

"That's right, Granddaddy. Keep going. That's right. *Very* good. You're doing fine. Great job. Now just cross the T.

Colton's hand remained motionless. The heart monitor lapsed into its prolonged beep. Natalie looked at her grandfather then said, "Quick! Everybody turn around." We all obeyed her. Instantly, she said. "Look! Granddaddy crossed the T." He signed the will." She held up the will. The room burst into sound: Laughing, crying, shouts of "Hallelujah," and "Whoopee," and everybody was shaking hands and hugging and slapping each other on the back when the nurse walked in the door, because of the heart monitor. We all froze in the middle of whatever we were doing. The nurse looked at us, then at Colton. She bugged her eyes at us, put her hand over her mouth and ran out the door. Jerry was the first to laugh, but before long, even Percy was laughing, his face dripping sweat.

In the embalming room at Morton-Albright, we each performed a task necessary to Colton's preparation. Natalie set his features, combed his hair, and did his makeup. In the chapel, the place of Colton's weeklong visitation, we held our own private viewing. Hundreds of flowers had already arrived, because of the hospital—

Jones had instructed them to tell everyone who called that Colton was dead, and he never told them to stop. We all helped arranging the flowers. Soon Colton appeared to be sleeping on a cloud of flowers. Jerry stood at the head of the casket as we all filed past. After Denise kissed his forehead, Jerry suggested that we all say our own silent prayer. That was when the Presence swirled into the chapel. I could see it on the faces of the others—they felt it, too. Old John had come to call. He left us as quickly as he had arrived, leaving a shower of gold dust behind. Morton-Albright was ours forever.

"I think I'll just say Amen, if y'all don't mind," Ray said.

I pulled my MG into the carport at 23 Covington Place, my old home. Natalie pulled in behind me, driving Black Beauty. She stood next to me on the lawn. "You're really buying this place?" She asked.

"I'm not exactly buying it—Sophie Campbell made her brother-in-law sell it to me for legal costs and the taxes he paid on the property. It's my reward for killing Jimmie Blessing with my feet. I've only *started* remembering. I've got years to catch up on. I'm leaving my car here so it looks like the place is lived in. Tomorrow I'm hanging curtains, and I've hired a landscaper to take care of the lawn. When I talk to Margee, she'll send me the pictures. It's getting dark now. The night crew hits Central at eight."

At Jerry's house, Natalie bagged her photography gear. We both wore black clothing. Natalie said, "You don't look so hot. Are you feeling okay?" I coughed and said, "I've got Luden's cherry cough drops. I feel fine."

I felt terrible. We bounded down the staircase, right past Jerry and Cynthia in the living room. Natalie called over her shoulder, "Don't wait up." Jerry kept his eyes on his trade magazine, Cynthia's on her tatting. "You kids have fun," Jerry said.

I drove the car while Natalie kept checking her gear. I drove past Central; counted sixteen cars in the parking lot—they were busy, all right. I parked behind the adjacent warehouse. Natalie took the keys. She asked me, "Can you stop coughing long enough for this?"

I nodded and stuck a Luden's in my mouth. "Tie the tripod onto my back," I said. "We have to crawl."

"Crawl? You mean on the floor? Is it dirty?"

"Filthy."

"Aw, shit fuck piss damn hell. I'll bet it stinks in there too, doesn't it? Please tell me it doesn't stink."

"It doesn't stink."

Inside Central, we went down on our bellies and crawled beneath the racks, side by side. Natalie whacked me, then whispered, "It stinks in here. You lied to me."

"Sssh. We're almost there."

As we neared the embalming stations, the clink of instruments became audible, then, voices. "Last rack." I said. "We can stand up, now."

Natalie untied the tripod from my back and set it in place. She mounted the camera and focused the zoom lens. Bodies lay piled in front of each station. Men sliced at cadavers on the tables. My initial terror of bringing Natalie along faded as I watched her work—she had obviously done this before—she timed her shots with the clinks of the instruments. She jerked when a head went sailing into a laundry bin.

The scratchy feeling began in my throat, and worked its way into my lungs. I felt the urge to cough arising in my chest, that feeling you get when you *know* you're going to cough; you simply *must* cough, and there isn't a damn thing you can do about it. That cough now demanded release. I tried to pinch a cough drop from the slim box of Luden's. I couldn't see what I was doing, but I could feel that the cough drops were all kind of stuck together inside the box. I tried shaking the box gently against my hand. Cough drops scattered onto the floor. I bent down and found a lozenge, encrusted with sandy particles. When I opened my mouth, I coughed—four loud hacks.

Natalie whipped around. Her eyes were so big I could see their whites, even in the near darkness. The mutilators stopped mutilating and looked in our direction. I clasped my hands over my mouth. The men went back to work, all but Lester Boggs, Stark's assistant. He peered in our direction, then stepped to the end of his cubicle. He took a long look at the casket racks, then returned to his instruments. He sawed off a head and threw it into a bin, then slid the torso into another. He rolled the bin away.

"Let's get the fuck out of here," I said.

"No, wait," Natalie said. "Couple more shots."

"Fuck the shots. Let's go."

Natalie shushed me with a wave of her hand and put her eye to the camera. Boggs returned to the embalming area, accompanied by Lewis Stark. He spoke to the crew. I couldn't hear them—the tone of his voice was subdued, but his gestures were emphatic. The men abandoned their stations and followed Stark out of the embalming area. I told Natalie, "They're loading the retorts now. That takes an hour, then six hours to cremate. They're done for the night."

Natalie detached the camera from the tripod, took out the film, stuck it into her pocket, and inserted a new roll. "Keep a lookout," she said. Before I could stop her, Natalie trotted to the cubicles. I ran to catch up with her. She began shooting at the first station, walking backward down the line of cubicles, taking pictures. At the last station, she snapped a torso bereft of limbs and head.

"Run!" she shouted.

We turned to run, and found ourselves face-to-face with Lewis Stark. "Evening, folks," he said. "You must be Natalie Stiles, Jerry's daughter." Natalie stared at Stark's crotch, ready to kick him there and run, I thought. That's when I noticed the tubular bulge jutting from Stark's pants. He said, "You're a good-lookin' girl, Natalie, but don't flatter yourself. I'm not just glad to see you—I've got a gun in my pocket. Let's go. My office."

The three of us sat in the office, Stark behind his Mr. Spaceley desk. I coughed. "You've got that flu bug," Stark said. "Boggs heard that cough out in the warehouse. He came and got me. I sent the men to the break room, walked out the front door and came back in through the motor pool." He took out his Luger and pointed it at my head, then aimed it at Natalie. He opened his desk drawer, and put the gun away. "We don't need guns. Hell, we'll work this whole thing out, just like regular citizens. Let's have that camera, Natalie."

"No!" she said, clutching her Nikon close. Stark looked at Natalie like she had gone wacky. His hand went to the desk drawer. Natalie said, "You can have the film. Please don't take my camera." Stark said that would be just fine, he didn't want to seem unreasonable. Natalie yanked the film out of the camera, exposing it to the light. She threw it onto the desk. Stark thanked her, then said, "We've got six hours together. We're cremating right now. There's a refrigerated truck on its way for the other bodies. The crew is busy cleaning up. When we're done, y'all can go call the po-lice, or whoever else you like."

"You're just going to let us walk away?" I said. "Bullshit. You're just waiting for an empty retort. My guess is that you'll shoot us, throw us into the retort, *then* leave."

"That's a damn good idea, Casey. I'm glad you thought of it. Of course, I thought of it too, but I didn't want to ruin the surprise. You ruined my surprise, Casey. Damn. Might as well get yourselves comfortable."

Even on the night of her own execution, sleepiness crept onto Natalie's face. She nodded off like always: eyes and mouth half-open; breathing slowed. Stark gave me a look.

"She does that," I said. "Sleep disorder."

Stark nodded, like he knew what a sleep disorder was, but kept his eye on her. I closed my eyes, but cough prevented sleep. I peeked through an eyelid, checking Stark. He fiddled with his fingernails and scanned the trades. At 3:00 A.M., I sat up, bored with pretending sleep. I coughed a lot, my lungs now filled with flu. Natalie slept on. Her camera dangled from the strap wrapped around her wrist. Stark read his trade magazine. Natalie touched my leg—*awake*. She jerked a couple of times. Stark looked up, then returned to his magazine.

Natalie jerked again, moaning this time. Stark stopped reading and watched her. Natalie trembled, then convulsed, twitching and drooling. Stark got up out of his chair. "Seizure?" He asked.

I shrugged. Natalie gurgled like she was choking, sending Stark around his desk. He faced her now, and shook her by the shoulders. Natalie stopped twitching and resumed her former posture, still and quiet. Stark looked at me.

"Bad dream," I said.

Natalie swung the camera and whacked Stark in the middle of his face. He yowled and clapped his hand over his nose. Blood poured through his fingers. Natalie jumped out of her chair. "Run!" she yelled. I leaped from my chair and tried to run after her. Dizzy with flu, muscles aching, I lagged. Natalie waited for me at the steel doorway to the warehouse. I fumbled the keys, my joints electric with pain. "I'm hurting," I said. "When I open this door, you run like hell. Don't look back. I'll catch up." I twisted the key in the lock. Natalie shoved the door and bolted. I knew she'd make it, even when the bullet slammed into my back. I didn't hear the sound of the gun until I saw the bloody hole in my shirt pocket. The second bullet hit the back of my head. The floor slammed into my face.

19

Fluorescent light stabbed my eyes as I forced them open. My chest throbbed and burned. My head weighed a ton. I lay naked on a stainless steel embalming table. A face hovered over me, peering and poking me with a finger: Derrick Lott, the cremationist. "The fucker's alive!" he yelled. Detective Jones entered my vision. Natalie stood next to him. Her mouth formed my name, then Natalie disappeared.

I didn't hear any calm voices, summoning me toward the light. Instead, I rocketed upward through black space. I saw a flame ahead, speeding toward me—a man on fire. In his right hand, a gun. On his face, terror. His limbs flailed as he plummeted—Lewis Stark. I heard his scream as we passed each other. I looked over my shoulder, and watched the fire burn him to bare bones. The falling skeleton turned to charcoal, then disintegrated.

Then came the light. I stood in the middle of a road. I looked down at my feet. The road shone golden, smooth as glass. When I looked up, I saw a small glowing light, spherical in shape, about the size of a shooter marble. The light went prismatic. Colors shone from it in all directions. When the colors faded, he appeared—the old man: John Morton. "It's time for our talk, Casey," he said.

"Am I dead?"

"Look at yourself, son. You're a mess—bleeding all over the place. Nobody bleeds here. Besides, if you were dead, you wouldn't be talking to *me*."

"I'm here, but I'm not dead? Am I back there, too?"

"Sort of. It's complicated."

"Am I going to die?" I asked.

"Of course you're going to die. Everybody dies. You're asking the wrong questions, son. Next you'll want to know how many angels can dance on the head of a pin."

"How many?"

"None. Those fellas are ten feet tall—amazing, beautiful creatures. Now follow me."

I didn't follow him anywhere. Everything around us simply changed. We now stood on a dirt road—not dirt—gold dust. I remembered the line from the Ted Lewis number: "Gold dust, at my feet, on the sunny side of the street." I heard the sound of his clarinet. The music came from a blue-green Cracker home at the end of the street.

"That'd be your folks's place yonder," the old man said. I ran for the house, but no matter how fast I ran, Mom and Dad's house remained exactly the same distance away from me. "I want to see them," I said.

"You might, but they sure don't want to see you. All shot up like that? I thought I'd taught you better than that, son."

I stopped running. The music changed: everybody's favorite—"In the Mood," Glenn Miller. I knew exactly what Mom and Dad were doing inside that house—the jitterbug. I couldn't see them, not with my eyes—my mind did that for me: Mom, twirling in her long skirt and red lipstick, Dad in his work uniform, the one with the patch with his embroidered name: Rich. Mom's giggles and Dad's whoops punctuating their steps—they were happy. I smiled at John Morton. His glowing countenance faded, replaced by Natalie's worried face.

"He's awake!" she called out. Into my hospital room came Jerry and Cynthia, Ray and Denise. Ray's arm was around Denise's waist. I tried to sit up. Pain kept me from raising my head. Everybody stuck out their hands in the stop position. "Don't move," they all said.

"Pneumonia, and a bullet hole through your lung," Natalie said. "You almost lost your lung, and your life, too."

"Did I get shot in the head?"

"Not *in* the head, *around* the head. The bullet traveled in between your scalp and your skull. It came out the front, and you've got a deathy-as-hell scar on your forehead that's shaped like a star." Natalie stopped talking and started crying. "They said you wouldn't make it—not with the infection. Now you're back. Are you really back, Casey?"

"I'm back, Natalie."

She hugged me so tight, they had to call the nurse for painkillers. Natalie made everybody leave. We needed time alone. On his way out the door, Ray said, "You brought down JFT. The state's attorney ordered their slow-talking, cole-slaw-on-their-barbecue-eating, Crimson-Tide-rolling Alabama asses out of Florida, thanks to you, and Natalie's pictures."

"But I saw you take the film out of your camera," I said.

"You forgot the other roll, the first one I took, with the zoom lens. I stuck it in my pocket before Stark found us. The state's attorney has it now. JFT is finished, and so is Lewis Stark."

Natalie told me Lewis Stark was dead. "He tried to kill you," she said. "I ran to the car and drove to a pay phone. I called the ambulance, the police, and Daddy." With the authorities on their way, Natalie drove back to Central. She ran inside to find me. She watched Derrick Lott attack the JFT crew with a shovel. Stark fired a shot at Derrick. It ricocheted off the shovel. The police burst in. Natalie and Derrick searched for me. Derrick found me naked, on an embalming table. "They meant to cut you up and throw you into the retort."

Derrick and the police looked for Stark. They found him six hours later, when they opened the retort—a skeleton, crumpled in the corner near the door. The unincinerated pieces of the Luger identified him. Apparently, Stark had hidden in the retort when the cops showed up. Derrick admitted pressing the button on the retort, but told the cops, "It's my *job* to press the button."

I imagined Lewis Stark, hiding in the retort; the look on his face when the door slid downward; the *foomp* of ignition. Had he screamed and banged against the door? Danced in a squat when the floor of the retort became too hot for his shoes? Had he slapped at his clothing when it burst aflame? I shuddered. Natalie said, "They examined Stark's skeleton before they swept it. From the look of the skull, Kendall thinks Stark took the easy way out—put a bullet through his own head."

"How long have I been away?"

"We buried Granddaddy yesterday."

"Some funeral, huh?"

"That's what I hear. I didn't go. I've been here with you the whole time. You're turning me into a sap, death-man."

The next day, my family helped me into John Morton's bed. I spent two weeks recuperating. Margee called. She had come down for a few days, while I was unconscious. She contracted the flu, and went home to get well. She promised to come back when we were both feeling better. She promised to bring the pictures, too—all of them.

Ray came to visit me one afternoon. He said he was back in the arrangement office. He said, "Don't laugh at me, Casey, but when I nearly died from that flu bug, I had a strange experience. I'm talking spooky shit here—like a dream. I went to heaven and had a talk with John Morton."

I told Ray not to worry. I wouldn't laugh. He said, "John Morton took me to see a young boy, about ten years old, and as happy as the dickens. He whispered in John's ear. John said, "He wants to know why you're not happy."" Now, you may not believe this, Casey, but the boy was my son. I don't know how I knew it, but I did. I also knew if

I said that I was unhappy because I lost my only son, he'd think it was his fault that I was unhappy. I figured the kid wouldn't want his old man unhappy, so when I woke up from my dream, I woke up happy. I know it sounds crazy, but I swear—"

I interrupted Ray. I didn't think he was crazy at all, I said. I asked Ray if he trusted me. When he said, yes, I asked him, "Where is the body of Waldo Shipper buried?"

Ray's expression changed. He sighed, and fell into a slump on the edge of my bed. He said, "I did a bad thing, Casey." He told me that everything Lex had seen was true—but Lex hadn't seen everything. "I buried Waldo Shipper in that clearing," he said. "It happened right after Johnny Ray died, and I was all messed up. When I finished the burial, I got into the hearse and started back for the funeral home. I thought about Waldo Shipper's family, laying flowers on his marker, while he was lying out in the woods. I tried to tell myself that it didn't matter. It only mattered that they *believed* the man was in his proper burial place. Hell, Waldo Shipper didn't care. He was dead, but his family wasn't dead. They had entrusted me with the care of someone they loved, and I had failed them. That was when I realized what it meant to be a funeral man. When I drove that hearse out of the woods, I felt bad. Real bad. I walked straight into Jerry's office and told him the whole story. I didn't care if I lost my license. I didn't deserve one. Until then, I had only been here for Denise, and that's not a good enough reason to work in a funeral home."

"You told Jerry? What did he do?" I asked Ray. Jerry had arisen from his chair, and put his arm around Ray. Jerry accepted part of the blame. He told Ray he shouldn't have let him come back to work so soon after the baby. He shouldn't have let Ray lock himself up in the back room, with little contact with the living.

"Jerry told me to go home, put on some old clothes, and bring my truck to his house." Jerry loaded the truck with shovels and a spade, and accompanied Ray to the clearing in the woods. Together, they exhumed the casket bearing Waldo Shipper, and drove it to Fairview Cemetery, where Jerry explained the situation to Henry and Kip.

Jerry even offered to inform the Shipper family, to correct our mistake, and to ease Henry and Kip.

"They didn't even give us a second look," Ray said. "Henry got the backhoe, and we switched caskets in the shed. Waldo Shipper was in his proper grave, the same day as his funeral. See? John Morton himself had taken care of Henry and Kip's families, for generations. It was the good name of Morton-Albright that made those two men forgive our mistake, and help us in our trouble. On the way back, Jerry told me a Bible verse: 'A good name is better than riches.' "

"Do you know how the rest of that verse goes?" I asked. Ray shook his head, so I quoted, ". . . and the day of a man's death is better than the day of his birth. The heart of the wise dwells in the house of mourning."

A week later, I kept my promise to Natalie. On a Sunday afternoon, we drove to Fairview Cemetery. Natalie gave me a bunch of roses from her mother's flower shop. We followed the cemetery's directions to the area of Mom and Dad's grave. Natalie stopped, and told me to go on by myself. "Take a few moments alone," she said. "Then I'll join you. Just walk straight ahead."

I felt my palms going sweaty. My heartbeat picked up. Anxiety set in on me. Each step seemed to take longer than the one before. I stopped, and looked down at the bronze marker embedded in the grass, inches from my feet.

KIGHT

Richard　　Nancy

1927–1962　　1930–1962

Together Forever

I looked down at the marker. The pain began in my abdomen, sick and sore. I wiped the first tear from my cheek—Mom and Dad, smiling and waving from the airplane door. I knelt down and placed the roses next to the marker. I ran my hand over its raised lettering, then I lay down upon it. The bronze rectangle became my pillow. I clawed at the grass around the marker, wishing I could dig myself into my mother's arms, longing for my dad to rub my head. If I dug deep enough to uncover them, what would I find? Two charred bodies to hold me close. Skeleton faces for smiles and kisses. Stink for Dad's aftershave, Mom's perfume. I had spoken the words to others for most of my life: my parents are dead. But only now, without guilt, could I listen to those words in my own ears: Mom and Dad were dead, and I missed them. I could not bring them back. Only my own death could bring me to them, and I had come close enough to death to know that I wanted to live. That meant saying good-bye to them. I buried my face deeper into the marker and flooded it with tears. I remembered what I had lost: Mom's sweet smile, Dad's hand on my shoulder. I remembered their affection for each other, their love that brought me into this world. They wouldn't have wanted their only son spending his days dying, killing his own soul for that which was lost. They would have wanted for me what they'd had for themselves: a life, and love.

It was my love who placed her hand on my shoulder. My Natalie. I stood up, and held her close to me. She wiped tears from my face, then shed her own. She started with her giggling, her hand to her mouth. "I'm sorry," she said, "but your mother's name is spelled backward across your face." I ran my fingers across my face, feeling deep indentations from the bronze letters. Natalie opened her compact and showed me. "It's not backward," I said.

"Of course it's not backward. You're reading it in a mirror, ya goofball. So, aren't you going to introduce me? It's okay to talk to them. Talk to them like they can hear you. They can, you know."

I put my arm around Natalie's waist and cleared my throat. I felt embarrassed at first, but then the words came easy: "Mom, Dad, this is Natalie. We're engaged to be married. She's going to be my wife. I love her, more than anything. If you knew her, you would love her, too."

Even from the grave, I felt their love for me, giving me permission to live my life, and to let them rest.

I could retire at my leisure.